C. C. Uzoh, M.D., is Nigerian-born British who originally hails from Southeastern Nigeria where he draws his knowledge of the rituals portrayed in this book.

The trilogy, which began in *Children of the Shadows: Unearthing the Ritual* and will conclude in *Children of the Shadows: The Never-Ending Fear*, is intended to raise awareness of this barbaric practice which, while illegal under the African Charter, is still being pursued in the 21st century.

Dr. Uzoh lives with his family in Kleinburg, Ontario, Canada.

My inspiration comes first and foremost from Jesus, the Author and Finisher of my faith, and all the glory be to God in the highest.
I dedicate this book to all the children who hold a special place in my heart: Orla, Naeto, Ary, Adaorah, Lauren, Mimi, Urenna, Korinne, Kamsi, and Eli who were children at the time of writing this book, as well as all the children of the world. You are all capable of greatness.

"Fathers, do not provoke your children to anger, but bring them up in the discipline and instruction of the Lord."
–Ephesians 6:4

"It's the greatest poverty to decide that a child must die so that you may live as you wish."
–Mother Teresa

"For our fight is not against flesh and blood but against principalities, against powers, against the rulers of the darkness of this world, and against spiritual forces of evil in the heavenly places."
–Ephesians 6:12

C. C. Uzoh

CHILDREN OF THE SHADOWS: FIRMNESS OF PURPOSE

AUSTIN MACAULEY PUBLISHERS™
LONDON * CAMBRIDGE * NEW YORK * SHARJAH

Copyright © C. C. Uzoh 2022

All rights reserved. No part of this publication may be reproduced, distributed, or transmitted in any form or by any means, including photocopying, recording, or other electronic or mechanical methods, without the prior written permission of the publisher, except in the case of brief quotations embodied in critical reviews and certain other noncommercial uses permitted by copyright law. For permission requests, write to the publisher.

Any person who commits any unauthorized act in relation to this publication may be liable to criminal prosecution and civil claims for damages.

This is a work of fiction. Names, characters, businesses, places, events, locales, and incidents are either the products of the author's imagination or used in a fictitious manner. Any resemblance to actual persons, living or dead, or actual events is purely coincidental.

Ordering Information
Quantity sales: Special discounts are available on quantity purchases by corporations, associations, and others. For details, contact the publisher at the address below.

Publisher's Cataloging-in-Publication data
Uzoh, C. C.
Children of the Shadows: Firmness of Purpose

ISBN 9781645754619 (Paperback)
ISBN 9781645754626 (Hardback)
ISBN 9781645754633 (ePub e-book)

Library of Congress Control Number: 2021923473

www.austinmacauley.com/us

First Published 2022
Austin Macauley Publishers LLC
40 Wall Street, 33rd Floor, Suite 3302
New York, NY 10005
USA

mail-usa@austinmacauley.com
+1 (646) 5125767

My overwhelming and never-ending gratitude continues to go to:

My parents, Engr. Ray aka Eseluenuego, and Mrs. Marie-Pauline aka The Original Mrs. P.

My children, Orla aka my princess, and Naeto aka Tha Naeto Boy.

My sister, Chinwe, and my brothers, Obi aka Obyno, Chez aka Obele Agu, Ik aka Irishman, and Chux aka Nwachinemelu.

For your unending and unconditional love, I love you all.

To my most cherished beta reader, Daniel O'Connell, you remain exceptional.

To Joseph Adams, Femi Akilo, M.D., Anthony Anani, M.D., Alecia Brown, Rev. Fr. Song Eugene Chianain, Adekunle Ishola, Tosin Jimoh, Abraham King, Nonye Ndekwu, M.D., Ugo Nwaomu, M.D., Chinedu Okeke, M.D., Margaret Olaniran, M.D., Bohdan Pich, M.D., and CY Tse, M.D., thank you for your friendship, love, support, and prayers.

To my editors, you did another terrific job!

Dear Reader

Thank you for your interest in *Children of the Shadows: Firmness of Purpose*. The book in front of you is the second installment of a trilogy that continues a didactic story that began in *Unearthing the Ritual*.

I hope you will enjoy this as much as you enjoyed reading Volume I.

With best regards and thank you,
C. C. Uzoh, M.D.

Author's Note

Whilst the premise, as well as the low value that is placed on human life in the part of the world in which this book is set, are factual, references to all names of people, clans, villages, and majority of the events are fictional.

This book affirms life's value and emphasizes its impermanence and fragility.

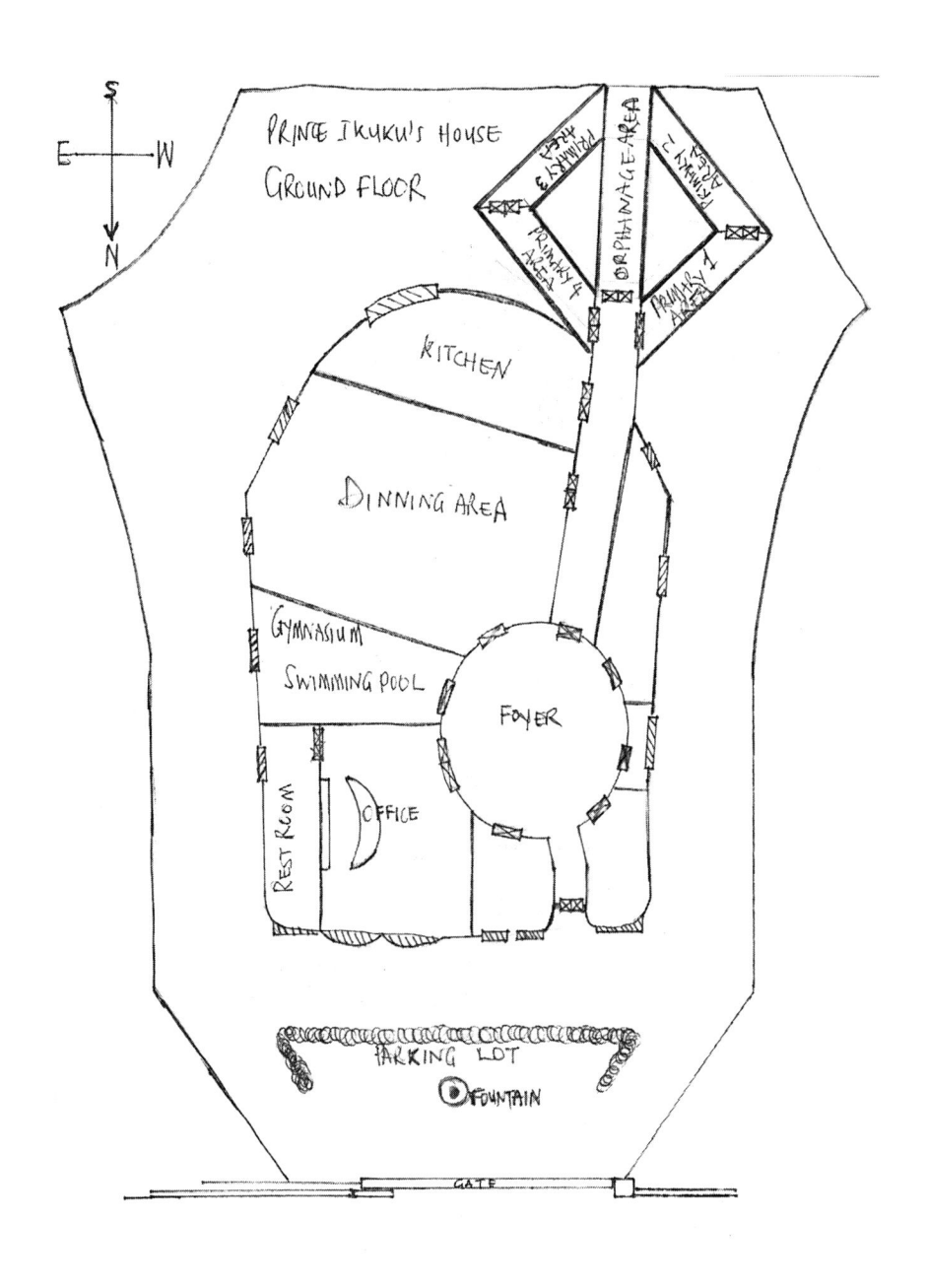

Diagram 1: Ground Floor: The Ikuku House

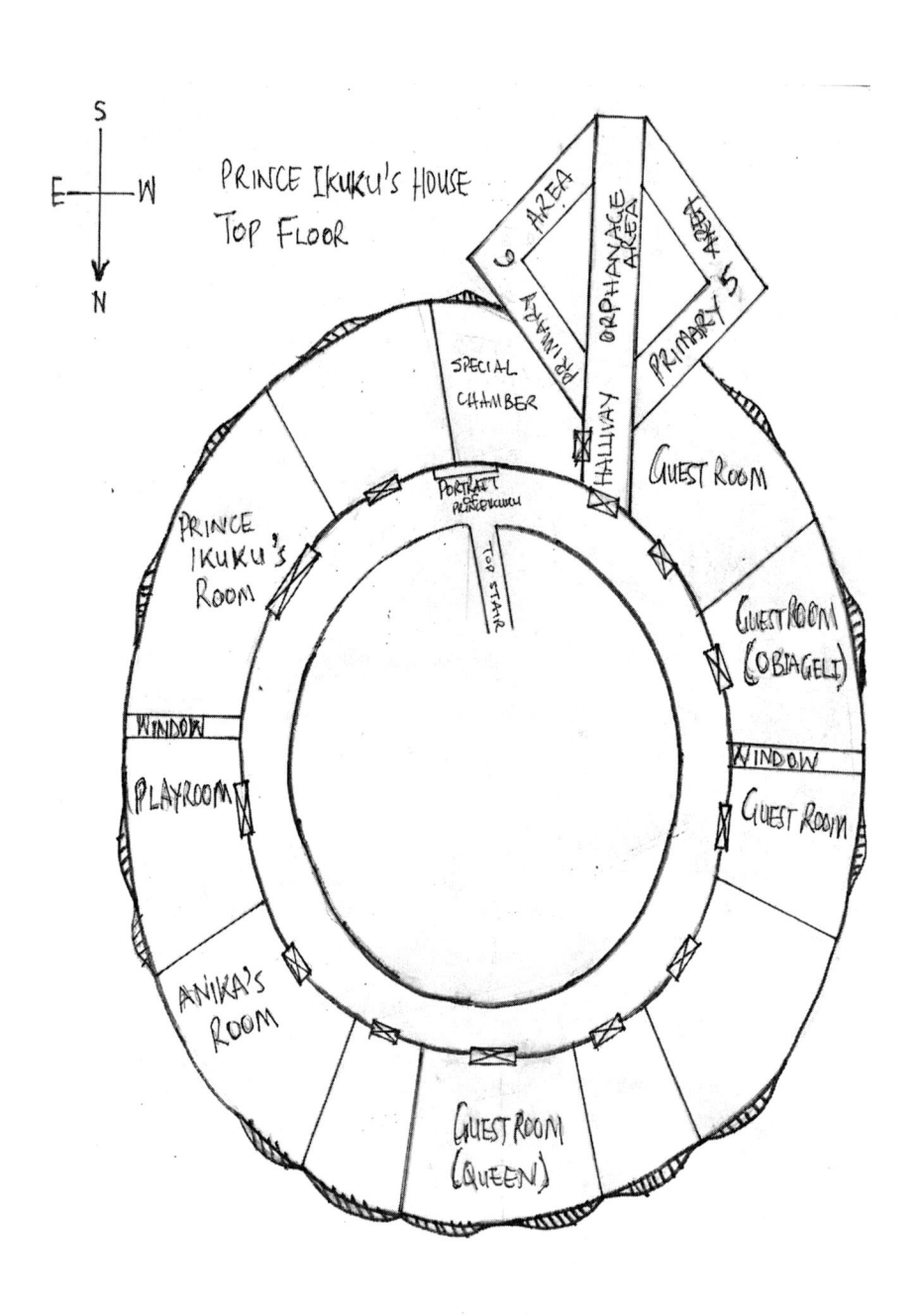

Diagram 2: Top Floor: The Ikuku House

**If it still exists,
then it can happen to you
or someone you know.**

A Peace Warrior's Rulebook

Section One
Subsection

1. During a spiritual journey, before speaking, acknowledge to whom you speak by their full name and title.
2. Only at the discretion of the most venerable one, may an impromptu meeting take place.
3. The sole reason for an impromptu meeting alone may be discussed at such a meeting.
4. A minimum of two peace warriors are required to call for an impromptu meeting.
5. Names of non-peace warriors may not be mentioned during a spiritual journey.

Section Two
Subsection

1. The process of the ritual rubbing out of a non-peace warrior **must not** be _watched_ by a non-peace warrior, so, better off carried out in a concealed shrine.
2. The process of the ritual rubbing out of a non-peace warrior **must not** be _broken_ by a non-peace warrior, so, better off carried out in a concealed shrine.
3. The process of the ritual rubbing out of a non-peace warrior **must not** be _countered_ by a non-peace warrior, so, better off carried out in a concealed shrine.
4. If the process of the ritual rubbing out of a non-peace warrior is unfinished, it may result in no benefit to the would-be peace warrior.

5. The process of the ritual rubbing out of a non-peace warrior **must** be done with the *athame*, and if carried out on a peace warrior's behalf, the consequence to the peace warrior will be the same if the rubbing out was caused by a being begotten by the *athame* or the peace warrior is in full awareness of the rubbing out.

Section Three
Subsection

1. No peace warrior should have within their personal or social space any non-peace warrior with *compunction/conscience*.
2. No peace warrior should have within their personal or social space any non-peace warrior with *an opposing spirit*.
3. No peace warrior should have within their personal or social space any non-peace warrior with *an opposing voice*.
4. No peace warrior should have within their personal or social space any non-peace warrior with *an opposing action*.
5. If a peace warrior directly or indirectly rubs out a non-peace warrior for the purpose of *wealth*, *strength*, *protection*, *vengeance*, *evil*, or, as determined by the Evil One, for any other *selfish* reasons, the length of that peace warrior's life will be reduced by the number of non-peace warrior's lives that that peace warrior rubbed out.

Section Four
Subsection

1. A peace warrior is expected to keep their *athame* safe and out of a non-peace warrior's sight. The process of its acquisition must be repeated to obtain a replacement.
2. A peace warrior is expected to maintain their *Ikengá* out of a non-peace warrior's sight except that peace warrior is in the process of becoming a peace warrior.
3. It is a bad omen for a peace warrior's *raven* to be seen by a non-peace warrior.

Section Five

Subsection

1. Disrespect for spiritual methods **must** attract punishment ranging from loss of all benefits to the rubbing out of that peace warrior's most loved one or that peace warrior themselves.
2. The rubbing out of a peace warrior **must** be accomplished by fire or roasting under the sun and that of their most loved one **must** be by the peace warrior's hands.
3. A peace warrior **must** exit the spiritual journey only when their candle burns down completely or just before the first light of day, whichever occurs first; there is no other way.
4. A peace warrior **must** walk humbly with their god otherwise they will be abandoned at their hour of most need.

Chapter 1

King Ajutu awakened with a start. All his egregious schemes had been askew—he'd realized through the venerable ones during his spiritual quest across Igboland.

He'd sought proof that the people he'd wanted killed were indeed dead. They'd simply informed him that there was no evidence that Odera, Obiageli, and I had passed on to the hereafter. They'd said no more than that since the three of us hadn't, in any way, shape, or form, caused the ritual any suffering visible to man in the human world or to them in the netherworld.

Refusing to cater to his megrims and what they considered to be mere assumptions by him that their group would flounder, as their secret had been brought to the light, they'd told him that taking our lives was in all respects his choice, although their decision would change in his favor the moment either or both of Odera and I began to fight against the deathly conduct.

As a result, King Ajutu had run his candle down fast and exited from the journey.

With his forehead vein engorging, nostrils flaring, and chest heaving, the perfidious monarch looked to his right, through the gap in the ornate drapes and out the window on the west wall.

The darkness was pitch black.

There was the reflection of the glimmering night-light that stood at the corner on the room's parallel side between his awe-inspiring grand dresser and the magnificent, handcrafted entrance-doors.

His hard and cold eyes flickered upward and leftward to the clock—it read 3:12.

Glancing over to his immediate right, the intervening space between him and Isioma was empty.

Grinding his teeth, he turned to the left to see Ijeoma and Adure. And all three maidens seemed to be deep in the arms of Morpheus.

"So, wherever Adaku has gone, she has gone alone and of her own accord, and has nothing to do with me…" he mused with a crisp tone, palming hard on his chest. "King Ajutu or her maker. The Queen of the Coast forbids them from doing anything alone unless at my behest, and it wasn't my will for her to depart this room whilst I slept."

Head cocked, he slowly shook it and flicked his gaze upward. Drawing a deep breath, he held it for a moment before puffing out in a slow manner. Pressing a fist to his mouth, he remained brooding, "If Adaku is lying with Namdi right now, I will be unforgiving. She must have assumed I wouldn't wake up until close to six as usual, but she should have realized that the last two days have been anything but usual. For how long has their secret liaison been going on whilst I slept? Did she lie to me to protect him because of this? Why does she force my hand? Does he even realize that he is involved in a nowhere affair with her?"

Creeping out of bed while almost not disturbing the silence, he donned his velvety, blue, regal robe. Knotting its cummerbund, he strode without noise across the cozy room toward the door. Purposefully drawing in slow breaths, he remained soundless whilst exiting the room.

The door shut.

Isioma roused soon after. Stirring Ijeoma and Adure, they arose in no time.

"The king has gone after Adaku," Isioma said. "She left not ten minutes before he awoke. I think she went to be with Namdi."

"We did warn her against trying to fulfill her fantasies with these henchmen," Adure said. "How do we help her though?"

Gazing at the dresser, Ijeoma said, "I will alert her," springing out of the high-sitting, king-size featherbed.

"That's wise of you—since he's the only one who activates our stars, she'd realize that he's now awake," Adure said. "And it's kind of you as well to help her despite her disregard for you yesterday."

"That is bygone. Besides, we must have one another's back regardless," Ijeoma said, skipping across to the dresser and thumbing the gleaming star that was uppermost on the handle of the king's *Akupé*; and, with this, she leapt back into the bed.

They all lay down and stared at the ceiling, breathing heavily, and waiting for events to unfold.

****

With heavy breaths, King Ajutu swept down the two flights of stairs from his great chamber[1] and strode onto the west passage that extended from the southwest section of the palace toward the staff living area on the ground floor of the three-storied northwest section.

Arriving at the northwest passage, he saw Adaku leaving the staff common lounge, and their gazes met. She was unfazed. His curiosity as to why she hadn't reacted to the element of surprise that his being awake at that hour presented, fleeted. He gave her a black look as his eyes flashed.

"So, your frolicking with Namdi has evolved into sexual relations under my very nose?" he roared with an orotund voice.

"Your Majesty, it's not what you think. I had a feeling that he'd checked out of the palace for good, and I came to confirm. I didn't want to bother you—not that there was a way I could arouse you from sleep during these hours anyway," Adaku replied whilst her face fell, and a look of terror moved fast across it as she recalled the king's intent.

"Don't you dare patronize me!" he stormed, stomping past her as she neared him, and headed straight into the lounge toward Namdi's room.

"Open this door at once!" he coughed out with a dead-serious tone as he arrived at the door and planted his feet wide apart. With his chest thrusting out, he cracked his knuckles and glared at the door.

With feverish haste, Adaku dashed to the door and unlocked it. Turning the knob, King Ajutu flung the door open. The knob on the inside of the door hit the wall hard and dented it. A little amount of fine dust from paint and filler material fell to the floor.

Leaving Adaku just outside the doorway, he strode into the room, looking around. It looked unlived-in. The wardrobe was open and empty. The bed was stripped. The table was bare. Walking across the room, he opened the door to the en-suite. He gave it a look, but Namdi wasn't there. He peeked behind the open door to no avail. Pulling the shower curtain aside, the shower was empty, too. Huffing out his irritation, he spun around, pounded his fist against the tiled wall and cracked a tile. He felt no pain.

"Bastards! How dare they have the sand to stand up against me?"

---

[1] Diagrammed on page 12 of *Children of the Shadows: Unearthing the Ritual.*

He stormed off, flinging away, livid to the hilt, feisty on an idea. "It is now clear that I can't leave this to these double-dealing henchmen—good riddance that half of them are dead. Time to look for new ones—supernatural kinds," he murmured under his breath. "Beasts I can better control; ones who stand a better chance against Odera."

Striding back through the doorway, he flashed Adaku a glance and yanked off her waist bag as he shoved past her onto the lounge. Its buckle broke and fell to the floor.

Arriving at the northwest passage in no time, "Go after them! Find them wherever they may be. Rub them all out—and don't even dare serve me again in bad faith. And then return to tell me why you, of all people, would tell me a barefaced lie and why I shouldn't send you back," he roared, his chthonic voice pealing, causing the birds feeding within the courtyard garden to take to the air in uncountable numbers as a shudder racked through Adaku's body.

Fury making him drift in and out of invisibility, he left the northwest passage and entered the north passage that led to the northeast section, slamming the door with a bang behind him. Marching through the dim passages, he headed toward his caucus room, leaving all doors open, his strides bounding.

****

Experiencing a rush of feeling for King Ajutu's displaced anger, shamefaced Adaku took in one sniff of the air in Namdi's room to determine its scent and pulled the door to shut with force. The key dropped to the floor of the lounge.

Leaping across from the lounge to the northwest passage, she barged through a door into the northwest veranda and kicked the door to slam shut as she began to morph.

Moving with a sensuous slink across the veranda onto the courtyard that was a theatre of chirping crickets, she purred, growled, then snarled as she, in every respect, transformed into a gorgeous black leopard with faint ghost stripes of circular dark spots.

With hackles raised, the sleek feline flipped its long, sturdy tail over its back, looked around once and leapt with prowess, grace, and stealth from one garden furniture to the next until it landed nimbly, on all paws, atop the roof terrace between the two west sections then, with all possible haste, up to the roof of the northwest section.

With its amber eyes glinting and narrowing, the smooth cat flared its nose in one direction after another. In the air that felt dry, it cast with fury for a trace of Namdi's scent, then as its eyes focused on a path wafting with vanilla-tinged cologne, its lingering tail rose with its tip twitching from side to side.

Setting off to spoor Namdi, the master of the shadows ghosted westward into the overhanging trees as they exhaled mists of early morning and descended a trunk, headfirst, and, in no time, dropped about 11 meters to the undergrowth of tangled, rampant vegetation and recumbent shrubs.

Evincing the terror of an animal in extremity, it purred past tree trunks with swift twists and turns until it disappeared through the cooling shade of the Stygian Forest[2], into the starless and faintly moonlit darkness of the small hours.

---

[2] Diagrammed on page 11 of *Children of the Shadows: Unearthing the Ritual*.

Chapter 2

All het up, King Ajutu squeezed himself through the widening gap between the half shelves within his caucus room before they each ground to a halt.

Forgoing all entry politesse, he arrived at his shrine front-first. His face still shooting a black look, he drew his mouth into a thin line. Biting on his lower lip, he tugged on his robe and closed its open top.

Then he postured and knelt before his *Ikengá*. Staring at it and pointing his right forefinger at the sun's eye that was painted into the concave south wall, "I implore thee to bring forth the Most Venerable One," he said in a shrill and commanding tone of voice.

In a wink, the purple, open human eye blinked once, and a voice boomed, "You do not approach the *Ikengá* front first, with your eyes open, without your Akupé, then summon the Venerable One with such a tone. It is not our praxis. Subsection four of section five directs you to 'walk humbly with your god.'"

"I know, Your Most Venerable, I mean no disrespect. My spirit is troubled. I need four fugitives to be rubbed out."

"Of that much I know, but your troubles are avoidable. You fight a needless battle. Your number will further increase if those four fugitives die for your protection—"

"Your Most Venerable, would that still be the case even if they die in the hands of others?"

"So long as they die for a reason by your *athame's* creation or the killer is under your tutelage, it will be recorded as a rub out in your name—section two, subsection five. You know this, but your indignation makes you ask. You are not thinking right," the Most Venerable One's voice was sonorous. "Though we know your will, we still need your words. So, what do you require?"

Evincing a haunted countenance, King Ajutu's wide, unblinking eyes appeared glazed as he rolled his shoulders, "Your Most Venerable, I require four supernatural henchmen."

"You know we cannot create living beings out of nothing, and you are quite specific on four, why?"

"I have only four bodies to give up at this time, Your Most Venerable, and I need them with immediacy."

"Good. So, go on and profess their names."

"Batu Ofuzo, Diko Ibaga, Jadue Efudu, Kadiye Imuno, Your Most Venerable."

"And what will be their nature?"

"Your Most Venerable, surprise me like the Queen of the Coast did two decades ago. You know better what will best serve me. Bestiality over beauty, this time, though. Then, I needed tireless, subservient, and vivacious servants. Now, I need fearsome warriors."

"The Queen of the Coast got demoted two ranks for going with just what your mind harbored and not demanding your words also. I need your words."

After a long moment of contemplation, "Chimeras of the most powerful animals of the sea, land, and air, and of all locomotive abilities, and capable of faster regeneration than the maidens, Your Most Venerable."

"I should not be dissuading you, but because you have been a loyal servant of the Evil Chief and we want you to stay in the human world to continue to serve him, I owe it to you to say that what will better serve you is to walk away from this witch-hunt."

"Walk away and remain troubled, Your Most Venerable?"

"You will be troubled regardless, but you will have more years to serve him. Again, I must ask, have you kept your eyes on your *Okiké*?"

"Not lately, Your Most Venerable."

"For 20 odd years since your malevolence against four of your previous henchmen, you haven't. Of course, you had no need to. Your memory may fade, but the elephant never forgets. Your number is rising. Your *Okiké* keeps the count."

"What is my count?" He cleared his throat. "Remind me, Your Most Venerable, I am frazzled at the moment; my memory is not serving me that well, and I prefer not to break our connection just to check the *Okiké*."

"It is not my duty to remind you. But your count is nine. With these four henchmen, it would rise to 13, and with the fugitive four, 17. Your creator supports something in the vicinity of three score years and ten, other things being equal, and with your strength and for not honoring your parents, especially your mother, we agreed with your maker on no more than four score years. Right now, you are at 71, add the four or eight to come and you will be at 67 or even 63. Remember that with each life you give up to the Prince of Darkness for the purpose of greater strength, evil, vengeance, protection, or wealth, yours shortens by one—section three, subsection five. The Evil One gives nothing for free. It is always at a great cost. As you stand, the Evil Chief will rub you out the moment you are 71—that is approximately ten years away. Keep your eyes on your *Okiké* the entire time. The four new names have been marked. Your ordained *athame* awaits—section two, subsection five. You know the observance. We await their *lifeforces*[3] for exchange. But be warned that there could be problems as they go through *the zone* if you give their lives up outside of this shrine. Remember the first three subsections of section two. And how quickly the body will regenerate depends on how long the body stays lifeless before it is *negergized*[4]. The shorter the duration, the faster they regenerate," the Most Venerable One's voice reverberated for the last time and the room's ambience dissolved to instant quietude as the sun's eye turned stock-still again.

He rose, and without observing his usual procedure for exiting his shrine, rushed to the caucus room's west wall and inspected his *Okiké*. There were nine vertical ridges spaced half a centimeter apart, beginning at the pointed end of the tusk and moving toward its wider end.

Counting on his fingers, "My son, the four young women who lost their lives to give life to my maidens, and the four henchmen whom I had to rub out lest they went against me after their role in kidnapping the four girls and witnessing me rub them out," he muttered to himself amid herky-jerky movements. "But I need these henchmen. I'd rather have just the next two years to live as the king than the next ten as a castoff with a blot on my escutcheon."

He strode back into the shrine, front first again, and stood still for a long moment. "Batu is weak from his injuries and should not be difficult to bring to the shrine, so I will take him first," he murmured. "The three others will be difficult. It was easier two decades ago. The unsuspecting henchmen were already in the shrine. It was easy to make them pass out by infusing fumes of

---

[3] The spirit or energy that gives life to living creatures; the soul.

[4] The process of giving a person's lifeforce overwhelming evil tendencies. This takes place at *the zone*.

chloroform into the shrine after locking them in it. These three may suspect foul play if I invite them to the caucus room at this time of the morning. What would I say is my reason for the invitation?"

Reaching to his right, he opened a shoulder-level cabinet and grabbed a glass container out of it. The transparent can had in it a thick piece of cloth within a colorless liquid. "Making them pass out in their rooms and carrying them one after the other to the shrine seems the obvious way out. For chloroform to work this time around though, the doctor did say that the mouth and nose must be exposed to it for no less than five minutes. Can I overpower them for that long? Diko is the strongest of them; perhaps I will take him last," he pondered for a moment. "And if this does not work…" He transferred the canister to his left hand and strode to his *Ikengá*, stooped, reached toward its back, and grabbed his *athame* whose handle was inscribed with the sigil of the purple-eyed sun, sticking it behind his cummerbund. "They die in their rooms, and I will deal with whatever problems may arise."

Carrying himself straight and with assurance, he marched out of the shrine, leaving it open. Grabbing Adaku's waist bag from the conference table with his right hand, he stuffed it inside his robe, behind the cummerbund, and secured it from dropping. His dark, malefic eyes glinting, he stormed out of the caucus room whilst his right hand pulled out his *athame*. As the hand clenched around its helve with its veins bulging, he seemed to harbor no doubts about the wisdom of his scheme.

Chapter 3

Meanwhile, with thick clouds obscuring much of the moon light, the starless welkin remained pitch-black.

Beneath the dusty haze of mid-January, the immediate vicinity of the cave[5] had a nigh-on peaceful ambience—though disturbed without end by the faint tinkle of cool water flowing down walls, the gently babbling streamlet, the thrum and plash of the resulting waterfall as well as chirping crickets, and, at irregular intervals, by the echoes of rasping *'kweek'* and series of sharp *'tsks'* from accidental nightjars across the dells, the ruffling of leaves by a gentle breeze, and the swish and faint hum of distant light traffic, some of which carried loud and clear across the landscape.

A trilateral door made with fronds of palm and sticks appeared to have secured the rock shelter's entrance. It'd taken Odera a little over an hour of skill and style to come up with the—two-meter tall, one-meter wide at the base—barrier, which he had completed moments before Namdi would arrive much to a welcome surprise. Namdi would help Odera install it. The bond between them and mutual respect evident during the half-hour process. Obiageli and I had contributed to the task by taking turns to hold up Odera's beaming flashlight.

Inside, attired in makeshift pajamas, we were all dead to the world—aided by the external sounds being muted by the door. Lying on a mat on the floor of the reorganized eminence, I was next to Obiageli who snored with little noise whilst my shut eyes made rapid movements. Odera seemed at peace as he slept face down on the cushioned bench between the mat and table. Namdi dozed atop several layers of his clothing, which were spread out on the

---

[5] Diagrammed on page 11 of *Children of the Shadows: Unearthing the Ritual* and on page 13 of *Children of the Shadows: The Never-ending Fear*.

pavement next to the cave entrance, his folded arms that rested on his kitbag pillowing his head, his bush machete sticking out beneath the bag.

Bute and a rather-subdued Dike, both of whom seemed to be growing closer, had their eyes respectively focused on the interior of the cave, even more so with Dike.

"I still can't believe that your mother fixed up that cave all by herself," Bute said. "Was she not scared of wild animals, or hoodlums?"

Shrugging, "She is as fearless as she is determined," Dike enthused.

"I probably won't understand why," Bute said, "but you seem to wonder if she has begun to let go of her interaction with you—"

"I am a little concerned, though I hope not. I do not want my story, at our gathering, to be like those of the others."

"I was right; that is why you did not attend tonight's gathering."

Dike nodded with feeling.

"I know how you feel—I felt that way, too, during my earlier periods here when all I wanted was to stay talking with the ones I loved…The ones who loved me…Something I took for granted while still human," Bute said. "But I don't think there is anything to worry about. It's not been long you last connected. Though I will use this opportunity to say that nothing lasts forever—"

"So, you would not mind Namdi forgetting you?"

"Though there were long spells of no communication between us during the past 16 years, he has not forgotten me. I'm just saying that everything in that world, our past world, is fleeting. Things can sometimes be fast-paced and, at other times, be slow, constant then irregular, up then down. Whatever it is, be prepared for what may come, and, at the same time, hope for better."

"You sound much like Somto."

"He will rub off on you pretty soon. And if you asked him, he would tell you about his early period here. He said he wasn't always like he is now. In any case, don't fret. A lot has happened to your mother in less than two days. She can't possibly speak to you through the night with all the exhaustion. She needs rest. Beyond everything, you indicated that you two have a strong bond."

With a smile building on Dike's face, "We do," he said.

"So, trust that that is good enough to keep you two talking for a long time to come," Bute spoke with airiness, then began to drift away. "Catch you later. It is no use watching Namdi as he sleeps. He has never awoken at night to speak to me…He is a sound sleeper. I came only to check up on you after not seeing you at our meeting."

"What will you then do?"

"Chat to the others. Continue to learn a thing, or two about the creativity they possess…That I can muster. I have a feeling Namdi, and Odera will need a lot of it from me soon and for a while to come."

"I will stay watching. My mother never sleeps through the night. She will be awake soon."

"Well, if like you said, you were the basis for her not sleeping through the night, then I see no reason why she would wake up now that you are no longer human; never mind her tiredness. For what it is worth, give her another squeeze. She should know it is you this time."

"I did try, but no amount—or tightness—of hugs yielded any results."

"Keep trying, or else give her some time to recoup her energy levels," Bute began receding from view. "Remember, with low expectations come little, or no disappointment."

No sooner a gust of emotion slumped Dike in deeper dejection than he heard me let out a sigh and watched as I turned to back Obiageli. Facing the lantern beneath the table whose dim light softened my face, I still didn't awaken. In double-quick time, I felt a tight hug and opened my eyes with a start, knowing it was Dike. There and then, I expressed the wish to see him.

Dike materialized in no time just as I sat bolt upright. Crossing my legs, I faced the foot of the mat.

"Mama, I was so worried that you had forgotten me," his voice thick with desire and overcome by impetuous passion.

With an expression of harassed fatigue and eyes straight away devoid of sleep and, I responded with a nonchalant shrug, "Not while I'm still alive. I'm just very tired. I was disturbed by a bad dream. But, my son, it's not been long we last spoke."

Dike pursed his lips in a self-satisfied smile, "I know, but I miss you so much. I realized that you were in a lighter sleep and tried to wake you again. I had been trying. What was your dream about?"

"I miss you, too. I think whilst reliving the concatenation of events that led us here, I saw your father in a miserable state."

"Hmm, Somto said that dreams gratify one's thoughts and wishes…That it also can serve as conduits through which one's concerns get channeled, showing images from one's subconscious or reflecting one's desires."

"Hmm, interesting. Did he say anything else about dreams?"

"A lot…And what got me concerned was him saying that negergies may also cause dreams to occur to haunt us or spur us into detrimental action. That they can do this by showing us what has happened in the past, which we may not have been privy to, making us grow eager to know."

"I see. Can I connect with this Somto who seems to know a lot about little-known subjects? You said he wished to meet me."

"Shall I go get him?"

"I think I see him already," I said as he appeared to my left, floating on Dike's right-hand side.

"Finally, I meet the mother of the year!" Somto gushed, his eyes shining with excitement.

"Hello there, Somto!" I raved. "Thank you for your warm approval, but you didn't have to. And thank you for looking after Dike."

"Not at all," he replied, glancing at Dike, beaming with pleasure. "Thank you for agreeing to meet me. I have been wondering if you would be willing to help some Pneumas exit from our world."

Looking to my right at Dike, I said, "He doesn't waste any time, does he?"

"I told you he is a straight shooter."

Somto remained smiling as my gaze shifted back to him.

"Dike talked about finding and burying the bodies of the spirits who want to leave your world. We would've to discuss it with Odera and Namdi. I alone won't be of great help."

"Pneumas," Somto corrected. "Can we talk with them now?"

Glancing at Odera, then down from the eminence at Namdi, I shook my head.

"Okay. Can we talk with them first thing after they wake up?"

Smiling, I glanced at Dike who shrugged, "We'll see about that," I said. "But I don't think that it'd be what's foremost on their minds when they wake up—making our way to Agudagu will be paramount. Dike said you hailed from Amandizuogu."

"Yes, from *Umudima* clan."

"I've never visited. I heard that they are trying out a ruling system without the monarch having so much power or existing at all as Agudagu has been successful at doing."

"Yes, for two years now, my brother did say so. If it will help its economy be like Agudagu's, I'm all for it," Somto said with no whisper of interest. "I've got to go now. It has been an honor to chat with you."

"We'll chat again soon," I replied but not faster than his disappearing act, then I looked at Dike who shrugged again.

"That's Somto for you, but you bypassed me and took the shine off the first meeting between you two. You should have allowed me to introduce you."

"I'm sorry, it wasn't done on purpose. Please forgive me."

"You don't need to apologize, Mama. I am only learning how to vocalize what I would, as a human being, typically have clung to as a grudge. I'm learning not to be as stubborn and misconceiving as I used to be. Somto told me to deal with the issues there and then with whomever offends me so that I bear no grudges."

Smiling, I nodded. "He seems good for you. But I must tell you that I have mixed feelings about your decision to not be buried at this time. Your body will be more and more unidentifiable as time goes by."

"With what has happened in Akagheli these past two days, with all we have uncovered, you will soon realize that you need me to be around. I will not be the only one whose body will be beyond recognition. If when it is time for me to leave where I am, whenever that is, and I am hoping a long time to come, and my body, along with those that are where mine is, has disintegrated, then a mass burial may be the way to go."

"It saddens me that I won't be able to give my son a proper burial on the one hand, but happy that he's still with us on the other hand."

Dike grinned, "I am glad to still be around."

Chapter 4

Even as Dike and I spoke, Batu couldn't care less who'd opened the door to his stark room.

Groaning and holding onto his throbbing head as his dwelling lit up for a moment, he tried to find a suitable lying position that wouldn't aggravate the ache in his body.

Sneaking in, King Ajutu didn't light up the room. Pushing the door to hang ajar, the area was thrown into semidarkness. Prowling away from the doorway, he lifted his chin and hovered near the foot of Batu's bed. Out of sight, behind his back, one hand bore his athame and, the other, the jar of chloroform. Able to see by a chink of light from the lounge through the cracked open door, which cast his shadow on the wall behind him, "You seem to be in a lot of pain…" he said, his words ringing hollow.

With labored breaths, shirt and pants clad, Batu lifted his head a touch. Fighting the bruising and swelling that marred his face, he peered with his bloodshot, brown eyes at the king as he continued to speak: "Come with me to my caucus room, and my personal physician will make you feel a lot better. He is on his way."

"Thank you, Your Majesty," Batu said with a groggy voice and rose from his single bed. "I can't see very well…and I am sorry to be asking, but, please, will His Majesty be able to help me?"

As a ghost of an evil smile grew on King Ajutu's face whilst his dark, malevolent eyes glinted, he stuck his knife in his flank, behind his cummerbund, and set the jar down on the floor by the wall he stood before.

Helping Batu out of bed and onto his feet, he guided his hobbling henchman out of the room, through the lounge and the passages, to arrive in the caucus room shrine.

With Batu still clung to his left arm, King Ajutu thumbed a button on his right that was adjacent to the cabinet. Grinding out of the floor of the room's center, a fine block of marble grew to about 80 centimeters.

Looking up at his king, "Thank you, Your Majesty," Batu just about managed to let out.

Nodding, King Ajutu helped him lie atop the slab.

And no sooner had Batu settled facing up to the vaulted ceiling than King Ajutu with a maleficent stare at Batu, in an instant and with a swift, forceful motion whilst intoning cryptic incantation that spoke of offering up one lifeforce for another, plunged his athame, with both hands, into Batu's heart. Though able to protect his face, the king didn't manage to avoid the spatter of blood onto the front of his robe.

At the same time, Batu's disfigured face assumed an even more grotesque distortion. Arching his back in horror for a moment, he collapsed back, hard, onto the rigid surface and went wide-eyed at his king whose hands continued to push down on the knife's handle. As blood spilled out of Batu's heart, Batu let out a series of whimpers that faded little by little to silence.

King Ajutu yanked out the weapon and as blood dripped from it and his hands, he leapt to kneel before his Ikengá, within the space between it and the head of the table and pointed the knife at the eye on the wall, "Your Most Venerable, you now have Batu's life in exchange for the lifeforce of your creation. I await."

He dropped the weapon on the floor. Wiping his hands on the flanks of his robe, he stood and swung around to face Batu. Twisting his wedding band around and around on his finger, he watched Batu from the head of the slab.

In a snap, an ominous green-blue light emanated from the eye on the wall, split into two, and entered each of Batu's eyes.

Screeching with agony suddenly, Batu began to ripple and lengthen whilst his muscles twitched, bulged, and ripped apart his clothes that were becoming tight-fitting; his injuries passing from sight.

In a quick sequence of movements, Batu lifted his upper body off the table and swung his legs to dangle them from the edge for a moment before he sprang off it. Turning counterclockwise in the air, he landed secure with slyness and postured before the king with his head hanging. Whilst his right knee, left foot, and clenched right fist pressed hard against the floor, he flung his left arm to position it across his back.

"Your Majesty," he said with a deep, bass voice. "Your humble servant awaits a name."

"You shall continue to be known by the name your body's owner bore as has been my tradition. You may arise now, Batu," King Ajutu said and strode out of the shrine, the bottom of his robe swaying about his legs. "Come with me. I will show you to your room. You will be there until I need you."

"Yes, Your Majesty," Batu said as he looked up, and his new, unclouded, green-blue eyes twinkled.

Rising, Batu turned on his heel and marched close behind his king, towering over him.

Glancing in the direction of his Okiké on his way out of the caucus room, the king noted that an additional ridge had appeared. Screwing his eyes shut for a moment, he heaved a heavy sigh.

Upon arriving before Batu's room, King Ajutu looked up at him and pointed to the door. Bending his head forward, Batu walked in and perched on the edge of the bed. Entering after him, King Ajutu grabbed the canister, strode out of the room, shut, and locked the door.

Arriving in front of the room to the immediate right of Batu's, he pushed its door open, and Jadue was fast asleep, facing up. Unscrewing the transparent container as he, at irregular intervals, held his breath to limit the volume of fumes he might inhale, the king pulled out the wet rag and laid the jar on the floor just beneath the bed. As liquid dripped down between his fingers onto the floor, he replaced the glass can's lid.

Sitting his full weight astride Jadue's midsection, he pinned Jadue's arms down with his knees before placing the rag over Jadue's mouth and nose. Pressing down on it with the heels of both palms, he tightened the fabric over Jadue's lower face as its fluid streamed down Jadue's cheeks and neck.

Chilled by the occurrence, Jadue opened his eyes wide, and King Ajutu assumed invisibility in an instant. In a bid to be free of the fumes that stifled him, Jadue tossed his head, in a vigorous manner, from side to side, but no amounts of struggle without his hands availed him. And once he was dazed, King Ajutu materialized and stuffed the rag back in the canister.

Lifting him up over a shoulder, the king plodded to his shrine whilst huffing and coughing. There, he laid Jadue on the marble top, performed a similar ritual slaying and Jadue would transmute into a taller version with a Herculean build and glinting, green-blue eyes.

"My lungs definitely cannot stand the strain of another heavy lifting without my inhaler," deliberative King Ajutu muttered to himself under heavy breathing as he pressed the button on the shelf to shut the shrine. "But I don't have the time…"

He guided Jadue to his room.

Exiting from it with his canister, King Ajutu entered Kadiye's and managed to make him pass out as he did Jadue. Striding out of the room, he pocketed the canister and entered an adjoining dwelling.

In the darkness, save for the light from the lounge, he tapped on Diko over and over, "Rise up, Diko," he said time and again, panting.

Jumping out of bed to the sound of his king's voice, Diko adopted a single genuflection with a tilt of his head, "Your Majesty," he said. "What do you require from your loyal servant?"

Puffing a little, "I need your help to get Kadiye to the caucus room. He has taken ill, and the doctor is on his way to see him," King Ajutu said as he walked out of the room. "Come with me."

Carrying Kadiye over a shoulder, Diko wondered about the pungent smell Kadiye reeked of, which also, to an increasing extent, choked him as he coughed and trundled toward the caucus room behind the king.

In the room, King Ajutu arrived before the shelf and pointed to the floor next to it, "Set him down there," he said as he stepped away from the area.

Coughing, Diko was hardly able to orientate himself and keep his eyes open as he laid Kadiye down.

With his heart heaving, the king lifted the chair that was allotted to Chief Madu. With both hands and with a right to left swing, he clouted the right side of Diko's neck with the stile of the wood furniture.

Spewing out blood from his mouth, Diko went limp and let Kadiye land with a solid smack.

As Diko fell forward over Kadiye, King Ajutu, baring his teeth and with extreme force, struck Diko's temple with the bottom of his clenched left fist and rendered him unconscious. Still puffing, the king opened his shrine and thumbed the button that lowered the marble slab. Dragging Diko onto it, he pushed the switch again to raise the table, then repeated his ritual routine.

Chapter 5

Masses of dark clouds, out of which lightning crackled and fizzed, had blocked out the setting sun that glowed the sky red as a torrent of rain, blown by the wind that howled about the palace, poured down and pitted the bare earth; the speedy drops spattering and pattering against the steps, windows, and steel gates as well as a black car whose engine thrummed whilst it sat parked across the open palace gateway.

The shrubs on the building side of the fence were a blaze of color.

Heading for the palace front doors as the first pearls of thunder rolled across the airspace, Ajutu had his left forearm around a boy's shoulder. Exiting through the double entry door whose left half was open, they were greeted by a man in uniform who stood in front of the right half and appeared a little older than Ajutu.

Atop the stoop, Ajutu patted the boy on the head, squatted down before him, then collected a wristwatch from the man. Showing Odera the timepiece, "Odera, my son," Ajutu crooned. "Ejizu said you are the only person he would ever share this with. So, let me strap it on for you."

Odera stretched out both his skinny arms, smiling as he swayed on his feet. And Ajutu, looking as keen as mustard, placed the watch on Odera's left wrist.

The watch's case back had no sooner induced pain in Odera than Ajutu's body twitched to his own surprise at the same time, unbeknownst to him, a silver color flashed across the pupils of his eyes.

As Odera let out a yell that coincided with another explosion of thunder that resounded in the west and, on instinct, repeatedly stamped his rain-boot-shod feet on the concrete floor in agony, shaking his left wrist in a futile attempt to get the watch off, Ajutu's face remained a study in confusion as he persisted in fastening the straps, cinching it as tight as was possible.

Then Ajutu gathered Odera to his chest, his mind whirling, "Shush! Shush! That's okay, my son…It is well now," he said, succeeding in muffling Odera's cry.

In a flash, the pain spread through Odera's left arm toward his left shoulder, neck, then his heart, and, in the fullness of time, exploded within him, giving rise to a sudden chill that was accompanied by shivering, an elevation in body temperature, and copious sweating. And within the space of five heartbeats, he felt normal again.

"Papu, you may get in the car now," Ajutu whispered. "You can see that it has happened as they wanted."

With a head bob, "Your Royal Highness," Papu replied.

Papu had descended the steps and entered the driver's side of the car when Ajutu released Odera from the embrace, making a show of checking him over, "I am sorry, my son, it was static electricity that caused the pain. You will be fine from now forward. Show it to your mother. Tell her I gave it to you, but do not give it to anyone. Ejizu will not be happy if you do. Take it as your sixth birthday present in advance, if you like—"

"Is it not too early? My birthday is not until the end of next month," Odera said.

"Just cherish it, okay?" Ajutu demanded. "And keep it safe."

Odera nodded, "I am sorry for yelling, Your Royal Highness, thank you," Odera said, then looked skyward. "Thank you, Ejizu."

"You are a strong boy for not crying," Ajutu said as he pulled the hood of Odera's raincoat over his head and pecked him on the forehead. "Run along now, Papu is your new driver and is waiting to take you home. We will see you again tomorrow after school. He knows to be there waiting for you; Princess Nena will give you lunch, and I will see you when I return from work in the evening, and we can have supper together as usual before you go home."

"Bye," Odera turned around.

Odera ran down the concrete steps and opened the door to the Mercedes' left backseat. Settling into it, he waved at Ajutu as he pulled the door shut.

Ajutu returned a wave at the car as it drove away, then got to his feet when the car had disappeared from his view. As he turned around to enter the palace, something about the set of his shoulders suggested that he'd felt accomplished though his mind continued to wonder what had also momentarily happened to his own body.

As beads of cold sweat appeared on Odera's forehead, his eyes snapped open with a start, brightening a little in the inky darkness. Despite Obiageli's snoring and Nkem's muted voice as she remained in conversation with Dike, all Odera could hear was the pounding of his own heart.

Feeling an ache in the entirety of his left forearm, though less so than he'd felt straight away after installing the cave door, he rubbed his left wrist, glancing at his wristwatch, and the time was 04:47. Lying awake for some time, he puzzled over his dream.

And with an unfocused gaze, he turned his head toward the cave entrance and the door seemed to stand secure. Flashing a slight knowing smile, he faced the opposite side again, shut his groggy eyes and went out like a light.

Chapter 6

By the time Dike caught sight of it, it had ripped off the raffia door.

With an uncertain crack to his voice, "Mama, a black—" he'd shrieked.

Startled by the sudden crash in the doorway, our connection ended before he could complete his sentence.

Gasping, I stared and babbled, "God help me—us! Dike, help!"

A chill ran down my spine as the hairs on the back of my neck stood on end, and it had nothing to do with the draft through the then-door-less cave mouth. A charging black leopard, which yowled and grunted with anger, had barged into the cave, and had landed on the pavement next to Namdi. I was certain that it was only a matter of seconds before it'd maul Namdi to death, then come after us.

The continual guttural sounds overshadowed the outside ambient noises, which were no longer muted.

As my gaze fastened on the pair of glinting, amber eyes that surveyed the area, Obiageli turned around on the mat, insensible to the developing situation. Overwrought, I grabbed and shook Odera's arm with feverish jerks, "Odera, wake up!" I yelled in loud whispers, pointing at the cave entrance as my breath burst in and out whilst my heart leapt into my mouth and my lips trembled. "A wild animal! And it's near Namdi."

With a sudden deluge of alarm that seemed to rise within him, perhaps due to the panic in my voice, "What? Where is he? Is he okay?" Odera whispered as he sprang off the bench and felt around the top of the table. "Shoot, I hung it on the bike after making the door."

Grabbing the flashlight from the table, he beamed its light at the cave entrance. Seeming to ignore the dazzle, the sawing panther remained astride motionless Namdi, looking down at him. Namdi's damp, bulging eyes were filled with blind panic as he stared at the large carnivore's faintly spotted and lustered somewhat purplish underbelly fur, avoiding its eyes. As the sound of his heartbeat thrashed in his ears, Namdi tried to grab his machete from under his kitbag. Appearing to growl its displeasure at Namdi's attempt, the large cat also appeared content with just standing over him. More confused than terrified, Namdi didn't freeze. His forehead beaded with perspiration, runnels of sweat formed on the sides of his face.

I cradled Obiageli's head in my arms against my bosom, hoping to muffle her snoring and protect her ears from the loud echoes of the animal's sounds.

Moments on, having had enough of the glare from Odera's flashlight, the felid cocked its concave earflaps and appeared to be confirming the noise that it'd detected from us. Sniffing Namdi once—its long whiskers stroking his face, it licked Namdi's lips whilst connecting eyes with him. Then it purred and moved fast with impetus, toward the eminence, hissing and snarling.

Seeing this, bemused Odera's voice rose many octaves as he roared, "Namdi, my machete, now!"

Confounded Namdi rose in an instant, forward rolled, and grabbed the cased weapon—that Odera had said was fashioned from a super alloy made in the main with nickel, copper, chromium, and titanium, with varying and tiny fractions of iron, manganese, silicon, carbon, and zirconium, according to what Papu had told him—off the motorbike's handlebar.

"Bute, help! Help Odera, help us," Namdi whispered as he flung the blade in the direction of the light source.

Odera jumped onto the table and caught it at the top of its flight with his right hand, aided by light from his torch. Landing back onto the floor, he unsheathed it between his left flank and tucked-in left arm. The weapon's metal scabbard clattered to the stone floor, and as an eerie sound resonated within the cave, he postured, stood—feet planted and wide apart—behind the bench, before Obiageli and me, shielding us.

With the flashlight in the tight grip of his left hand and machete clasped in the other hand, he hyperventilated, and his broad shoulders heaved, "I told you I saw one of those," Odera whispered with a tremor in his voice as his leg muscles tightened.

More interested in Obiageli's protection rather than any 'I told you so', I held her closer.

Guided by its perfect vision, the noisy and furious feline bounded without effort, up the steps that had been hewn into the rock wall. Arriving atop the eminence, it made a sharp turn to its left and stopped. Locking gazes with

Odera whose flashlight shone into its mid-face, its pupils that were dilated to the hilt narrowed a little. Crouching, it snarled, forming spume of spit in its mouth, and swishing its tail with ferocity. Poised motionless, each voluntary muscle in Odera's body tuned only to winning the looming clash.

With the tension reaching a high point, in a blink, the majestic cat leapt across the table and pounced with outstretched claws, aiming for Odera's neck with its jaws and knocking him backward.

On instinct and happening in rapid succession, Odera jerked his head back, blocked his neck with his left hand as he shoved the flashlight toward its furious face and, in no time, drove the point of his machete upward into its underbelly with a powerful thrust and twist, puncturing through and through the artery that pumped blood from its heart.

Sinking its jaws into the device, its canines caught parts of Odera's fingers just as he withdrew them; and as he fell onto Obiageli and me, he swept the weapon in a downward slash with both hands, tearing the said blood vessel's whole length.

As the hefty feline landed with Odera, a shadow departing from it, moving through the air like a bat out of hell, the torch was jammed between its jaws; its light pointing at a diagonal toward the ceiling. With minimal effort, Odera pushed its suddenly cold, lifeless body away, knocking the bench over. Standing up, he pulled out his weapon whilst applying counter pressure.

Wielding his machete, Namdi leapt up the steps as Odera turned around and gathered us to his broad chest. As I felt the side of my face pricked by his two-day-old bristles, I couldn't tell whose heart pounded faster. And Obiageli would awaken because of the extra squeeze from a well-muscled man.

Namdi arrived at the landing and as his eyes widened in the instant he pointed at the body on the floor, his mouth dried up and his tongue clove to the roof of his mouth.

The dead body's face had become lit up in part by the dim lantern beneath the table. Falling out of its shrinking jaws, the metal flashlight clanked against the stone floor and jolted us. Readying his weapon without conscious effort, Odera turned to face the source of the rattle.

Seeing Namdi transfixed, Odera set his machete on the table in less than no time, picked up the torch, and flashed it at the carcass, "Adaku!" Odera shrieked, leaving his mouth agape and eyes widened.

"You were right," Namdi said as he shuffled back a step with his head down and took a moment to reflect. "You are always right."

"The reason it spared you," Odera said as I let go of groggy Obiageli, sidled to him, and wrapped my arms around his right arm.

"She certainly wanted me for herself," Namdi said, jerking his head back and away from the sight. "If not, I would have been on my way to where Father is."

"The affection she had for you was her weakness," Odera said. "That weakness probably got her not thinking right and contributed in no small part to saving us all—"

"What is going on, Mama?" Obiageli said as she arose from the mat whilst idiosyncratically rubbing her eyes.

Hugging me around the waist, I draped my right arm around her shoulders as three of us stared at Adaku's nightgown-clad, lifeless body that spilled blood and bowel from the whole of the front of its torso through a significant rent in her clothing as the body slowly changed its overall appearance.

"What now?" I said with eagerness.

Deviled by a newfound fear, "We leave this cave immediately," Namdi said with a voice that rose in its pitch as he hurried down the steps. "There are three more where she came from and those ones have no fondness for any of us."

"Who is that Mama?"

Still confounded, Odera felt pain in his left hand and lifted it. Shining his light at it, it was bloodied but seemed not to be bleeding. There were cuts across the distal parts of the three middle fingers.

I took the light from him and handed it to Obiageli. Picking up the bench, I stood it over the body. Guiding him to sit down on it, I set his hand on the table and lifted the lantern onto the furniture. Turning it up, its flickering glow projected our shadows on the stone walls. The entirety of the front of his shirt was blood red and so were my and Obiageli's clothes. Parts of his right Caligae sandal were also smeared with blood.

"I need more light," I said, rushing to the kitchenette. "Oby, please, point it to the table."

Grabbing a bowl, I stuck it into the water that descended the east wall of the eminence and half-filled it. Setting it on the table, I displaced Odera's wristwatch as far as it could go up his forearm so as not to get it wet. Noting that the time was 05:19, I dipped his trembling, ill-manicured, hand in the cool water. As the water turned an instant crimson color, my eyes alighted on a circular black scar—where the watch's case back had been in contact with his skin—debossed with a symbol that was just about visible.

Our gazes meeting for a beat, I tore off a small portion of my wrapper and swathed his fingers in it as he gently pushed the watch down to cover the circular blotch.

"That must hurt, Odera. Did that lady, over there, cause it?" Obiageli crooned.

"Yes, Oby, but she can't harm him, or us now that she is dead," I said. "Odera made sure of that."

"Lucky it's my left hand," Odera said in a muted voice. "I can still fight with my right one."

Locking gazes with him again, "You think there will be more fights?" I whispered in forlorn hope that he'd refute my suspicion that the fight had only just begun.

With his eyes flashing, "Think?" he whispered and shook his head. "I know. I told you what the queen said—you heard what Namdi just said. This is just the beginning. He will not stop until we are silenced for good. Based on what he told me before directing me to…you know," glancing at me, then at Obiageli. "Going by what he told Namdi when he commanded him to go after us with the other henchmen, he entertains no shadow of a doubt that you, and anyone on your side, threaten his reign as king, so he will be firm in his purpose for going after us with everything he has, and it could be any creature as you have seen. Who knows what those other maidens can turn into? You can never get King Ajutu to eat crow. He is going to be the very devil to defeat."

Finding certainty, a renewed fire, and refuge in his eyes, "Then we have to run to Agudagu immediately," I said and hurried around to gather our belongings.

With a strained smile, "My immediate older brother in North America would have said, 'Why couldn't you see the reality of the situation; better wake up and smell the coffee,'" Odera said. "Namdi, we cannot spend another minute here. We should have left for Agudagu the moment you mentioned what Adaku had told you."

"I am fully awake and the coffee smells strong," Namdi said. "I am good to go. No time to dwell on the past."

Chapter 7

Unbeknownst to him that his eyes had flashed amber once a little while earlier, bone-tired King Ajutu arrived before his great chamber's doors and gestured his four, new, tall, and fearsome henchmen to wait at the top landing of the southwest section.

With a quick glance at their maximal muscled physiques, which were on full display, "Get acquainted with one another as you wait," the king commanded with towering anger as he pulled the doors open. "Our forthcoming mission of great import requires unity."

Walking through the doors, he removed Adaku's waist pouch from within his robe and flung it toward his dresser. In the darkness, he squinted at the bed as the doors shut without much noise. Adaku wasn't in bed, and the other maidens seemed to be as he'd left them. With the covers down at their heels, he caught sight of their perfect figures as well as the gradual rise and fall of their firm and symmetrical breasts…Nonetheless neither of them had Adaku's kind of effect on him and the tension in his stomach loosened not a bit.

He strode toward the right side of the dresser and entered his closet that was full of a variety of articles of clothing including printed shirts and footwear all made with baroque exuberance. Swapping the bloody robe for a clean one of the same color and dropping it on the floor, he contemplated for a moment.

Proceeding deeper into the adjoining restroom, he looked out of a high-arched window on its south wall. Seeing his queen's house in pitch blackness, he curled his lips. He returned to the room and sat in a chair, facing the dresser.

With his head down, he leaned forward and set his elbows on his thighs. Lacing his fingers together and rubbing his palms, he tried to calm his sense of foreboding.

Chomping at Adaku's whereabouts, "And why is she not back?" he muttered, lifting his head to glance at the clock above the entrance on the east wall. "5:23."

He looked toward the top of his dresser, and saw, in alphabetical order of names, four gleaming suns on the handle of his Akupé. As a wide grin grew on his face, he drummed his shoeless feet against the soft floor and reached for it. He grabbed it, spinning the handle around to the opposite side.

Struck dumb for a moment as his smile changed into a bark of laughter, he gasped. With an incredulous stare, he jerked his head backward as giddiness came over him. Squeezing his eyes shut for an instant, he opened them to look again. Still, only the bottom three of the four stars sparkled. The topmost one remained extinguished.

Experiencing a coldness that went right to his core, his grip on the fan's handle tightened for a moment before he dropped it back on the dresser as if it seared. Turning his head away, he stood up with a stiffened posture, shook his head and, with an exquisite kind of agony, emitted a short, mournful squall, "Noooooooo!"

Clutching at his chest, he hunched over and tried to catch his breath.

Then he rushed toward his night table. Stumbling as his right foot caught the leg of the bed, he grabbed his puffer, shook it once, inhaled the first time, then one more time.

Tossing the device aside as he dropped to his knees, he uttered a yelp of disbelief and sunk his head in the bed as tears streamed down his cheeks. "Just because I was angry, I let her go after them alone, despite knowing Odera's strength. Why? Why? Why? Why have I done this to myself?" he sobbed, gnashing his teeth as he pushed a fist into the bed.

Rising, he leapt across the room to the east wall, flicked a switch. After the room lit up, he strode to the dresser, ran a thumb over the four suns from the top to the bottom, then grabbed his Akupé. Taking up a position in the center of the room, he paced back and forth.

Batu, Diko, Jadue, and Kadiye, in that order, filed into the room and stood before the adjoining east wall.

The king pressed the three stars on his Akupé, and the naked maidens launched themselves out of bed to take up positions before the west wall.

With their heads bowed, all seven chorused with differing cadences: "Your Majesty."

Setting his Akupé down on the bed, King Ajutu faced the maidens each of whose hair still remained in a perfect chignon, "For those of you who knew Adaku, she is no more," he noted, and each of the maiden's interest sharpened as they stiffened and exchanged furtive, wide eyes at one another with their rich faces glowing with emotion. Turning his neck to look at the henchmen, "And for those who had not even a nodding acquaintance with her, she was my irreplaceable number one. She has been executed by the very people you have now been created to hunt down and rub out. Batu, Diko, Jadue, and Kadiye, this is your mission, your reason for existing, and it behooves you to not fail me. Be wise and attack in twos. No lone wolves, and do not all rush in like fools. Odera is not an easy target. Adure, Isioma, and Ijeoma, you will go with them. Act as the second line of attack. Stay concealed. Only get involved if it heats up. And what is our motto?"

"United we stand, divided we fall," the maidens said in unison.

"Henchmen, take note," the king barked.

Striding to the dresser, he grabbed Adaku's bum bag, sniffed it and closed his eyes, sinking his face in it for a moment. Then he squeezed it with a mixture of anger and frustration.

He unzipped it and poured out its content on the bed with keys clinking as they tumbled out, "Take this…" he said, and, with scathing glitter in his eyes, he tossed it to Diko. "Let it guide you to wherever she is and to only the people she left her scent on—two men, a woman, and a little girl. No more, no less. The maidens will show you them if need be, and make sure to return the bag to me along with her body…" He paused for a long contemplative moment. "Now, go," he roared, delivering the words with finality.

Bobbing their heads, they left the room in a wink, with Ijeoma leading the way. Jogging down the stairs and through the passages, they arrived on the west veranda, then stopped. Each of the brazen-faced henchmen, who were clad in undersized t-shirts and shorts and stood well over two meters tall, looked a question. Leering at the unclothed, young women, for a moment or so, attraction seemed to crackle between the two groups.

Protecting their modesty by natural instinct and as one, the maidens placed their right arms and hands over their busts, left hands in front of their private parts as their right thighs moved a little over the left—then transformed.

Adure turned into a sturdy, heavy, compact, black morph forest jaguar with powerful jaws on a broad head, short, stocky limbs, and dappled with few, large, solid spots on the head and neck, which grew thicker, larger, and rosette-shaped on the body. Ijeoma reshaped into a slick and tall, golden leopard bespeckled with numerous, solid, black rosettes. Isioma converted to a tawny cougar with flecks of black at its tail's tip, face, and behind its ears, and white below its eyes and around its mouth.

Chuffing at each other, the felids loped onto the garden and leapt onto one item of furniture after another to arrive on the roof ahead of the henchmen who had followed in turn.

They then, for a moment, stood, side by side, in file—Batu on the far right, Kadiye on the far left, and in between them, Adure, Jadue, Ijeoma, Diko, and Isioma in that order from left to right.

Scanning around for an instant and following Adaku's scent, they sprang off tandem into the forest. Causing small birds to flit about in the tree branches, they landed steady with their feet on the ground cover. And without breaking stride, they hared off, weaving between the trees, remaining abreast.

As they galloped along, alert Jadue saw, with his glistening, aqua eyes that seemed capable of nighttime vision, a tentative squirrel that lurked scores of meters ahead. Projecting a clear fluid from his mouth at breakneck speed, he directed its range to pour down on the unwary animal. Whilst the rodent underwent gradual disintegration with continued sizzling, Jadue leaned back and looked rightward—over the felines of Ijeoma and Isioma and around the back of Diko's head—at Batu, "What have you got?" he said, rushing his words with a bubbly baritone.

Darting an upward glance toward his left, Batu exhaled at a tree branch. In no time, fire from his nose and mouth ignited the offshoot and consumed it.

Tightening the squeeze of his right hand around the waist bag, Diko looked back and doused the fire with a blast of steaming water breathed in jets from his mouth and nose, "Our mission does not include starting a bushfire that might rub out someone we are not meant to," Diko said with an officious, deep, bass voice that had an edge to it amid intermittent grunting and deep roaring from the felines as well as the rustling of leaves and cracking of twigs underfoot.

"So, I make acid, Batu produces fire, and Diko hot water. What will Kadiye bring to the fight?"

Straight-faced Kadiye turned his head rightward, over Adure's Jaguar, and eyed Jadue. Then, he twisted his neck 180 degrees around to look back. With a quick streak of lightning from his eyes, he struck down the smoldering twig. Eyeing Jadue one more time as he turned to face forward again, he roared an earsplitting crack of thunder. This, rumbled with strong claps that shook the area, fell some trees and triggered a racket of animal cries dominated by the squawking of numerous birds and fluttering of their wings as they took flight.

With a nod, "Impressive! This already has the makings of an exciting operation," Jadue enthused as he pulverized, with one step, the fizzing pile of dissolving rodent bones under his bare right foot. Feeling no pain as he ran on, the abrasion on the sole of his right foot healed in a snap.

Their interest enkindled, they shot off. And scenting the breeze at every pace, they followed Adaku's whiff with a pertinacious drive. Bounding the rugged terrain, they scrunched the underbrush, flattened foliage, and bent thin woods. Skipping watercourses, they disappeared into the black forest whose trees and shrubs were mantled in dust and glittered with dew.

Chapter 8

At the same time, some sixth sense continued to tell Somto that their world, from which he'd long accepted there was no return, had taken on a different sort of verve.

"All this while, I've considered myself a master of this crossroads world—certain that there can't be anything new here to discover or explore," he soliloquized. "How pleasantly wrong have I been?"

Throwing a further glance at the entry portal, there was still no indication of a new arrival. Gliding a significant distance, Somto approached Dike.

Dike was watching us four as we tore away from the vicinity of the natural cavern, sending up clouds of dust into an air that was tainted by fumes from vehicles. Slowing down, we forced our way into the shimmer of myriad lights from the stream of heavy, rumbling, and almost-gridlocked expressway traffic as impatient motorists blasted their horns, scowling and letting out expletives whilst making sudden swerves. With each of us dressed in our outfits from the day before, Obiageli was sandwiched between Odera and me as he rode on the motorbike, atop patchy and potholed asphalt, slaloming in and out of slower road users. Namdi, who journeyed along on the dirt surface that was contiguous with the blacktop, rode my bicycle with our baggage and their machetes in its posterior carriage and just managed to maintain our pace because of the slow-moving, balking motorists. Avoiding glaring eyes from the passengers all around us and turning to look back, again and again, all the while, at the unlit blackness over Akagheli, Odera, Namdi, and I were fearful of what may be coming after us.

"Do you sense something new about this place?" Somto said. "Like a gathering force—a growing energy?"

Without looking at Somto, "I have not been in tune—have been concerned about my mother and sister's safety since their encounter with the black leopard," Dike said with nonchalance. "Why do you ask? Do you feel something?"

"Yes. Not quite anything I've felt before—even as a human. I can liken it to what Buka describes to me regarding his growing sentiments toward his love interest at work. So, I think with a high degree of certainty that a Pneuma, not quite like any of us, has settled here."

"How do you mean?" Dike said whilst his unblinking gaze remained on us.

"A Pneuma of the opposite sex—a female," Somto said.

His interest kindling, Dike shot Somto a stare. "How could that have happened? You said only people who died like us end up here and only boys go to glory like us."

"For Mkpátáku, yes, only boys," Somto said. "But it is possible that it goes deeper—there could be more on this issue than meets the eye."

"So, what now?"

"We find out."

"I am afraid, but you would have to do it alone or find Ijezie. I want to be ready for when Mother calls."

"Catch you later then," Somto said and disappeared in no time.

Having negotiated the patches of highway that were damaged to a large degree, as fast as was possible, we continued on the first stretch of better-maintained road to Agudagu, which pursued a straight course due northwest over scrubland and had faster traffic.

My eyes ranged beyond the sprawling hills, dense green valleys, and, on the whole, jackal-berry dells, which were around three kilometers due north-northwest, toward a landscape on the outskirts of our destination that shrank storied buildings to just dots of light. And my mind began counting off each second of the 90-odd minutes Odera said would be the minimum time it'd take us to arrive at the center of the said town where Prince Ikuku lived.

****

In a far-removed region of the crossroads world, Somto glimpsed a hunkered-down, shimmering human figure, which lurked just within his range of vision. Reappearing as he closed in on it, his eyes glittered with excitement,

"Aha! Adaku Ofor. I knew I was right," he raved, stilling his demeanor to observe her closely.

Projecting a calm image, the slender female Pneuma, with wavy, silvery-gray hair that flowed over her shoulders, cast Somto a glance, then stood up to face him, "Yes, Somto Odinaka," she said with an inner light, looking Somto straight in the eyes. "Right about what, your feelings?"

Struck by her ethereal beauty, Somto nodded, "You have to have been taken to a shrine and killed a certain way with the killer intoning a certain rune to be in our elusive world," he said.

"And that's how I came here. Your point being?"

"I didn't see you arrive the usual way—"

"You don't see everything. Only The Almighty does."

Nodding again, "I agree," he said with a distant, unfocused smile. "But not a single Pneuma saw you descend; I would have discerned you otherwise."

"That, I can agree with you on."

"Did you just arrive, then?"

With a half shrug, she shook her head, "I've been dead for many years."

Tilting his head to the side, he gazed at her with focus. "For what purpose?" he said. "Mine was for wealth. Every Pneuma here, by the way, all of whom come from every one of our country's three lands, died for the sake of wealth."

Lifting a single brow, she asked, "You've met every Pneuma here?"

Somto gave a crisp nod and thumbs-up as he moved closer.

"There can't be many of you, then," she said.

Somto sniggered and shook his head, "A few thousands."

"You are quite meddlesome, aren't you? To have interacted with thousands of Pneumas," she moved back a pace to increase her personal space. "Well, in my case, King Ajutu said it was for the purpose of his protection."

"I've been here longer than most and was able to welcome a lot of them. Just a few tens were still here when I arrived," he said. "Why am I just sensing your presence though? When did you arrive here?"

"Why so many questions?"

"Curiosity," he said with a blithe, smiling face. "Besides, what's there to do here most times than to talk and interact?"

With a wooden expression, she pondered, "Maybe 20 years ago or so," she said.

Somto contemplated.

"While my body was in use..." she continued, "my Pneuma must have remained subdued considering that now that the inhabiting lifeforce is vanquished, my Pneuma has become free and why you sensed my presence. The lifeforce was one of King Ajutu's maidens just because you are wondering—you know, the king of Akagheli."

Nodding, Somto observed her with the wonder of a child, "Though I wasn't that well-attuned to my surroundings for an extended period after I arrived here, still, I was vigilant about the comings through the portal for the simple reason that I continued to look for a way to go back. So, it can't be that I didn't see you arrive here. If you were subdued as you said, then you most likely came here in an inert and dispersed form rather than compacted. This, I believe, explains why I didn't see you enter. Pneumas need to be conscious and in control of their faculties for their lifeforce to stay compacted into human form. So, another lifeforce knocking yours out of your body, as your body expired, probably left you insentient."

With a shrug, Adaku began to drift away, "Perhaps, but doesn't matter now," she said. "You cock of the walk. Sounds like you know a lot and don't give up easily."

"Seems like it took you no time to be in full control of your creativity," he quipped. "Nonetheless, curiosity is the gateway to learning, and one can't give up when one hasn't accomplished one's quest."

"What's your quest?" her tone was deadpan.

"To eventually leave here," Somto said. "And yours?"

"No idea. As you hinted, I've been dead to this place since I arrived," her tone was becoming more expressive.

"And where are you going?"

"To attune myself to my surroundings," she had a hint of a smile.

As Somto chuckled to himself, Adaku turned her head around and grinned, and, for a moment, he felt an irresistible connection growing between them.

"You may be the spark that this place has needed for a long while."

"You are turning up the pressure. I hope, for your sake, that I don't disappoint," she returned as her smile faded, and she looked forward again. "I don't think our form will make it possible to engage in what you have on your mind at this moment in time."

With a silly grin, he caught up to her and asked, "What were you doing crouched down?"

Arching her brows, "Tried to see how far down this place goes," she said. "I'm surprised you didn't glean that for yourself."

"I was more concerned about who you were," he said. "Nonetheless, any luck?"

She shook her head.

"It's a void with no limits," Somto added.

"I figured. Was just wondering how I was able to walk on a level without there actually being a floor, or ground."

"Two words: energy and concentration," he said. "If one concentrates one's energy, one achieves a function. I often tell new arrivals that walking—or doing anything for that matter—in this void is akin to Jesus being able to walk on water whereas Peter would start to sink the moment he doubted. Faith—or, in our case, focus—does it."

"Then make sure to tell the Pneuma your mind just switched to that it is possible to shake hands contrary to what you told him when he first arrived."

"And that would be Dike…I should, and I will. Silly me not to have realized all this while that it's in fact possible to touch one another if we focused on it."

"And you are definitely right. After I became aware of my existence here, I rose, floated, and moved about erratically—like a bubble. But when I focused on staying still, my feet seemed like they suddenly touched a transparent surface. I bent over to check, then—"

"Along came Somto," he said, essaying a smile.

She chortled, "Don't even think that being able to finish my sentence makes us soul mates," she said. "My thoughts are transparent to you and so are yours to me."

Shrugging, "Never mind soul mates…Pneuma-mates happen to be the best kind of mates ever," he said and did a cheerful little jig.

Chapter 9

Within her little nondescript room, Queen Nena took her time to awaken in her bed that sagged in the middle to the beat of repeated hammering on her front door.

Sighing, she rolled over to her left and fumbled for her night lamp. Turning it on, she squinted at the wristwatch on the table, "If that's Ezinne, then she must have a good reason for staying out all night without my sanction and waking me up way before six on a Sunday morning, banging the door like she is possessed."

Expelling a hiss of annoyance, she dragged herself out of bed.

Staggering to her plain, wooden wardrobe that wasn't bursting with clothes, which had, on the wall to its left, a full-length framed photograph of her in a long, narrow, close-fitting, and flowing, silvery-gold, satin robe with a diadem atop her head and a scepter in her hands, she picked out an open-fronted, fur-trimmed, floral, silk housecoat and slipped it over her nightwear. Knotting its fabric belt, she walked out barefoot.

Through a short, chaste hallway, she arrived in the living area as the banging on the door rose in viciousness. In haste to open the door to rap on the knuckles of whomever it was, she didn't light up the area.

Barely unlocking the door, it burst open, knocked and sent her sprawling backward to land thump across the short-piled carpet. Looking up, she saw King Ajutu's dark figure in the doorway, clapping his Akupé against his right palm as though he was applauding her for a deed well done.

As he stared down at her with a face that was livid with anger, her heart pounded with fright whilst her mind flitted from one thought to another as to why she was being faced with that situation.

A beat of five seconds later, he loomed through the darkness toward her, "Woman, you will come with me immediately, like it, or not," he spoke with startling ferocity. "Sparing you 30 years ago was the worst mistake of my life."

Wincing at the animus in his voice, she pushed her elbows against the floor to lift her head from her recumbent position, "What have I done, Your Majesty?" she cried out, looking up at him. "Please come in…Let me turn on the light so that we can talk about it."

Grabbing her thick and full, sable hair with his right hand, he swung her around on her rump, then tugged and lugged her through the door, onto the patio and into the chill, gray predawn as a breeze sighed in the garden trees and, along with the mist, also whispered in the dry grass.

As he dragged her through the lawn, goose pimples specked her skin for more reasons than just the cold. Screaming in desperation, she pulled at his arm to soften his yank that almost tore her scalp off her skull, wrenching in vain to set herself free of his firm grip.

Moving through the south and southwest passages and all the way toward a room that was on the floor below his great chamber and to the right of his forever-lit pigeon room, Queen Nena bruised her heels and the entirety of the exposed back of her legs.

Chapter 10

Inside of the room that allowed access after furnishing a keypad with the right four-number code, King Ajutu rammed Queen Nena to the wooden floor and pushed the steel door behind him. It slammed shut with a clang and locked itself.

In the relative darkness and without taking his piercing gaze off her, he pushed a button on the wall behind him and the floorboards pulled away from him, revealing an oubliette.

She peered down into the cold, inky blackness only just illuminated by a bar of light that shafted through a draped window on the wall the room shared with the pigeon loft. To her horror, she found Ezinne who was still in the t-shirt and jeans from the previous day and was curled up in a fetal position in the inner right corner of the almost-unaired cuboid space—an enclosure that was at least hundred square meters in extent, bare of plaster, and leaked an evil smell.

Still aghast, "How long has she been there?" Queen Nena croaked, and as she turned to look up at him, he withered her with a look and gave her a hefty shove with his right foot.

Pitching forward headlong, she tumbled down the stairs. Feeling her knees and shins scrape against the concrete finish and flinching in pain, she arrived at the bottom of the 11 steps and landed with a thud on her side, next to Ezinne, on the dusty earth that was besmirched with blood and likely other bodily liquids.

Try as she did, Ezinne couldn't stand on her legs, which felt heavy to lift. Giving up, she crawled at a slow pace on her knees and hands toward her queen and tried to help her up, "I'm sorry," Ezinne said with hebetude.

"What are you sorry for? What did you do?" Queen Nena muttered with pain in her cracking voice as she pulled herself up to her knees, managing to straighten her rucked-up nightgown and house coat.

Pacing the top edge of the dungeon, placing his hands on his waist, then crossed before him, "Silence," the king's strident voice interrupted. "You will only speak in answer to my questions."

Glancing all over his Akupé's handle, three stars and four suns still sparkled. His lips wearing a sardonic curl, he returned his stare to the opening below, "Now, what did you tell Odera?"

"How do you mean, Your Majesty?" Queen Nena crooned.

"Do not play dumb with me. Ezinne told my maidens that Odera was at yours with a 'mother and her daughter.' So, what did you tell him to make him disobey me and cause Adaku's demise?"

Queen Nena turned her gaze from him toward Ezinne whose head inclined. Lacing her fingers together, "I'm sorry," Ezinne murmured as she stared at her mucky fingers.

Looking up again and holding her palms up and out, "*Bīkó*," the queen said. "Please, Your Majesty, leave her out of this. She is only a child who did not know what she was doing. Let her go. Let us talk as king and queen should, Bīkó, please."

"Shut that dirty trap of yours," he bellowed with rage. "What did you blab to him about? If you do not talk—"

"We only talked about Ejizu," the queen interjected.

"If you give me one more false reply, I will lock you both down there…" he said, "so that you can experience as she did—or she can share with you—what it is like to spend an evening and a night down there without food, water, or much air, and with a chill, plenty of dust, insects, and the smell of dried blood, vomitus, urine, and excrement…You decide."

Quailing at his heartless words as he spoke, a sudden coldness crept around the queen's core. "Damn the day I left Ikuku for him," she mumbled to herself.

"I said no talking or murmuring," he said with a lot of asperity.

With a flash of inspiration, the queen exhibited saint-like submissiveness, "I will tell you everything you want to know if you let her go. Besides, you don't want her to hear what I told Odera, do you?"

Raising his brows and massaging his temples, he clenched his jaws and set his teeth, "Get her out of here and away from my sight before I change my mind, and meet me in the caucus room," he barked with a sharp tone. "And if what you tell me displeases me, the four walls of that hole will be the last things you will see in this world."

He keyed in his access code, flung the door open and charged out of the room, leaving it gaping.

Injured Queen Nena and weary Ezinne helped each other to clamber up the steps. And upon arriving in the room, they sat beside each other on the surface of the top stair.

Checking Ezinne over, Queen Nena embosomed her, "How did this happen?"

With a powerless voice that came through flaky lips and looking down with blurred vision from sunken eyes, "When I told you I was just going out for a stroll yesterday evening, I lied, and I am sorry," Ezinne said. "I went to be with the maidens—was bored and didn't want to be alone. They asked me about my life living with you, and not having much to say, but wanting to feel among, I told them about the only interesting thing that has happened to us in recent times—that Odera came with people to visit us. Then Adaku told me to wait and she left. When she returned, she said the king told her to take me somewhere, and I ended up here."

"Did you tell them anything else?" the queen murmured as Ezinne hanged her head. "Look at me, Ezinne, please, it's important. Did you?"

Ezinne looked up as tears coursed down her depressed cheeks and shook her head.

"Are you sure?"

"Yes. I didn't hear anything you talked about with Odera, as I was busy listening to Obiageli, so I didn't have anything else to tell them."

Smarting because of her wounds, "I warned you about those maidens, but it's okay," Queen Nena said as she eased away from the embrace and arose. "Let's go and get you some water to drink—your lips are very dry…And to wash your face, too."

Fighting tears of frustration, she stood and helped Ezinne up.

As the Ezinne got to her feet, "But why did he make Adaku keep me here?" she said, with bitterness edging her hollow voice. "What wrong did I do?"

"Maybe he didn't want you to tell me about your encounter with the maidens," the queen said as she hobbled out of the room, arm in arm with Ezinne.

Doddering along, Ezinne gave slow nods.

As Queen Nena slouched alongside Ezinne, "Damn this awful man who cares only to be one step ahead—to control all things," she added under her breath, then shut her eyes as she looked up. "God, have I not longed enough for the punishment for evil to be meted out quicker? Will nemesis continue to be so slow?"

Chapter 11

Expectant King Ajutu stood before his Okiké, frowning. Time and again, his eyes moved between it and his Akupé. The elephant's white tusk had since grown four extra ridges and his hand fan still had seven sparklers.

There was a sharp knock at the door.

"Come in," he barked. "And do not break my door."

The door opened.

Chin down, shoulders hunched, Queen Nena stepped into the lair, trudged forward a few paces, and knelt down before him; her slatternly appearance striking a discordant note with the opulence of the caucus room. She'd been in the room only once before, a few days prior, during the celebrations of the 30th anniversary of the king's accession to the throne when he took his guests on a tour of the upgraded palace and she had to tag along, playing the loyal queen.

Gazing at her as the door shut, he flashed a frozen smile and seemed glad that she didn't look her old self.

Perhaps the way she looked when he took her away from Prince Ikuku.

"Definitely not missed a thing by not being with her all these past years," he said under his breath, pulled his chair back to a vantage position and sat in it.

Looking toward the Okiké, he nodded before he draped his right leg over the arm of his chair and placed the Akupé in the space between his thighs, "I'm all ears," he said with a sharp tone, appearing absent-minded as he kept an eye on his lap.

Rising, she attempted to take a seat. Looking up, he shot a disapproving glance at her.

"I did not invite you to sit down, so remain on your knees before I cut those legs off," he said. "And don't waste my time with your dawdling. Tell me what you told Odera."

Going down on her knees again, she rested her buttock on her heels and looked him square in the face.

"Ajutu, how did things get to this state? Where did I go wrong? Was I not the queen—the woman—you wanted me to be? Why do you treat me this way? Eh, *Obim*, my sweetheart, why?"

Mellowing down, somewhat, "This is not what you are supposed to be talking about, Woman!" he hissed.

"This is the first time in 30 years that we have had the chance to talk one-on-one, and we will get to what I am supposed to be saying," she said. "Accord me this opportunity to speak freely, please. At least, if I'm going to die today, grant me this last wish to air everything I've held onto for a long time."

King Ajutu stayed quiet, avoiding her gaze.

She assumed that she hadn't lost the ability to get him where she wanted him; the same way she was able to get him to bring Ejizu's body back from the shrine. Being unsure how long that seemingly better mood of his would last, she knew she had to act fast.

As she lifted her left hand and the diamonds on her finger winked in the room light, she gazed at his left hand, "Our eternity rings are still on our fingers. We are supposed to be one, Ajutu; we agreed that it would be for good, or for bad; those were the words you made me say instead of what I originally planned to say. Why have you reneged on them? Though Ejizu died and we both know how, we were supposed to deal with it as one. You were supposed to ask for my forgiveness, and though it would have been difficult, I would have gotten there. Instead, you left me all by myself and lay bare and carried on the life of a bachelor with no thought for me and found yourself new lovers. It hurt me so much that we are married yet I am alone, but you are not alone. Nobody has been there to meet my own needs. Everything that made me a woman, a wife, and a mother, I gave for this marriage—my womb, my submissiveness, and my child. You took all of these for granted..."

Sensing a pause in her speech, "Are you done?" he said as he peeked at his Okiké again.

She was unaware that piling on the guilt was of no use. His heart had long since turned to stone.

"No," she replied. "Have you ever wondered who will replace you as the king? Do you know what will happen after your reign? Do you know that you brought this all on yourself—on us both? Disregard that as a king you could afford to be wrathful and get away with it; and never mind your brutality, but your selfishness has made it such that your lineage might end with you."

Standing up, as her words seemed to strike a chord with him, he paced the room, holding his Akupé; and his bleak, almost vacant eyes grew remote. She was unobservant that she was further setting his teeth on edge.

Sensing her chance for what she'd thought could be a killer act, she stood and approached him. Face to face, she hugged him and rested her head on his chest for a few heartbeats, then looked up at him, "I have never stopped caring for you—even now, after everything. We can end the standoff between us now and reign as one for however long we have left. What is there to this life that we should nurse many aches in our hearts?"

He wriggled out of the embrace, having heard enough, and pushed her away with such might and main that she flew backward a few meters and smashed into the shelves. She hit the floor, face down, with a strong smack, and heavy books tumbled out and landed on her head and body. Lifting her head, large tears brimmed in her eyes and dropped to the floor. As she winced in pain and clutched the left side of her chest, he approached her.

Standing over her, "Have you still not learnt that obedience is better than sacrifice?" he roared. "For the last time, what did you tell Odera?"

Still and quiet, her heart ached. The spark of hope had in every way vanished. That whatever confidence she had about saving her marriage had been eroded by the humiliation she'd faced that early morning, she wept in silence.

Snuffling a little, "That…that…" she sputtered, then paused, trying to quell the acid that was developing in her voice. Trembling all over with her gaze planted at the floor, her face dripping tears, she shut her eyes, and as she took a moment to gather herself, delicate lines rayed out at the corner of each eye. Then she unscrewed her eyes. "That, notwithstanding that you swore to uphold the laws of God at our coronation, you remain a murderer…That you killed our son for money…That you promised to kill me if I told anyone…That you are part of an evil spiritual organization that gives you powers…That he should run as far away from you as he possibly can," she cried out. "But what I forgot to tell him is that hellfire will be too nice of an end for you."

She looked up and locked gazes with the only man she ever knew intimately, the one who had led her a merry dance.

Fuming, he raised his hand as if to strike her, and she lowered her head on instinct.

"Love brings out obedience…And since your love is far away from me, I have nothing more to live for, so make it quick," she sobbed. "It was only you and Ejizu. And, as of today, Ejizu has been gone from me for 11,143 days, and I had hoped that after all these years, we could still save our union, but I have lost you as well."

For some reason, the king seemed to think better of knocking her into the middle of next week and, instead, set his Akupé on the conference table, yanked the door open, and slammed out of the room.

The self-closing door shut after a little.

Chapter 12

Barely a dozen seconds later, with her confidence all but withered away, still, Queen Nena sobbed no more and slowly got herself up slowly. Holding onto the left part of her chest, she picked up the books one after the other and put them back on the shelves.

With an ache in her legs and ribs, she hobbled as she made her way, as fast as she could, out of the room, down the east and south passages, through the garden, and into her home.

She hastily shut her front door and locked it, "Ezinne," she cried out. "Have you finished?"

"No, Your Majesty, I will be done very soon. I'm just finishing up."

"Okay…Just the bare necessities," the queen's voice wavered as she shuffled her feet into a pair of flip-flops that were set close to the entryway. "The state we are in won't allow us to leave with heavy bags. Not that I am sure of how we will be able to leave this prison, but I will sort through my things shortly."

Listless, she pulled open one of the French doors and stepped onto her back porch. Closing the door, she hobbled through a path and onto Ejizu's bordered grave—his resting place whose earth had eroded and hollowed out over time and surrounded by a rose bush whose stems trailed over its low marble-finished edges.

Slumping on her knees, she squinted for a beat at the headstone that read:

Prince Ejizu Ugodi; September 5, 1961 - July 17, 1967.

With a sob of despair, she threw herself face down against the uneven bed of loose earth and sniveled, "You were the only valuable I could truly call mine, but you left me before you even knew me, before I could really know you," she said. "I've been torn between running away from your father and ending my life, and though it took me a long time, I've got to the point, and I choose to end my life because there is no way out of here for me, and where would I even go? I wish I could see you again—to be with you again and to never part. And I want to do it here on your grave before Ezinne tries again to stop me."

Sniffling, she arose on all fours and scrabbled around the depression for something, anything she could use to get herself to the life beyond the grave.

Moments passed, then, all of a sudden, near the foot of the site, her fingers felt a hard matter just under the earth. She grubbed over and around it until it poked out of the soil.

Gasping in consternation and in a quick combination of movements, she flinched, shut her eyes as she plunked herself down on the dark-brown sand and scooted backward a few paces on the butt of her housecoat.

She opened her eyes, and saw, sticking out and contrasted against the ebony of predawn, the dry bones of the distal part of a foot bare of skin and flesh but stained with murk. Elevating her eyes above the skeleton, she saw a wraith appearing from a gray mist and floating in the cold air. Casting her gaze down at the four, pale-brown, unequal-sized, partly degraded phalanges, which were in two sets of two and just clung to each other by hard, brown material, she noted that the length that protruded was the exact shape of the levitating shadow.

Realizing what was happening, her heart fluttered, and her eyes glazed over. As her muscles lost tension and she held her breath for an instant, her lips parted. Heaving in delight, tears welled in her eyes anew. Whilst a smile grew across her face, she leaned in to touch the apparition but failed in her attempt. Still and all, "I am not going to be alone for much longer," she shrieked. "Ezinne! Ezinne! Please come out…To the back yard. Quickly."

With a sudden unexpected surge of nervous energy, and in earnest, she got to her feet. Leaping over the low rose bush, she ran to a wooden shed beside her house and pulled out a shovel. Running back to the grave with newfound determination, she began to dig at a frenetic pace.

Chapter 13

Somto was absorbed in his rap about the finer points of existing in the crossroads world as they drifted alongside each other at just a little faster than a snail's pace, hence Adaku was the first to spot a homogeneous presence.

She pointed and Somto caught sight of it out of the corner of his eye. The specter's edges were sharpened even so and its energy was more boosted than would, as a rule, be expected for a normoactive Pneuma.

Cocking his eye, "That's Ejizu!" Somto gushed in a matter-of-fact manner. "He has been unburied. After three decades? And he appears to be in a conversation with his mother, the queen of Akagheli. But for what purpose has his grave been opened?"

"How do you know that he speaks to his mother?"

"Dike, the Pneuma I told you about, said his mother told him the story of the current queen of Akagheli and her son," Somto said as Ejizu remained oblivious to their presence. "It was how we were able to learn that proper burial is the way to help us leave here. Also, it's almost always with mothers that Pneumas converse, so it's not that difficult to make an educated guess."

"I see," Adaku said. "He looks around five, or six years of age."

"Yes, he told me that he was almost six when we met more than 30 years ago," Somto said. "He would give Tochi Bioma much-needed company."

"Who is Tochi?"

"Our latest male arrival. He told us at our meeting that he had celebrated his sixth birthday about three weeks before he was sacrificed. He needs Pneumas his age to talk about what they tend to talk about at that age. He appeared wet behind the ears during our last gathering; I think he'll be happy to meet Ejizu."

"Well, we don't know why his grave is open and how long that would be for," Adaku said. "Let Tochi not get his hopes up too high."

"True. We'll find out soon enough after he is done with his mother. But do you know what I'm now excited about?" Somto said.

"Absolutely! Apart from my arrival," she enthused. "You are looking forward to finding out from Ejizu where he had been for 30 years."

"Yes. To figure out where we might be going from here," Somto grinned and blew her a kiss. "Where had you been all my life?"

"Let me see. You were sacrificed at the age of 16, 30 years ago. Mine was at age 14, 20 years ago. So, 34 years ago, you were 12 years. This means I was born when you were around 12, and I would have been around age four at the maximum before your life ended," she said. "Therefore, I was either non-existent, in the womb, suckling, or toddling around my mother during your lifetime. No chance that we would have ever had this sort of connection during that period, so there you go."

Still grinning, "Your approximations have been spot-on," Somto said. "But it was just my way of saying that I want you around me always."

"Oh, I see," she said as they flowed past the area surrounding Ejizu.

"My mother used to say, 'Life is what happens while we're busy planning,'" Somto said. "Two things I consider very important to me, which I have thought about a lot and sort of even made plans for have so far happened by chance. Discovering how to leave here and someone I can have a different kind of connection with."

With a self-conscious grin, "And the latter, would that be me?" Adaku mumbled.

"Uh-huh," Somto said. "Tell me about your family of seven. You mentioned your mother. What about the other five?"

"Yes, there were seven of us; father, mother, two younger brothers, two older sisters, and me."

"You must want to connect with them, right?"

"I would love to," she said. "I see all of them. They are all grown up now. All married with kids and seem happy. Father and Mother live close to their oldest child and must be in their 80s now. He was a blacksmith, and she was a seamstress as well as a choir mistress. But I don't want to bring them back to the sorrows they must have dealt with over the last two decades."

"You said your sibs seemed happy, but you didn't say the same for your parents."

"It's difficult to say whether the look on their faces is due to their wrinkles, or sadness. But they don't look happy either way."

"You should contact them. Most parents never get over the death of a child. They often live with the expectation that their children would be the ones to bury them, not the other way around. They will be happy to learn that you are in a good place."

Looking at him with pleasure and a twinkle in her eye, "I can see why every Pneuma would be happy to talk with you," she said. "It makes me remember the part of the Holy Book that talks about sharpening one another as iron sharpens iron. So, how do you reckon I go about it?"

"Show them a sign that you are present so that they may wish to see you."

"I think I know what to do," she said. "Before we were kidnapped by King Ajutu's men, four of us friends were on our way to a cultural event. I had on me a purse that I liked a lot, and they have kept it all those years. I will grab it and move it around in front of them and hope they somehow decide to see me and not get spooked."

With a shake of his head, "I think they will get spooked," he said. "Rather than that, first try connecting with your closest sibling after which they will tell your parents what to say to make a connection with you happen. Use whatever you two liked to do in common. Like, with my brother, just before I died, he was eight years old, and we used to build paper airplanes together. I found one somewhere in the room we shared and made it fly. He saw it and cried, 'I want to see Somto. Where is Somto?' then I appeared to him."

Nodding, "I will," she said. "My immediate older sister, Adaugo, liked to twist and pull on my hair, and whenever she did it, I would wait for when she was asleep to play out my revenge. I would twist and pull on hers in return until she awoke and chased after me. I'll do just that. So, where are we going?"

"Where do you want to go?"

"I would like to meet the others."

"Really?" ecstatic Somto said, and, following an emphatic nod from Adaku, he forced his breath through a small hole between his lips, producing a loud puff of air that whistled through the void. "Make sure to tell us all about your three friends who were also killed like you; to give at least three others hope for a female companion. Who knows, their Pneumas may be making their way here soon."

"And you are concerned that some Pneumas may become jealous of you."

Somto gave a few quick nods, "And might compete for—"

"My attention, I know," she interjected. "But I've got free will, and I prefer to be with the cream of the crop."

"And how do you know that there is no Pneuma you might fancy more than me?"

"Unless you disappoint," she said. "This shy Pneuma has already made her pick."

Gazing at her for a long moment, Somto crowed with delight.

Chapter 14

King Ajutu returned to the caucus room and didn't find his queen. Appearing unperturbed by her absence and with a half shrug, "Unless she has climbed over the three-meter barbed bulwark," he muttered to himself in a reassuring manner. "She has no other way of leaving the palace without the escort of a henchman."

The rifle in his left hand at full cock, he tightened his right fist. With furrowed brows and lips pressed together, he stormed out and walked with purposeful leaping strides through the passages and out of the palace's main building.

Arriving before the door to the queen's place of abode, he twisted the knob and pushed but couldn't budge it. He took a few steps back, planted his feet in a wide stance, aimed his rifle at the lock, and fired once with a jerk.

Cracking across the terrain with many hills, the shot blasted the hardwood barrier wide open.

Set back on their heels as they bagged the rest of Ejizu's bones from the shallow burial site that also contained parts of his all but decayed coffin, Queen Nena and Ezinne froze for a moment, almost jumping out of their skins. Cowering for cover on instinct, in the depthless dugout, behind the rose bush, Queen Nena motioned for Ejizu to offer them protection.

Moving to hover in front of them, he faced his mother, "That's Father with his hunting rifle," Ejizu said with calm.

"He is here to kill me," frantic Queen Nena whispered as she struck out near the bush and scrambled for the bones-containing bag that gaped open, dragging it toward her position and crouching down back in the hollow ground. "Though I wished for death earlier, now I don't."

"Then you will not die; not now, and not by him," Ejizu replied. "Let Ezinne stay behind you."

Motioning to Ezinne, "Hide behind me," the queen whispered. "But how will you stop him? He's a very determined man, and you are only a young spirit."

"Being a young spirit means that I have a lot of youthful and creative energy," Ejizu said. "You remember Somto, the one I told you about before I was buried?"

Queen Nena nodded in a flap, "That's one of the names I've tried to remember all these years," she murmured. "What about him?"

"He taught me how to concentrate my energy to do anything I desire; so, there are many irons in the fire for me. All you have to do is relax, wait, and watch."

"How can I relax in the face of death?"

"Okay, continue to panic then," he said with a facetious demeanor and impish grin. "As long as you keep your eyes open to see my moves."

"Looks like someone is eager to show off," the queen said as she broke out in a cold sweat. "You haven't changed one bit—still full of mischief."

Meanwhile, trooping into the darkness of Queen Nena's living room, King Ajutu groped for the light switch and flicked it on. Rifling through the house with his gun at the ready, the search availed him a packed travel bag in Ezinne's room as the only relevant find in the entire house. Furious, he tossed out its contents onto the floor and walked out, "Stupid people," he said as he strode through the hallway. "Where do they think they are going? The only place they will go is out of this world."

Reaching the living area, he looked out the windowed patio door as he approached it, but the illumination in the living room nullified his view of the garden. Walking toward the door-less entrance, he thumbed the switch on the adjacent wall and turned off the light.

Bullheaded Ezinne's first instinct was to stand up in the grave and tried to move closer to her queen, "The king has switched off the house light," Ezinne said over her breath. "I think he might have left after not finding us in it."

"Shush! Do you want him to hear you?" the queen whispered, unaware that Ezinne had stood up.

Lurking in the darkness, King Ajutu closed in on the laminated glass doors again. Appearing from the shadows, he peered out one more time.

Moving back a few paces, and from about ten meters away, he pointed his gun and squeezed the trigger. The rifle kicked as the bullet exploded, spiderwebbing the glass with splits that centered at a hole, the slug cracking fast through the air.

His aim was perfect; and collapsing backward across Ejizu's grave, Ezinne struck the back of her head against the marble edge of the burial site and snapped her neck, expiring instantly.

Still hunkered down, Queen Nena looked back at Ezinne in shock as she lay on the earth with blood oozing from a hole that gaped in the middle of her forehead, her unblinking eyes becoming glazed.

Seeing the same as his mother froze and shed a tear, furious Ejizu began to concentrate his energy.

In the split second that it took the king to sense that his queen must be hiding close to Ezinne's body, he pulled open the double French doors and made a dash for the garden with his gun in position, "Come out now! You foolish woman," he roared. "Now is the time for you to walk that road that annihilates the one who walks it. I should have been over and done with this 30 minutes ago rather than waste my time thinking twice about it."

As he arrived at the disinterred grave, she drew herself up and looked up at him from within the pit, next to the bones-containing bag, wiping tears that ran down her cheeks, and full of indignation that he should presuppose to judge her.

Training the muzzle on her, not farther than 40 centimeters from the center of her forehead, "What are you doing with Ejizu's bones, you witch? Why are you digging up his grave? I can see that you are fast becoming a mad woman, and I will now help you out of your misery."

Stung by her husband's scorn, she shut her eyes and hung her head as though surrendering to him.

With his face attempting a sardonic smile, he fired a shot, and a shudder racked her body, though he wasn't as quick in discharging the weapon as Ejizu was in suffusing the space between the end of the barrel and the top of his mother's head.

Unseen by his father but still visible to her as she sensed his shield and looked up, Ejizu absorbed the blast, bullet, and all of its ballistic shockwave through his hands that were held apart.

Gasping, King Ajutu coughed for air. Confused to the core about what had happened, he fired a rapid succession of bullets, his body jerking with each crush of the trigger to the recoil of the rifle until there were just the disappointing clicks of an empty chamber.

Still, nothing happened. His queen remained untouched.

His face assuming a rictus of repulsion, he tried to pound her face with the butt plate of the long-barreled firearm's stock, but he met the same resistance.

Ejizu's fury grew, and he concentrated his energy even more.

Standing up and looking up at her king, she engaged in a stare-down with him until the bewildered expression that had crossed his face converted into contempt and he spat in her direction, the chill breeze scattering the spittle away. He tried again to hit her and, this time, and unexpectedly, he was thrown back by a strong push from Ejizu.

Landing in the rose shrubbery opposite the left foot corner of the grave, his gun tumbled out of his hand. Feeling no pain, though without doubt demoralized, he scrambled out from the densely packed plants and plashed hedge and took to his heels toward the palace, his robe streaming behind him. Stumbling again and again, he continued to look back with wonder.

Chapter 15

Entering his caucus room, King Ajutu grabbed his Akupé. Flashing a passing glance at his Okiké, he arrived at his shrine and, whilst keeping to all etiquette, summoned the most venerable one.

In high dudgeon, "Your Most Venerable," he said as soon as the eye on the wall blinked. "Did you see what just happened? Do I no longer possess the most powerful evil force in the land?"

"Ajutu, you are a Leviathan in more ways than one, as are your two other compeers who, with you, make up the three pillars on which the Evil King's rule takes a stronghold in Naïjerland," the voice resounded. "Though, overall, you are supposed to be second only to Overlord Tamir of Wusaland given his superior rub out count, you at least possess the most powerful negergies in Igboland to be specific. However, what just happened did not come from one of us. The lifeforce that caused the event is a kind one; a protective one—a type of posergy. They look after their loved ones and all who treat their loved ones well. And there are many of them—all children. It is rare to find a child spirit that is inherently evil even though you adult humans sometimes refer to children as such. You adult humans are often the ones who expose children, theirs or others', to evil."

"Whose spirit is that, Your Most Venerable?" Ajutu wheezed out. "My son's?"

"Yes, Ajutu, it's your son's spirit," the voice thundered again. "To subdue it, he has to stay buried. All of them have to be buried to end their activities. We don't have any power over them in the afterlife not least because they've long figured out how to evade our notice, so I'm afraid we can't help you here."

"Your Most Venerable, how did the queen know that unburying him would release his spirit?"

"She did not always know. She stumbled upon that knowledge because you drove her to the extreme," the voice rumbled again. "Having succeeded in keeping her away from your personal space completely and for the most part from your social space, you should have let things be. But you remain the architect of your own misfortunes. You should have left her in peace, considering that she also agreed, while in your company, not to entertain any thoughts or utter any words about what she witnessed—Ajutu, she managed to keep her promise. So, unless your son's bones are buried, she will be protected by him, and what you just witnessed is only an arrow in the quiver of these oft-called 'Children of the Shadows.'"

"I also just rubbed out another, Your Most Venerable. How does this affect me? Will my years further decrease?"

"Your Okiké should tell you that," the voice roared again.

"My Okiké did not increase my count, Your Most Venerable."

"Then the rub out wasn't for any of the reasons for which the Okiké keeps count. The young woman wouldn't have affected the course of your life in the grand scheme of things, so need not have been rubbed out. But you let your anger control you."

"I thought the netherworld would be happy with additional rub outs, Your Most Venerable."

"It doesn't matter to us that you rub out good people. In fact, we prefer that saved people live to maintain the chance of them reverting to a sinful nature, then we can claim their lives then. Death is gain for the likes of her, according to the Holy Book, as she is now free from the evil we deal out to your world."

"I see, Your Most Venerable. Why would you accept the rubbing out of a good child but not that of a good adult? Why did Eke's good wife have to be rubbed out?"

"Like I already alluded to, an adult who walks with The Almighty still knows good and evil and may still choose evil at some point with constant temptations from the Evil Chief, especially if they are at a fledgling stage in their walk, as the young woman was, so we want to give them that chance. The Prince of Peace said His Kingdom is for the likes of children. Though we are not allowed to touch them, humans can. So, we accept children in sacrificial offerings because we prefer that they don't live on. Living on means that they might influence adults to be like them and help adults make eternal life promised by Him. And I shouldn't be telling you all of these, but the Prince of Darkness needs only pledged servants like you who have drunk deep of traditions like Mkpátáku and shown over time that they will not accept the

Prince of Peace. Eke's second wife was good on the surface, but, beneath, she bore a constant grudge against her sister wife—the sun went down on her anger many a time; of course, she would have been exceptional had she been amongst good people. Of her own free will, she remained around Eke and his first wife, and this made it difficult for her to be firm in her worship of The Prince of Peace and The Almighty One and to grow in Their Spirit."

"I see. Thank you for your patience, Your Most Venerable. You are a great teacher, and I learn each time I entreat you," the king said as he assumed invisibility. "That would be all for now. I must now go and retrieve Ejizu's bones."

"Over the last score and ten years, I've not seen you this subdued, Ajutu, this weak," the voice resonated. "Your body is ailing from your pigeon disease and your other mistreatments of it. The negergies you possess, and, ultimately, the negergies of your eight creatures, need a strong body. They cannot operate at full capacity without one, and all of them together may be too much for your body as it is. So, be careful what wheels you set in motion. Don't strain yourself with this needless campaign, or else you will spend your force before we are even at the kernel of the situation, and you may end up needing to be salvaged. I hope that you haven't forgotten what this might mean for you."

King Ajutu remained silent.

The shrine shut, then, moments later, the caucus-room door opened and closed.

Chapter 16

Meanwhile, with no evidence of being at strain or feeling any fatigue, the henchmen and the felids exploded onto the area outside the cave.

In just over an hour, they'd raced through the vast and dense forest about 60-odd kilometers on a great-circle distance. The vicinity was in a state of bleak and dismal emptiness, deserted of life and ponged of death.

Within an atmosphere of chuffing sounds and led by Ijeoma's leopard, they entered the cave in a single file, crunching the wrecked raffia door underfoot.

Arriving at the eminence, they moved the bench away. Standing in an arc, they gazed, for a moment, at the body that they suspected was Adaku's dead body even though it no longer looked like who the three felines had once known. Smell of gore in the air making Ijeoma's leopard queasy as all three cats glanced at one another, they assumed their maiden forms. Loosening their chignons to let their flowing hairs fall over their bare bosoms, they ripped Adaku's nightgown off her body.

Tearing the fabric into parts, they made them into six broad and long sheets, and each tied one at the armpit across their bust and another at the hip as a loincloth.

At the same time, looking over to Batu and handing Adaku's waist bag to him, "We need to deal with this part of our assignment quickly and get on with the rest of it," Diko said. "The fastest way to get her body back to the king is by air. You are the one with the wings and the tight grasp, so over to you. We will wait here until you return."

Without a word, Batu grabbed the fanny pack. Knotting its buckle-less grips, he hung it around his neck. Picking up the remnant shreds of Adaku's clothing, he bound her midsection to contain her internals. Lifting the body as if it were weightless, he bounded out of the cave.

Exiting just as the atmosphere behind him produced the first sight of light from an invisible sun and gave the clear sky its blue color, he launched the corpse in the air. Promptly, he morphed into a prodigious, demonic, wing-flapping, black eagle with a dark-brown lion head and mane, and a dark-tan Inland Taipan snake for its featherless tail. The more-than-double, life-size beast with a feathered body went up, up, roaring fire and leaving trailing tentacles of smoke in its wake.

Swooping down on the mortal remains and with the sleight of feet, it plucked it out of the air in a vice-like grip with its pair of four extremely muscled, oversized, powerful, and featherless talons sunk into the body's flesh moments before it would have impacted the ground.

Opening its wings that spanned more than three-meters-and-a-half, it lifted with ease, circled up into the air, banked 90 degrees clockwise, and soared northward on the dry north-easterly trade winds.

****

Back in the cave, the sextet had split up in singles and scoured the entire space, checking out and destroying the chattels that were left behind.

After this, the restless henchmen sat on rocks at different parts of the enclosure, whilst Adure and Isioma huddled up at the table and Ijeoma used water that came down the walls to wash Adaku's caked blood away, gagging time and again as she did.

As Diko grabbed fish from the stream, above which midges flitted, and shoved them in his jagged and crooked-toothed mouth, Jadue teased glow-worms out of crevices with his forked tongue and chewed on them, whilst Kadiye licked the water that descended the walls with blazing fast movements of his large, rose-colored tongue.

"What do you think he'll do with her host body?" Adure said with keen interest as Ijeoma joined them.

"No idea," Ijeoma casually said. "Maybe see if he can use it again."

"But can he use it again?" Isioma said. "Has it not been unused for too long for it to still be able to accommodate another one of us?"

"I am not sure how these things work," Ijeoma said. "We will find out in time."

"That's if we make it out of this battle, alive," Adure said.

"Why do you think we will not make it out alive?" Ijeoma said.

"Well, Adaku didn't make it," Adure said.

"It was just her against Odera and Namdi," Ijeoma said. "This time, it will be seven of us against two of them. And do not forget that our henchmen now have special powers, and, apart from that, they are also no longer loyal to either Odera or Namdi."

"Ijeoma is right," Isioma said. "We will live to see what he does with her body."

Staring at Adure and their gazes meeting, "Something tells me you harbor a fear," Ijeoma said.

"20 years is a long time, and I'm at home in the palace with you two," Adure said with fervor, hanging her head. "If we don't make it, there's no guarantee that we'll all be sent to the same place or into human bodies. Our maker will most likely separate us."

Patting Adure on the back, "Yes," Ijeoma said. "But we are not supposed to get involved initially, and I trust that these vicious henchmen…" she gestured down from the elevation toward the trio, "will do the job so that we do not get involved at all."

Adure nodded, "But if we don't make it and are never placed together again, I want you two to know that I enjoyed every second of our two decades together," she said. "You never know what will happen. We weren't expecting not to see Adaku ever again."

"Adure is right," Isioma said. "And I enjoyed every moment three of us shared. Thanks to Adaku. She always engaged the king, thus allowing us time to play with one another and bond well."

Overcome with acute nostalgia, Ijeoma shed a tear, "I do miss Adaku," she said. "Having always wished, more so lately, that she would disappear off the face of the earth to allow the king to pay me more attention, I never thought I would long for her to be around. She knew how to handle any situation. She danced attendance on the king, hence why he took to her. I should never have been jealous. She would have been a true leader if ever we needed one."

With the air around them loaded with wistfulness, Adure experienced a flash of inspiration, "Do we have to get involved in this mission?" she said. "Can't we skip it?"

Wagging a finger and shaking her head, "We cannot disobey him," Isioma said. "Our maker would know, and our end will be the same as if our bodies died in the mission. Our only chance of sticking together in these bodies is to obey him, fight together if needs must, and ensure that our bodies stay alive."

Arriving at the cluster of maidens, the henchmen perched on the bench. "What are your names?" Jadue said.

"Did you lose your memory in exchange for your powers?" Ijeoma said with a hint of derision as she turned to face them, flanked by Isioma and Adure.

Poised, each maiden folded her arms across her chest, "We've known you all for many years," they said all together; their motive seeming only to test them.

"Well, we were meeting you all for the first time a short while ago," Diko said and Kadiye nodded.

Turning her neck to the right, then to her left, Ijeoma exchanged respective knowing glances with Isioma and Adure, "We are Isioma, Ijeoma, and Adure," Ijeoma said, gesturing from her right to her left. "Who did you come from?"

"The most venerable one sent us into these bodies," Jadue said.

"What was his command?" Adure said.

"To do only what the king says," Kadiye said, yawning. "To not let our own will dominate his."

"Do you know Odera and Namdi?" Adure continued.

"Who are those?" Diko said with slow, even breaths.

"Two of the ones you were created to destroy," Adure said.

Facing his palms up, "We don't care about names," Jadue said with half-lidded eyes as he focused on picking his teeth with one of his long fingernails. "You ladies are supposed to show them to us and leave us to do the rest."

"Did he command you to have one another's back?" Adure said.

Diko nodded.

"Did he tell you what would happen if you went against the commands?" Adure said.

"We will be removed from these bodies and, at best, taken to a new body, though we are not sure what type of body, or, at worst, locked up."

"Those were the exact orders we were given," Ijeoma said. "We are indeed of the same nature. So, welcome."

The henchmen got to their feet and exchanged firm handshakes with the maidens. Following this, Diko pushed his large hands into his tight pockets and stood, looking bored; Jadue sat back down with a posture that sagged and picked at his ugly fingernails and cuticles, whilst Kadiye ran down the steps.

"Off to find food," Kadiye said with a flat voice. "Sensible to store up energy for the battle ahead."

Chapter 17

At the same time, reappearing atop the sandy knoll, King Ajutu wheeled around in a frantic scan of the vicinity.

The area in and around Ejizu's gravesite was empty. Ezinne's body was not visible, the grave was a mound of rather wet sand, and his queen, his rifle, as well as the bones-containing bag, were nowhere in sight.

As his left hand clenched and unclenched in turn around the handle of his Akupé, his index finger tapped against it many times over, "Why would Ejizu choose her over me?" he mused—his words filled with malice and admixed with an ignoble pang of jealousy. "I am much more powerful than her. We could have combined forces and ruled with unimaginable dominion."

His breaths slow and loud as his shoulders rose and fell, he crossed his arms in front of his chest; and as his gaze flickered upward, due west, to the blue firmament, his eyes narrowed. Not far flung from each other, two life forms were airborne. As one got closer, the other whizzed farther away. The beast that came winging had a body in the claws of its huge bird-like feet and approached the palace at speed. Though seemingly unsure which henchmen it was, a shadow of a grin grew on King Ajutu's face as his eyes danced over to Adaku's body.

Then his smile faded as his sight refocused on the disappearing figure and he heaved a heavy sigh. The vertically inclined outline was in full flight and was, needless to say, making a headlong getaway from turmoil and had a bag in the grasp of their right hand.

As his breaths shortened and quickened, he paced up and down in clear exasperation, not knowing where to look or go, "Ejizu? Ejizu!" he barked. "How could you help that woman fly away with your bones?"

He paused for a long, contemplative moment, "I must get those bones. I must find a way to get his bones! I must own them!" he mused, and stiffening his neck and jaw, and with gritted teeth, he added with a sharp tone as the lion-headed eagle descended with a deafening whirr to lay Adaku's body on the downslope before him, "She will live to face me again. Wherever she is fleeing to, as long as it is in this world, she cannot hide from me."

Modifying to human form, Batu genuflected with praying hands and a hanging head for a moment. Then he removed Adaku's waist pouch from around his neck, reached out his hand, and offered it to King Ajutu whose stare had darted, for a moment, to him.

Contemplating, King Ajutu took the bag and hung it around his neck, "You have done well," he said as his gaze moved again to his queen who'd become no more than a dot in the cloudless sky; and with a shake of his head murmured to himself: "If Batu goes alone after her for the bones, Ejizu might destroy him…If Batu kills her, my years will further decrease. I better leave her alone for now. Can't afford more setbacks." Then he cast a fearful glance around the handle of his Akupé before directing his eyes down at Batu whose head was still bowed. "You may rise now, worthy servant. Go and join the rest. Your assignment still waits."

Wasting no time, Batu leapt into the air, transformed, then took flight.

Tucking the handle of his Akupé behind his cummerbund, King Ajutu knelt before Adaku's almost-bare body. With a jerky hand, he caressed the body's face, which no longer looked like that of the Adaku he knew, then carried her in his arms and made his way back to his nest.

Chapter 18

Still beset by fear, Queen Nena's eyes remained shut. With her elbows pressed into her sides and her right hand clasped tight around the khaki bag's grips, they sailed over the part of the forest whose trees glassed themselves in the dark creek to arrive above a view that was, for the most part, agrarian.

"I can't thank you enough for saving me from the clutches of that man; from that prison," she said with trembling lips. "And thank you again for letting me bury Ezinne in your grave and for helping me with the rest of the digging as well as filling it up."

"It is okay, Mama. Though we belong to each other, I have no other belongings in the world you are in. The grave doesn't belong to me," Ejizu said as he maintained his focus on not letting his mother accede to gravity's demands. "Just promise me that you will keep my bones safe. He has figured out that burying them will cease my activities, and I can't help you if I'm not active."

"I will protect it with all my life; better than I looked after you," she said. "This is my second chance, and I will not let you down."

"You looked after me well," he said. "There was no way you would have known what he had planned back then. Quit being hard on yourself."

"Thank you, my son, for understanding," she said. "I hope Ikuku will be as understanding and also forgive me. I expect that he would realize that I have nowhere else to go."

"You would have to let the occurrences speak for you," Ejizu said. "Let him know what you witnessed and experienced with Father. That should be enough. You are not merely going over there to beg for him to take you back. You are going there to seek help for Akagheli. Father is going to be relentless; he has shown that much. Had your eyes been open, you would have seen the beast that flew past us not that far away. It is one of the creations he asked for. I heard him brag to himself about how he will use them to fight everyone who has come up against him and anyone who is yet to. He not only has continued to wink at the deathly ritual, he is also preparing for serious bloodshed."

"What if Ikuku doesn't listen to me?" she said with stress in her voice. "What if he is angry deep down because I jilted him, and our interactions last week were, on his part, mere superficial courtesies of diplomatic exchanges?"

"Quit being skeptical, Mama. This is bigger than just about you, so stop making it about you. If he doesn't listen to you, then I will speak to him," Ejizu rapped with feeling. "If you tell him to wish to connect with me, he will be able to see me and hear me speak. He will no doubt listen to a messenger from the afterlife…I hope."

"Okay, my son," she said with an uncertain tone, her breaths bursting out and in. "Are we almost there?"

"You will know when we get there," Ejizu said, suppressing a giggle.

"I know they can't see you, but are there many people watching me?"

"There are pockets of people here and there pointing. But the forest behind gives us good cover."

"Well, until we get over the expressway to Agudagu, which, I imagine, will be teeming with travelers," she said.

"We are traveling over uninhabited land as well as farmlands that have only a handful of people on them; and, also, at the height we are, no onlooker will be able to tell that it is you, so stay calm."

"I'm sorry for acting like this and asking all these questions," she said. "I'm just a mixed bag of feelings and emotions—of fear, anger, joy, worry, tiredness, anxiety, loss; you name it…"

"Relax, Mama," Ejizu said. "The time for going to pieces has now passed. You have escaped his evil embrace. But Mama, how did you manage to dig up that grave so fast?"

"My son, it beats me, too, but all I can say is that when you're hell-bent on something that fear sets your heart on because it is sure to save your life, and you are racing against borrowed time, adrenaline kicks in, giving you all the strength you need, such that any- and everything suddenly becomes possible to accomplish. Let us not forget that Ezinne helped, too."

Chapter 19

With his Adam's apple bobbing, King Ajutu laid Adaku's corpse on the marble top within his shrine and summoned the queen of the coast as should be done.

As the eye on the wall blinked, "Can she be brought back, Your Venerable?" he said in a hurry and with a wavering voice, nodding toward the body.

"We cannot create something out of nothing. The Almighty alone can," the alto voice said. "She cannot be brought back. The body is no longer habitable. Were it a native body, the zone might have fixed it, but it was a borrowed one…So, you would have to end another life for the negergy that you knew as Adaku to return in that new body. Is this what you require? The negergy returned in another's body?"

His gaze clouding, "That would be another rub out," he said with a faint hope for a different answer. "Further reducing my years?"

"That would always be the case," the voice stated without regret. "Either that, or you remain its host or you find a willing host for it. We made you aware of this fact two decades ago."

"What about taking it back or destroying it?"

"We cannot take it back," the voice said with certitude. "The negergy we earmarked for you and, to create your maiden, needs a body once it has been stripped off the Evil Chief, and in the absence of one, you, as the reason it was begotten, must be its host unless the negergy is being punished for disobedience when it is either locked up, or forced into an animal's body or you no longer exist when it would have to wander about until it finds a willing host. It is not debatable. We have not the ability to destroy lifeforces. The Almighty alone can and has promised to do so, with permanence, to all evil lifeforces at the end of time."

Clearing his throat, he turned away and knelt down. Deep in thought for a moment, he then muttered to himself: "I had hoped that she would bear my heir. It would have been a supreme combination of her beauty and elegance with my powers. I wonder why she couldn't conceive. If that body was barren…good riddance!" Darting his gaze back to his Ikengá. "Is reducing my years further not worth it for an heir? Well, um, Your Venerable, let me think about it some more."

"She was not barren. If I were you, I would check the part of her that pleased you the most. And by and by, you are endowed with the freedom of thought and action," the voice said and the eye on the wall forthwith blinked for the last time.

Darting a glance at Adaku's wrapped, gruesome midsection for a moment, "Not now," he muttered to himself and, with a sudden notion, strode out of the shrine into the caucus room.

Approaching the northwest section, he ascended the stairs to the top floor and banged on Papu's door. It flung open in a blink of an eye and the seemingly charmless Papu, whose tiny face was shrunken and eyeballs were a little prominent, adopted a single genuflection in the doorway.

Without acknowledging Papu, "Get me Chief Madu this minute," King Ajutu said, then stomped off.

As the king gathered distance from him, Papu shut the door and passed out of sight within his dwelling.

Arriving back at his lair, King Ajutu shut the shrine. He seemed to have descended to self-pity, and his hair appeared to have faded to a dusty gray within a few hours.

Standing on his left foot with his right foot set on his chair, his right hand supporting his chin and right elbow resting on his right thigh, he gazed at the ceiling and contemplated. Rubbing the back of his neck with his left hand, he said, "Is ignorance not bliss? Do I really want to find out?"

Then, he nodded and walked to the shelves. Opening the shrine again, he padded toward Adaku's body.

Chapter 20

The dark skies of the night had, by and by, given in to my wish and made way for the rose and gold of the peep of day, fresh and invigorating.

A half-hour or so later, the town center welcomed us with an atmosphere of suburban tranquility. Admixed with the consonant din of soundproof power generators, there was sparse and quieter traffic on the minor roads that branched off as forks from the Akagheli-Agudagu expressway. Granted that there was a network of electricity-conveying poles unlike in Akagheli, which, for all intent and purposes, was off the grid, still, the supply of hydroelectricity all the way from *Naïjer Dam*[6] was, as anticipated, still precarious. Nonetheless, with close-set houses, which were strung along the warren of wide minor roads, Agudagu was well-planned with gridded streets.

Approaching from the south, which was lined with shops and offices and also had a police station and a few hotels, I noted as we exited from the highway onto the main town road that the east side sprawled with well-maintained flats likely for single people whilst the west side provided for townhomes I presumed to be for families.

North of the said road, a church whose bell was almost ready to begin tolling for early morning mass, was set amongst trees on a hill in the distance, and further down from it, to its right, was the framework for a terminal of a railway station under construction.

Not a cloud obscured the deep calm as the picturesque sunrise over the crest of the hills echoed the fine layout of the township my heart very much desired; and though it no longer was dark, still, there wasn't a serene place within me as I continued to wonder:

---

[6] A dam that exists along the stretch of the Naïjer River as the latter flows between Orubaland and the eastern aspect of Wusaland. See map on page 14 of *Children of the Shadows: The Never-Ending Fear.*

What next will the king send our way? Is it right for us to be holing up in the 'town of trees' and pouring out our troubles on it?

"This is not usual for Agudagu's urban center," Namdi said on noticing how lost for words I was. "Only because it's a Sunday…Any other day, even at this time, it would have taken at least an extra half an hour to strike here, as the cosmopolitan bustle would have been everywhere around us."

Looking back at Namdi, "I'll take Agudagu any day and anytime," I said in a hushed, awed whisper as I managed to find a way to wrap my arms around Obiageli's neck in the tight space she was in.

She'd been, in a way that was not habitual, quiet during the entire journey, and had kept her arms folded across her chest. With her entire front nuzzled up against Odera's back, her eyes, which were, on the whole, empty of expression, had stared at one side of the freeway or the other.

I had passing thoughts as to whether she was missing her father and brother, which I could do nothing about, was, like me, indulging her usual woolgathering, which was fine with me, or was reacting to the Harmattan nip in the air, which I didn't do anything about, as my mind had flitted fast that I ended up not giving it enough consideration to have asked Odera and Namdi to stop in order to pick out a wrapper, from my baggage, to provide her with an extra layer of clothing. I trusted, however, that she'd have voiced that out had that been the case.

Looking over his right shoulder at Namdi, "Her name ought to be changed to Nkem Agudagu," Odera said with a solid grin as he maneuvered the motorbike comfortably into a narrow and empty, idyllic street whilst somewhat-enervated Namdi remained close behind us.

Namdi would have been more fatigued had he not, time and again, clung onto the motorbike to be drawn by it during the trip.

Cuffing Odera playfully on the back, "Whilst I love Agudagu, I'd prefer Njoku," I said and, in that instant, brought about an air that became charged with awkward quietude.

Shining through again was my aptitude for spoiling moments with my passionate desires. Nevertheless, still thinking about Odera, my mind drifted to the black mark on his left wrist. I wondered if it had been the reason that he almost never took off his wristwatch during the time we'd been together or even sported one for that matter, considering that most of the other henchmen wore none.

Heading further north, we rode past the collegiate church that was as old as the hills.

Nine kilometers or so later, on the outskirts of the town center, eastward from the church, and without coming across any dirt road, or clogged-up gutters, we arrived at a cul-de-sac.

To our left, a solid, jet-black, steel gate, which stood almost two-meters-and-a-half-high, closed off a great arched and curlicued, wrought-iron gateway.

On either side of the isolated and fortified enclosure was a patchwork of open fields sprinkled with small groups of jackal-berry trees. On the opposite side of the paved blind alley that's known as Ikuku Close, an orchard that bore a prolific collection of the said trees, catty-cornered about 25 meters rightward from the gate.

Revving the motorbike a few times, as there was no visible bell to ring nor did he have the patience to search for one, Odera set his feet on the ground as the engine rasped.

The gate slid ajar unmanned after a little and an armed camo-uniformed man, who was built like a tank, donning a black beret and had a transmitting handheld, which was attached close to his left shoulder, stood in the way. Appearing to speak into the device, "Yes?" the dark, tall, lean, and broad-shouldered man spoke with a gruff voice that had a faint but unmistakable *Middle Belt*[7] lilt, sounding skeptical. "Who are you all and what do you want?"

"Good morning, sir," Odera said. "We are Prince Ikuku's visitors. He is expecting us. We are messengers from his brother, King Ajutu's."

"He did not instruct us that anyone was coming to look for him," the officer with several tattoos across his neck said and puffed on the half-cigarette in his left hand, smoke curling up from it. "I am not sure that he is ready to receive guests yet. But if you are from the king, then you might want to wait for him."

Still looking exhausted, "We will wait for him," Namdi replied before Odera could, sensing that the clean-shaven, angular-faced, army man wasn't

---

[7] A geographical region of Naïjerland around a waterbody that runs obliquely from the nation's east south-east end (Wusa-Igbo channel) to its north north-west (downstream of the Naïjer River). It essentially forms a transition zone between Northern and Southern parts of the nation.

difficult to please. A situation I'd learnt was uncommon amongst military men, thus hinting at the possibility that His Royal Highness, whom Odera had described as genteel, might've rubbed off a little on him, suggesting to me that he'd been in the prince's employ long enough.

"Okay, come in then," the seemingly friendly man with three stars on each of the rank insignias on either shoulder patch said, then thumbed a button on the inside of the pillar to his left, letting the heavy gate slide fully open.

To our right was a watchhouse; and before us was a massive, terrazzo parking lot that was bordered by rose hedges on its south, east, and west sides from surrounding, long, tarmac driveways that forked toward the sides of the building[8] as pleached walkways and converged at the gate. Wide enough for three vehicles stationed side by side, the drive paths also had a flagstone-paved sweep.

Within a stone fountain at the front third of the terrazzo-finished area, water purled, plashed, and tinkled.

At the front of a substantial and, without question, baroque-style edifice, there was a huge array of armored military jeeps, a technical vehicle, and shiny black sedans with tinted windows. The stone building's convex facade had half dozen columns of bi-level windows, some with pulled-apart drapes; and below the top middle two windows was engraved *The Ikuku House*. On the back of the west side of the roof, a chimney belched out wisps of dry smoke.

Boorish soldiers in battle fatigues were armed to the teeth. With automatic rifles at port arms and hand grenades hanging from their garbs, they ran hither and yon: nipping from bottles, sipping hot tea or coffee or gulping *Kunu*[9], snorting tobacco and hocking a luggie, or smoking cigarettes, or were just in huddles: playing cards and tattling in whispers. Being within hail of some of them, I noted that they, for the most part, spoke in *Hausa*[10], and I tried my best to ignore some of their peevish and sensitive remarks about me; the 'sexiest adult female' within the vicinity.

Riding up the paved track, we parked the motorbike and bicycle to the left of the massive structure. The captain shut the gate, leapt over the rose bush,

---

[8] Diagrammed on pages 12 and 13 of *Children of the Shadows: Firmness of Purpose.*
[9] A drink made from grains; popular amongst northern people of Nigeria.
[10] One of three major tribes in Nigeria. Also the main language spoken in Wusaland, northern Naïjerland.

and dashed across the terrazzo. As he approached the entry doors, we dismounted.

Subdued by the environment, I held on tight to Obiageli's hand as we stood close behind Odera and Namdi.

"Come with me," the officer said, glancing backward as he walked past us. "By the way, I am Captain Iduto."

"Nice to meet you, sir," I said with a subdued voice as he halted at the double steel doors that offered ingress into the building and keyed in an access code. "I'm Nkem."

Moving aside as the doors jerked and began to swing inward, he bade us enter, "Someone will meet you at the atrium," he said, yet again, into his radio. "Nice to meet you, too, Madam Nkem. I hope you have brought good news from the king. The prince does not like trouble. He is a good man."

Groaning deep down at him for calling me 'madam,' I nodded, then pondered on how someone would've known to receive us until Obiageli looked up at me, "Mama, that soldier is recording everything he says."

And it struck me that the person, who would welcome us and perhaps a number of other people, must've been on the other end of the handie-talkie and heard everything that transpired. I thanked the heavens that I hadn't reacted on the outside to being called 'madam.'

A good way to run a security unit, nonetheless; but why are there many armed men from the north of the country? Why is it important that everyone is aware of every other person's utterances?

"He wasn't recording…He was saying it to other people," I said as we walked through the expansive entryway—which featured an exhibition of luminous orbs descending at various lengths from a standard ceiling—into the mansion, to the murmur of unseen staff, servers, and children, and to note as we arrived onto a wide and circular, lustrous, marble-floored foyer that wherever there were walls, they glowed with a satiny sheen.

The vestibule had eight doors ranged around its lateral limits, one of which was a set of windowed, French doors. On its south side, the opening also served as the bottom landing for a pair of curved, marble staircases with banisters that met at a central mezzanine before continuing as straight stairs with a central and a top landing.

On the top landing, at an average adult's eye level, a medium-size color photograph of the prince's head, shoulders, and chest hung in a polished frame on the south wall. Curving east and west and lined at its inner limits with patinated, chocolate-colored, carved wood balustrades that joined up on the north end of the area, above the entryway behind us, the landing ringed the top floor as a two-meter wide circular gallery.

Allowing light stream into the area, a floor-to-ceiling window was in each of the arching east and west walls such that an imaginary line that joined the two glassed in apertures would divide the circular top floor into two equal halves. Whilst there were five doors on the south semicircle, seven doors lined the northern side.

Hanging down the center of the hall from the high and windowed ceiling, a chandelier spread a circle of light to the impressive space.

The atmosphere within the house, whose architectural style was 18th-century European, was casual with a dash of elegance and decor that proclaimed a chic tapestry of western taste, Asian custom, and indigenous cultural tradition.

He is indeed a well-traveled, and probably inquisitive, man.

As the entry doors shut, another one to the immediate right of the eastern window, second to the left of the prince's portrait, inclined inward, and a pinafore-clad, headset-wearing, youngish, and trim, biracial lady, who grew her sheeny black hair long and had about her a niminy-piminy air, walked out.

Descending the central, then the eastward staircase, her large, keen eyes darted from one of us to the other and seemed to wonder whom to address, "The prince will see you, but he has just awoken and will be getting ready for church," she said with a rather reflective Southern African twang, nodding to Odera as he stepped toward her. "Can I take a message to him?"

"Tell him that church can wait," Odera started, drawing further furrowing of naturally arched brows from the lady as she flared her pert nose. "But the reason we are here can't. I don't mean any disrespect, but what is your name, young woman?"

"Miss Anika—" she began to say as she landed on the foyer, and it was clear that Odera was taller than her by no less than 20 centimeters.

"Hello, Miss Anika, nice to meet you, too," Odera interjected, walked to her, and put his right arm around her right shoulder as a look of confusion crossed her elegant, oval-shaped face, and she gazed up sidelong at him, tightening her shoulders. "You see, we have traveled many kilometers to arrive here this early for a reason. If you look there, my right-hand man, whose eyes are red because he rode a bicycle on the long and unforgiving expressway to get here, is expecting nothing less than to see the prince. So, Prince Ikuku will hear that reason directly from our mouths, and, after that, if he still chooses to go to church as his next line of action, then so be it. But you will tell the prince that Odera Njoku, the lead henchman of the king of Akagheli, King Ajutu's royal guard, has a life-and-death matter to discuss with him." Helping her turn around, Odera walked her back to the bottom stair, nudged her upward, then continued. "Unless you want me to run up those stairs and find him myself. But I am sympathetic to creating an awkward situation for you over this. My first way, or my second way; choose one."

Ascending the stairs, Anika took much longer than it had taken her to descend it, looking back with wonder at Odera's imposing frame the while. And Odera's piercing gaze remained trained on her until she disappeared back into the room out of which she'd materialized.

Chapter 21

Startled by a loud, deep roar, the quintet of Ijeoma, Adure, Isioma, Diko, and Jadue stared at the cave entrance.

Strolling in was a dark-tanned, gigantic, lion-headed horse whose tail was a black-and-dark tan banded king cobra that made a growling hiss. The beast had a dead hare dangling from its fearful and gaping maw, transfixed by one of its large and pointed lower canines.

Jadue sniffed the air with nonchalance, "That's Kadiye," he said at first blush, and they all paid it no further heed.

Gagging on seeing close up the bloody and headless prey as its predator arrived at the eminence, Ijeoma sprang off the bench and bolted down the stone steps. Hard on Ijeoma's heels, Adure and Isioma wondered what the trouble was with her.

Ijeoma bent over the brook and vomited into its clear water as the other maidens arrived beside her. Standing on Ijeoma's left-hand side and rubbing her back whilst Isioma held her hair out of the way from the other side, "You don't look okay," Adure said with a nervous disposition, looking about her. "What do we do? Do you need anything? Is there even anything of use around here?"

"I wish Adaku was here," Isioma said, holding Ijeoma's right arm and whilst keeping Ijeoma's long hair away from her face as Ijeoma continued to heave. "She would have handled this with calm and masterly finesse."

Flustered, "Of everything she taught us and provided for us, it was those diaphragms that I like the most," Adure said. "I couldn't even provide proper care for an adult who's vomiting much less a helpless child if I ever convinced myself to bear one."

"So, you used it?" Ijeoma said as she straightened up.

"Why not?" Adure said. "Adaku instilled fear in me when she said that the king was trying to get her to bear his heir since his queen couldn't, and she didn't want to be pregnant because she feared the 'unwanted effects it might have on her will.' I had to—"

"I stopped using it," Ijeoma interjected as she wiped her mouth with the back of her left hand, then on her loincloth. "It became, hum, discomforting after a while to keep putting it in and taking it out each time."

"Well, if we go by the emotions you showed yesterday when Adaku took the garage key away from you and again just a few minutes ago—emotions we rarely see…You vomiting yesterday morning while we were in the shower, and again now, and add that you have been sleeping with the king without any form of protection, I will say with a hundred-percent certainty that you're pregnant," Adure said, then leaned back to look at Isioma. "Tell me you use yours."

"I do," Isioma said. "I did everything Adaku asked us to do."

"Good," Adure said, straightened up, then fastened her gaze on Ijeoma. "How long do you think it's been?"

Looking down at her bare lower abdomen, "Well, I have not started showing, so definitely not up to five months," Ijeoma said. "And according to the books I checked up, the fact that I am vomiting tells me that I am definitely not less than one month into the pregnancy."

"You were worried?" Adure said.

Avoiding eye contact with Adure on purpose, she said, "Not really. Just developed an interest in the whole pregnancy thing after Adaku mentioned it."

"Did you not know when you stopped seeing your monthly—" Adure said.

"It had never been regular," Ijeoma interjected. "I had, in the past, gone several months without seeing it, so I could not determine by that."

"This means you're not going to be fighting with us then," Adure said.

"What if our maker punishes me for disobeying the king?"

"Well, even though she probably already knows that you're with child, still, she's going to summon us before ever she punishes us, so we'll have the chance to convince her that another of hers and the most venerable one's kind is growing within you, who potentially could help extend their powers in the human world," Adure said, darting her gaze between Ijeoma and Isioma. "She dared not take you away and leave the offspring with no mother to look after it, could she? Would she?"

Isioma shrugged, facing her palms upward, "Who knows?" she said under her breath. "She is evasive and completely unfathomable."

"What if you two fight and then die, who will help me through the rest of the pregnancy, birth, and early motherhood? I cannot do this on my own."

"Well, you already said that we will not die," Isioma said. "Why do you now doubt?"

"I do not know," Ijeoma said with a strain in her voice. "Jangled nerves and emotions of a maiden who just all but confirmed that she is pregnant, I guess."

"Okay," Adure said and motioned toward the steps. "Let's go and get you some rest."

Shaking her head, "No," Ijeoma retorted. "Not up there. Kadiye's meal will make me sick again. Let's go outside for some fresh air. The stench from the trickle of blood is about to make me gag again."

"Do we tell him?" Isioma said.

"If we don't tell him at the first opportunity, the queen of the coast would, and he wouldn't like it," Adure said. "He's going to find out soon all by himself anyway. We aren't allowed to sleep in his bed wearing any form of clothing."

Barely outside the cave, the maidens would see Batu changing from his beast form as he touched down and shuddered to a halt, spraying sand at them from under his feet.

"Ready to go?" he said.

The maidens shook their heads; not merely to get sand out of their hairs. "Ijeoma needs some time to get herself feeling better," Adure said. "We'll be back when Kadiye is done with his meal."

Nonchalant Batu disappeared into the cave as just out of sight, more and more birds piped, warbled, and cheeped as they continued to rejoice in the new day whilst the maidens settled down beneath a jackal-berry tree that had shadows of its leaves dappling the ground.

Sitting with their backs leaned against the tree trunk, with Isioma on Ijeoma's right and Adure to her left, they shot blank stares for a moment, then drank in the scenery, making out the silhouettes of treetops in the distant horizon.

"Where do you think they are…Odera and Namdi?" Ijeoma said.

"At Prince Ikuku's," Adure said. "Aside from the fact that he is the only one with the means to protect and perhaps help them against what's coming, the way all three of them cozied up to one another during the king's anniversary events leaves no doubt in my mind."

"What do you think Adaku did with Ezinne?" Ijeoma said.

"Adaku abhorred Ezinne," Adure said. "I can't imagine anything less than locking her up in the dungeon for her to die. Isn't it what she did to that laundry lady who burnt her outfit, who later died from dehydration and suffocation? And she would end up dumping her body in the forest?"

"Adaku could be mean at times," Isioma said.

"Adaku's meanness was second to none a lot of times if not all the time," Ijeoma said. "She was a bad girl many more times than she was not."

"Who're we to judge?" Adure said. "I think that as long as we haven't been good, it really doesn't matter how much bad is done. We all haven't been good."

"Is it our fault that our free will tends our nature toward being bad?" Isioma said. "That we are good only to the king by his control and sometimes to our kind for reciprocity?"

"Not sure I know the answer to that, but does free will not mean we can choose to do good?" Ijeoma said.

Gazing at Ijeoma with wonder, for a while, "You are definitely pregnant, Ije," Adure said, and Ijeoma looked a question. "I can't believe you're talking about choosing to do good… Ije, who always likes to fight. Your maternal instinct is clearly coming to the fore. I can't say that I'm not impressed."

Furrowing her brows, "I disagree, in a way, on the fight issue," Isioma said. "Though she has always been wicked to humans as expected, it has only been in the last few weeks that Ije has shown a propensity to have quarrels with us and disobedience to the king, which ties in nicely with a surge in her hormones."

"Perhaps," Adure said.

And as a smile grew on Ijeoma's face, "I was only wondering why we do not choose good if there is free will."

"I don't believe we are capable of choosing to do good once the zone has settled what our inclination ought to be," Adure said. "We can talk about it all we want, but when it comes down to the nitty-gritty of acting with goodness, we tend to drift toward evil—"

Sighing, clearly not of a mind for the topic in question, "And when this fight is won, you might even become the next queen of Akagheli," Isioma interrupted. "And we would become your court ladies."

Filled with varied emotions, Ijeoma's eyes welled up. Seeing this, Adure and Isioma nestled against her and rested their heads on her shoulders, each placing a consoling hand on the back of either of Ijeoma's hands.

Gazing eastward at the sun as it crested the distant horizon in the blue skies that were without as much as a wispy cloud, its blinding rays hadn't the slightest effect on their glistening, amber-colored eyes.

Chapter 22

Prince Ikuku took his time, but when he showed up on the gallery and leaned over the railing, it was there and then clear to me that he wasn't cut from the same cloth as his twin, and I felt a further pull of his abode's tranquility.

To mention a few reasons: he didn't induce fear, didn't seem fettered by tradition, didn't have an obvious proud port of a prince, was debonair as could be, and, overall, seemed gently born.

Having huddled up below the chandelier, we'd shot the bull about our encounters up to that point and tried to come up with reasons as to why Prince Ikuku's house was guarded to a great extent.

"Odera! Namdi!" Prince Ikuku enthused with an even temper. "What a surprise! Little did I know to expect you so soon after suggesting that you checked up on me. And what is this grave matter I hear you are burning to get off your chests? You thoroughly scared the living daylights out of my personal assistant, and I had heard that *Herero* people do not scare easily."

Looking up, "Prince Ikuku, we can't talk here," Odera said in an officious tone, clearly not in the mood for pleasantries.

Tugging on Odera's shirt, "Shouldn't he be addressed as 'His Royal Highness' to his face?" I whispered.

Looking back at me, "He specifically asked not to be referred to that way," Odera whispered with a crisp tone. "He prefers 'Prince Ikuku.'"

With his freshly shaved chin up, broad shoulders squared, the prince padded along the gallery contemplatively. Though he had a cautious, academic mien, carried the patina of old money, and, at that time, displayed the comportment of a person at peace, there was a hint of confusion across his face as he descended the stairs, unconsciously fixing his magnificent, blue robe.

Arriving before us, "Prince Ikuku at your service," he said with a strained smile as he shook hands with Odera, Namdi, and me, then bent over. "Young girl, why did you let these adults take you out of bed so early? Remind me to tell you how to make them think twice the next time they try, okay?" he continued as he placed a patient hand on her hair and stroked it whilst she nodded and swayed from side to side. "Also, tell the person who styled your hair that way that I will give them a job to make those of all the young girls in our…" pointing to the first door on the west gallery to the right of his photograph, "orphanages."

Following the prince's left index finger for a moment, Obiageli glanced up at me, and I flashed a self-conscious smile.

Rising, Prince Ikuku nodded to me, then gestured us toward a set of doors on the east side of the ground floor, to our left. Following him as he strode toward them, I couldn't help but focus on his strange-looking leather *Zōri*[11] that slapped the floor.

Pushing the tinted-windowed, French doors open, he motioned to the seats, we walked in after him and he shut them.

Inside, well-lit by motion-sensing ceiling lights, the workspace, which had a thick-piled carpet that was wall-to-wall, was uncluttered and its fragranced air was conditioned warm. Four, ritzy, leather, comfort chairs with accompanying ottomans ranged around a coffee table to the left, and a set of draped, twin, bay windows was further down. Ahead, there was a grand floor-to-ceiling bookshelf that took up half of the east wall whilst leaving the remaining half equally distributed on either side of it. With at least 15 serial weighty tomes on each of its seven levels, and a wood plaque that commemorated a sort of achievement in archery making a brave show at the center of the middle shelf, the striking bookcase had before it a grandiose mahogany desk of the same length and color: with an in-box at its front-left side that had a sheaf of papers and to its right stood a shut, carved, wood door.

It was an office that provided comfort for no more than four people at a time at the maximum.

We sat in each of the three chairs that ranged on the guest side of the massive desk that was convex on its outer aspect and concave on the inner side. As Obiageli sat on my lap, Prince Ikuku settled into his armchair and drew it closer to the desk.

Leaning back in his seat, he crossed his legs at the ankles, set his hands whose fingers were laced together on his lap, and nodded to Odera, "I'm all ears."

---

[11] Thonged Japanese sandals with flat soles.

Without hesitation, "One word, Mkpátáku," Odera shuffled to the edge of his seat and started. "Does it mean a thing to you?"

Prince Ikuku pondered for a moment, and as he opened his mouth to speak, Obiageli blurted out, "It's a game men and boys play," looking up at me. "Mama said so."

"Shush!" I uttered with a snappish tone, quelling her with a look.

Prince Ikuku smiled, cast his gaze on Obiageli for a second as she shied away from further words, then he leaned into the two-way radio that was set on the inner long side of the in-tray, next to a corded, analog telephone set.

Thumbing one of the many buttons on the radio's cradle, "Anika, I need you here please," he said. "A young girl needs a shower, change of clothes, breakfast, entertainment, and anything else she might want. Also, see if someone can rustle up cups of coffee for four people."

Reclining in his chair as the radio continued to blink, "So, young girl, what is your favorite meal for breakfast?" the prince said.

Obiageli shrugged and rested her head on my chest, "My name is Obiageli, and I like cereal."

"Then you will have whatever type of cereal you want, Obiageli. And anything else you find in the dining room, just point it out to Miss Delvue and she will let you have it, okay?"

Nodding, she said, "You mean Miss Anika?"

"Yes, Anika will give you all you want. She is a nice lady and loves kids too."

"She looks it," Obiageli said. "Where is she from?"

"She hails from a tribe known as Herero in Namibia," Prince Ikuku said. "Do you know where that is?"

Obiageli shook her head. "Why did she leave there? What is she doing here?"

"Okay…Ask her to show you where it is on the map," the prince said. "We met on my travels almost five years ago…When she heard of our orphanages, she volunteered to help us out for free for a few months. But after I realized how good she is with children, I couldn't let such a talent go, so I convinced her to stay, train as a teacher, and earn a living working at our school. Formerly a nun, she has also been instrumental in reintroducing me to church, and I hope I will not be late today."

Then there was a rap on the door before one of them cracked open. Appearing in the doorway, Anika held the door wide open.

Helping Obiageli down, "Please, Anika, don't take your eyes off her," I said, and Anika nodded as Obiageli walked to her and took her waiting hand.

We all watched as Anika squired her away, shutting the door with minimal sound.

"God bless your daughter, madam," the prince said.

"Nkem," I said. "Granddaughter of Ebubedike Okanka, not 'madam,' sir."

"Wow!" he voiced. "The great Okanka's granddaughter? You are most welcome, Nkem. This day is turning out better than Anika made me think. And it's Prince Ikuku, not 'sir.'"

"Yes, Prince Ikuku," I said.

But don't be too quick to conclude about today…

I thought, amid the intermittent crackling and hissing of static and trenchant, Hausa-speaking men's voices coming through the radio receiver.

Setting his jaw with intent, Odera cleared his throat, "Does it mean anything to you?"

"Sorry, Odera, I was getting there. Pardon my rudeness," Prince Ikuku said after turning the volume down on the radio receiver. "Father, on his deathbed, abolished it as of January 14, 1968, exactly 30 years and four days to this day—the day my brother ascended the throne in my stead—and made him promise to keep it abolished in Akagheli and to help abolish it across Igboland. What about it?"

No sooner had the prince finished speaking than commotion crackled through the radio handset's cradle, "We have an approaching unidentified flying object! What should be done about it, Prince, sir?" the captain said.

Prince Ikuku whipped up the handset as he stood, then dashed to the bay window that looked out on the palatial parking lot. Parting its elegant drapery, he canted his head and peered out. Not catching a good sight of the situation, he excused himself and ran out of the room.

Chapter 23

Exiting the mansion, Prince Ikuku gasped and stared on in disbelief at the outline in the sky. One that wasn't a bird, or an aircraft, and was blurred by a sudden blast of cold and buffeting air, getting bigger as it closed in fast on the compound.

Preparing to give a command through his handset, he glimpsed its full figure as the rush of wind passed and it struck him like a bolt out of the clear, blue sky to realize it was Queen Nena coming down through the air.

Flummoxed and speechless, he didn't reply to the barrage of, "Do you read me, sir?" the captain continued. "What is the command, Prince, sir?"

Civilians in trees and atop vehicles on the road adjoining the blind-ending alley, and armed soldiers with weapons at the ready within the enclosure alike continued to gape at her. And as her silken finery swayed and rustled in the gentled breeze, Queen Nena alighted on the terrazzo ground in her flip-flops.

Opening her eyes, "Thank you, my son," she mouthed as she limped toward Prince Ikuku whose mouth was wide open.

She picked the walkie-talkie out of his motionless right hand with her left hand and spoke into it: "Soldiers, port your arms! Your visitor is the queen of Akagheli."

Moving with a gingerly slink toward the open entrance to the house, her right hand tightened around the grips of the bag of Ejizu's bones.

Chilled to the marrow, Prince Ikuku turned around. Shaking his head, he found himself following behind her with interest etched on his face.

"I'll follow your lead," Queen Nena said, slowing down.

As he strode past her toward the building, looking back at her, he remained bewildered.

Entering his office, he stood aside on the inside.

Having heard her voice through the handset's cradle, I'd gone down on my knees in her honor whilst the brothers forever hanged their heads. I remained on the floor as she walked into the office and stopped, staring at us, her brows lifting in surprise.

I inclined my head.

"Your Majesty," we said as the prince shut the door, strode across the room, and pulled out his chair for her.

Padding across the area and ensconcing herself behind his desk with a somewhat-bewildered look on her face, she stood the radio device back within its cradle and stooped down to settle the bag on the carpet, beside her left foot and out of everyone's view.

"You all should sit down, please," the queen cooed as she leaned forward with a slight grimace and sighed with relief, lacing her fingers together. "Thank you, Ikuku. I feel so much at home already."

Prince Ikuku walked away from the desk. And as he paced up and down the space between us and the doors, his right hand cupping his chin and the left arm moving across his upper abdomen, one of the doors opened again without a preceding knock.

Walking in with a rattling tray of teaspoons, cups, milk, sugar, coffee, and a jug of steaming water, a female servant set it down on the coffee table. Exiting the room, she shut the doors without as much as making eye contact with anyone.

Still pacing as the strong scent of coffee wafted through the room, "How is it possible…What just happened?" Prince Ikuku struggled to construct his sentence.

"The handiwork of the spirits of those sacrificed children who remain unburied," I said as I settled down.

Coming to rest and staring at me, "Say what?" the prince said.

"Ejizu helped me fly," the queen said. "At least you saw it for yourself. This wasn't hearsay."

Darting his gaze at the queen, "I don't know what just happened with you," Prince Ikuku retorted. "But I know Ejizu is dead!"

"Okay, yes, so his spirit helped me escape Ajutu. The king had tried to kill me this morning because I helped Odera escape. He was going to kill them all…" the queen nodded to us as she spoke, "because Nkem discovered that the Mkpátáku ritual did not stay abolished…And I told Odera that he killed Ejizu for it and that's how he got all his money. And as if that was not enough, he decided to kill Ezinne."

Slouching and burying our faces in our hands, Odera, Namdi, and I clutched our pearls in horror over the news that Ezinne was no more.

"Wait, wait, hold on," Prince Ikuku said. "Let me get this straight. You all are saying that the ritual my father abolished a score and ten years ago is still being practiced? And my brother got his wealth by killing his only son? My only nephew?"

Sitting upright, I said, "Yes, my husband killed my son too on its account two days ago."

With his eyes flashing and his expression speaking disbelief, "This cannot be true," Prince Ikuku bellowed. "Unbelievable!"

"Ikuku, unbelievable to you, or not, it happened," the queen said. "'Seeing is believing!' was one of your favorite phrases back in the day, right?"

Prince Ikuku nodded with an absent mind, and I realized that we were succeeding in arousing his curiosity.

"Since you and Ejizu had a connection, I implore you to please make a wish to see him," the queen said.

"This is ridiculous," Prince Ikuku said, and after a quick dip into his thoughts and with a half shrug, he said, "Well, I would like to see you, Ejizu, please show yourself to me."

"Also ask to be able to hear him," I added.

Sighing and rolling his eyes, "I want to be able to hear you as well," Prince Ikuku said.

In no time, Ejizu's apparition appeared to Prince Ikuku to his bewildering surprise.

"Everything they've said so far is true and only the tip of the iceberg," Ejizu said.

With wide eyes that didn't blink and wide-open mouth that didn't speak, Prince Ikuku stared at Ejizu's specter for what seemed like an eternity, then, "I had absolutely no idea that these things were happening," the prince uttered.

"Neither did we," Odera and Namdi proclaimed.

"You'd proved yourself to be a fortress of moral rectitude," the queen said. "That's why we've all come here. I had no idea that they would be headed here, and they as well as I had no inkling that I would end up here. This looming disaster that your brother is orchestrating must be stopped."

Looking at the queen, "Ajutu and I were sundered by many differences," Prince Ikuku started. "If what you say is true, then it surely has to be the final straw. Not that I have an idea about what I am going to do regarding this bombshell, or that what I would eventually do, I would be doing for revenge or anything of that sort, but Ajutu effectively forced me to relinquish my birthright and took you away from me. The most annoying part of it all is that both these things he snatched from me, he has not used, or treated well. He has indeed remained the black sheep."

"He is getting even blacker now," Queen Nena said with feeling.

"As we speak," Ejizu added.

"Did you know that Ajutu caused Mother's demise?" Prince Ikuku continued. "He thought it was a joke at the time. He had said he could get Mother to dance anytime he wanted, so, one morning, we must have been six or seven…He poured soapy water all over the path from her room, hoping that she would just shimmy, but she slipped, fell, and had a bleed in her brain in addition, and the rest is history. What a naughty little devil he was. He liked to control everything, even other people's emotions and feelings."

"Wants everyone to dance to his tune; more so now that he has become the devil incarnate," Queen Nena added as an air of gloom descended upon the room. "Whatever has to be done about him, we all have to band together."

"As the rightful heir to the throne and as decreed by my forefathers, it is my bounden duty to create a brave new world for Akagheli," Prince Ikuku said. "And I don't think it is wise to involve everyone, especially you ladies."

"How is it your duty and not ours as well?" Queen Nena said. "We all have a stake in the wellbeing of our fatherland."

After a long moment of contemplative thought, Prince Ikuku grinned, then paced up and down with his hands behind his back, one in the palm of the other, "Please indulge me while I tell you all a story that my father many times told me as a child," Prince Ikuku enthused. "My great-great-grandfather, King Igungu, had to carve out regions from Igboland as Igboland expanded and named them Akagheli, Amandizuogu, and Agudagu due to the fight between all three sons as to who would be king at a time that there was no system of an heir apparent. Akagheli became king of Akagheli, and clans would choose if they wanted to be part of a kingdom or not and which king they wanted to remain with if so. Four clans, Utolo, Itoga, Amakwe, and Ozumba stayed with Akagheli, while the others either resettled with Kings Agudagu, and Amandizuogu or resettled in other parts of Igboland, choosing to self-govern. King Akagheli would change the rules in Akagheli so that the first son would be the heir apparent. He was then succeeded by his only son, Mbanegu. Mbanegu had two sons, and Otubu, the older son, our father, became king. Before then, however, King Agudagu had decided to make the monarchy in Agudagu ceremonial and to have an elected person as the leader. This, many believe, contributed in several ways to Agudagu's progression from a village to a town and now fast becoming a city. King Akagheli saw how well Agudagu was doing and decreed, after he was unable to convince Mbanegu to accept a ceremonial role on succeeding him as king, that if after three generations of kings, Akagheli still trailed Agudagu in progress that Agudagu should invoke the right to annex it, and that the existing king himself must surrender the kingdom to Agudagu's right to effect this annexation and if the existing king cannot be trusted to do it, for the closest in the line of succession to take the mantle. So, it is my duty to force this through, as there is no chance that Ajutu will surrender willingly."

Standing up, "Thank you for your trip down memory lane, on a subject that's mostly enshrined in our laws, but I disagree on parts of your reasoning, Prince Ikuku," I vociferated, thumping the top of the table with my right index finger. "These 'ladies' you refer to happen to be in tune with their dead sons' spirits, who each, in turn, have connections with the rest of the Children of the Shadows, whom we need for success in this endeavor. We can't win any fight against the king, who obviously commands supernatural forces at will, without help from the invisible world. This is not just a battle against flesh, bones, and what we can see, but also against spirits, shadows, and many unseens…"

As he observed me, listening to my passionate rap, Prince Ikuku postured and sunk his hands deep in his front pockets. It seemed to have struck him to a realization that he wasn't as au courant with the situation in and around Agudagu as he'd thought.

"For this reason, the queen and I must be made front and center in this operation—an operation we can't afford to be flimsy about, one that would require resolute determination and strength of character. This is not a joke. This isn't about sinking the differences between you and your twin. This isn't about fighting over who has the right—or wields the power—to carry out a decree. This mustn't be politicized. For this, we must be firm in our purpose, and the purpose is to end this evil practice, which has permeated most of our villages and affecting lives left, right, and center, now and for the last time. So, don't tell me we're not fit to be involved simply because we're ladies or because some decree says you should carry it out. These 'ladies' lost sons to this deathly ritual."

Nodding and smiling, his eyes showing open admiration as I sat down, "Nkem, you seem to me not just an intelligent woman but one who has a will of iron and who will not be fazed in taking this fight to Ajutu however he plays his hand," Prince Ikuku said as he backed away toward the door. "You have shown that with passion—and not just with talent—one may dine with a prince and a queen…and fight alongside them against a king, so kudos to you; you will take the logistics of this fight forward…And Nena can partner you. I'll be right back. A robe is of no use right now. I should clean up and dress up like Odera or Namdi, although they need fresh clothes, too. You all can use this time to freshen up. Make yourselves at home as Nena has done. You may call Anika to guide you all. She's always on line two and ready to help. I'll meet you all for breakfast in an hour, or so after which we will draw up a plan for action. And, Odera, tell Anika to help you with proper first aid on the injuries to your left hand."

Exiting from the room and leaving the doors wide open, Prince Ikuku bounded up the eastern stairs.

Chapter 24

Chief Madu was decked out in his official outfit and wore a frown across his pear-shaped face as he materialized in the caucus room to a pacing King Ajutu who couldn't look him square in the eye.

With a passing glance, "You took your time," King Ajutu had audible stress in his tone as he turned his back to his chief and ambled to the shelves with his hands crossed behind him, his Akupé dangling from his right hand.

"It wasn't easy convincing Adane of why I had to heed your call on a Sunday morning," Chief Madu said without regret as he stood behind Chief Jokum's allocated seat. "It isn't even eight o'clock yet, and she wasn't happy that we are disturbing her routine that mandates that we stay in bed till at least ten on a day of rest, especially after making up following our disagreement on Friday on account of that Okanka woman. I was also upset at how you kept me dangling on Friday. So, pardon me for not rushing here."

"Personal feelings must be severed from official duties," King Ajutu said. "Responding to your king's summon is one such duty."

Stroking his white goatee, "Hence the reason I came at all," Chief Madu said, standing before the door and still looking daggers. "What's going on?"

King Ajutu arrived at the shelves and turned around. Leaning against them, he hung his head, "The Okanka woman is still alive and—"

"We knew that from last night," Chief Madu interjected with a sharp tone as he placed his hands on his hips, the end of his *Mkpó* pointing backward diagonally from his right hand and striking the door. "What's new?"

With his head still inclined, "I am worried that more people would become aware sooner rather than later—Ikuku most importantly, if he doesn't already know as we speak," King Ajutu said as he cast glances at his Akupé's handle, then toward his Okiké. "He has a mind like a steel trap. You and I know what his pedant self would do with this information."

"How do you know that Ikuku will soon become aware or might already be aware?"

"Nena has flown to him."

With an incredulous gasp, "Flown?" Chief Madu said.

"I figured that is where she would have gone. He is the only one who can provide her with the kind of protection she needs right now…Plus, they were once lovers and probably still are. Moreover, where else would a figurehead queen in distress go?"

"How could she fly when she is not even allowed out of the palace on foot to start with? Is she a witch?"

Knitting his brows in disapproval, "Ejizu's spirit made her fly before my very eyes," King Ajutu said. "Have you or your wife had an encounter with Emenozo?"

Staring at King Ajutu, confusion seeming to befog his brain, "I haven't and Adane has not indicated such, though she brought him up again on Friday," Chief Madu said. "I will specifically ask her about it later. But Ejizu's spirit? How?"

"Yes," King Ajutu said as he lifted his head and looked at his chief with a pained stare, the skin around his eyes bunching. "No matter what happens, do not let her, or anyone else for that matter, unbury him. That is how."

"Why would anyone want to do that?" Chief Madu said, cracking his knuckles and inadvertently scratching the door with the end of his Mkpó. "What are you concerned about?"

"I don't know if your wife has any plans to do it considering that she brought it up. Maybe she has heard from others who have. But that's the way to unleash his lifeforce," the king said. "It appears the angered lifeforces of the children we sacrificed for Mkpátáku will be keen on helping anyone who is prepared to fight against the ritual. Is she now aware of how he died?"

With his interest piqued, Chief Madu walked to his allotted chair. Pulling it out, he plunked himself down on its edge, "I have never mentioned it to her, and I don't think she has been made aware by anyone else because if she knew, she would have confronted me with the knowledge. Instead, all she has done, on several occasions, is try to get me to talk about how he died. Regardless of it all, I hope that this time around, you will involve me wholeheartedly in whatever plans you have."

A hush descending over King Ajutu, he seemed to consider Chief Madu's words.

"As the only surviving chief from your father's era after you disbanded and exiled the others for pushing you to help get Mkpátáku abolished beyond Akagheli…As the only chief of yours ever to accept your invitation to Mkpátáku, who knows almost all—if not all—there is to know about the extent of your spirituality, my loyalty should never be questioned. It, therefore, behooves you to include me totally in this."

With slow nods, "Well said," the king said. "We have to find all of the Mkpátáku shrines and mass bury the remains of the sacrificed children to end the activities of their lifeforces. Without this, I don't think we stand a good chance in our fight to keep the ritual alive."

"And how do you propose this should be done?" Chief Madu said, crossing and uncrossing his legs. "Do you realize it would involve combing every nook and cranny of Akagheli and other neighboring villages?"

"We would have to call an impromptu meeting with the venerable ones and invite everyone to go to the shrine of their Mkpátáku sacrifice to bury the remains of their children if they had not done so previously," King Ajutu said. "And there would also be the need for me to supervise each one of these committals or, at the barest minimum, confirm that they have been done. After betrayals from Odera, Namdi, and Adaku, my trust level has gotten so low, to the point of near non-existence."

Following a moment of contemplation, Chief Madu said, "That's a starting point, but what about those members who have passed on? Who will locate their shrines?"

Tilting his head to the ceiling and with an impatient huff, "The venerable ones will direct us," King Ajutu said.

"I thought they made it clear that they would only get involved when there is proof that the ritual is being fought against?"

Rolling his neck, "I still don't understand what they mean by 'proof,'" King Ajutu said. "I sense it, and that should be enough. It might be too late to keep the knowledge of the ritual under wraps if we keep waiting for an all-out assault from them, which I don't think would happen.

"From what I observed with Ejizu; they tend to be more reactive than active. We must be many steps ahead. Besides, the most venerable one is aware. He told me that burying them is the way to cease their activities. Well, if they still refuse to partake in it, I'll do it without them. You may not know this, and I didn't want to tell you initially, but I have the map of the whereabouts of all the shrines in Igboland.

"So, since we have to be at least two in agreement to call a meeting, section one, subsection four, I have asked for you so that you partner me in this request."

With a grimace and a slight shake of his head, "Though it would be a Herculean endeavor to port to all shrines," Chief Madu stated and shuffled his feet inanely, tilting his head from side to side for a few moments. "I say let's do it. Shouldn't we call Eke too?"

Pushing the button that opened the shrine, "He will be useful but not to initiate a spiritual journey," King Ajutu said as the shelf parted open. "We haven't the time to go chasing after him now. We will enlist him during, or after the quest."

"Can this operation be accomplished with secrecy though, to prevent tongues from wagging?"

"We can do it at night up until midnight if push comes to shove," King Ajutu said as he got inside the shrine with his back first, ahead of the chief who also backed in.

Still facing the exit, the king pressed another button to his left and the marble top ground apart into two equal halves as they turned around to face the concave wall. Posturing a single genuflection before his Ikengá, the king pointed his Akupé at the eye on the wall.

Catching a glimpse of Adaku's mummy-like body as it dropped into the space between the half slabs, Chief Madu assumed a similar position behind his king, protecting his nose from the malodor that suddenly took over the room.

The body landed with a thud as against a background of grating sound, the marble top closed and sealed itself tight with a loud whoosh to become whole again.

Shutting their eyes as sweet-smelling vapor wafted out from strategic vents at each of the two corners of the room, the king's left hand reached out backward to interlock his fingers with those of his chief's left hand, and Chief Madu placed his right hand on his king's right shoulder.

Then King Ajutu started, "Your Most Venerable, where two, or more have agreed, we may engender a journey; please accord us this request, send fort for all members and let the process begin."

The eye blinked, and the most venerable one's loud voice came through, "We hear you; we see you, and we acknowledge you. May the journey of the negergized-lifeforces of all the peace warriors, wherever they may be, with no exception, begin."

And no sooner had he uttered those words than two, large, raucous birds, with glossy, black plumage and wedge-shaped tails, appeared out of thin air.

Hovering at each man's right side, fluttering their wings, and using their feet, like magnets, they, in a snap, pulled each man's negergy-subjugated lifeforce out of his body's side—an undertaking that resulted in an instant generation of a whirling sphere of discrete, gray, electromagnetic force field around each raven.

And as each of the lifeforce-less men collapsed with a flop, sideways on their left, with King Ajutu's Akupé remaining in his right hand's tight grip, the two thick-billed, 60-centimeter-long and large-bodied ravens spread their wings, which spanned just under a meter-and-a-half, and with steep, flapping rises, they approached the ceiling.

Folding their wings, they dipped at speed before diving vertically with ease to disappear through the marble floor and down, down into the earth they went, heading for the underworld.

Chapter 25

Arriving at the vast concourse of boisterous Pneumas, Somto threw his thoughts back to a time when he would've seen them as they were. Looking to his left at Adaku, "I've never seen our group this blissed-out and it should make it easier for you to speak to them," he said in haste as his eyes danced around in search of Dike.

"Still, I can't say that I'm looking forward to this despite all of your assurances."

"Start with talking about your friends. That should make it easier."

Nodding, Adaku leaned in toward Somto, "I've never been one to address a crowd," she said in a quiet mumble. "In all honesty, being part of a group of four from my late childhood up until my demise was a way to cover for my bashfulness."

Motioning to the horde, "They can hear you though," he said. "You'll be just fine. I'll stand aside and leave you to it."

Positioning herself high above the gathering, her eyes passed from one unturned Pneuma face to another, and she suddenly felt out of place. With her cheeks flushing, she cast down her eyes at Somto as he stood somewhere at the front of the mass, then inclined her head to allow her flowing hair to flop over her eyes. And the events that led to the loss of her life flashed through her mind.

The four men had come out of the thick bush to the horror of her and her three friends. Taking to their heels down the bush path, they'd scattered and had gone like lightning in four different directions when the men began to chase them down. Adaku would run through the bushes and had turned her neck around as one of the men breathed down her neck, "I know you are one of the king's henchmen," she'd screamed as the man tackled her to the ground. "Please, leave us alone…We're only children."

The henchman would carry her deeper into the bushes where he pinioned her, and the last thing she'd remembered in her fruitless struggle for freedom was that the snide man, who had his entire weight on her naked midsection, fondled her breasts with his left hand whilst, at the same time, grabbed a rock with his right hand with which he'd struck her on the head.

Drifting toward her, Somto stood to her right and faced the crowd, "I'm sure you all know that this is Adaku," he said with a stentorian announcement, jolting her out of her reverie. "Being the only female Pneuma here, she's a little overwhelmed. She's got news about female Pneumas who might be joining us anytime soon, and she needs all our support."

"You are most welcome to our world," the horde burst into an uproar of approval, and Adaku, with her head still down, peeked from behind her hair to see how appreciative the group was.

With a defiant toss of her head and feeling wanted, she buried her feelings of timidity and embarrassment and lit up like a light, "We were four friends. The others were Ijeoma, Isioma, and Adure," she said, rushing her speech. "We were all 14 and grew up down the road from one another and had been best friends since we could talk. We loved to go out and do things together. We were kidnapped as we were on our way to watch *Ágábá*[12]—or 'let's go'— masquerade around Christmas time. Though I wasn't aware of what the negergy that inhabited my body did all the while before I became active here, I'm now able to see the negergy-inhabited bodies of two of my three friends who refer to themselves as 'maidens' and all their activities. I'm not sure why I can't see more than the heat signature of the maiden they call Ijeoma. At any rate, under the command of King Ajutu of Akagheli, they are preparing for battle against any human who is in contact with us Pneumas. He's worried that he, as well as the ritual through which he got his powers, are about to be exposed. Therefore, we must be ready. I'm not exactly sure yet of how they will go about it, as I'm not privy to what else the king might be planning, but according to Adure and Isioma, he has converted four henchmen into supernatural beasts for the fight—"

"How do we get involved? How do we help?" many from the assembly vociferated.

"We can—" Adaku started.

---

[12] A type of masquerade event.

"For those who can, please contact your folks," Dike interjected as he appeared out of nowhere on Adaku's left, winking at Adaku. "I am sorry for cutting you off." Giving Somto cause for elation, Dike continued, "For those who can't, let them use their creativity to help those who can. My mother and the queen have been allowed by the king's twin to look after the human-Pneuma connection as it may relate to the battle ahead, and I will be helping my mother and my sister. Ejizu will help the queen, and Bute will help his brother, Namdi, as well as the man who used to be the lead henchman of the king of Akagheli, Odera. I am sure Bute has mentioned his brother to you all at some point."

"I'm of the notion that you all have gleaned that Ejizu is back here with us," Somto said, evidently pleased. "There is a myriad of us—we are now well over three thousand. If we work together, we can achieve anything. Since Dike's mother and Ejizu's mothers are going to lead this, we have to take our cue from them."

"Does it then mean that we shouldn't be talking to our folks about finding our bodies for burial?"

"No," Ejizu shrieked from behind the gathering. "My father, the king of Akagheli and the foremost spiritual leader of the evil practice in Igboland, is now aware that burying our bodies or bones is the way to silence us, so we must not make this easy for him. Therefore, let your folks not go in search of your remains just yet. Your fathers would probably still go in search of them for committal. Though it's risky, let your mothers and/or siblings do whatever they can to stop that from happening. Right now, and I'm sure many of you are also aware, as we speak, that my father and people like him, your fathers, are meeting with the Evil One's minions on how to go about doing away with us."

"And how do those of us who have the only person that can stop our fathers from burying our remains cast aside, or locked up like Rapulu's mother, help?" another Pneuma asked.

"They have to be set free," Ejizu said. "I will inform my mother or Prince Ikuku. We need all the human hands we can get."

"Though they might not be in the right frame of mind to get involved, still, they need their freedom," Dike added.

"Nice to see you, Ejizu, welcome back if I'm allowed to say," Somto said as Ejizu flowed toward the front of the gathering whilst, on instinct, his eyes ranged over the multitude in search of Tochi. "I never thought I'd see you again on this side of the afterlife. I'm burning with questions for you about where you had been for 30 years."

"I'm happy to be here with you all and fighting for a cause as important as this," Ejizu said as he slowly levitated toward the front. "There's no place else I'd rather be. So, 'welcome back' is in order. About where I have been, I'm sorry to disappoint you, but I can't remember a thing right now. Those 30 years have been a blur. To me, it's like I left here and returned in a blink of an eye."

"Never mind, Ejizu," Somto said with some brio to his tone. "It's all for the better you said that. It makes me a lot happier to remain here for as long as is necessary, without further longing to be someplace else."

"So, as we speak, I gather that the three maidens and the four beasts are preparing to continue on their journey to where their targets are," Adaku said.

"By targets, do you mean my sister, mother, Odera, Namdi, and the queen?" Dike said.

"Perhaps, but I heard them mention only Odera, Namdi, and Prince Ikuku," Adaku said.

"They are headed to Prince Ikuku's home then," Ejizu said as he halted, wheeled around, and flowed away in a wink. "I must warn them."

"Alas, a battle looms," Somto said with his hands aloft. "One I never thought was possible; one none was brave enough to instigate until Mrs. Nkemjika Odimegwu came along. Long may she live to witness the victory that, I believe, we will achieve not merely because we think ourselves younger or more equipped, but because, in the end, the light will always overshadow the darkness, and good will always trump evil. Dike, we await your signal."

Following Somto's cue, and as Dike flashed a winning smile, the Pneumas all swayed, hands overhead, and shouted, "We will stand victorious over all forces of darkness."

Adaku drifted toward Somto among the raucous, "I don't think this Ejizu that I see is at Tochi's level of maturity. He speaks like he is some multiples of six in age."

Somto nodded, "It seems that wherever Pneumas might be, they continue to advance in all ways except in chronological age."

Chapter 26

Meanwhile, somewhere in the depths of the earth, the arrival of the peace warriors in their meeting place would end half an hour after the call had been placed by the most venerable one, and the gates to the arena were sealed with a bang.

The inside was shadowy and was in opposition to beyond the enclosure due to a vast array of coruscating candles and name displays that all but illuminated the area.

"Ózò Ajutu Ugodi and Ózò Egu Madu have called upon you warriors," the most venerable one boomed from the center of the expanse. He was flanked by his four other venerable ones, as was usual. "May they give all and sundry an explanation for this summon. And we may only discuss such matters as are the sole reasons for these impromptu gatherings; section one, subsection three."

"Thank you, Your Most Venerable," King Ajutu's voiced carried from within his cubicle. "The existence and continuance of Mkpátáku ritual are threatened by the lifeforces of its victims who have not been buried and are helping humans who intend to fight against it. We need to find the remains of all the children who have not yet been inhumed and perform burials for them. It would entail each of us visiting the shrines where we conducted the sacrifices."

"These shrines, like mine, for instance, may contain remains of several of these children and it would, therefore, be difficult, if not impossible, to isolate the remains of each child," Mr. Eke Isigwe roared. "Will a mass interment suffice? Or do we need to lay them to rest individually."

"I should think that as long as earth covers them all, that burying them en masse would serve the purpose," King Ajutu said.

"How do we go about getting the remains out without creating a pervasive stench? One that will make our village people alert to what we are doing," Mr. Amechi Duru said. "You know how quickly bad smell and bad news spread."

"That is a good point, Ózò Amechi Duru," Chief Egu Madu said. "My suggestion is this: since most of these shrines are basement ones, to pull down the portions of them that are above ground, cover them up with sand, compact the sand, and seal the entire area with concrete."

"Ózò Egu Madu, I think your suggestion makes practical sense," King Ajutu said. "And the ones that are not a basement and have side rooms for storing the remains, we just bulldoze them into the ground."

"By all means, we will rebuild the shrines at a later date," Chief Egu Madu said. "All ritualists must, as soon as this meeting is over, go ahead and remove all personal effects from their shrines in readiness for this operation."

"Also, everyone must be on the lookout…to make sure we prevent new unburials from happening," King Ajutu added.

"Does it matter who buries the body?" Mr. Amadi Bioma asked. "Is there a difference if a family member does it versus a stranger? I ask because I don't think I am ready to go back to the same shrine where I sacrificed one of my sons not quite one day ago."

"I don't think it matters, Ózò Amadi Bioma," King Ajutu said.

"What do we then do about new intakes?" Mr. Eke Isigwe asked.

"Anyone wishing to partake in Mkpátáku would have to do it after the shrines have been rebuilt," King Ajutu said. "So, sad as it may seem, there will be no new intakes for as long as it takes to win this battle. Therefore, we must bring a halt to the recruitment of would-be members for now. Sometimes we must stop or take a step back to leap even further. And, of course, we would have to rethink how we dispose of the remains of our child victims going forward."

Deafening silence ensued for an innumerable period as the atmosphere of evil and death grew tangible.

"And as you already are aware, the netherworld does not yet see the need to get involved in this fight. Though we would love to, but we can't begin striking humans just for the fun of it. It is entirely your fight, Ózò Ajutu Ugodi. You have what you requested," the most venerable one boomed. "Does any warrior have something more to add on this issue?"

"No, Your Most Venerable," the multitude resounded, then cheered: "Long live Mkpátáku ritual!"

"This assembly is adjoined until midnight," the most venerable one roared and as his voice faded away, he vanished along with the other venerable ones.

In no time, the doors flung open to welcome a massive inrush of a slew of ravens.

Enveloped by their assigned peace warrior's negergized-lifeforce, they exited. And with a few flaps of their wings, the ravens soared upward in droves, with the gray lifeforces faintly contrasted against the unlit darkness of the deep chasm.

Arriving in the caucus room, each of King Ajutu and Chief Madu's ravens hovered over their bodies, released their respective lifeforces and vanished into thin air.

After the lifeforces thrust themselves into the men's bodies through their right sides, King Ajutu and Chief Madu lifted their upper bodies.

Sitting on the floor of the shrine, "Whose was that body that dropped beneath us?" Chief Madu asked.

"Adaku," King Ajutu said as he got to his feet.

"Really? Didn't recognize it…And who took her life?"

"Odera, or Namdi. But my money is firmly on Odera, and he will surely get it. I will curb his abilities."

"He is a grade 'A' example of one biting the hand that feeds one. But from what I remember, didn't the most venerable one warn that he couldn't be checked once he was endowed?"

"The most venerable one said that whatever abilities Odera has acquired cannot be reversed, but he can be prevented from obtaining new ones. What he cautioned me against was that the process of preventing him would be complicated, if not impossible, and that weakening him is perhaps the only way to do the same to the ones to whom he gives his powers."

"Well, since it is not a hundred-percent impossible, we have a chance. So, what do you intend on doing with this shrine? With all the mortal remains below us?"

"Nothing," King Ajutu said huffishly, pocketing his left hand. "I haven't, beneath us, any remains from Mkpátáku that needs burying. It was just Ejizu."

Rising to his feet, "You are assuming that its only sacrifices for Mkpátáku that we need to worry about," Chief Madu said. "What about those henchmen of many years ago? You should consider evacuating and burying every remains down here even if you want to retain your shrine."

Patting his forehead with his Akupé, King Ajutu took his time before he responded, "I am concerned only with getting Ejizu's bones," he said with a half shrug and padded out of the room with a posture that sagged. "The lifeforces we will be fighting against are those of children…Those henchmen were not children. Besides, I must be careful not to further expose myself, which will be the case if I bring anyone in here to begin an evacuation."

"But most of us will be exposed in doing this," Chief Madu said as he walked out, following close behind his king. "We can give a plausible explanation to the potential workers. Our people are gullible."

"And what would that be?"

"The same line we have always fed them," Chief Madu said. "That they died of a deadly disease and had to be quarantined."

"Hmm, it didn't take Nena long to realize it was a lie," King Ajutu said and exited from the caucus room ahead of Chief Madu. "It won't bode well for me. Go and get Mr. Isigwe. I need a shower."

As they arrived at the caucus-room-area passage and the king headed down the east passage, Chief Madu looked around, and as the coast was clear, he vanished into thin air.

Chapter 27

At the same time, hesitant Ejizu summoned up pluck and squeezed his mother.

Lifting her head from the desk, he was right before her, levitating cross-legged above the desk. As their gazes met, she grinned, and he forced a smile.

"Sorry, my son, I dozed off."

"I didn't mean to disturb you, Mum. I saw that you were sleeping and went to Prince Ikuku instead. He was undressed, and I didn't want him to worry about me seeing him that way, so I had to come back to you."

"What worries you, my son?"

"You know that I hear everything Father has said since the moment I became active again, as had also been the case during the few months between my being sacrificed and proper burial?"

"Yes, my son."

"Father had sent creatures after us before you unburied me, and one of the Pneumas confirmed this and that they know you are here. I'm sorry for not warning you early enough."

Queen Nena stood up in a frenzy, "Like the creature you saw?"

"Yes, like a lion-headed eagle that roars fire."

"I must tell Ikuku at once!" Queen Nena screeched, dashing out of the office with Ejizu flowing close behind her.

Arriving at the top floor and guided by Ejizu, Queen Nena barged through the second door to the left of Prince Ikuku's portrait.

Chapter 28

In the intervening period, about 43 kilometers away from our whereabouts, as the crow flies, the henchmen and maidens started out of the cave.

Setting off at a jog, quickly, they got a whiff of Adaku's smell. Following it north-northwest, they sprinted across the savanna-like strip of land. Then, in an instant, zoom, they disappeared amongst the thick tree-covered terrain just as the maidens metamorphosed into their felid forms.

Chapter 29

The prince's dwelling was nearly as big as Queen Nena's entire home at the palace, with the best decor that money could buy.

Prince Ikuku had donned a pair of navy-blue jeans and a tight-fitting, buff, turtleneck, woolen pullover and was sitting at the foot of his bed. With his right leg crossed over his left knee, he slipped on his second sock. Looking up, his eyes swept over her delicate visage, and she appeared worked-up as well as sheepish, staring at him apologetically. As she held onto the gold knob of the inwardly open door for a moment longer, he gave her a smile.

"Come in and close the door," he casually said, adjusting his position on the bed that was dressed in an eight-piece, plum, white, and faux fur bedding set. Patting the bed beside him with his left hand, he added, "Sit by me. Everything will be fine."

Turning around, she locked eyes with Ejizu for a long moment, then shut the fumed oak door without a sound, winking at him. As she approached the bed, Ejizu turned on his heel and flowed away but didn't disappear. Restless, he opted to roam around the entire house.

Queen Nena settled down beside Prince Ikuku with a round-shouldered slouch and gazed at her left palm, the fingers of her right hand massaging it with light strokes.

"How have you been?" he said. "I wasn't able to really find out last week."

"Not good," she said. "But I came to tell you that Ajutu has sent beasts after us, and they are coming to your house. Ejizu told me."

"I've been pondering on an approach against whatever he sends. Ejizu mentioned how he saved you from his gunshots."

Glimpsing the prince out of the corner of her right eye, "He told you?" she said.

"Yes. He said you slept off a little after I and the others left the office. He squeezed me just before I got in the shower, and I indicated a wish to communicate with him. I think he just wanted to stay talking. He, as it were, showed off his abilities—like how he would gather everyone in the living room to show us what he could do with a football."

Queen Nena couldn't suppress a wistful smile, "I missed him so much," she said as she lifted her head and met his eyes. Nerving herself, she added, "I missed you, too."

Gazing at her for a few beats, he looked away, "You are still married," he said with a shade of longing in his tone.

"Perish that thought! Will you?" came Queen Nena's peremptory response. "That marriage ended more than 30 years ago," she pulled out her wedding band and threw it across the room. "I should never have left you."

Still looking the other way and ostensibly amazed at the strength of her feeling, "It was my fault," he said. "I wasn't ready to settle down, but you were."

"I should have waited till you were ready," she said whilst looking at him with yearning and through a mist of tears. "Is it too late?"

As she wiped her wet eyes, he got up and ambled across to where her ring had landed, adjacent to his grand dresser. Picking it up, he turned around and stood staring at it, rolling it between his fingers, contemplating. "It is never too late for love," he said. "The question should be: do I still love you that way?"

Straightening up, she continued to look at him with desire, searching his face and eyes with expectation. Raising his head, he caught her eyes, which had continued to soften and glaze over. And not a word passed between them for a little.

"Do you?" she asked, relaxing her posture.

"Though I wasn't ready to settle down, I thought you would be by my side, to travel the world, to grow together, to discover who we were before settling down," he said as her toes began to point upward. "I kept wondering if things might have been different had I been intimate with you as you wanted—"

"You didn't believe in intimacy before marriage, and I understood," she said. "It wasn't that at all; and before you refer to those university women again, it wasn't them either. I have accepted that it was all Ajutu's beguiling schemes, and I was naive to have fallen for them. How old was I then? Late teens? Early 20s? What did a girl with a sheltered childhood know? All that mattered to me then was to settle down and be like others who were planning families—buckling under pressure, I guess."

"You were four months short of 22 years when you married him in February 1961," he digressed from his train of thought. "But I couldn't find anyone like you during all my travels, and it's not because there weren't worthy women. There were very many of them to choose from. I discovered that I subconsciously didn't give myself the chance to be with another woman because I truly love you. We had this pure connection that people never find, and if lucky, may find just once at the max in one lifetime."

Rising to her feet as a smile slowly built, she walked with light, bouncing steps to him, and picked out the ring from between his fingers. Flinging it away, she moved in and embraced him.

Touching her head, he felt her hair and sighed. Resting his chin on the top of it, he held her by her hourglass waist, "He hasn't looked after you well," he said with a slow shake of his head. "You always took great pride in your hair. It has surely lost its healthy gloss and feel."

Shutting her eyes, "Coming here, I thought it would be difficult to win you back…I believed that as time passed, your feelings toward me had changed, and I was prepared to do whatever it would take to make you mine again, but you've made it so easy for me," she said. "I always wondered if you had any resentment toward me, and, last week, when you didn't show any, I thought you either were pretending, or you had suppressed it in the harmless form of your good works in Agudagu as well as your travels…and I don't know why I felt the former was more likely."

"Despite that you gave me my congé because of him, and I hoarded the memory in my heart because I was hurt as was to be expected," he said. "My heart hasn't hardened toward you. True love is easy, my one and only, and I still choose to love you…Never stopped, and never will that change."

Pulling back, she locked gazes with him, then grabbed the sides of his head, stood on tiptoes, and kissed him once on the lips. Looking him in the eye without blinking and with a deep, savoring breath, "I don't know the number of people who get a second chance with their first love after losing them the way I lost you. I was also afraid that I had spoiled your very capacity for love. But thank you for making this straightforward…I didn't know what I was doing back then with all the persuasion from Ajutu, my parents, and my friends."

Staring down at the floor, "The traveler will always return home," he said. "And with what's coming, would I pretend when my last moments in this world could and should be filled with desires for the only woman I've ever loved?"

Lifting his chin, "Look at me, please," she said. "Make love to me here and now."

Adopting a Pecksniffian tone, "You are still married," he said. "We are not married, and I shouldn't even be kissing you or confessing to you."

With a constrained smile, "I don't know why I expected that your response would be different. Your father did an exceptional job of scaring you from having a child out of wedlock."

"One that would have created problems for the monarchy," he quickly added.

"It's different now though; you are no longer in the line of succession to the crown."

Flashing a weak grin, he looked at her a long moment, "There is one secret you must know about Ajutu."

Rolling her eyes, she said, "I'm all ears."

"Even though at face value he would seem like a gentleman, he was into sleeping with women against their will—"

"You mean raping them?"

Prince Ikuku looked away and nodded, "I learnt that he had continued doing so even after he married you. His henchmen at the time bragged that he would get them to capture women of all ages from the streets and take them into the bush where he would do his thing and then sometimes, they would have their turn after him."

"There's clearly no accounting for tastes," she shook her head and all but fumed as a slight degree of petulance crept into her voice. "But why do you tell me this when I'm telling you that I want to be with you?"

Forcing a smile that wavered, "He might have an heir out of wedlock, thus another reason why we must end the monarchy. And he might also have given you an infection."

"Yes, he did, and I got myself treated. But all I want is to be with you," she said with feeling. "Though I'm very interested in what becomes of Akagheli, I'm not the least bit interested in what happens to him or the monarchy going forward. I realized early on after we got married that he wasn't who I thought he was, but it was too late. He is the clearest example yet of the discordance between inward reality and outward seeming. He also mistook my love for weakness, and I'm done loving him."

"After this is over, if we survive, we can look into being together," he said.

Still in each other's arms, "The only way I can marry you is if Ajutu dies," she said. "Otherwise, he wouldn't allow a divorce to happen."

Grasping reality, he pondered over her words for a long moment, then let her go, "Well, the only way we'll be alive after what's coming ends, and as hard as it is for me, his flesh and blood, to fathom, is that he dies. There's no way he and us can be alive after this," he said as he walked back to sit on the bed and pulled on his black combat boots, avoiding looking at her. "So, we will have to get as many of the spirits like Ejizu to act as shields for us just as he protected you…Then my military men can deter and destroy the creatures with their weapons."

Turning and leaning against the dresser, "Yes, the likes of Ejizu can certainly do that, but I don't think that Ajutu will be sending creatures that mere bullets can destroy," she said. "And why do you even have military men from the north guarding you? They guard your house like it is where Agudagu's wealthy stash away their money."

Smiling, he rose to his feet. Folding his arms across his chest, "Although the orphanage and elementary school, both of which adjoin this house require protection, as well as one or two other material things within this house that are also valuable, being guarded was at the town manager's insistence. He said that 'I am a pearl amidst the everyday,' and too valuable to Agudagu not to have round-the-clock protection from the finest military personnel afforded him by our land's military governor. Most of them are Hausas from Wusaland, or Hausa-speaking Middle Belters as you might imagine considering that we Igbos are behindhand regarding having enough people in the army. And not trusting these northerners completely because of the Biafran thing, I insisted on English-speaking ones and open communication networks so that, though they still communicate in Hausa from time to time, I'm privy to most of what's been said amongst them, as I have a good feeling for the language."

Nodding, "The same Ikuku of old, who seems to have no care in the world but yet concerned about what people say about him," she said. "And what are these one, or two valuable things?"

"It's important to know who one's well-wishers are so that one doesn't waste one's limited time on earth in the company of negative people."

"Certainly," she said. "You've always said that. Odera might have an idea what to do in case the military folks don't succeed. Before I slept off, he did mention that he killed Adaku with just his machete. She had attacked them in the form of a black panther."

"Wow!" he uttered and shook his head as he approached her. "So that's how he got that bloody wound that wasn't well-wrapped up; I was wondering…one wouldn't have thought that any of those maidens had it in them to attack anyone, let alone alter into a wild animal. Wonders, they say, shall never end. It's almost nine o'clock. I'm famished. Let's go and eat breakfast; we can talk some more with the others about our mode of attack. And pardon me for saying this, but you look exhausted."

"I am and need more nap time…Worrying about Ezinne's whereabouts all night affected my sleep, but my sense of duty impels me to keep up appearances."

"Anika will take you to one of the guestrooms. I'll take you to her. You can take a nap there rather than strain your neck on my desk."

"Not while Ajutu is planning evil," she voiced. "Nothing a reinvigorating shower can't fix."

Taking her left hand in his left hand, she looked up to her left and gazed a long moment at him, then stroked him on the cheek with the back of the fingers of her right hand, "I know how perfect you are at maintaining a semblance of calm even with an inner turmoil. Like how you seemed unperturbed during your father's burial but would cry so much to me afterward."

"Well, my father had drummed it in my ears that kings don't show their emotions that might make them seem weak to the outside. I had been under enormous pressure to please him—pressure that began before I was even five and would trigger the series of events that led to my abdication of the throne."

Sighing for days gone by, "I wish things were different," Queen Nena said, her voice faltering with a hint of uncertainty.

"However difficult it might seem; we have to just let the past be and let the present bloom."

Interlocking their fingers, he put his right arm around her waist, and, together, they headed out of the room. Leaning toward the right side of his face as his touch seemed to set off a wave of excitement within her, "You haven't forgotten the good old days," she whispered in his ear as they arrived at the gallery and stopped.

His eyes twinkled in amusement as he shut the door.

"I should say a word or two to the others before I go and sort myself out…"

Prince Ikuku nodded.

"But not before you tell me what these valuables are," she said.

"Your curiosity does not seem to have wavered one bit," he said. "And you still don't forget easily. I thought that ignoring it the first time you asked was enough to permanently dispel your desire to know—"

"Well, we know each other too well," she said.

"Two human skulls…" he said, drawing a furrowed brow from her, which made him quickly add. "They are made of crystal. I got them from Germany last year. The scientist in me was intrigued by what some people had said they could be associated with, but I haven't managed to test their suppositions yet."

"Hmm, you have truly been bored," she said. "I'm glad to again be that distraction that you've always craved…before loneliness leads you to build human bodies out of crystal, considering that you've already gone and bought two heads."

Chuckling to himself, he nodded again. "They are skulls…But you couldn't be righter."

"It just occurred to me that I heard you and Ajutu talk about 'crystals' last week. Are those skulls what you were referring to?"

"Yes. I mentioned it by chance, and, initially, he didn't seem interested until one of the other dignitaries commented that he had heard that they were associated with paranormal phenomena, then Ajutu wanted to know where they were."

"Did you tell him?"

Nodding, "I did…and I can tell you, too, if you want to know. They are in my special chamber," the prince said. "But I didn't think anything of it at the time."

"Now you do?"

Prince Ikuku nodded.

"Hmm, it beats me why he's interested in it," she said. "What will you do, considering that he has been to your house?"

"About what?" he said. "About Ajutu coming to my house to steal them?"

"About why he became interested only when he heard the word 'paranormal' and that he also knows where they are?"

"Well, with all we have just learnt about him, it should surprise nobody that he is in the least interested in anything that is linked to the paranormal," he said. "And what we are going to do about it all is currently dogging our consciousness."

Chapter 30

Meanwhile, as Ejizu completed his switching of realms, Somto, Dike, Adaku, and Ijezie were huddled together and deep in conversation. The almost-vacuum around them was saturated with voiced thoughts.

Stealing furtive glances at Ejizu as he approached them with his head down in dismay, and eyes shut in a bid to exclude their discourse from his mind, they made space for him to join their circle.

Somto turned his head toward Ejizu, "Adaku just said that one of the maidens is pregnant with your father's child."

Following a moment of sullen silence, as he closed in on the group, Ejizu opened his eyes as he lifted his head, "I heard Adaku, and I'm surprised it's only one—and not all—of them who is pregnant," Ejizu said with an askance attitude without making eye contact with any of the quartet. "As I flew my mother across to Prince Ikuku's house, she gave me an earful of everything, not least his infidelity."

"You should tell her immediately," Somto said.

"We're assuming she doesn't already know," Adaku added.

"She isn't aware and probably would prefer that it stays that way," Ejizu said. "She wouldn't dare welcome the thought, let alone the actuality of another woman, who is not a wife let alone the queen, producing an heir in her place. It would be much too humiliating for someone who sees herself as having pride of place in Akagheli's history—the queen that was when Akagheli appeared to be making some progress toward prosperity."

"All the more reason for you to let her know," Adaku said. "Not welcoming it entails that she would work tirelessly to stop it. As heir to the throne, the child might be a menace—"

"If your mother and co. don't vanquish the negergy that's in the maiden and, in so doing, end that pregnancy," Somto interjected.

"Will a monarchy still be in existence after this fight is over?" Ejizu said. "With the possibility that every villager would have caught wind of my father's evil acts and his failure to keep the ritual abolished? That offspring won't have any loyal subjects to rule over if Prince Ikuku helps bring about democracy in Akagheli."

"Still, Igboland is better off if that child is not born," Dike said. "It may still cause far-reaching trouble regardless…whether it is able to rule or not. In fact, my instinct tells me it would become quite dangerous the more it is unable to rule; and ruling by force and fear would not be out of the question for it. How can you tell a potentially powerful heir apparent that he or she can't rule after their father?"

"I know you all are worried about what nature a child coming from my father, who it seems, can bring the Evil One into corporeal existence, and a maiden, who is an ailuranthrope, will assume," Ejizu said. "But knowing my mother, such news will be a distraction to her, considering that she will be working hand in glove with Dike's mother in the looming war. If after the hostilities end, the maiden is still alive, and hopefully my mother and co. are still alive, then we can tackle it then. Furthermore, I don't want to add to her misery. Her face has lost its usual bloom, and she needs to heal first and that's going to take some time."

Nodding, "Makes a whole lot of sense," Ijezie said. "I say we don't tell her yet. Adaku, do you have an idea when the child might be born?"

"I heard the pregnancy may be around four months at the most."

"That gives us at least five months to rid it from their world if it so happens that the maiden survives what is coming," Ijezie said.

"You are assuming that the pregnancy has to last nine months," Adaku said. "These are not mere humans, Ijezie…It could be far less than that."

"The body is human, so I will take nine months for now, or deal with it as and when things change," Ijezie said, glancing at Adaku. "Be sure to let us know."

"Yessir!" Adaku said with a hint of a smile, then faced Ejizu. "Do you have an idea what your mother and co. have as a counterattacking measure? The maidens and the henchmen are making a headlong dash toward them, and we need to come up with propositions quickly and put them into action."

"They are getting to it, though I must add, slowly, due to my laid-back uncle not appreciating the full extent of what the others had witnessed," Ejizu said. "But we can't work at their pace. They don't see what we see. So, to start with, I say we provide them with the first line of protection, to allow them more time to come up with an attack strategy. We will form an invisible barrier around the house they are in—"

"That's an awesome idea," Somto said. "Linking hands, we will form a ring around the premises, then concentrate our energies and impetus and merge them into a force field to protect the house and deal with whatever firepower they would wield."

"Somto!" Ejizu said with a steady, low-pitched voice, his mouth curving in a smile. "Thanks for stealing my idea."

With a brusque nod, "Yes," Adaku said with a clipped tone, giving Somto a funny look. "He's got this happy knack of helping himself to everyone's thoughts."

"You can't blame me," Somto said and twirled gaily. "This is a very exciting moment. I'm so fired up. Before Adaku arrived, then this battle that's coming down the pike, the most adventure I ever had, here, was helping my brother scare off some bullies when he was about ten years old—by making his bicycle chase them without a rider on it. Of course, I was the rider…they just didn't see me. He is 38 now, so we are talking 28 years ago. Wouldn't you all agree that I'm overdue an adventure?"

"You clown," Ijezie said. "Many of us have had no thrills since arriving here. I know you well, and all you are doing is showing off to Adaku."

"Well, every Pneuma will be thrilled to the core and in an unforgettable way with this one," Somto enthused, turning toward Adaku. "Adaku doesn't mind me drawing attention to myself, or do you?"

Adaku shook her head.

Chomping at the bit, "Those seven will be in for a sensational shocker," Dike said. "Somto, make the call to all Pneumas, and I hope they won't be irritated at being summoned again so soon. Let's get down to the nitty-gritty of protecting the house. Adaku is right. We don't know how much longer we have till those creatures show up. Better to lie in wait than get there late."

"I agree—least said, soonest mended…My mother would have said," Somto said and began his whistling call.

Chapter 31

Moments on, amidst clinking of cutlery against chinaware, Prince Ikuku and Queen Nena arrived in the bright dining room that had all the modern conveniences whilst Anika hung back in the doorway, holding Obiageli's right hand in her left hand.

Throwing a glance at me, to where I'd sat directly opposite him, Odera nodded leftward toward them. Glancing rightward, I could see that the connection, which had once existed between the prince and the queen, as Odera had alluded to, hadn't waned notwithstanding the passage of time. The view also confirmed to me that Anika was to the manner born with children, and I wondered if she had any of her own and, if so, where they were.

Darting my gaze back at Odera as we dropped our forks and arose, I smiled at him as I experienced a passing thought about what my and his relationship would be like 20 years from then.

On our feet, atop the dark, walnut-colored, thick-pile carpet, around the tablecloth-less, highly burnished, long, rectangular, solid-wood table that could seat ten people, Odera, Namdi, and I bowed our heads to the queen.

"Please sit down," the queen said as she glanced around, admiring the decor of the grand hall; at the tea carts and polished sideboard on the south side before her eyes rested momentarily at the room's east end as strong white-and-golden sunrays shone through between the mullions of the two floor-to-ceiling windows, showcasing the beauty of the thick mohair that created the curtain's fabric. "I don't have much of an appetite, so I'll be leaving you all to freshen up and attend to the aches and pains I feel. Carry on with drawing up a plan as you must. Let's not waste any more time. See you all before long."

As Namdi and Anika engaged in a brief, mutual gaze that ended with him winking both his eyes at the same time and holding them shut for significantly longer than a normal blink, "Yes, Your Majesty," we said, all together.

And Namdi would reopen his eyes with a winsome smile at Anika just as the queen gave Prince Ikuku a peck on the cheek, which appeared to thrill and excite him. As the queen slunk toward Anika, who was grinning for the first time, to my notice, since our arrival, I waved at Obiageli who was dressed in a different outfit. Smiling and with her eye on a toy in the grip of her right hand as it hung by the wrist from Anika's hand, she waved back with her left hand.

Just as we all settled down in the ladder-back chairs with woven seats, Prince Ikuku dished out a full English breakfast and poured himself some of the coffee Anika had rustled up, which I'd transferred to the dining table.

As he ate, "Thank you for Oby's dress," I said. "She looks like a princess."

"Doesn't she?" he said with a cheerful grin. "Nobody would have guessed that that dress is second-hand. We get them free from Europe to clothe our children."

Gnawing my under lip in reflection, "About that," I said. "I struggle to understand how a town this prosperous still has many unplaced orphans. People surely have the wherewithal to adopt these children."

Leaning sideways, "That's an interesting observation, and I can't think of any reasons why they don't adopt…Also we have strong reasons to believe that at least 90 percent of the children in the orphanage that adjoins this house are not real orphans, but abandoned children who come from neighboring communities—"

"I can never grasp why parents abandon their children," I said.

"Well, local studies have shown that having parents who are alive and want their children depends to a great extent on what the economic situation is with any particular family," the prince said.

"Considering that there is poverty within Agudagu's neighbors, it does then seem like they dump their children at Agudagu's doorstep on purpose," Namdi said.

"It does seem that way, but what do we do?" Prince Ikuku said. "These abandoned children, all of whom are boys by the way, never asked to be born, and they deserve no less than the ones who weren't abandoned. All we do is give them a good start at life and ultimately educate them as a way out of the ruck as well as the best defense against despotism."

"Must be difficult to give those children names," I said.

"Not quite," the prince said. "I was told that, strangely, many of the boys, the 90 or so percent I alluded to, have what is assumed to be their first names tattooed on them, so that made it easy. For the girls, and the rest of the boys, we assign names in an alphabetical order, much like how the west names their weather systems while leaving out alphabets that don't have meaningful names that they begin."

"What you are doing deserves a lot of commendation," Odera said.

"It's the least I could do. I made a lot of contacts on my sojourns across the globe who helped me realize that running these charities is important. I had thought that Ejizu passed away out of the blue from an unforeseen illness and felt the desire to ensure no child died because of avoidable reasons like good health, food, love…You know, all the essential stuff. It was also my way of having children around me since I had none of mine and was not an uncle anymore."

"You couldn't have said it better," I said. "But I also did wonder how you sustain these charities."

"Agudagu is a town that depends heavily upon the wood industry. Three decades ago, I invested most of the money I got from Ajutu, which I now know was ill-gotten, in the planting of tens of thousands of jackal-berry trees, which you can now find everywhere, and I oversee. Though an untitled and a non-executive member of Agudagu's Administrative Leadership Team by choice, I can influence plans, actions, and laws making, so I fought to enact an ordinance whereby for every tree that is felled, five are planted in turn, and for every tree that is sold, five percent of the proceeds go toward these charities. There is also a nursery where we grow them in readiness. We've also recently just got awarded the federal contract to provide termite resistant wood toward the construction of a major railroad. So, for as long as jackal-berry trees are in existence and in demand, the orphanages are catered for…Even if I were no more, it would require an amendment of the law to get the arrangement overturned."

"Interesting forward planning," I said. "And correct me if I'm wrong, I think that someone in Amandizuogu took a leaf out of your book—"

With a knowing smile, he said, "Yes, I heard that Pará rubber trees began to sprout up everywhere in Amandizuogu around the same time as my trees put forth shoots here."

"It's good when people copy the right things; I wonder why someone didn't do the same in Akagheli," I said. "But how do you look after all the trees to ensure they aren't cut down illegally considering that this behavior is rife, certainly in Akagheli?"

"Oh," Prince Ikuku said. "We have rangers, foresters, and botanists who go around in patrol vehicles. Nothing to worry about there. All catered for."

"You will go down in Agudagu's history books as a pioneer extraordinaire," Odera said.

Sitting upright, "Perhaps, but right now, Akagheli's future is what concerns me," Prince Ikuku said. "Charity, as the fella says, begins at home."

"So, how can we do this without alarming the populace?" I spoke. "I fear that if it's mishandled, people might flee Akagheli, and that's not what Akagheli needs."

"I don't see how we can keep it a secret," Odera said. "I think a better way to handle this might be to send a word out in a controlled way to people so that they are not alarmed by sudden exposure to what has been going on."

"You mean let it filter through like a rumor?" Namdi said and Odera nodded.

"We are assuming that people don't already know. Anyway, there's no time for that," Prince Ikuku said. "Ajutu has already sent out his squad of supernatural goons."

"He has? For certain?" Odera croaked, rising, and working himself up. "And we are here chewing the fat?"

Leaning back in his seat, "Settle down, Odera," Prince Ikuku said. "No battle has ever been won without proper planning, and no good planning can be done without good nourishment. Ejizu and his group will buy us time by shielding my house—Ejizu suggested it. Let's see what his lackeys have got. I have top-notch military men who are always ready, and you didn't do badly with the panther that attacked you. But in the end, fretting about it will not move the needle on what we hope to accomplish. By the way, Anika did a good job on your finger injuries."

Feeling a sudden uprush of proprietorial instinct, "Odera is much more coordinated than he appears to be right now," I said as Odera glimpsed his fingers and sat down, and I reached out my hand toward his left hand. "His encounter with the panther has left him a little anxious."

Looking across the table, at me, Odera smiled and stretched out his left hand to touch mine for a beat, then resumed eating. Continuing to stare at him as the moment our fingers met remained emblazoned on my mind, I sensed true repose begin to grow within me regarding the upcoming battle and it was all thanks to him. I was glad that he'd been the one who'd ushered me into the palace. My daughter and I might have been dead and forgotten had he continued to practice with Namdi in the dojo and allowed us to wait until noon to see the king, at which stage any of the other henchmen may have let us into the palace and most likely would have obeyed the king's command. It had to be him since all matters that were out of the ordinary needed his sanction as the lead henchman.

Or was it just down to Papu's quick thinking, or God's plan?

Noticing a connection between Odera and me, Prince Ikuku leaned toward his meal and picked up his cutlery. Pausing for a moment, he gazed at his plate, then looked up at us, "When this is over and we are still alive, you all are welcomed to live in my house until you settle down. Nkem, you could take charge of looking after the hairs of the orphanage's girls while Odera and Namdi can join me in contributing to Agudagu's economy and the rebuilding of Akagheli's," Prince Ikuku said, then focused his gaze at Namdi who was sitting to Odera's right. "And Anika is so ready to say goodbye to solo life. Nice fit for any good man—28 years old and no children yet."

A smile built across my and Odera's face.

And with a swill of black coffee, Namdi chortled behind his left hand and sat back, "She does seem nice," he said as he chewed a mouthful of sapid sausage, and love seemed to be kindling within his bosom. "It gives me one more reason to stay alive."

A ripple of laughter ran around the room from Prince Ikuku, Odera, and me against a background of intermittent static from the handheld at the head of the table where the prince sat.

Looking at Prince Ikuku, "I don't think the queen will allow you out of her sight again, so you might as well start planning a permanent move to Akagheli," I said.

Raising his brows, Prince Ikuku shrugged, "We'll see. I'm largely a sinecure here, if truth be told…Hopefully it won't be long until Akagheli no longer is ruled by a monarch so that she can move here with me…Unless you lot don't mind being my protégés," he said and sipped his coffee, making a wry face as he spat it back into the cup. "It beats me that you lot don't mind your coffee cold."

Setting the cup down, he reached for the walkie-talkie.

"Anika said the school that's part of the orphanage is a good one," I said. "Can Obiageli begin there tomorrow?"

Nodding, "Certainly, Anika can sort that out for you," the prince said, then spoke into the device, "Anika, please let someone know we need hot water in here."

Chapter 32

Wrapped in a towel and holding another in her right hand, Queen Nena exited the bathroom.

Arriving at the window that looked out over the mansion's front yard, she pulled the curtains further apart to allow more sunlight into the lavish guestroom.

Outside, between the near-naked branches of the clump of trees ahead, she sighted the gently rolling hills not that far-off and, with the side vision of her right eye, scores of people who'd taken to their heels on the street that turned into the dead-end road.

Paying no heed to why people were scattering, she ambled back to the bed. Settling down on its edge facing the window, she gave her hair a quick rub to wet the towel, then bent down to massage the back of her heels and legs, where she had large bruises, humming delightfully to herself.

When she looked up again, her eyes were suddenly wide with shock. The black eagle with a dark-brown lion head and mane, which Ejizu had mentioned, was approaching the property at speed, flapping its huge wings with brute strength, swaying, and tossing its snake tail violently, and roaring fire.

With a dart of panic, she was thrown off balance. Tightening her grip on the towel in her hand, she got to her feet in a snap and backed away toward the exit, still gazing at the monster.

As she shrank away and turned to run, uncertain whether to get dressed first, or leave the room in the all-together, out of the corner of her left eye, she noted that the creature's movement had halted without warning as it received an instant discharge of electricity throughout its body and fell toward the ground.

Slinking to the window, she looked out. Down on the eerily deserted, tarred road side of the high fence, the *lieagle*[13] writhed for a moment, then rose to posture with wrath, roaring at the building. Through the double-glazed glass that excluded most of the external sounds, she was certain that she saw hell in its huge, cyan eyes.

Petrified by the sight, her eyes flickered. And it wasn't toward anything better. Further back, she descried three monstrous creatures sliding out from behind the trees. There was a lightning-roaring black horse with the same-colored mane, whose tawny lion head had eyes that also flashed lightning and whose tail was a King Cobra. On its left was a white lion that boasted a large olive and jet-black banded tiger snake for a tail and had a white mane of hair around its black, double life-size Komodo dragon head whose forked tongue dripped fluid that seemed corrosive. In between those gruesome beasts was another with a tawny body, front half of which was a lion and back half a hippopotamus, with a coal-black crocodile head and mane, and a black mamba as its tail. And each snake seemed to evince an autonomous disposition.

With wide-open eyes, "Satan has an active role in this world and has clearly stolen Ajutu's soul for his bidding," she whined as she dashed for the walk-in closet where Anika had laid, for her, a selection of clothes.

Dumping the towel in her hand, she tugged off the one her body was wrapped in, revealing just a pair of underpants. Forgoing her brassiere and almost tripping, she scrambled into a pair of black jeans and a sky-blue close-knit, woolen pullover. Grabbing a pair of lace-less sneakers, she eyed for a beat, the bag of Ejizu's bones, which she'd placed at the innermost corner of the clothes room, then rushed out.

Leaving the guestroom door open, the most central door on the northern side of the top floor, she bounded around the gallery as she slipped on her footwear, then, in a succession of flying leaps, arrived down the eastward stairs.

She sprinted into the dining room, noting that the previously occupied seats were pulled away from the table with one overturned, but no-one was in there. Her instinct was to dart for the work room whose door was wide open.

---

[13] A massive (more than double life-size) eagle with a life-size head of a lion.

Chapter 33

Within the home office and in a cold sweat, Prince Ikuku, Odera, Namdi, and I were at the bay windows, looking out as the military men drew themselves up in battle array, ready for if and when needed.

"What the heck happened to that creature?" Queen Nena shrieked. "Did you see the other three?"

"No," Prince Ikuku started. "We saw just one—"

"After a frantic call came from the captain, we rushed in here and saw the flying beast drop out of the sky and fall toward the ground behind the fence," I said.

"And that's Ejizu and his group," the prince continued. "They formed a field of energy around us. So, there is probably no way for those creatures to enter."

"No way, yet," I said. "They are giving us time to get our acts together. They don't know for how long they can keep the barrier going. It depends on what the creatures have as weapons."

"That's true," Queen Nena said. "Ejizu said he felt drained of strength after absorbing the multiple shots from his father, hence the reason he took me out of the palace as fast as possible lest he lost more 'impetus' and became unable to lift me up in the air."

"But we can't fire any weapons through their barrier," Odera said. "How do we attack?"

"We would have to communicate with Ejizu, Dike, and Bute," I said. "They can create openings through which we can fire. They can then close up again when we are done—so open, fire, shut, and repeat until we are done."

"We must be careful though, as communicating with them might distract them and take away from their energy, weakening the barrier overall," Namdi said.

"Ejizu was able to fly me and talk with me as well even with him being drained."

"The younger spirits have more resilience than the older ones," Namdi said. "From my understanding, the majority of them are older spirits who lost their lives at least two decades ago—"

"We ought to try though…" Prince Ikuku said. "Unless someone else has a better idea than what Nkem has suggested."

"We must act with caution," Queen Nena said. "They all have snakes for tails, and each snake appears to have a mind of its own."

"Are you saying that they are detachable?" Odera said.

"Yes," Queen Nena said. "They could easily fly through an opening in the barrier and come for us."

"Did you get a glimpse of the other three's weaponry?" Odera said. "We know the flying one uses fire."

"And of no consequence to the barrier," Prince Ikuku said. "I don't think it can generate high-enough temperatures needed to affect the barrier."

"One of them dripped a liquid from its mouth that fumed and sizzled as it hit the ground—" the queen said.

"That's definitely acid," Prince Ikuku interrupted. "Still, it would have no effect on the barrier."

"Another flashed lightning from its eyes as well as roared the same…and the last one didn't show what it had," the queen said.

"The one with lightning worries me," Prince Ikuku said. "One strike can generate enough heat that may very well destabilize the balance of the barrier."

"And how do you know all of this?" I asked.

Smiling, Prince Ikuku tried to reply.

But forestalling him, "One of his majors was physics," Odera and Queen Nena said without exception.

Nodding, "Over to those who can communicate with their departed ones," the prince said, striding toward the exit as Odera, Namdi, and I continued to look out the window. "Let me instruct my men to open the gate. Nkem, please be the one to point out where the gaps in the barrier would be. Take that handset. I'll pick up the one in the dining room."

Grabbing the prince by the arm, "Before you go," the queen said, her words laced with anxiety. "Why didn't those vicious creatures turn themselves loose on the people I saw running helter-skelter up and down the road?"

Contemplating hurriedly, "Not sure," Prince Ikuku said. "I've got to turn that over in my mind before I can give you an answer. Nkem, Odera, or Namdi might know."

Reluctantly letting the prince go, Queen Nena faced us, "Does anyone know?"

Gazing out the window with the handie-talkie in the tight grip of my hand, we shook our heads without as much as a glance in the queen's direction. Nothing but the looming ill wind that blew no good had taken over our minds.

Chapter 34

In the interim, the bracing morning wore on in Akagheli, and within the caucus room, Chief Madu and Mr. Eke Isigwe awaited King Ajutu's arrival.

The chief was in his usual seat, leaning back, rapping his Mkpó on the carpet, and glancing at his wristwatch time and again. Eke was seated next to the chief, hunched forward with his elbows on his lap, hands apposed, and fingers laced together, tapping his feet.

"We have been waiting a while," Eke said. "This is not what I planned to do today. Is there anyone we can send to let him know we are here?"

With a shrug, "His henchmen and maidens aren't around," Chief Madu said. "We just have to wait for as long as he takes. He is our king and spiritual leader after all and can cool our heels for as long as he sees fit while we are under his summon."

Looking around, Eke got to his feet and padded toward the north end of the room with his hands pocketed, admiring the king's mosaic. As he passed the door, it flung open, missing him by centimeters. Striding in, King Ajutu made for his chair.

Facing the king as the door shut, Eke bowed his head for a moment. Settling down, King Ajutu rested a set of keys and his Akupé on the table.

"Take your seat, Eke," King Ajutu said. "Thank you for coming."

"I am happy to be here, Your Majesty," Eke said as he returned to Chief Jokum's chair. "You look different in those getups. I have never seen you wearing chinos, a sweater, a face cap, and dark glasses."

Wearing a frozen smile, "The occasion and the weather call for them, and you two got your garbs spot-on too," the king said as Eke leaned back in his seat, shaking his head, and smiling. "You don't want people to easily identify their king as he roams the streets unguarded, do you?"

"But you are capable of becoming invisible, Your Majesty…We all are," Eke said. "And that should take care of things."

"It saps my energy to do that. I like to reserve it for when it is really needed," the king said.

"Hmm, I agree, Your Majesty," Eke said.

"So, as the only occultist in this neck of the woods, we will start with your shrine, then seek out the rest. Roughly how many remains do you reckon there are in your basement?"

"163, Your Majesty," Eke said.

Furrowing his brows, "I wasn't expecting you to be exact," the king said, then his eyes darted from one peace warrior to the other. "With that number, we have to go with mass burial. Agreed?"

Eke and a contemplative Chief Madu nodded.

"Have you removed all of your belongings?" King Ajutu continued.

"I did that soon after our impromptu journey before Chief Madu came calling, Your Majesty."

"Okay," the king said as he stood up, sliding the set of keys over the table toward Chief Madu. "Off we go. You will drive us to any builder's site you know. We must commandeer a bulldozer."

"I know your henchmen and maidens aren't here, Your Majesty. Why don't we go with any of the other palace workers?" Chief Madu said as he hesitantly picked up the keys and sprang to his feet.

"I do not trust any of them. What about your boys, can we go with one of them?"

"Your Majesty, Izundu packed up and went back to his family yesterday. Onuka locked himself up in his room and I don't think he has eaten or spoken to anyone for close to 24 hours now."

"Your Majesty, if we need someone to run errands for us, we can make a stop at my shop and collect one of my boys," Eke said. "I trust them."

King Ajutu nodded. Motioning toward the door for his guests to walk out ahead of him, he picked up his Akupé. Glancing at its handle and at his Okiké in turn, he flashed a brief smile, then followed the men out of the room.

Turning his head to look backward as he stepped onto the adjacent corridor ahead of the chief, "But, Your Majesty, how do we figure out where the other shrines are?" Eke said.

Preempting the king, "As the Supreme Peace Warrior of Igboland, His Majesty was given a map of all the shrines within his domain," Chief Madu said. "The problem, however, is that of time. His Majesty does not trust that the occultists will do a good job and wants to supervise their burials himself."

Darting a glance at the king, "That will take many days to accomplish," Eke said. "You indicated that we don't have that amount of time, Your Majesty."

"That's where using our teleporting abilities will come in handy," King Ajutu enthused.

"Still, it would take days, Your Majesty," Eke said. "Our energy levels need to be recouped after each instant travel—depending on the real distance covered—before we can repeat."

After a long moment of considered thought, "I guess you are right," King Ajutu said. "How could I have quickly forgotten how sapped of energy I was after the only time I ported?"

"Trust me, Your Majesty," Eke said. "I use it daily and, many a time, I am too tired to even eat that I have to sleep it off for a couple of hours to regain my strength, and we are talking after merely going from my home to the shrine or farthest, close to my shop."

"We'll just have to wait and see how everything unfolds," the king said. "My henchmen and maidens may just put this matter to bed in a matter of minutes for all our anxieties."

"I am sorry to say this, Your Majesty," Chief Madu said as the three men arrived at the east passage striding abreast, with the king in the middle, heading toward the garage. "But have you considered that you may be acting too much on instinct rather than by logic on this issue? As a man who prides himself on having the patience to always think things through, I feel that you are letting personal feelings cloud your judgment."

Turning to his left, "Are you developing cold feet?" the king retorted, his eyes wide with revulsion at the chief.

"Though we have been warned twice by the most venerable one, I am with you all the way, Your Majesty," Chief Madu continued. "I am just concerned that it is too simplistic to assume that doing all these rapid-fire burials wins us the war."

"It is simple—stop the activities of those spirits and the humans are defenseless," the king said with huffishness. "It is not that complicated."

"Yes, Your Majesty, you are a hundred-percent correct," the chief said. "But what if these burials do not stop the spirits?"

"Ejizu was not active until he was unburied!" the king protested.

"Let's assume that he wasn't active, Your Majesty, remember that he was buried with the proper rite of passage," the chief said. "What if the ceremony matters as well?"

"If rite of passage is relevant, then we get an official to perform as many as are needed."

"What if a coffin is important, Your Majesty, as part of the rite?" the chief continued, causing the king to come to a halt. "Think about it. If we mass bury, then realize that a box is necessary, what do we then do? Start to dig again? It could become really messy."

Standing with his arms akimbo, frowning, "So what are you suggesting?" King Ajutu said as the two men also halted.

"That we bring the remains out, Your Majesty, lay them in caskets, then perform a normal funeral ceremony. It is all about respecting the deceased. What do you think, Eke?"

"You have a point, but—" Eke began to say with a cracked voice.

"Let's do that then," the king interjected as he hurried on. "You take the lead, Chief Madu."

"I don't know where the limit would be," Eke said. "What if, as part of the ceremony, it is important that at least one bereaved family member is present? What if the grave must be no less than six feet deep? What do we tell people who see us doing all these and begin to ask questions?"

King Ajutu heaved a long sigh of tiredness and their conversation lulled. "No more 'what ifs'… And don't bandy words with me anymore. Let's get down to business," the king roared. "Get a few coffins and cram in as many remains as each can contain and get a pastor, or priest as well and pay them whatever they ask for. Everyone has a price."

Chapter 35

At the same time, basking in the salubrious weather but poorly concealed within one of the bare jackal-berry trees across from Prince Ikuku's home, the feline forms of the maidens were at a vantage point.

Seemingly disinterested and unable to see into the compound, they watched as the beast guises of the henchmen remained on the prowl in front of the private property, with Kadiye grumbling thunder and flickering lightning.

Altering back to human nature one after the other, they sat astride separate tree boughs, with their backs against the tree's bole, lolling at ease. Ijeoma was at a level below Adure and Isioma who backed each other.

"What do you reckon is going on in there?" Isioma said, swinging her long, slender, and hairless legs. "This impasse cannot continue. The flies that all these rotten fruits around us attract irritate me with their bumbling, and I cannot wait to leave this place."

"It's clear that Prince Ikuku has an invisible barrier protecting his house," Adure said. "What do you suggest we do instead of stating the obvious?"

"We go home," Isioma said. "After all, we were not created for him to be used in conflicts."

"We're asked to obey him and that overrides everything else," Adure said. "There must surely be a way around it. Kadiye's lightning is the most potent weapon we came with. He should strike."

"And who will go and tell him?" Isioma said. "I don't want to be an easy target. Since they have an invisible barrier, they might also have a stealth missile."

Letting herself drop from the tree, being closest to the ground, "The sooner they accomplish this mission, the sooner we can all go home, so I will go," Ijeoma said as, along with some jackal-berries that thudded to the ground, she landed on the greensward and rolled forward out of the trees as crisp, yellow leaves scrunched under her full weight.

Arriving onto the tarred road and without breaking her motion, she arose, scampered to the lion-headed horse, and whispered in one of its large ears.

Following Ijeoma as she turned around, the *liorse*[14] loped along by her side to the edge of the orchard. There, it stopped as she disappeared into the trees and did an about-face.

With the building at a good target range, it lifted its front limbs. Balancing on the hind ones, the lion-headed stallion focused its huge aqua-colored eyes at the house. From them, it discharged rapid forks of lightning that sizzled and spiked through the air toward the middle of the structure.

Producing a sheet of current that traveled in all directions, the multiple strikes lit up the entire barrier, revealing a massive scintillating dome that was at least thrice the size of the somewhat-circular edifice and covering all of its aspects.

---

[14] A life-size horse with a life-size head of a lion.

Chapter 36

Within the crossroads world, the effect of the extreme heat generated by the lightning flash was instant. All Pneuma eyes, which had already been shut, screwed up even more.

With a dump five times more than any of them had ever experienced, no communication, thoughts, feelings, or emotions passed amongst them.

Whilst their edges glowed almost as bright as the sun's corona, one after another, the energy they received began to drain them of their impulsion.

Venturing harder and harder to cling on to one another, it seemed as though the stronger their attempts were, the lesser they achieved, as an unseen force contrived to pull them apart much like similar poles of electromagnets would be expected to behave. It seemed that it would be only a matter of time before they wilted, and that time came before we knew it.

Chapter 37

Whilst each of our fear-filled eyes continued to gaze up toward the sky, Prince Ikuku arrived onto the driveway sweep. Watching as the coruscating film over the house began to dim in a patchy spread, it wasn't long before the barrier was no more.

Experiencing a sinking feeling, despairing Prince Ikuku glanced at us from within the front yard, and no sooner had he turned to face forward again than he was rattled. The lion-headed eagle had flown over the fence and landed on the terrazzo.

Heaven help us!

Turning into a rolling ball of fire that scorched flowers and ignited the closest ironclad jeep to it, it halted before the prince who blenched. As it reworked to become Batu, Prince Ikuku struggled to regain his composure, looking up in horror and expecting to be reduced to ashes.

With a minatory look, Batu sniffed the prince once.

As the big fire burned, giving off much more heat than smoke, Batu scanned around whilst scenting the air until he sighted the mansion's main entrance.

Realizing that it would take an act of God to get any commands from his petrified boss, "Soldiers, open fire, now!" Captain Iduto ordered his troop who forever had their weapons at the ready.

Batu bounded to the heavy metal door under rapid-fire that did nothing to hinder his pace or cause him to change his determined course of action, or retaliate with a fire of his own, yawned a burst of fire at the door, reduced it to a molten wreck, and whipped onto the foyer.

Dashing into the office as the innumerable bullet wounds on his body healed, he saw Odera, Namdi, Queen Nena, and me before the windows. The queen and I had cowered behind the brothers forever.

Prince Ikuku and his captain bolted toward the house whilst the other soldiers ran for cover just before the burning jeep underwent a violent and destructive shattering that sent shrapnel everywhere; the explosion mushrooming into smoke and flames as it resounded round the eerily deserted street.

Looking up at Batu as he closed in on us and sizing him up, Odera cried out, "Batu, it is us, Odera and Namdi, your commanders. Have you forgotten that I spared your life yesterday?"

Curling his upper lip in disdain, "I don't know who you are, and I wasn't in existence yesterday. I have only one commander, King Ajutu, who requires that you all die," Batu roared as Prince Ikuku arrived to stand in the doorway along with Captain Iduto. "Where is the little girl?"

Before anyone could utter as much as the start of a word in response, Batu exhaled a blaze of fire over us and made a swift turnaround to face the doorway. Seeing Prince Ikuku staring past him, at us, and smiling, he followed the prince's gaze.

Facing us again and realizing that his flame hadn't done what he'd expected, he flared another blaze at us with fury.

It was again absorbed by Bute, Ejizu, and Dike.

Further angered by his continued inability to reduce us to a pile of ash, Batu rushed into hand-to-hand combat, coming up against the duo of Odera and Namdi whose chins dropped on instinct as their arms and hands went up with elbows tight to their bodies.

Absorbing with tight guards and doing their utmost to stay locked down against Batu's heavy pummeling, Odera and Namdi moved around counterclockwise and slowly backed out of the room, luring Batu toward the spacious hall.

The prince motioned for the queen and me to leave the room, then thumped Batu's flank again and again; most likely as a distraction since his punches didn't appear to carry any weight, whilst time after time his captain shot into Batu's body at close range with his six-shooter. But those attempts were to no purpose in the practical matter of defeating the newly improved Batu.

Feeling no pain, Batu's interest remained only on Odera and Namdi.

Chapter 38

As Queen Nena and I scurried away and headed upstairs, two things bothered my mind.

One was the immediate need to have my daughter in the safety of my arms. The other was, though it seemed that Odera, Namdi, Oby, and I had been the main targets, why the heck had Batu spared the soldiers despite that they had opened fire at him, as well as Prince Ikuku who he'd first come up against?

Arriving at the gallery ahead of the queen whose bruised legs seemed unable to draw any more propulsion from her survival instinct, I shuddered to a crash overhead. Recoiling at the sound as masses of building material slammed against—and cracked—the gallery's marble floor, I felt the temperature within the home drop quickly.

On the side of my eyes, I saw a massive hole in the middle of the front of the house, above the entrance door, and an even bigger exit hole on the opposite side. A bolt of lightning had traversed the house and had ripped out the walls, allowing in more draft than the gaping entryway alone had afforded.

Below, scattering away momentarily as huge chunks of masonry smashed to the floor, spewing up white clouds of dirt and sending cement shards in all directions, the quartet circled Batu and stood poised. An epitome of calm, Batu's eyes twinkled and roved around his opposition as they huffed and puffed from exhaustion.

As I stood frozen with horror, inhaling white dust, Queen Nena caught up with me, seized my left arm with her trembling right hand, pulled me along as she fought a coughing fit, and barged into the nearest room; the one to the immediate east of Prince Ikuku's portrait.

Glimpsing Kadiye leaping through the entry hole as the queen banged the door shut, two doors further north from ours, Anika briefly poked her head around the penultimate door on the eastern side of the gallery to see what was going on.

Making a mental note of where my daughter was as Anika briefly havered at the threshold of the door, peered down the foyer before she withdrew into the room, shut, and dead-bolted the door, I knew I had to get to that room as soon as it was possible.

Landing beside Batu, Kadiye stood with his back against Batu's, "And who are the targets?" Kadiye whispered.

"The two at the ends," Batu replied in an undertone. "You go right, and I'll take left."

Ignoring Prince Ikuku and his captain like they weren't there, Kadiye rushed toward Odera whilst Batu forward rolled to Namdi. And the brothers in arms lifted their heels a touch more to stand steady on the balls of their feet.

Rising, Batu leapt toward Namdi, and as he pounced, Namdi caught him on the chin *biff* with a right-handed uppercut that sent a whine of pain through his head and quickly followed it with a left-handed blow to the side of Batu's face that sailed him afar.

Landing as Namdi seemed to marvel at the sheer force and outcome of the punches he'd landed, Batu hit his head on the corner of the concrete debris and his vision *seemed to tunnel*. Sitting up in no time, he shook his head once, then roared a cone of fire at Namdi.

Bute took up the blaze.

Frustrated, Batu got to his feet and hurtled toward Namdi.

In the meantime, Kadiye closed in on Odera at speed with a left-handed superman punch. Odera dodged the attack with a spinning punch, double-striking Kadiye's jaw with the back of his right hand and the heel of his injured left hand, giving off muffled thuds and a *whap* and sending Kadiye up, over, and sideways onto Batu's path with a *whump* as Kadiye's eyes glazed.

Lurching wildly, both supernatural henchmen careened backward with their upper backs stopping *crack* against the wall between the pair of staircases. Blood welled up in their mouths and they spat out.

Dashing rightward to the prince, "Prince Ikuku," Odera whispered, drawing him aside from his captain. "Do you know why they are not attacking you two?"

Prince Ikuku shrugged, his eyes flashing wide open.

With his drawn handgun reloaded and aimed in turn between Batu and Kadiye, Captain Iduto remained focused but unable to decide which of them to shoot at as they hurtled toward the brothers in arms, or perhaps wondered about the need to further waste ammunition.

At last discharging a shot into Kadiye, "Watch out," the captain screamed as Kadiye leapt into the air, unaffected by the bullet that lodged in his chest.

Still unmanned and distracted by talking to the prince as well as not appreciating how nimble the latest version of Kadiye had become, Odera was caught on the hop. By the time Odera saw it coming, it was too late to fend off, as Kadiye's flying head-butt *whacked* and knocked him back a few meters toward the entryway, and he landed *splat* on his back, his eyes tearing as he groaned and rubbed his forehead.

Kadiye followed quickly with a forward roll that continued with slamming both heels of his sturdy feet into Odera's crotch, causing Odera to further screech with pain as he lifted his head and grabbed his private area.

Diving onto Odera, Kadiye gave him the evil eye and a chokehold, then discharged a streak of lightning toward his face. Odera, on instinct, turned his head rightward, and Bute would suck up most of the strike, a flash singeing Odera's left temple hair.

At the same time, Batu exploded forward at Namdi with a jump-inside kick that missed Namdi, as Namdi moved back a few paces, delivering, as Batu landed, a long-range left-fisted uppercut that sounded *boff* on impact, locked up hard, and went right through Batu's chin, cracking Batu's jaw.

With his lower jaw dangling, Batu's fury grew, and he metamorphosed into his beast form, releasing its Inland Taipan snake, which searched around for a moment, then slithered, with agility, up the eastward stairs to spoor Obiageli and me.

Possessing no potent jaws to bite, or properly roar and somewhat weakened, the lieagle dropped to its knees, with his head drooping. Sensing his moment of triumph, Namdi wrapped his arms around its neck.

At the same time, disturbed by his lack of success at frying Odera, confused Kadiye, without will, loosened his chokehold on Odera. Not wasting any moment though, Odera kneed hard into Kadiye's crotch, then struck him hard against the chin with the point of his right elbow, knocking off some teeth and making Kadiye spew more blood. Pushing Kadiye off his body, Odera scooted backward on the butt of his pants for a few meters, then stopped to gulp in drafts of air into his laboring lungs, patting his left temple and glad to see no blood on his fingers.

Stung by the loss of his teeth, Kadiye adapted into his liorse form, sprang from its hind legs, then detached its tail. The king cobra bared its fangs as it made a loud, growling hiss and reared up the upper part of its body, extending its neck. Attempting a long-distance attack on Odera, the snake missed as Odera rolled away to his right and rose in a snap.

Dashing toward the lion-headed horse as it lowered its forelimbs following its prance, Odera hopped onto the concrete mass and leapt off it to bestride the creature with the finesse of a born horseman, though he wasn't one. Wrapping his muscular arms around Kadiye's beast form's neck as the king cobra curved a swift turnaround and made a beeline for him, Odera squeezed as hard as he could with one eye on the speedy snake.

Thrashing around, the beast turned its long neck left and right to clasp any part of Odera it could catch in its ferocious jaws to no avail. Attempting a roar and a bolt of lightning, it could only muster a series of strangled gasps as well as tiny sparks from its eyes. Snapping its jaws one more time at Odera as it fell sideways to the floor, Odera saw life fade away from its eyes as they rolled up and the lids struggled to blink.

And just before it impacted the floor and went over, stone dead like a log, its tongue lolling out, Odera sprang off it and dodged the king cobra's flying strike. Landing, Odera forward rolled in the direction of the snake's travel, up onto one knee, and caught the snake in mid-flight. Putting up no wiggle of resistance, the snake easily succumbed to Odera's squeeze.

Using both hands, Odera ripped it in half down its middle with Herculean tugs. Splashing blood around, he flung the two ends away in different directions lest they joined up again.

Odera arose and ran toward Namdi who still had the lion-headed eagle in a headlock, "They are weaker without the snake," Odera whispered. "And the snake is weaker without them. Finish it off! Now! I am going after the other snake."

As Namdi released the chokehold, then pulled the beast's jaws further apart, before wrenching its neck and it went limp to land smack against the floor, Odera darted past the captain who turned with Odera's movement.

With eyes wide open, "Who are you guys that you would defeat massive and deadly creatures with just your bare hands?" the captain said.

"Though size matters, a skilled fighter can still dominate," Odera roared as he ran up the eastward stairs. "Natural elements for weapons aside, they floundered due to their lower skill level and rashness. They should have listened to me and spent more time in the dojo."

"Airway, breathing, and circulation," Prince Ikuku said as he watched Odera ascend. "Affect any of these and a living, breathing creature with blood running through its vessels will always succumb."

"But our shots did nothing," Captain Iduto said.

"They were capable of self-healing, so those shots could never have caused them to lose significant amount of blood except one puts a huge hole in the big arteries that drain the heart of blood, or the heart itself. So, it had to be their easily accessible airway and breathing. Smart guys these two," Prince Ikuku said with a benevolent smile, then gestured the captain toward the top floor "You may just have one more chance to again try your luck at killing the snake with your gun if it's indeed weaker now."

"One curious mixture of an unpredictable king, two monstrous creatures and three large cats await us on the outside," Namdi stated as he looked around at the wreckage. "No time for quips. It is not over by no stretch of the imagination."

Chapter 39

Arriving at the eastern aspect of the gallery whilst trying to shake off the aggravated pain in his left forearm and hand initially caused by the respective injuries from the previous day and earlier that day, Odera came face to face with the world's most venomous reptile.

The small-scaled snake had made futile attempts to enter either of the rooms that Obiageli or I was in.

Watching as Odera clenched his fists, the supposedly placid snake raised its fore body in a tight, low, S-shaped curve with its round-snouted head facing him.

In no time, it flew toward Odera and quickly wrapped its three-meter-long body in coils around him. Snapping its jaws as it moved in to strike Odera's prominent, left, jugular vein, Odera heard a loud thud the instant the snake's head shattered into a myriad of pieces. There had been a single discharge from the crack shot Captain Iduto who stood at the central landing of the straight staircase.

The captain blew at his pistol's muzzle as Odera freed himself from the headless serpent, "My weapon spoke at last," he said. "Loud and clear."

"That was close," Odera said. "Thank you."

"Yes," the captain said. "The snake almost had you."

"I meant your bullet," Odera said, dashing onward.

"If at first, you don't succeed," Prince Ikuku proclaimed as Odera slammed his right shoulder into the door the snake had hovered before, but it didn't budge. "Try and try again."

Banging on it, "Open up," Odera roared. "It's me."

Flinging the door wide open, I stormed out of the room and ran slap into him, embracing him hard. "Is it over?" I whispered as he half hugged me with his right arm, the left one somewhat limp by his side.

Odera leaned back to avoid smearing me with the bloody debris on his face, gazed into my eyes and shook his head. Letting go of him in that instant as my eyes widened further in horror, I darted for the door behind which I believed Obiageli was in.

Exiting the room, the queen ran down to Prince Ikuku. Embosoming him, she bit his open mouth. Making him weak in his knees, she engaged him in a prolonged and sensual lip-lock kiss. On his part, it was as clear as night and day that still waters ran deep, whilst on her part, it was either she was trying to make up for all the time she'd lost with him or was yearning to experience again what King Ajutu had denied her for more than three decades. In any case, I could slip right into her shoes, and they'd be a perfect fit.

Perhaps to give the two love birds some privacy, Namdi and Captain Iduto motioned to head out of the building.

"I better check on my men and get the vehicles ready, should we need them," the captain said.

"I'll grab the machetes," Namdi said.

Continuing to pound on the door, "Let me in, Anika, I want Obiageli," I barked. "Why are you taking so long?"

Squeezing myself into the room the moment the door cracked open, I ran toward Obiageli as visibly shaken and increasingly pale-faced Anika slammed the door shut, "Is it over?" Anika said with a tremble in her voice.

Turning my head around, I shushed Anika with a finger in front of my apposed lips as I shook my head. Facing Obiageli again, I scooped her up as she stood from where she'd sat amongst a cornucopia of toys. Closing my arms tight around her, I stood rooted to the spot for what seemed like an eternity…well, until Odera barged into the room.

Chapter 40

Odera shut the door with a bang and closed in on us with precise strides whilst pushing up his sleeves.

"We have to lure the remaining creatures away from this house, to protect Oby, Anika, and its other inhabitants—" he whispered in my ear.

"They aren't after Anika and other people in the house," I croaked with a low tone as I set Obiageli down and wheeled around to face him with my arms akimbo and becoming a little dewy-eyed. "They're after us, Oby included. I'm going to stay here with her. I can't lose my one remaining child. I would be much too grieved."

With a basilisk stare, "You are being emotional about this and not thinking like the person who convinced Prince Ikuku about being involved," Odera said as Obiageli ran off, deeper into the room, toward another set of toys, and Anika followed close behind her. "We need Dike, so you have to come with us. You are overreacting by talking about losing Obiageli. That won't be possible if Dike is close by."

Returning my own silly version of a lethal gaze at him with a sheepish grin as his words sank in, he forced a smile, then looked away, appearing too exhausted to be exasperated. Scanning around the massive children's playroom and with his left arm tucked in by his side, Odera strode to and looked out the two windows on the east wall, one after the other, pulling the drapes apart with just his right hand. I could see a wave of treetops that stretched to the horizon.

Not seeing what he'd hoped to see, my guess being the rest of the creatures that I'd thought were at the front of the house rather than at the side, he returned to the room's center as I mulled over whether or not to go with him and the various possible outcomes if there was another attack like the one we just survived.

Perching on the edge of an island worktop where there was also a sink and a tap, facing me, he seemed to need a few moments to recuperate, as his adrenaline rush, in the fullness of time, waned.

"You are supposed to be a co-leader of this operation's connection with Dike and the likes of him," he added, his captivating, deep voice rumbling.

Granted that I'd become accustomed to the frisson of excitement and serenity that his presence gave me, and not wanting to be left alone and wondering again whether he was dead, or alive during another separation, I couldn't resist leaving with him. Still, an opportunity had opened for me to coax him into assuaging the unease that bubbled up inside me about his left wrist.

Sidling to him, I leaned by his left side, against the marble countertop, "I'll go with you if you tell me about the black scar," I whispered as I lifted his left hand and stared at the watch. The time said six minutes past 11. "When did it happen?"

With a surge of self-pity and seeming not in the mood to argue about whether I was right, or not in using my sort of blackmail, or feminine wile, "A few weeks after Ejizu passed on, I am not now sure how many…Have to really think about it to be certain, but it was still during the rainy season," Odera rapped in muted tones. "King Ajutu gave me the watch—though he was not king then—and I allowed him to wrap it around my wrist. You see, I had learnt then that nobody could argue with him and certainly not as the little boy that I was at the time. The moment it touched my skin, its metal back gave me a serious shock. Later, while in his car that always took me home, I pulled it off and saw a red burn mark that would become black over time. I had no idea why it happened. Papu, who had given the watch to the king, reassured me that everything would be fine while driving me home. As time went on, I realized that if I didn't have it on, my left wrist would hurt, and it is often unbearable."

"Even now…After all these years?"

With a slow nod, "Even now," he seemed to murmur.

"So, that's why you have it on all the time."

"Yes, most of the time. I just endure the pain when I must take it off for a shower or a swim or when I am in the dojo, practicing hand-to-hand combat with Namdi. If it breaks, I will not then have a way to take care of the pain."

"Have you ever tried wearing a different watch? Or using an armband to see if just keeping it covered is all that matters?"

"Armband, only when practicing. Watches, many different ones, but this is the only one that keeps the pain at bay. All I've been able to do, over time, is change straps," he said as he laced the fingers of his left hand into those of my right and jerked forward, pulling me in tow. "We really must get going before the remaining beasts crash into the house, and time is running out."

Ignoring him for a moment, I stroked his left biceps with my left hand, "Is that why your left arm looks stronger than the right much as you are right-handed?"

"How do you know that I am right-handed?"

Screwing my eyes at him, "I've been with you for at least 48 hours now, and my eyes haven't been closed all the while."

"Perhaps," he said with nonchalance as he towed me along by the hand. "I find that I fight better with my machete when it is in my left hand. I may have subconsciously worked my left side more to see if that would take the pain away. Who knows?"

Looking back at Oby and Anika as introspective Odera gazed ahead, "I'll be right back, Oby, okay?" I voiced. "Anika, please keep the door secured like before."

As Anika nodded with her thumbs up, Obiageli gave a little friendly wave without a glance in our direction. Having not owned as many as one toy all her life, she'd become surrounded by several.

For her to, at long last, spend some time away from my boring and regimented self is a welcome development. Living here will be great for us. With the many servants to wait on us, not only will I be allowed the opportunity to properly weep and wail my son, I'll also not be without helpful companions. This is certainly the life…where progress is possible. I can't wait.

Arriving at the gallery, Odera pulled the door shut behind us.

"Have you considered that all the creatures may not follow us. One might stay back to finish off Obiageli," I said, causing Odera to come to a standstill.

Shaking his head after a long moment of contemplation, "Oby would be a distraction if she went with us. If any of the maidens stay behind, they should be an easy gun kill for the sergeants. The beasts on the other hand, if they do not follow us as we head out of the premises, then we will go after them. We play it by ear."

Chapter 41

As his gaze flickered away from the handle of his Akupé, King Ajutu shifted with unease and regarded Chief Madu with a cold stare, "If you stepped on it, we might get to wherever we are going much quicker," he bellowed with a wavering voice as his eyes twinkled turquoise once, then again, a beat apart, then he looked around wildly.

With a faltering smile, the chief glanced in the rearview mirror as bars of sunlight shafted through the sunroof, "I don't know any casket maker or construction site, hence why I am driving slowly so that if there are either of those on this road, we may spot them as we look around," the chief said with a low and intimate voice, looking back intermittently. "It would be nice if we searched with three pairs of eyes rather than two."

Sat alone and behind Eke who rode shotgun in a black, up-to-the-minute Mercedes, the king swallowed hard and shuffled again in the backseat that was upholstered with the hide of a black, morph leopard. Looking like a sinking man, a sheen of sweat populated his chin, cheeks, and forehead despite the not-so-warm climate within the enclosed, four-door, custom sedan.

Falling into an unwonted quiet and avoiding eye contact with his chief, the king rocked back and forth in anguish. Refraining from looking at the hand fan a second time as it laid on the seat, to his left; his restless left hand moved to flutter over it whilst his right hand pressed on his lower abdomen.

He picked up the Akupé and fanned himself as his right hand pushed down on a button that lowered the window.

Looking out the window, the sun had continued to ride high in a cloudless sky. And at a significant distance away from the right border of the northbound service road, scenic on the horizon rose knolls of various sizes that were crowned with trees and seemed to move in the opposite direction to the king's favorite vehicle.

As a rush of breeze cooled his face, he pulled the dry, dusty air deep into his lungs. With each inhalation deeper than the one before, he seemed to succeed at curbing his impatience.

Musing because only the middle two suns and the lower three stars still sparkled, "Two more negergized-lifeforces to host. I wonder what my Okiké's count is…I should have brought it along. If the four runaways are still alive, will I ever be able to win against Odera, the very thorn in my side? No doubt that he has had a hand, or two in the rubbing out of two of my special henchmen. Odera and Namdi are proving too hot to handle by any other. It is fast becoming a certainty that I must fight the war all on my own. If Odera is still alive, is it solely by virtue of his triumphs, or are my own failures to blame as well? To what extent have the lifeforces of the child victims of Mkpátáku been of help? Why did I put my head in a noose like this, eh?"

Eke gave Chief Madu a puzzled look, "Is he always like that?" he said under his breath.

"He soliloquizes time after time," the chief whispered, then looked in the rearview mirror. "Is everything okay, Your Majesty?"

With a sad, musing, downward gaze as a cloud passed over his face, the king ignored his chief, ground his teeth, and continued to murmur to himself: "I should have done things differently when Ejizu returned from school after his first day in primary one to say that there was a classmate whom everyone said looked like him and was only five days older. Why did I become so interested to the point that I would drop Ejizu off to school the next day to catch a glimpse of Odera who, indeed, bore striking resemblance to him? Also, had I not decided to stay and discover who Odera's mother was, I might be in a better situation right now. Why did I push Ejizu to be close to Odera? Why did I encourage Nena to invite him over to the palace often? I was such a fool to have been magnanimous toward Odera. Why did I, after sacrificing Ejizu, beg the venerable ones to modify Odera to not just be a look alike but to look exactly like Ejizu in every way, shape, and form, and Ejizu to assume the likeness of Odera to deceive the queen and to lie to Odera's parents that Odera had died? I was so stupid. Yes, I was desperate for an heir, but nothing could have stopped me from using Ejizu for unimaginable wealth, nothing. I can't feel bad about that—I mustn't. If only the venerable ones had not refused my first request and again when I asked to be made physically powerful but tell me that they would honor another plea if I made it. Why did they say they agreed to my third request because of my unwavering loyalty to their mission on earth as was the tradition but did not apply that same reasoning to my first and second ones? Had they granted my first or second wish, I would not have needed to make the third and would not seem toothless right now. In making the third wish, I had hoped that Odera would forever remain loyal and, one day, also become a peace warrior. If only I had not asked them to irrevocably endow Odera with the exceptional abilities that I had wanted for myself…One that would have enabled me to quickly master and enhance, with, or without practice, whatever skills set I, as much as, desired. Then another to allow me to bring forth from within myself the most extreme form of whatever as much as connected—or made contact—with me visually, physically, mentally, emotionally, or spiritually, be it good or evil. And then for me to unwittingly be able to pass these powers onto anyone with whom I developed bona fide and requited affectionate bonding, for the sole purpose of continuity…Had I not achieved these things for Odera, unbeknown to him, at a time he wasn't even six years of age, I would have had no need to keep tabs on him…To the point that I not only sent people to entice him into choosing to be my henchman as the surest way of maintaining a relationship with him, giving him gifts and exposing him to wealth he couldn't have imagined, but I also, senselessly, furnished his parents, in secret, with money to educate him up to secondary-school level and perhaps beyond, had he not given in to working with me instead of furthering his studies…Why did I give him a clear path to making a good living? Had this not been the case, he would not have given up on the pursuit of university-level education and I would never have been close to him."

With rapid lip motions and perchance in need of someone to displace his growing agitation toward, "It's a Sunday, Chief Madu, there are not many motorists on the road," the king fumed impatience. "Step on it!"

Chapter 42

Odera shut the door as we stepped onto the gallery and ambled toward the stairs and looked over the railing to assess the situation below.

Whilst chatting with Namdi who had his hands closed around the hafts of his and Odera's machetes whose distinguishing features, at face value, were like night and day, and had the latched belts of each of the machetes' scabbards circled around his left shoulder, Prince Ikuku and Queen Nena were still in each other's arms, and it was clear that he topped her by at least 14 centimeters.

In the place of the creatures were the lifeless human forms of Batu and Kadiye.

As Odera and I arrived downstairs with my arms wrapped around his left arm, "Whoever made those creatures could never have delighted in their creation," I said.

"Made in desperation," Odera replied. "He never planned for this. Now I realize that he invested everything—time, effort, and money—in me for my loyalty and is clearly running out of options and desperately clutching at straws."

Pleased to see each other again, Namdi dropped the machetes with a clatter as Odera eased off my hold. Locking eyes for a moment, the brothers forever then engaged in a bear hug for three in-and-out breaths. Releasing each other, they bowed once with each clenched right hand palmed against the left side of its bearer's chest. Knocking the backs of their right hands three times, they clasped hands as they patted each other three times on the upper arm with their left hands.

It was another well-executed bond greeting. I'd first seen it after Namdi's surprise arrival at the cave.

"You fun guys have got to teach me that," Prince Ikuku said. "In fact, I've got so much to learn from you—like those moves you two executed on those creatures."

Facing the queen and giving a little bow, "Your Majesty," Odera said, looking increasingly more confident by the second, then faced Prince Ikuku for a moment before he picked his machete sheath-belt off Namdi's shoulder. "It will be an honor to teach you when the time is right. Now, we have more pressing matters."

As Odera and Namdi girded the belts across their bodies, "About that," Prince Ikuku started. "You and Nena were wondering why they did not attack anyone else."

"Oh, that," Odera said whilst focused on latching his belt. "I figured that out already. It has to do with the years that he stands to lose. If he is directly or indirectly connected to a human death and his spiritual organization deems that the life lost would have in any way impacted the course of his own life, he loses a year—a life for a year. I am more concerned about why all the beasts did not attack at once—why they paired up."

"That's easy," the prince said. "Being a twin, he was fascinated by everything that could work or operate in pairs. Tag-team fights were his favorite thing growing up. On the streets, he would always force me to fight on his side against others."

"That makes plenty of sense now," Namdi said as he picked up the machetes from the floor. "His vehicles are in pairs…He had always wanted his ten junior henchmen to work as five pairs…His four maidens often stood in pairs, and he liked for us to be two to ride on his motorbikes."

"A creature of habit," Queen Nena added as Namdi handed Odera's machete to him, "and of control."

Guiding their machetes into their respective sheaths, Odera and Namdi headed for the gaping exit, marching side by side. Unsure of Odera's exact plan, we followed close behind them in a snap.

"And how do you know this, Odera?" Prince Ikuku said.

Opening his mouth to speak, Odera at first hesitated as though he didn't want to divulge what he knew, "Hmm, after I overheard him say it to Chief Madu on one occasion during my earlier days as a henchman, I did my research," Odera said as he walked on the paved driveway sweep with lengthening strides toward the motorbike. "Nkem, you will ride in one of the military vehicles with Prince Ikuku and Queen Nena unless they choose to stay behind as their lives aren't in danger.

"Namdi and I will ride on the bike. Prince Ikuku, please command your men to open the gate and get the Technical out in front. We will ride behind it for cover. We have no clear idea of what is behind that gate. Let some of them follow our lead in their vehicles. For whatever it is worth, the rest should stay here and guard the house."

Prince Ikuku and Queen Nena gazed for a moment at each other and with nods of agreement, "We wouldn't miss this fight for the world," Prince Ikuku said. "Our lives may not currently be at stake, but our society is!"

Skipping down the portion of the driveway to my right, I plodded alongside Odera. As Namdi dropped back most likely to allow me some time with Odera, Odera maneuvered the motorbike in the direction of the drive path that arched toward the gate, which had several bulletproof jeeps stationed ready for a motorcade.

"What are you thinking?" I cooed. "What's the plan?"

Stopping at the front of the line of vehicles, "To stay alive—to give Igboland's firstborn boys the chance to become grown men," Odera said with aplomb as he bestrode the motorbike and key-started it, the engine sputtering before it shrieked into life.

"Captain," Prince Ikuku roared as he strode toward the armored jeep behind the motorbike, towing Queen Nena along by the hand. "Get someone to open the gate and do all that Odera has ordered. We will be riding in your vehicle behind him. Let's move. Also, get Sergeant Cruzo to inform the general manager of housing and urban development about the damage."

Revving the two-wheeler as Namdi arrived and mounted the passenger seat, wrapping his forearms around Odera's midsection, "Can't possibly plan anything else with any significant degree of success against an unpredictable king," Odera continued, gazing at me as I lingered on their right-hand side. "First, we lead the remaining five creatures away from here, then we continue to play it by ear. Whatever we do, we must be careful to avert a civil war, which, I fear, is in the wind. Go, get in a jeep. You will be safer in one."

Chapter 43

The beast forms of Jadue and Diko prowled the road about three meters from the three felids who were resting in the tree as they appeared to be waiting for Batu and Kadiye to exit the premises.

Soon, the trio's ears rose, then their heads as their eyes darted toward their 11 o'clock position at the gateway as its barrier jerked to begin sliding open.

As the gun truck screeched and drove off, turning a sharp right before the gate came to a chunking halt, it became evident to the creatures realized that Batu and Kadiye were gone for good. Despite in danger of crashing into the beast forms of Jadue and Diko, which were about 22 meters down the road, the gun truck hurtled on, revving.

Unperturbed by the loud engine roar, the creatures stood immovable in the middle of the road. Wasting no more time, the gunman let fly wildly in rapid succession from his mounted automatic rifle, and slugs zinged with whines through the air. Not running for cover, the creatures advanced amid the storm of bullets whilst the flinching large cats leapt off the tree, landed with stealth, and sped away like lightning across the lush greens, disappearing amongst the trees.

With fast gallops, the mamba tailed *Ammit*[15] leapt onto the hood of the truck, then to its roof in quick succession. Denting both parts of the vehicle in turn under its hefty mass, it blasted steaming water over the gunman.

As the gunman jumped off the truck and rolled away toward the orchard, the beast struck quickly with a bite that delivered a massive amount of pressure that wrecked the mounted gun, twisting its barrel into a spiral.

At the same time, jamming on the brakes, the truck driver stopped instantly, and the tawny beast's momentum flung it off the vehicle and over the motorbike as it released its fast, slithering, black, mamba tail.

---

[15] Crocodile-headed creature with front half of a lion and back half of a hippopotamus.

Landing and careening to a stop on the edge of the border stones that dead-ended the road, about eight meters away, the tawny lion arose and charged at speed, baring its jagged teeth toward the still-accelerating motorbike whilst all injuries it'd sustained healed in a wink.

As the scalded sergeant ran back into the compound, peeling off his wet uniform to minimize his risk of further burns, the mamba made a flying charge off the ground toward Odera and Namdi.

Seeing the snake approaching from ahead of them and the tawny Ammit from behind, Namdi drew Odera's machete with his right hand. And no sooner this happened than Odera pulled on the brakes, sending the motorbike into a fishtail that lifted the hind wheel as the motorbike arched clockwise for a moment on its front wheel. With a swift flick of his wrist, Namdi severed the head of the serpent, which was unable to change direction in mid-flight as it aimed for the position the bike had occupied a moment earlier.

Simultaneously, the Komodo dragon-headed, white lion charged toward the jeep Prince Ikuku, Queen Nena, Captain Iduto, and I were in as it came to a stop due to the commotion ahead involving the motorcycle and the gun truck.

Arriving at our vehicle, as all four of us frantically rolled up the windows, the massive, chimeric, white lion ejected its acid to pour down all over it and, in one quick maneuver, lifted it toward its left side with its hind legs. As the vehicle slewed and the beast spun around and began to rip out the tires on the right side, the queen and I screamed on top of our lungs, clinging onto the headrests of the front seats for dear life. It was a wakeup call to us both that the children of the shadows mightn't be able to shield us from all elements.

Seeing all that was unfolding, the brothers in arms jumped off the motorbike, as its hind wheel lowered, and it crashed to the ground. Lobbing Odera's machete to him and arming himself with his own, Namdi sprinted toward the oncoming tawny Ammit whilst Odera chased down the *komodion*[16] as its short-tempered, fearsome teeth began tearing our jeep's bottom, violently rocking the vehicle back and forth, probably in a bid to turn it turtle, and allowing leaking gasoline spray about. Inwardly, I thanked God that neither the fire-breathing nor the lightning-striking beasts had been alive. We'd have gone up in flames.

With his machete, Odera quickly chopped off the white lion's tiger-snake tail and the angry beast turned counter-clockwise to face Odera. In no time,

---

[16] A life-size lion with a double life-size head of a Komodo dragon.

Odera slid beneath it and, with one slash, severed its head from its body with a little amount of acid dropping from its huge tongue onto the rucked-up sleeve over his left arm. Experiencing a moment of sudden impetus in that instant, Odera let go of his weapon as he retreated and quickly pushed his sleeve further up. Spitting into his sizzling, melting flesh, he wiped the area with his right hand as the Komodo dragon head tumbled away, altering into Jadue's head.

At the same time, Namdi jumped above the galloping, tawny lion and turned head over heels in the air. Landing on his feet behind it as it decelerated to a shuddering stop to make a sudden turnaround, Namdi split its tail-less hindquarters into two, near-equal halves. His timing was split-second. With blood gushing out, Namdi quickly leapt, broke off a hunk of a branch from the overhanging jackal-berry tree, and shoved it into the bleeding space; and the gaping wound failed to close and heal, tried as it might. Not long after, the creature exsanguinated and transformed back to Diko as it crashed to the ground.

Whilst the acid continued biting into the outer layer of our flipped-over, steel-plated vehicle, Prince Ikuku managed to push open the front passenger door. As Odera motioned to help him out of the vehicle, he signaled for him to stay back.

Sniffing the air once and holding his breath intermittently so as not to be asphyxiated by the fumes, "Hydrochloric acid without question," the prince murmured to himself as he clambered out, doing well to avoid direct contact with the jeep's outer surface. "We were saved by the body panels' armor plates. A different scenario, and there would have been enough heat to cause a fire and an explosion."

Making the sign of the cross as he stood on the vehicle's frame, Prince Ikuku tugged off his belt, ran it under the handle of the backdoor, and pulled it open. Stretching out his strong hands, he hooked the queen under her armpits and dragged her onto the frame.

As she jumped off to land on the ground, the prince helped me onto the vehicle. His palm felt very smooth. Also giving Captain Iduto, who was already clawing his way out, a hand, "It's advisable to hold your breath for as long as you can until you are further from this vehicle," the prince yelled as the captain, and I dashed away. "If not, then breathe slowly and deeply to minimize inhalation injury."

Namdi approached to stand by Odera whilst wiping his machete clean against the front of his shirt. Ramming his machete into its sheath, "Five down, three to go," Namdi said as Prince Ikuku jumped down from atop the right side of the flipped-over, four-wheel drive, leaving his belt behind.

Standing with his hands deep in his pockets, the prince surveyed the damage, "You bike riders can swap your four-strokes for my state-of-the-art turbos. You can have one each," he said with an absent mind, then strolled toward Queen Nena.

At the same time the prince was speaking, noticing how scared out of my wits I was, "Four to go," Odera retorted, wiped his right hand on his top, picked up his machete, and ambled toward me as he sheathed it.

With an appreciative sigh, I threw myself at him, embracing him with all my strength, and he wrapped his forearms around me, even his left forearm. There was no doubt in my mind that he was the one I wanted to be with. I'd become a firm believer that exceptional circumstances bonded people in ways that years together mightn't.

For any future wrong he might do to me…For any hurt he might induce, he's already forgiven.

Letting him go after a long moment, I stilled my posture, and with rapt attention, "What now?" I asked with a soft voice and expression as I glimpsed the acid burn on his left arm that no longer looked fresh. Caressing it, he felt no pain. Lifting his forearm as he turned to look due northeast, the wound from the day before had also healed. Darting my gaze to his fingers, I noted also that the grazes from earlier that day were no more.

It can't have been due to Anika's ministrations.

Staring at him as confusion fogged my brain, "We can't continue to endanger more people by letting him send beasts here," he replied with certitude. "We will return these bodies to him—to let him know that we are no longer afraid…That we are now ready to take the fight to him…That we now mean business."

Chapter 44

Meanwhile, whilst their edges still shone a light that was feebler than normal, Bute, Ejizu, and Dike waited for their energy levels to normalize.

"Boy," Bute said. "Am I glad to be obtaining some respite from that entire negergy dump we got exposed to in the space of a few moments."

With a facetious demeanor, "You three seem to have had much more fun than the rest of us," Somto started as he and others appeared around the trio.

"Though I am glad to have helped out my brother and Odera," Bute said with a voice that dropped an octave, or two as he registered his sister's wish to connect with him. "I'd just as soon you were in a position to take the negergy dump that we received. I'm sure you would have thoroughly enjoyed it."

"Was only kidding," Somto continued as Bute attempted to change realms, glitching as he tried. "You lot did well. I'm sure there will be a lot of less energy-draining action to come. Ejizu, Tochi is here to meet you. He's welcome to roll with us, having shown a stronger will than most despite his age."

Ejizu managed only a nod in Tochi's direction, and bashful Tochi gave a little wave, remaining quiet.

"Somto," Ijezie said as he sensed Tochi's thoughts. "Tochi has told you again and again that the fact that he was the last to stop providing the barrier over Prince Ikuku's house had nothing to do with his will, but you still won't listen. Before the lightning strike, when I could still sense every Pneuma's will, his was no more than any Pneuma's. I am sure you would have known that too. That he lasted the longest is because of being the youngest Pneuma here…Meaning that he possesses more creative energy."

"I agree with Tochi," Adaku said. "Ejizu was the third to the last to let go, I stopped just before Tochi and Dike right before Ejizu. This lends to what Tochi is thinking. Though Ejizu passed on three decades ago, he was only active as a Pneuma for two-thirds of a year, or so, according to you, Somto, hence didn't dissipate his creativity much. In my case, I hadn't used an iota of my creativity, thus why I lasted longer than Ejizu; and Dike has been here for less than three nights, and so on."

"Though it is clear that our earthly ages matter with regards to what our Pneuma threshold energy is…" Somto said. "It also is plausible that on top of this threshold level of energy, which is necessary for basic functions, there is a varying amount of additional creative energy that gets emitted, albeit in tiny quantities, with the passing of time as we remain active—the loss increasing in amount linearly with the level of creativity. Does this then mean we need to be more selective in the use of our creativity?"

"We can all tell that you have been speaking with your engineer brother about this," Ijezie said. "It isn't like we have been using our creativity willy-nilly. I don't think it is that simple. I know for certain that our creative energies do replenish, as I am beginning to feel energized again, and I'm sure every Pneuma is. Though it is possible, like you said, that it is doing so in a diminishing way, we cannot jump to any conclusions just yet."

"If making sure that this deathly ritual is abolished for good uses up all my creativity, it would have been for a just cause," Dike said with a voice that sounded muted and faraway.

"One would have thought that an energy dump would cause excitation and increase our energy level…" Ejizu said with a mellow tone of voice. "Not leave us nearly inert."

"I'm not entirely sure," Somto said. "But having pondered over it after I recovered my energy, following our barrier going down, I remembered something Ejizu experienced during his first stint here and had a chat with my brother as I observed how Ejizu, Bute, and Dike took in the fire, and Bute the lightning, and I've deduced that it had to do with the dump being a negergy—much like feeling uncomfortable around toxic people in the human world. And that after we absorbed these negergies, we transmuted them to *posergies,* then emitted them. The transmuting and emission processes probably accounted for the draining effect we experienced."

"Yea, like how I felt around Ijezie's dad," Dike said with a less-feeble voice.

"We all felt like that around him," Ijezie said.

"I bet I looked funny as I absorbed the fire," Ejizu said as his edges all but lit up as normal and he touched Bute, transferred some of his impetus to him, and nudged him into the action of connecting with Azuka.

"Not really," Somto said. "It was noteworthy. With your eyes shut, you three instinctively stretched out your hands, allowing a gap as wide as the width of your Pneuma form—like you were creating a field between two poles. You then moved around to ensure that the fire or lightning entered the field near the center, streamlining as it did…And once this happened, the energy split into two to travel to the center of both hands, then through the arms to the body, effusing through your edges into our void. It happened in the twinkling of an eye."

"Interesting," Adaku said. "At least we are getting our void filled with posergy not negergy. That's a decided plus."

"Isn't it then possible that the energy I regain is the same positive one I or another Pneuma emitted?" Dike said. "Is it not true that energy cannot be created or destroyed? Only changed from form to form?"

Somto nodded as a smile took time to grow across his face.

"If that's the case," Dike continued. "Then though we may get drained quicker the older we are when we arrive here and the longer our Pneuma forms have emitted energy into our void, we won't necessarily get to the point where we are not able to regain our creativity."

Gazing with focus, "Could this energy exchange amongst us explain how we are able to glean one another's thoughts, feelings, emotions, and so forth?" Adaku said. "How we were all able to provide the barrier despite that most of us don't have any connections with the people who live in the prince's house."

Somto continued to nod. "Marvelous," he enthused. "I'm glad to roll with you insightful Pneumas. And to crown it all, let us, therefore, try our utmost to be positive at all times."

"I hate to rain on this positive moment, but my father is making his way to a shrine with a bulldozer behind him," Ejizu said. "Whose ritual took place at a shrine that's close to the palace?"

Being able to discern voices of scores of Pneumas who were far-off as they chorused, "I was," and not only hearing the same words from Ijezie and Dike, Ejizu knew that he was fully recharged.

"Dike, you must do something with regards to what my father is about to do if you want to remain with us. The time is now for you to work with the other Pneumas whose bodies are also in that shrine."

With a wide grin and a wink at Somto who also gleaned what Dike had in mind, "I know exactly what we will do," Dike said as he drifted away from the group. "Please, could all Pneumas whose ritual sacrifice was conducted by Ijezie's father make an appearance at our meeting place?"

Chapter 45

The skies had managed to stay azure; the sun was almost at its highest above the horizon, and the Harmattan chill wasn't stinging.

Looking skyward as he arrived at the little gun truck with Namdi, "That evil king's unpredictability seems the only cloud on the horizon," Odera mused, and with a hard swing, they thumped down Diko's gruesome body across the intact bodies of Batu and Kadiye as well as Jadue's decapitated body; the resulting agitation making Jadue's head roll back and forth a touch.

"We will be free of him soon," Namdi's tone was reassuring.

Pulling a tarpaulin over the bodies, they secured it with ropes.

Clearing runnels of sweat from his temples, Namdi sensed Bute's attempt at connecting with him. Obliging, he paid attention to his brother's distressing words.

And in the split second it took Namdi to digest the news, he felt he'd had a hand in the event Bute described. With vacant eyes and rounded shoulders, Namdi slumped onto the edge of the truck's tailboard as he shook his head.

Glancing at Namdi, Odera could tell that something was amiss. The first time he'd seen Namdi in such low spirits was after Bute passed away. The last time Namdi was similarly under the weather was when Namdi's father departed. Odera wondered if something bad had happened to either Namdi's mother or Azuka or both.

Turning around and perching beside Namdi, Odera's knees hitched a little, "What did Bute say?" Odera said, looking rightward at Namdi.

Namdi took his time, pondering, searching for a way to conjure up the words to say what needed to be told.

Soon after we'd arrived back on the premises, I'd gone to check up on the soldier who'd sustained thermal burns and learnt that he was Sergeant Dago. Anika, who, it turned out, had some training in first-aid administration during her stint in the convent, was attending to his wounds at the time in one of the ground-floor rooms. His beret and sunglasses had protected much of his head and face from burns, his thick khaki clothing had minimized the scalding on his body and his high boots had ensured it didn't affect his lower legs and feet.

Meanwhile, ambling toward the gate on leaving the building to see what help I could accord Odera and Namdi, there was the scratch of a match lighting a cigarette as I was accosted by a handful of the soldiers. Rugged though they were, and some even had piercing, somewhat racy eyes that unnerved me, for some reason, they all suddenly seemed amiable.

Surrounding me on the driveway, some of them casually loaded, locked, and checked their rifles.

"We betted that you have Fulani blood," one of the privates said as he stuck a cigarette behind his right ear. "Do you?"

Nodding with unease, "Private?" I asked.

"Private Dabir," he said as he took a long pull on a cigarette that was between his left index and middle fingers and, in a casual way, blew a succession of smoke rings up into the air.

"And I can speak Hausa too, Private Dabir, though my accent is quite unintelligible," I said. "And I heard at least one of you say something that I found offensive when we first arrived."

Glancing at one another, "It was Private Imala who said it," another private said with halting words and a northern accent, pointing to Private Imala. "He has no girlfriend and is always full of fantasies about any beautiful woman he sees."

And everyone lapsed into a long moment of awkward silence.

Staring down at his feet, "It looks like your father passed on this morning," Namdi said with a voice that cracked, then lifted his head to look at Odera, patting Odera consolingly on the back. "He was unresponsive when Azuka went to wake them up a little while ago. I am so sorry."

Letting out a long, low sigh, Odera went quiet for a long moment, then: "It was always going to happen. Death is inevitable," Odera said with a thickening voice, shrugging. "It was better in his sleep than any other way. Who knows if the stress of yesterday played a role?"

Rubbing tears off his eyes as his head dropped, Odera patted Namdi on the left shoulder and squeezed it a little as he stood up. "We will make a stopover before heading to the palace," Odera said and padded away on heavy legs. "I will inform Nkem and others. In case I forget to tell them, please let the soldiers know that we would need a chainsaw."

"They will be calling a doctor to confirm before they take him to the mortuary," Namdi said as he got to his feet. "I wish I had better news for you and that the issues of yesterday didn't happen."

Odera nodded his acknowledgment as he rounded Captain Iduto's overturned jeep, aiming for the gateway.

Swinging around to face the vehicle and with a sharp pang of frustration, Namdi lifted the tailboard, slammed it shut, and fastened it. Rapping on the truck's bodywork, "Take your position. You are good to go," Namdi said to the driver in a low voice and headed toward the compound.

"I told you all that she is Fulani and might be able to understand Hausa, but you didn't listen," clean-shaven Sergeant Fric, who had a chiseled look and a one-centimeter, vertical, facial mark of identification on either cheek, blurted out. "Anyway, do you know why those beasts did not attack everyone? Word on the streets has it that in making their way through town, they ran on the roads and streets, jumped over vehicles, climbed rooftops and trees as people ran away from them, but that they did it very peacefully."

"Yes, their sender specifically ordered them not to kill anyone other than the four of us who first arrived here," I said happily as I caught a glimpse of Odera stepping onto the premises, looking sad, and subdued. Raising my arm in salute, "I've got to go, soldiers."

Returning my salute with smiles, cheers, and whistles, "Master Odera is a lucky man," many of them choroused.

Private Imala crossed his arms behind him, "I am very sorry, madam," he said with a bow. "Please don't tell the prince."

With a self-conscious smile on and in a hurry to depart from their company, hence not bothering to ask that Private Imala didn't refer to me as 'madam,' I bade Private Imala and the rest of them farewell with a wave of my hand. Wheeling around, I walked toward the one for whom my heart whammed away, my eyes filling with longing and love as I went straight into the safety of his arms.

Chapter 46

Scores of kilometers away, the triumvirate of Chief Madu, Eke Isigwe, and incognito King Ajutu, who had the best protection from the sun's blazing heat, arrived at Eke's shrine as trees swayed, creaked, and groaned in the wind.

Also, in attendance, with a handful of them straggling toward the area behind the rest, was a troop of, at the least, 40 men who mostly had wan and bitter faces. In pairs, most of them carried coffins, one had a hunting rifle at the port, and another was formally dressed in a black clerical shirt with a tab collar and had the Holy Book in one hand. They arrived to circle the closed gravesite whose girdling fronds of palm had all but yellowed.

Behind the group, coming from Palace Road East that also had several Peugeot 504 pickup trucks and Toyota Hiace vans parked on it in a file, a bulldozer crashed through the bushes and jerked a little distance toward the area as Eke waved its driver toward the back end of the shrine. Its tracks moving with ease over knobby tree roots and rocks, it came to an abrupt stop. With the powerful tractor's huge engine thrumming in everyone's ears, it lowered its front-based, broad, upright blade.

Milling about Farm Road, a crowd of fascinated and noisy lookers-on grew in number. Darting a passing glance around, King Ajutu could see through his dark glasses, men's faces peeking out from trees and on stretched necks from behind the bordering shrubs to observe the vicinity of the shrine.

Leaning toward Eke, the king gestured behind him, "Tell your boys to chase away those nosey parkers."

Walking across the area to the man with the rifle, Eke whispered in his ear, his manner with the gunman showing a familiarity. Turning around, the man aimed his rifle skyward above the position of the bystanders and rang out a sharp spatter of shots.

As the bullets whistled through the air and a flock of birds frantically winged their way toward the sky, the men in the trees either fell out of them, breaking branches with a crack and landing smack—or jumped down—onto the parched Farm Road. And the ones already on the earth path flattened themselves against the surface for a moment.

Then all of them, without exception, ran pell-mell in every direction.

Chapter 47

By the time Dike included himself and Ijezie in the total count, 163 Pneumas were ready for action.

Staring for a long, disbelieving moment at nothing, he shook his head slowly and turned to look at Ijezie, "Your father was involved in these many sacrifices? Destroying 163 families?"

"Surprise, surprise," Ijezie said. "Though I was the only one he killed in that shrine, the others having been killed by their own fathers; he has killed many people, like Mama Uche, outside of his shrine. So, he most certainly has helped destroy many more than that number."

"Does he sleep at night?

"He is often restless at night until midnight when his raven takes his spirit from his dust," Ijezie said. "He seems scared of the night. You should see how his eyes redden, and he yells at everyone as soon as the skies darken—like something fires up his blood during those hours."

"I did see a raven at the shrine, but not at night," Dike said. "I think I may have been concentrating too much on Mother around midnight, the only night my father lived after becoming a part of the unseen world's evil realm. It sure seems like they see our shadows during those times, and our shadows cause them some form of mental anguish. My father did not react well when he saw mine and ended up killing himself."

Shrugging, "Enough tales," Ijezie said. "Let's better get on with it. The bulldozer is about to begin clearing the ground."

"Swing into action, Pneumas," Dike said with a small yelp.

Chapter 48

Whilst sun-dappled, dusty leaves dotted shadows on the ground, King Ajutu, shaded by citrus-tree foliage, seemed the happiest he'd been for two days, as he watched on in expectation, swaying on his feet much as all the suns on his Akupé's handle had been extinguished.

Murmuring to himself, "I am definitely close to laying all my human opposition bare. If the supernatural henchmen were no match for the combination of Odera, Namdi, and those child spirits, then they lacked purpose and are better off not in existence. Good riddance. And very soon, the spirits of those children will be rendered inactive one after the other until it remains only Ejizu. Then I will go after his mother and everybody else that dares stand in my way, with all I have."

Sat in the windowed cab of the bulldozer was an elderly man who hummed a traditional song to himself. He seemed to enjoy what he did for a living. Going by the way his gnarled hands moved the control sticks back and forth, one could call him a master at his trade. Despite that at his age he ought to have lost deftness, it was with such that he maneuvered the blade at an angle into the ground of the shrine's back limit.

As the huge engine rattled and clunked and its beveled tool moved to depress the earth, the controls no longer budged. The old man's mood took an instant turn for the worse. *There's no way this could be happening*, his expression suggested.

Appearing to have minds of their own, the controls began to work themselves in reverse. The suddenness of it didn't seem as alarming to him as to why the sticks had begun to refuse his control in the first place.

"It has not even been a week since I spent plenty of my hard-earned cash to keep this equipment in good order. Eh? What is going on here? My only source of livelihood!" he muttered to himself. "It is unbelievable that it can embarrass me at this very moment…After I was able to get the best deal ever by taking advantage of their desperation and by the fact that what they wanted me to do was impromptu and on a Sunday. Did the mechanics cheat me, much in the same way I cheated these men? The same thing I tell my children and grandchildren not to do. Is this karma?"

With a shaky hand, he tried again and again to engage the controls, and, still, all attempts were to no avail.

Then, in fits and starts, the heavy-duty vehicle began to slowly move backward. It then dawned on everyone surrounding the area that something was wrong.

The wizened, weather-beaten man's face took on a smile. He seemed the happiest person within that vicinity. Making the sign of the cross, "Thank God—at least it still moves. I am going to take it back to the garage and demand that the issue is checked out and fixed, or they give me my money back. What arrant nonsense!"

At the same time, puckering his forehead, "What's happening? Why is that coot reversing?" King Ajutu whispered to Eke as his expression took on a touch of sadness, and he and his chief exchanged wide gazes.

"I'm not sure," Eke said, then shouted at the operator. "Hey, Old Man, what's going on here? Who told you to do that?"

Poking his head out of the cab, "It is not me, I swear," the elderly man retorted atop his voice amid rumbling vibrations, steady clicking, and grinding, then jumped out of the enclosure; probably not so much because of the fear of the unknown but to make his point. As the mechanical beast continued to judder backward, lacking any form of manual control, "See," the man who must have been nudging 80 said. "Not me."

Shuddering with horror, the tens of young men with coffins at their feet as well as the pastor and the man with the rifle, most of whose exposed skins had been weathered almost black, suggesting years of outdoor life, turned around and went like lightning, leaving the wooden boxes behind.

The king and his bumbling sidekicks knew what was happening, but they hadn't considered it.

Shading his eyes against the sun with a hand, as something immediately occurred to him whilst he watched the young men scattering, "I don't know what you men are doing here…" the gray, old man said with calm as his heavy equipment came to a quaking halt on Palace Road East, resuming its stationary humdrum sound. "But with those coffins, I am assuming you plan to remove some dead bodies and maybe use them for something untoward. It is clear to me, but I don't know about you, that the spirits of those bodies don't want you here. So, pay me my money and I will take my tractor away from here. I am no longer interested. If you don't pay me, my mouth will not stay shut."

As vehicles on Palace Road East shrieked to life one after the other and drove off, quickly reversing up the said road, circumnavigating the tractor, "Eke, pay him…I am walking home," the king sounded off as he walked toward the path the tractor had created through the bush, anger darkening his gaze. "Egu, bring the car home. These children are not jokers; they are on a high road to blackening my name, and I have to think about this more seriously."

Chapter 49

Even as the king headed toward the palace on foot, Namdi and Odera tore out of the prince's house, each riding a motorbike whose engines roared as if they belonged on a motorsport track.

I'd had the chance to catch a glimpse of a MotoGP race on Madam Tinkle's television and had heard how loud those bikes sounded. It'd been on one of the rare occasions Papa Dike had taken me out on a date to her beer parlor before Dike was born.

Prince Ikuku, Captain Iduto, Queen Nena, and I were in another armored jeep directly behind the brothers forever as they rode abreast. The bag of Ejizu's bones was on the floor of the backseat between my left lower leg and her right lower leg.

I'd wondered the wisdom in taking the bones to the same place she'd run from with them. But there wasn't a way she'd leave them behind, considering that she hadn't stopped blaming herself for Ejizu's death: "Things might have been different had Ejizu continued to sleep beside me; so his bones will always be by me," she'd murmured to herself time and again as I paced up and down the vacant space during the moments we'd spent together in the room between Prince Ikuku's and the special chamber as Odera and Namdi fought Kadiye and Batu.

As we followed behind the brothers in arms to get ahead of the little gun truck, skirting as they did, the quietly corroding jeep that had remained flipped on its side, I harbored mixed feelings about heading back to Akagheli. I hadn't expected to be going back that soon, especially without a good plan regarding how to stop the ritual, but I knew I wouldn't be there long. Obiageli was staying back in Agudagu with Anika and Odera had reassured me that we'd be back.

And I'd come to accept that Odera was often right.

Behind us, the motorcade continued with one other armored jeep following close before the gun truck joined in and tailed along in convoy. The second armored vehicle was driven by Private Imala, with Private Dabir riding in shotgun and carrying Sergeants Brymo—who was tall and thick-necked, with bony facial features—and Fric, both of whose rifles had their barrels sticking out through the open back windows. The gun truck was equally manned by two grunts whose names I never caught.

The adjoining street had begun to liven up following the earlier scare from King Ajutu's beasts. Captain Iduto's men had done their part to allay the fears of some of those who plied that route, telling them 'Everything was under control.'

In those days, if a person belonged—or seemingly belonged—to the army, their words and actions were seen as the be-all and end-all. Anyone garbed in green military uniform, or army camouflage was revered as godhead.

We joined the road's perfectly tarmacked surface with traffic droning up and down it.

Chapter 50

Every motorist on the expressway gave way to our convoy of military vehicles as we moved at breakneck speed when it was possible, breezing through police checkpoints and other traffic stops on the road, only decelerating at traffic slowdowns either caused by stretches of untarred road, or due to cracks, ruptures, or patches of potholes in the asphalt and briefly stopping only for gasoline.

As vehicular traffic dwindled to a trickle, we drove onto Village High Street. The digital clock on our vehicle's dashboard said 13:17. It'd taken just over an hour to travel between two geographically close neighbors separated by at least 90 kilometers of an expansive mixture of uninhabited miry farmlands, uninhabitable hilly terrains, and forested lowlands.

I'd never traveled between the centers of Akagheli and Agudagu to have been able to tell the trip's typical duration, but there was no doubt in my mind, considering how long it'd taken us to ride the shorter distance from the outskirts of Akagheli to the center of Agudagu, that the time it took us to cover the longer distance was much quicker than normal.

As we made our way onto Market Road and I looked out the windshield, I was beheld by a sight that surged within me the feeling that the evil conduct hadn't completely cast a pall of terror over the village, and a smile grew on my face.

Is there still a chance that we can end this without throwing any part of the village into a commotion?

Herds of perhaps homeward-bound, churchgoing men, women, and children of all age ranges poured from School Road. Maybe dressed in their Sunday best, they sang worship songs to themselves either cheerfully or in highly expressive croons, the older ones also holding, in their hands, either hymn books, or bibles, or both about them.

As we drove past them, the youth amongst them running alongside the motorcade, either touching them, or waving with alacrity at us, or doing both, and the queen and I returned their gesture, although the tinted windows prevented them from seeing us, the thought that some of them mightn't be alive in a few years from then, because of the deathly ritual, ruffled me and my face took on a sad expression.

Arriving at the building directly behind Odera's previous home, we were welcomed by locals who thronged to see the vehicles whilst conversing in low hums as a noisy, giggling group of children, with feet black from playing outdoors, romped around the neighborhood.

Dismounting their bikes as I exited the vehicle to a hint in the air of creosote, which must have been used in treating wooden parts of fences in the neighborhood, I joined the brothers forever and marched side by side with them toward a narrow earth track at the side of Odera's home.

Without as much as a glance in the direction of his scorched and still-smoldering bungalow, Odera strode into the back neighbor's house, accompanied by Namdi and me.

Gesturing for us to wait in the living room where the homeowners, Azuka and Namdi's mother had stood huddled together and had raised their eyebrows in conveyance of sympathy, Odera headed down the long passage for the room Azuka indicated was where his mother had been.

By-passing a wheeled walker, Odera entered the featureless room. His father wasn't there. His mother was slumped in a chair by the bed. With red, puffy eyes and downturned facial features, she reached out her arms toward him. Moving her walker away, Odera hunkered down and leaned into an awkward, warm embrace and felt a tightness in his chest as a chill coursed through his body.

After a long moment, she let him go. Perching on the arm of her chair, Odera slouched and, with a flat voice, "What happened?" he said.

With her chin, which had loose, unattractive skin, trembling, "I don't know," she said with a voice that broke. Sniffing, she wiped her nose with the back of her hand. "Adaku woke me up to say he was not breathing, and that was it."

Looking withdrawn, "He was a good father," Odera mumbled.

"He played the role well," she said, staring down at her gnarled hands for a moment, then out the window to her left whose parted drapes allowed sunlight stream into the room; her voice lowering and becoming more inward, "But he wasn't your biological father."

Sending Odera's world spinning the moment they came out, her words at the same time gave him a feeling that everything was slowing down. His stare grew empty for a little while, then he got to his feet, faced her, and crouched to level eyes with her.

"Mama, please tell me that it is your loss that is making you not think right—that makes you say this. Tell me it is a lie."

Shaking her head, she looked to her right toward the shut wardrobe. "I wish I could say that," she said, then paused. "He knew that he wasn't your father but begged me not to tell you while he was still alive. He didn't want you to not see him as such. I promised myself that I would tell you if he died before me and for Azuka to point you to a letter I had written to you about it all if I died before him. The letter was somewhere in our house. It is probably now burnt by the fire."

"Why would he beg you not to tell me? I would have thought it was the other way around where you would have begged him not to say anything."

Still looking rightward, "It is because of how it happened and who your real father is. Papa Doka was 55 then, and I was 42. We had agreed after your brother, Ileka, that we would stop at nine children. That's how come there are six years between your brother, Ileka, and you instead of just a year's gap as it is between the others. Even though you were loved and would turn out to be our breadwinner, we did not plan to have you. We were returning from our shop one evening when we were waylaid. He escaped and left me with the attackers who held me down. The leader of the group appeared out of nowhere and forcefully had his way with me during that event and it led to me becoming pregnant with you—"

"So, he felt guilty for abandoning you? Is that why he asked you not to tell me?"

Unable to maintain eye contact with her son, tried as she might, "Maybe, but I also think that after your birthfather knew, he threatened to make my husband's life miserable if you knew—just like he also threatened me. Your birthfather wanted to hide it. He had every reason to, but it had nothing to do with me. He thought that if you knew, out of excitement, you would tell everyone, as any child would do. I was convinced that you needed to know your biological father. I believe that every child needs to know their parents regardless of who nurtures them to adulthood."

"How do you know he was threatened?"

"Not just because I could see the fear in his eyes anytime I brought up your real father, he had also told me. He did it the same way he threatened me—sent hefty men to warn him."

With a pensive expression, Odera took a long moment to decide whether he wanted more information.

"Don't blame Papa Doka. If he didn't run away, they might have killed him."

With a slow nod, "Some women keep this sort of thing a secret and never tell their husbands. Why did you tell him?"

Looking down at her laced fingers, "Aside from the fact that he knew I was attacked, and our women rarely got attacked without being raped, we had practiced abstinence during my fertile days for five years with success. He knew he wasn't the person who got me pregnant."

"My birthfather, is he someone I know?"

Managing to once and for all lock gazes with him for a while, she nodded, "He is the king of Akagheli," she said, drawing a gasp from him as his expression clouded.

Standing, he shuffled a step backward and turned away as a rush of adrenaline tingled through his body. His heart hammering away, he paced the room. Not knowing what else to feel for a king that he already detested, his feelings fleeted. For a moment, he felt embarrassed for his mother, then his face twisted with rage at the man he knew as his father for not protecting her.

Stopping midstride, he faced her, "Tell me…How did the king know?" his voice rising in its pitch. "I am assuming he knew and that is why he made sure I was close to him."

"Yes, he knew because I sent him a letter through errand boys after you returned home on your first day in primary one and told me about Ejizu. I wanted you to be close to them partly for selfish reasons and partly because it was the right thing to do, and you were also very happy to meet someone that looked like you. After that, he took it upon himself to provide for us because of you and to keep us quiet. This, I believe, also contributed to why my husband didn't want you to know. We would not have achieved all we did with just artisanship."

"Why have you chosen now of all times to tell me this? Why didn't you let me bury him first?"

"You would have asked why I did not tell you earlier if I had left it late. This is the first chance I must tell you without any hindrances from my husband. We lived only for each other after you all left home. Now that he is gone, nothing says I will not be gone very soon. And my letter to you is destroyed. So, I couldn't wait any longer to tell you. And how will I see you again after now since it looks like Agudagu will become your new base?"

Rushing to her, Odera knelt before her and rested his head on her lap. "Don't say that Mama. I will eventually take you with me to Agudagu. Things are better there."

Resting her palms atop his head, "Go to your father and let him know that I told you. I have nothing more to live for. My once-heavy heart is now free. You are his prince and heir to the throne. Today should be a joyous day for you, never mind the death of Papa Doka. He lived a good life till old age. The only way out of this world is to die. The young shall grow, is our hope, and the old shall die, is a given. So, rejoice."

"Mama, there is nothing to rejoice about; the king is not what we all thought he was. He and his group do not give some young boys the chance to grow into men. But I understand what you are saying," he said as he raised his head, his tear-soaked eyes meeting her bleary eyes. "I will go to the mortuary and pay him my last respects, then send word to Doka and co. to come and bury him. I will be back to take you with me before you know it."

Nodding, she said, "Go, my child, and do what you must."

Chapter 51

Descending from the palace's west terrace onto the courtyard, the felids transformed into their human forms and seemed overwrought.

Appearing glum, "We've committed the worst sin anyone could against the king," Adure's voice was tense as they dashed through the door that connected the southwest veranda with its passage. "By not engaging in the fight when it got heated, we've disobeyed and defied him."

"We had a good reason for getting out of there," Isioma said. "So, I am not at all troubled about it."

"If you are not troubled, why did you make us continue to stop in the forest at the least excuse?" Ijeoma said. "You made us waste a lot of time there just to 'consider all options.'"

"I did it for Adure's sake," Isioma said. "She was panicking."

"I see," Ijeoma said as they entered the southwest section.

With flying leaps, they swept the stairs abreast and quickly arrived before the great chamber's doors. Slowly pushing them open, they entered, looking around. Their demeanors showing how quite relieved they were not to see the king in there, they headed straight into the shower.

****

A while later, they exited from the washroom clad in their usual inviting outfit; their pearl beads necklaces, wristlets, and anklets scratching and jingling as they walked.

"I hope these clothes would send the right signals to the king as is often the case," Ijeoma said.

"All my fingers are crossed," Adure said. "I still can't help but wonder if things would remain be the same with him without Adaku."

"We will soon find out," Isioma said.

Glimpsing the clock that showed the time as a quarter to two, "Still within his lunch hour," Ijeoma mumbled, leading them as they departed the room. "I believe he will realize that we are the only people he can truly trust and hence remain nice to us."

"There is no rhyme or reason for him not to treat us well," Isioma said. "If not, I will kill humans and make him run out of years to live."

"He knows that that is hit-and-miss," Ijeoma said. "It only counts if the venerable ones say so. Remember that he told us that the woman Adaku killed did not affect him."

"Seems like he has us exactly where he wants," Isioma said.

"Literally under his thumb," Ijeoma said as they went down the stairs.

"Again, stating the obvious achieves nothing for us," Adure said. "Maybe we should tell him about the pregnancy. It might soften him."

"Perhaps," Isioma said. "But it's your call, Ije."

"Or make things worse. I will think about it. I am concerned that if it turns out not to be a boy, he might begin to detest me. You know how much he wants a male heir."

"And if it turns out to be a boy, you will become his new 'irreplaceable number one,'" Isioma added as they drew to a stand on the southwest passage. "Is that not what you have always wanted?"

"Yes, but that's a big 'if,'" Ijeoma said with a hint of a smile.

"He's going to find out soon, anyway," Adure said.

"Well, not if my plan works out first," Ijeoma said, chewing her top lip.

"Since when did you have a plan?" Isioma said. "And what sort of plan are we talking about?"

"Since we were loitering in the forest," Ijeoma said. "And you will find out when it is solidified."

"I hope you don't do anything rash that would put all of us in the queen of the coast's bad books," Isioma said.

"Whatever I do, it will be to keep my child safe."

Gliding through the south, southeast, and east passages, they arrived at the entrance to the dining area on the ground floor of the northeast section and tentatively filed into the room.

Stewing in his own juice, King Ajutu was at the far end of the room, at the head of the long, rectangular table with 12 chairs ranged around it, feasting alone on prodigious quantities of a variety of local food and devouring what was on his plate.

He glanced up as he sniffed a familiar combination of fragrances that a slowly rotating, ceiling fan wafted toward him, saw the maidens approaching and studied them with keen eyes.

Maintaining flawless facades that masked their inward worries and curtsying, as usual, the trio settled on either side of the king. With Isioma and Ijeoma sitting respectively to his right and left, whilst Adure sat to Ijeoma's left. As they tried at dishing out meals for themselves, his face twisted into an expression of annoyance.

The king set his cutlery on the side of his piled plate, sat back in his seat and steepled his fingers. Propping his elbows on the chair's armrest, he tilted his head back, then looked leftward out the windows that had pulled-apart curtains, "I know full well that you have not completed your assignment, so why did you return and not consider giving me a briefing?"

"Your Majesty, we are sorry," Ijeoma said. "We had planned to do it after lunch—so, they had a military back up with guns, and we did not stand a chance. We do not heal fast enough, so we felt it was better to retreat and figure out a way to go in with a better chance against them. Plus, the henchmen, who were many times more powerful than us, did not make it."

Swallowing chewed food, then letting out a cough into his cupped right hand, he picked up the glass of red wine to his left and took a sip. "Is that so?" King Ajutu said as his Adam's apple bobbed, glanced at Adure, then turned his neck rightward to look at Isioma.

Isioma and Adure nodded.

The king set the glass down, "If that is the case, then you did the right thing. I don't want to lose any more allies. It is clear that I cannot cut any corners in plotting Odera's demise. It must be as directed by the most venerable one. I need to have him captured, and I need to possess his machete. So, you all are welcome back," he said, then, with a grandiose hand movement, gestured at the selection of dishes as he leaned forward to resume eating. "Eat! There is plenty of food. You need the strength for what is to come."

"Thank you, Your Majesty," they chorused.

"Your Majesty, is it true that he can only die by his own machete?" Ijeoma asked. "I heard you say it to yourself again and again last night."

Shaking his head dismissively, "More complicated than that," he said, his voice rising. "Is there anything else I ought to know?"

Disconcerted by the unexpected change in subject and tone of voice, "Like what, Your Majesty?" Isioma said, exchanging surreptitious glances with her fellow maidens.

King Ajutu's stone cold eyes darted from one maiden to the other before it flickered to his Akupé, which rested on the table on his right-hand side. Sighing, he lifted it, "Like that," he said with the heel of his tremulous right hand resting on the table.

Atop the table, next to his right hand, previously concealed by the hand fan, was a small, light-brown, cap-like device.

Evidently seething at Adaku's slight to his authority, "This Dutch cap belonged to Adaku," he added, glowering at them in turn. "What about you three, do each of you have yours?"

"I do not," Ijeoma said with certitude.

Terrified that the king might read deceit on their faces, Adure and Isioma cast down their gazes.

Following a moment's hesitation, "Neither do I, Your Majesty," Adure and Isioma said all at once.

"Okay. Each night, before I sleep with any of you, I will ensure that you do not have it in place. None of you will deny me an heir like Adaku succeeded in doing, understood?" he said with determination.

"Yes, Your Majesty," they replied of one voice.

Watching him for a long moment, "Are you porting somewhere, Your Majesty?" Isioma asked, perhaps due to her eagerness to soothe her guilty conscience.

Without looking up from his plate of food, "Why do you ask?"

"You are supposed to be dieting, Your Majesty," Isioma said. "And the last time you ate this much food, you were preparing to port to Europe because you suspected that your business partners there were being unscrupulous. Are you going to Europe again?"

King Ajutu dropped his cutlery and picked up his Akupé with his left hand. Sweeping one of its faces with the palm of his right hand, he dropped it on the table further before him. The top face was showing a map in real time on a fluid background and with numerous twinkling lights, much like a night, blue sky dotted with stars.

"By the time I would have covered all those 700-plus shrines across Igboland that you can see there," he gestured to the map. "I think I would have surpassed the distance I ported to Europe and back."

"When will you be going, Your Majesty?" Adure asked.

"As soon as I'm done here," King Ajutu said as he continued to rush his food.

"For what purpose, Your Majesty?" Ijeoma asked, seeming ill at ease and appearing to wonder what the father of her unborn child was about to get himself into.

Following a long moment of silence that was only broken by munching, gulping, the soft hum of the rotating fan, and the clinking of cutlery against chinaware, "We can talk about it upon my return," he murmured.

No longer eating, "When will that be, Your Majesty? When do you return?" Ijeoma purred.

His feathers seemingly ruffled by his meddlesome maidens, "Before midnight or maybe earlier, depending on…Never mind. I'll be back soon," the king bleated incoherently.

Unheeding, he gulped down the rest of his meal and chugged his wine. Pushing his chair back, he grabbed his Akupé and vanished in a puff of blue smoke.

Distraught, Ijeoma flung her cutlery across the room and dropped her face in her palms, sobbing.

"What's it?" Adure asked as she and Isioma set their spoons aside. "More pregnancy drama?"

Gathering some courage, "Using the diaphragm was not a problem," Ijeoma looked a little discomposed as she spoke. "I stopped using it because I wanted to get pregnant. One of the books in the caucus room detailed on how allowing a life grow in bodies occupied by the likes of us can help us avoid control by the netherworld and help our nergergies to remain within our host bodies for as long as the body stays strong as determined by health as well as age. I should have told you."

Isioma and Adure thought in inscrutable silence for a long moment.

"Well, thank you for eventually telling us," Isioma said. "But why the tears?"

"How will you two get pregnant if the king is not around?" Ijeoma said. "How will we stay together?"

"Why won't he be around?" Adure said.

"He looks out of sorts, out of control, and I fear that he will make a wrong move and Odera will finish him," Ijeoma said. "I wonder if he would survive what is brewing in view of the ammunition Odera and his group possess, and whether or not he still matters to me in the grand scheme of things. I have tried but could not get into the hinterland of his mind as only Adaku could. I sense that his cloak-and-dagger ways are beginning to catch up with him."

"Well, as I see it, if getting pregnant is in our favor, then it doesn't have to be by the king," Adure said, winking at Isioma who smiled as Ijeoma lowered her hands, her expression brightening a touch. "Women aren't the only ones who can get press-ganged into copulation in the bushes around here, you know. We'll be irresistible to any of the local men, so worry not."

"And what sort of child will come out of that?" Isioma asked.

"I don't really care," Adure said. "If we can exist on our own terms, then that's all I'm interested in. So, I'll either abandon the child or give it up for adoption."

"Allowing a were-jaguar to end up living outside of the palace and uncontrolled amongst humans either by giving it up for adoption, or abandoning it is a crazy idea," Isioma said. "Better to kill the child."

"Then I'll kill it."

"It is interesting that you two will talk about killing it. The book also mentioned that the negergy-dominated body that discovered the phenomenon had also contemplated killing the child but ended up bonding with it."

"We'll see about that," Adure said. "But how did you manage to find the time to read this book you are talking about?"

"Well, during the last time he ported to—" Ijeoma began to say but stopped as she grew flustered by the sound of pattering and heavy breathing from someone coming down the east passage toward the dining.

Following Ijeoma's gaze, Isioma's and Adure's eyes fastened on the doorway. As Papu appeared in it, stopped, and looked around, they rose to their feet in a snap.

"I thought the king was here," Papu croaked, sneaking a glance at his lapel watch. "Never mind, but the queen, Odera, Namdi, that lady from two days ago, and some military men are outside, and Odera is threatening to take aggressive action if I don't open the gates. What do I do? The king ordered me not to let them in."

Pressed into the limed oak table, Adure's fingers began to morph, and Ijeoma placed her left hand on Adure's right shoulder, "Not in front of him…Plus, you may be shot, and since we are not capable of rapid regeneration, it may be life-ending. There is a better chance of us staying alive if we confront them in human form," Ijeoma whispered, then raised her voice. "Thank you, Papu. Don't get involved. Go back to your post and secure your door. We will inform the king."

Wheeling around, Papu ran back toward the northwest section.

"Ijeoma," Isioma started. "Are you insane? You want us to stay and wait for Odera? Do you think he will walk in here and give us a pat on the back for coming to the prince's house with those henchmen? He is here for revenge, so we are better off if we skipped the palace."

"What do you think, Adure?" Ijeoma asked.

"Isioma is right. Let's do it…Let's run."

"Caucus room, first!" Ijeoma said. "Let me grab that book!"

Chapter 52

The sky had taken a sullen turn, though there was still enough sunlight to keep the Harmattan chill from dropping any significant degrees in temperature.

With bright eyes, a set jaw, and tightened fists, Odera bounced on his toes behind the two sergeants who operated the chainsaw. He'd proven to me beyond any doubt that he was a mixture of talent and dogged determination in the pursuit of what he felt was right.

The *'brum-brum-brum-brrrrrrrr'* sound made it difficult to hear my own voice screaming to Odera, through Queen Nena's wound-down window, that Papu was back to his post and was peeking from behind the wall to the right of the window in his room, suggesting to me that the king had been made aware of the developing situation and might be planning a surprise.

But as Odera remained focused on what he was going to do, I rested my case. A distraction wasn't what I wanted to become. In addition to that, I no longer fretted about anything as long as he was with me. He'd also proven to be proficient at handling unforeseen circumstances.

Glancing again at Papu's window, he was no longer there.

Soon, the right gate's bottom hinge at the pillar gave way just as the top one did moments earlier.

The two sergeants stepped aside for Odera who was as eager to enter the palace as he'd been to leave it two days prior and returned the gasoline-driven cutting tool to the trunk of their armored vehicle, behind us. Grabbing their rifles, they slammed the trunk shut and stood around our jeep, providing us with cover as planned.

Swinging the heavy metal on the hinge of the left gate, Odera pushed what had become one long piece of steel gate open as wide as it was possible and waved the little gun truck to reverse into the compound.

Neither he nor Namdi had the keys to the palace. Namdi, after receiving it from Odera, had left it with Papu before he fled the palace. I wasn't privy to what reason Namdi had given Papu as to why Odera no longer needed the keys.

As the driver brought the truck to a stop close to the front stoop's bottom step, I caught a glimpse of the feline forms of the maidens arriving at the rooftop.

Ruffling the golden leaves of the surrounding forest canopy, a breeze also creaked the overlapping, almost-bare branches as they blew around.

Furiously winding down in full, my window that had been halfway down, and sticking my head out above the top of the vehicle, "Odera!" I shrieked from within our vehicle as Namdi followed my pointing finger. "The maidens…They're on the roof…In their large cat—"

Sudden rat-a-tat-tats from the semi-automatic rifles belonging to Sergeants Brymo and Fric rattled me, and I didn't complete my sentence. They'd followed my pointing finger as well.

Odera would turn on instinct, toward the direction the spurts of gunfire had traveled. "Did they get hit?" he asked with a steady, low-pitched voice, certain that they'd fired at the maidens. The command had been to shoot at them on sight.

Shaking his head as I sat back down in the jeep, "They were too quick for us. They leapt off into the top of the trees," Sergeant Brymo replied. "Go after them?"

Odera was anything but pleased about the sergeant's response. He knew that the chance to kill them had gone.

"Not unless you are ready to be remembered as 'the late Sergeant Brymo,'" Namdi said as he casually dismounted his motorbike at the front of the Farm Road-facing queue of vehicles and walked toward the gateway holding the two machetes. "They blend in well with the forest better than your camouflage can afford you—not called masters of camouflage for nothing. Let them be. We will meet them again. The king is our main target."

Grabbing and clinging onto the bag of Ejizu's bones, Queen Nena felt a sudden wave of depression, "I couldn't for my life understand how I wasted nearly four decades of my existence with Ajutu. Next month, it will be 37 years of being married to him. How did I continue, against reason, to be holed up in that palace after I knew who he was, hoping to play happy families with him so as not to be hot with shame? Ikuku was right…I should have traveled the world with him. May the heavens blast this awful place," the queen agonized, clearly gulping back her tears.

With a curt nod toward the motorcade, "Okay, let's go," Odera ordered and clapped twice as the captain stepped down from his vehicle and walked into the compound with fast-paced strides. "C'mon, Namdi, Brymo, Captain…Let's go as planned. Fric, stay put."

Bounding the steps, Odera, Namdi, Sergeant Brymo, and Captain Iduto arrived at the front stoop, and Namdi handed Odera his machete.

Stepping away, "Sergeant Brymo, the door," Odera's words couldn't have been more pointed.

Posturing with his feet in a wide stance, the sergeant blasted away wildly at the doors' locks, the report of the gun cracking across Palace Road East. The shots creating holes where the latches had been, and the doors flung open. With this, Odera waved us out of the jeep.

Keeping her bag tucked in under her arm, frantic Queen Nena alighted from our vehicle before Prince Ikuku and me. Dashing toward the building behind the queen, we looked around furtively as Sergeant Fric followed close behind us, backing toward the open gate with his weapon in position. Aside from the four bungalows across the road, there was nothing else worthy of note—no onlookers in sight, no beasts on the prowl or in the air.

Running past Odera, Namdi, Brymo, and the captain, who all stood two on either side of the doorway like in a guard of honor, we headed through the entryway.

"Privates, step out of your vehicles and follow them with the corpses," the captain ordered, drew his handgun into position, and checked that his walkie-talkie remained active. Then, he gazed around the vicinity from the top of the stoop as Odera and Namdi joined us in the hall. "Sergeant Fric, take up position and man the gateway. Nobody enters. Nobody leaves. No conversations with anyone—might be a distraction tactic. One warning shot only, then shoot to kill."

Poised motionless on his feet, "Sir, Yessir!" Sergeant Fric responded whilst his rifle remained at the ready.

"Sergeant Brymo, man the doorway," the captain said. "Provide cover for Sergeant Fric. Keep your radios alive."

"Sir, Yessir!" the sergeants chorused.

"Odera," Queen Nena said as he waited for the privates to arrive in the hall with the corpses. "Ejizu just informed me that he can't see where Ajutu is—said he is capable of becoming invisible."

"What?" Odera whispered loudly; a certain frustration visible in his demeanor as the scope of what we were about to deal with seemed to have suddenly become clearer in his mind. "So, he could be anywhere watching us?"

"Or setting a trap," the queen said, paused for a moment, then nodded. "Ejizu also said that he no longer feels Ajutu's presence within the palace. Okay, my son, please just stay close and protect us."

"Dike, please be on the lookout," I said and met Odera's gaze, but I was unable to read his eyes. I wondered a little about his true feelings regarding going up against his father. He'd told Namdi and me of his encounter with his mother, Evelyn, and in the cold light of day had reassured us that he wouldn't put off the evil hour in the fight for justice for the Children of the Shadows.

"Bute, we are counting on you three," Namdi added.

"I will stay ahead of you all; Dike and Ejizu will bring up the rear," Bute said to Namdi just as the four, gloved privates walked onto the hall with the bodies over their right shoulders, the one carrying Jadue's body also holding Jadue's head in the palm of his left hand.

Walking in a file behind Odera, we all headed down the main passage, aiming for the caucus room. At the back and with his gun ready for action, the captain faced the direction of the exit, slowly backing his way down.

Chapter 53

In the intervening period, the felids leapt off the roof terrace into the canopy of the trees that not just overhung Farm Road but also extended to the roof of the palace.

Whilst the cougar lost its footing and tumbled through the trees, missing various attempts to grab at the trees' offshoots, the black, morph jaguar and the golden leopard quickly zigzagged down.

Transforming to Adure and Ijeoma respectively as they arrived at the forest floor ahead of the cougar, Ijeoma removed the weighty tome with *Theurgy* on its spine from the grip of her jaws. And as they galloped away, Ijeoma held the hardcover volume secure in the tight grasp of her right hand.

The branches, which had been made brittle by the dry air and broke off *tch, tch, tch* with ease, nonetheless broke the cougar's fall as it changed back to a ferocious and upset Isioma. Trying to save herself from falling further by making a grab for the nearest bough that seemed likely to hold her weight, though it all but snapped off as she neared the ground; Isioma dropped to the duff that was soft and damp with old leaves thick in the soil.

Shutting her eyes in anguish as she felt the heaviness in her right foot and the weakness in her right leg, Isioma tried to gather speed to catch up with her compeers. To her horror, she felt increasing pain and saw blood streaming down the outer side of the leg.

With a wince, "I got shot," Isioma cried out, then her knees buckled as she grew lightheaded.

On the ground, her right thigh throbbed. Loosening her chignon in a fit of petty rage to rest her occiput more comfortably on the forest floor, she shut her eyes.

Amidst the near and far sounds of gently burbling brooks, crisp chirping from birds, and croaking frogs, Adure and Ijeoma halted and turned around, heading back in a trice.

When Isioma opened her eyes again, they'd arrived where she lay splay-legged, with her right, lower limb twisted outward all the way from her spoon-shaped hip.

Giving Isioma's lower limbs a once-over, the duo noted three bullet holes along the side of her right thigh, just below the hem of her mid-thigh-length short skirt.

Squatting down by her right side, Adure tried to lift the limb. Isioma boomed out a scream that traveled and a quiver shook Adure's pear-shaped frame and she in a flash withdrew her hands with terror. Gazing up at Ijeoma who stood at Isioma's feet with one hand on her toned, mildly curvy hip, "She most definitely can't walk," Adure's voice was with a tremble. "We've got to carry her."

"How?" Ijeoma said.

"Piggyback her in turns."

"Might be easier if she changed to her cougar," Ijeoma said.

"How easier?"

"It is a long trek to our destination. If we get tired, she can hobble on three limbs. In human form, she will not be able to hop for long on one foot. I think it is better for her to change now. It might be more and more difficult the weaker she gets."

Darting her gaze to Isioma, "Can you change back?" Adure asked.

Isioma made one attempt, then a second before she gave up.

"Too weak to do it," Isioma said, her voice dropping as blood loss continued. "Let's stop the bleeding first, then I can try again. Put your hands around my thigh, above the topmost hole to reduce the blood flowing down to the leg."

Looking green around the gills, "Okay," Adure said with a wobbly voice and a brittle smile. "Ije, please go and look for something we can use to apply pressure over the wounds—or on second thought, come and hold it; let me go. I don't want to start panicking. You know how all thumbs I am when it comes to taking care of others."

Evidently convinced, "Sure, I will hold it. You go," Ijeoma said as she outstretched her well-built and toned arm and forearm toward Isioma's right thigh. "I need to stress myself less for my pregnancy, anyway."

Transmuting to her black, morph-jaguar form, Adure swept through the gently undulating mossy floor and disappeared into the cloud forest.

****

A short distance later, underneath tall trees that rose to brush the dreary sky, overgrown with vine and possessing small, thin, and soft leaves with dust, condensed fog, and resultant drips, and groaned to some degree in protest against a gentle wind, the jaguar's eyes sparkled as it caught something.

Conceiving an idea amidst the distant sound of people, perhaps mostly males, hewing timber whilst conversing indistinctly in teen-speak Igbo, it saw something of huge interest, and it stopped. Pussyfooting across the ground that was also covered with peat and humus, it closed in on its target.

In its line of sight, a swarthy, young man, who was probably one day of not eating away from being described as scrawny, had just finished relieving himself. Causing a few squirrels to scrabble their claws against tree barks, as they raced to their dreys at the top, the jaguar would give the crouched man the shudders to feel that something lurked nearby. And no sooner this happened than Adure materialized before him, flashing a wide grin. To her surprise, he didn't cover his nakedness as he straightened up, though he seemed in shock.

"This is definitely a step closer to what I want and need," she said to herself, seeming to savor the uninviting atmosphere within that part of the forest. Raising her voice and with slow, easy sway of her broad hips, "Hey," she said, fluttering her eyelashes, gesturing to her body, and suggestively baring her hitherto, unexposed, equally fair-complexioned upper abdomen. "Are you in any way, handsome man, interested in taking advantage of this, right here, right now?"

Giving her the evils in dismay, "It is definitely my lucky day that such a beauty as you, who could have the best men at her beck and call, would, on seeing a man as lowly as me in an environment that has a predominant stench of human excrement, become aroused?" he said.

"Definitely your lucky day," she replied. "And I hope you know how to please a woman."

Disregarding the chill in the air, he took off his pants and underwear, which had been three-quarters of the way up, and strode toward her, "I am assuming that you, too, know how to please a man," he said in a bubbly tone, quirking an eyebrow and smiling.

Winking at him, she shrugged off her beaded, short-sleeved half-top and tossed it onto the ground.

"We would've to find out, won't we?" she said in a slow manner as she unbuttoned his yellow shirt that clashed violently with his loose-fitting, red jeans and gently caressed his hairless chest with her fingers. Grabbing his head, she slipped her tongue into the depths of his mouth and purred. Then, she leapt onto him, wrapping her thighs around his waist, her legs crossing secure behind his dark, drawn buttocks with skin that was dry and cracked. Sensing him tumescent, she pulled her miniskirt up to her waistline with her right hand. Tucking it above her bum bag, she then grabbed his phallus as she felt a warm glow deep within herself. Parting the crotch panel of her blue thong panties, she shoved his manhood inside herself with a hard thrust, jerking as her open, watchful eyes widened even more.

Moaning, she bent over backward and pulled him by the back of his neck to bring his face, which was scrunched up with concentration, toward her ample bosoms. Dropping her back down to the uneven ground that was pocked with stones, radicles, and rhizomes, he landed smack on his knees and ignored the crushing pain that resulted within the joints. As her all but shredded, anterior, abdominal muscles fibrillated, she moved him in and out, aided by her toned thighs and legs, in a manner so quick that it was humanly impossible to achieve. And before long, his wide-open eyes winked amber as he got his rocks off and finished; the whole process lasting not quite one full minute.

Rising in a jiffy once it was over, Adure began dressing up as though nothing had happened whilst the young man remained on all fours, recovering from the experience, and seeming nonplussed. Dressed up, she grabbed his obviously white at-one-time underwear and helped him up with a hand underneath his armpit, "We need your underwear and maybe your crumpled shirt, too. We'll decide when we get there. Put your pants on and let's go."

Still a little stupefied, "Where…where…?" he sputtered. "Where are we going?"

"My friend needs help to stop a bleeder. She got shot," she said, then murmuring to herself, "And also to get her pregnant…It's close enough to the middle of the month. We might just be lucky."

Picking up his trousers, he asked, "Why are you walking around here barefoot? Why are you dressed this way despite the cold?"

"Why do you ask? Do you want to give me your sandals and shirt? A gentleman would."

Pulling his pants up, he said, "Not a chance."

"I don't need them anyway…Thanks for not offering."

Zipping himself up, then buttoning himself into his shirt, he said, "My question is, why do you not need them? 'Cause if you did, you would have put on shoes and covered your body better before coming out here."

Stretching out her left hand, she grabbed his right hand and said, "You'll get scared if I told you, and I don't want that. My friends and I really need you."

As they walked abreast amongst the trees, scrunching dry twigs and crisp, yellow leaves underfoot, "And since we're asking questions, why were you taking a dump in the forest?" she asked.

Giving her a curious look, he said, "You seem not to be from around here, otherwise you would know that when you live in a compound that shares a pit latrine with another compound, as can sometimes be the case around here, you would have to find an alternative place to do your thing if someone gets to it before you…and you badly need to do it and they are taking their time, or someone bullies you and takes your turn."

"Hmm, interesting. You sound like anger is festering and growing in your heart toward this bully."

"That bully will eventually get what is coming to him."

"Why do you people even live in clusters? Living separately might help avoid this toilet sharing that seems to be causing you distress."

Flashing her an even more inquiring look, "It's something that is age-old," he rapped. "Even though you seem not to support how we live, there are more positives than negatives. For one: it is, in theory, far easier to maintain defense against dangerous animals or bad people in groups than as an individual—"

"Still, I beg to differ," she interrupted him. "But you're right that I'm not from around here. Aren't you scared coming in here?"

"Nope. I come here all the time. A lot of people visit the forest for the same reason."

"Yes, I can tell from the congeries of smells that have spoilt this otherwise-wholesome place. But I'd be scared if I were you."

Chuckling, he said, "You came in here, so you are obviously not scared. If a woman is not scared, why would a man be?"

"That's a good observation, but I'm not your average woman, or person for that matter."

"So, where are you from then, and what are you doing here?"
"Trust me…You really don't want to know."

Chapter 54

Meanwhile, not far away from a stretch of School Road that was straight with fields of grass on each of its sides, Papu appeared out of thin air. Walking through a side path created amidst common hawthorn hedges, he arrived in a compound with three reed-roofed mud huts and headed straight into the middle one.

In the hut whose reed-mat door was lifted over the roof, a plump, average height, rather insipid woman with a distinctive widow's peak, who looked older than her real age with hard miles on a pretty face and was breastfeeding her baby girl, glanced up, and just about managed a smile as he approached.

"It's been a while," she said. "I convinced myself that you had forgotten us."

Papu sat down on ridged-up earth as she cast her gaze back to her suckling child, connecting eyes, which were baggy probably with the fatigue of overwork, with her infant's eyes, "I was waiting for the right time," he said. "How is Ugochi?"

"Doing well—" she said.

"How are you?" Papu continued.

Shrugging and without any eye contact with Papu, "So-so," she said. "Enjoying the bonding experience of breastfeeding, I guess, while at the same time trying to not think so much about fifth of July, eight years ago. How is Nonzo?"

Smiling with a whiff of bitterness, "Hmm, I understand," Papu said. "Nonzo, my son, is there. He is not happy with just being a town crier and is upset with me for not letting him be one of the king's henchmen."

"I don't blame him," she said, still gazing at her child. "It is almost impossible to get a good job around here even with a university degree, talk less of with just a secondary school certificate."

With a heavy sigh, "For sure, he is limited on options without a university degree," Papu said.

"Did you make him understand why you didn't want him to be a henchman?"

"I didn't. I mean, I did, but not the real reason—just told him he wasn't muscular enough," Papu said. "I can't possibly tell him that his life would be at risk doing that job without giving him a full explanation. How is your husband? I didn't see his motorcycle."

"My husband, Amos, is fine. He should be at his garage, attending to his customers."

"Even on a Sunday?"

With a dismissive nod, she said, "That's what he said he was going to do when he left, and I am tired of arguing about the same thing with him every Sunday. And your wife?"

Perking up, "The love of my life," Papu grinned. "She is doing good."

"So, what news brings you today?"

"Prince Ikuku is in town with military men. I think this signals the beginning of the end for you-know-who."

With her eyes and mouth wide open, "Are you serious?" she said with a voice that suddenly rose in pitch, startling her little one into a cry.

"Yes, Mama Ugochi," he said as she began rocking her baby to keep her quiet, then he rose to his feet. "I have to hurry back now before a lot happens in my absence. I will return with more news."

Gingered up, "Thank you, Papu," she said with a hint of a grin as her baby grew silent. "I hope it will be more good news."

Standing with his arms behind his back, "Me, too," Papu said.

"You have my blessing to take as much time as you need before we see again, if that will mean you come with more pleasant news," she enthused.

Hurrying out of the little hut that had major signs of neglect as the smile on his face grew, Papu disappeared once he was sure that no-one could catch sight of him.

Chapter 55

Walking out of King Ajutu's shrine, Odera left it open as the four privates exited from the caucus room behind Namdi who was ushering them back to their vehicles.

The plan had been to lay the henchmen's bodies on the table once we got into the king's lair; however, through the queen, Ejizu would make us aware of the existence of the shrine to Odera and Namdi's surprise.

Arriving at the head of the long and ornate table around which we had convened, Odera prepared to speak, and I was afforded a clearer view of the shrine's interior. It'd been difficult to see with Odera, Namdi, and the lowest-ranked soldiers clogging its space.

From my sitting position in Chief Madu's designated chair, I looked past the four execrable bodies and a head, which were laid from left to right across the floor in the room's center, mentally comparing it with Mr. Isigwe's shrine. Granted that it appeared more modern, better finished, and less diabolical, still, it begot within me a similar feeling of horror, and although for some inexplicable reason I'd become better able at managing my emotions in that regard, I was prompted to rise to my feet in protest as the stench of death hung in the air despite the pleasant smell from the shrine. Leaning toward Odera, "If you would like me to remain in this room with you, then that shrine must be shut," I whispered in his ear.

Odera had scarcely raised his head to initiate a nod when I skipped over to the half-shelf on the right and pressed the button that began to move the shelves toward each other.

Watching me as I returned to settle down, Odera gave a quick-to-fade knowing smile before he faced forward again, his eyes darting from person to person.

Prince Ikuku was sat to my immediate left, whilst Queen Nena and Captain Iduto occupied the remaining two seats in that order from the prince. Queen

Nena had the grips of the bag of Ejizu's bones over her left shoulder and was obvious in making sure that she didn't set her eyes on the king's mosaic. The captain tapped his right foot on the floor whilst his gun remained in position in his right hand and his handie-talkie rested on the table. All of us gazing at Odera, we waited for him to share his thoughts.

Standing behind the king's chair, "Any update from Ejizu regarding the king's whereabouts?" Odera started.

Shaking her head, "Still the same," the queen said. "Ajutu is moving from shrine to shrine across the land and experiencing the same thing: the children's spirits continue to stop the occultists from burying their remains. One wonders whether he has to visit every shrine in the land before he comes to the full realization that these spirits mean business."

Pacing up and down before the bookshelves, with his forearms crossed behind him, inclining his head and doing his best not to look at the Okiké whilst his sheathed machete rocked, "Is Ejizu able to tell us when the king is on his way back here?" Odera continued.

"No. Ejizu said he sees him only when he has reappeared at his destination, or at a rest stop," the queen said.

"So, we must be ready for when he suddenly shows up in here," I quickly added.

And at the same time, drawing to a stand and turning his neck rightward, "Rest stop?" Odera demanded.

"Ejizu said it appears to be that teleporting saps his energy hence creating the need to stop for food from time to time."

And no sooner had the queen ended her speech than the door cracked open without a knock; the sudden sound of its inward swing startling most of us; the queen and I much more than the prince, though Odera, who was deep in thought, as well as the captain didn't as much as flinch at the noise.

With his sheathed machete tossing and him oblivious to the scare he'd caused some of us, Namdi walked in and stood on the other side of the table with his head up, shoulders straight and backward, and arms folded across his chest. Facing the direction of the Okiké, he made strong eye contact with Odera as Odera approached the table again.

Grabbing at the top rail of the king's chair and hunching forward as the door shut, "He could materialize anywhere in this palace," Odera said. "Shouldn't we cover all the possible places?"

Sitting back in his seat and making eye contact with Odera, "How many rooms are we talking about?" the captain asked.

"Well, there are only three places he would definitely be arriving at as his first stop, on a Sunday. Odera was hardly here on Sundays, so he wouldn't know this," Namdi said, glancing at an analog clock on the east wall, which said the time was 2:21. "His bedroom, this room, and his pigeon room, but he could also go anywhere else especially if he is unable to find his maidens."

"We didn't come with the manpower to cover all three areas as well as guard the front yard," the captain said. "Which is the most likely place?"

"That would be this room," Odera said. "I say we wait here and move according to Ejizu's directions. Ejizu will be able to see him wherever he is in the palace."

"That makes a whole lot of sense," the prince added. "But before any violence ensues, please let me talk with him to see if he will agree to quietly give up the throne and allow the process of transferring power to the people to be—"

Thumping her fisted right hand on the table, Queen Nena interjected Prince Ikuku; her reaction was all but explosive. "I would hedge my bets on suggesting that to him," she said with a catch in her voice, feeling frustrated and peeved. "I know that you often carry tolerance too far, Ikuku, by being charitable in your judgments and rarely censorious; nonetheless, now, you must not believe anything Ajutu says. We would have come all this way for nothing if you consider negotiating with that loathsome man. Even if he agrees, it's only to buy him more time to silence for good all who have been against him. Think about it…What would you expect him to be doing while democracy is ushered in? Fold his arms and do nothing?" she scoffed. "We must end this issue now. It is now or never. If given another chance and he doesn't end up killing all of us, he will at the least fit us up. So, choose one. If it was totally up to me, I would not cast another pearl before that swine."

Tightening his grasp on the chair and with flaring nostrils, "Prince Ikuku, with all due respect, the queen is a hundred-percent correct," Odera said with a deepened tone, glancing at Namdi who shook his head; perhaps suggesting to Odera that it wasn't yet the time to further reveal that the king was his father. "I came here to end King Ajutu's reign by force and not by any negotiations. He is your brother, and I understand that you may have an attachment toward him, but he does not have any attachment toward you or anyone for that matter.

He cares about his skin alone…He never fights fair, and I am here to fight fire with fire." Pointing at the shelves, he added, "We did not risk our lives battling those creatures to then come here and become cowering wimps."

"I did not mean to draw the ire of the two of you," Prince Ikuku said. "Nena, you obviously know him better than I do…Odera, you probably know him more than any of us here, and I don't doubt your determination, but I only speak as someone who has considered that for someone who teleports, his powers may be insurmountable…At least by any of us."

"Well," I said, plunging blithely into my speech without thorough consideration of my words. "We can only know that he is too great to be overcome after we have tried and not succeeded, not before."

"How do you propose we fight someone who can become invisible at will?" Prince Ikuku said.

Odera looked at Namdi for a long, thoughtful moment before he faced the prince, "I have absolutely no idea, but the alternative cannot be to let him get off scot-free," he said. "I have—we have the will…There must be a way."

"But he can't stay invisible forever, can he?" Namdi asked.

With a sudden flash of inspiration, "Not possible," Odera said. "And if Ejizu indicates that he requires energy for the process and energy is never in persistent supply, then—"

"If you cut off his supply of oxygen like you did those beasts, it will diminish his energy stores and should prevent him carrying out an energy-dependent action like teleporting and assuming invisibility," Prince Ikuku said.

"Makes sense," I said. "But one has to be very quick in doing that or else the opportunity would vanish as fast as it comes."

Chapter 56

At the same time, Chief Madu was leaving his house.

As he shut the front door with a pang of annoyance, "What head chief should require at least 15 minutes to convince his wife that looking into gunshots around his neighborhood is the right thing to do?" he mused. "Well, whatever it takes, I must stick it out. It is important to keep her happy so that my situation does not turn out like that of the queen and Ejizu and reduce the likelihood of her looking into how our son died and perhaps ending up exposing me. But who has King Ajutu and his people shot at, or who has shot at them?"

Exiting his compound, he looked around, then vanished into thin air.

Before long, he reappeared out of nowhere a few meters from Mr. Isigwe's house, his long caftan swaying in the breeze. Turning right off Farm Road, he strode onto the quiet compound. Rapping his Mkpó on the ground, he walked straight into Eke's room.

Exuding a powerful, brooding air, "What have you been up to?" the chief asked, searching for a way to get to the point of him being there.

Glancing up, "Nothing much," Eke said as his face took on a nettled look, then he gazed down. "Fixing this—just finished lunch. Earlier on, I transferred my ritual chattels back to my shrine. You look worried."

"I am," the chief stated.

"You changed out of your casuals," Eke said whilst remaining focused on fitting a filter to the mouth opening of the ritual mask that was on his lap.

"Did not think I would be going out again but had to hurry out when the need arose before Adane changed her mind about letting me leave home on a day of rest. You know how quickly she can change her mind."

Chortling, Eke nodded.

Sitting gently on the bed's edge, beside Eke, Chief Madu wasted no further time. Staring straight ahead out the doorway, he continued, "I heard several gunshots ring out from the palace, and I am worried about the king; about the wheels, all these things he is doing are setting into motion. He seems overly disturbed and has become rattled, even erratic. He may likely end up exposing us all the way he is going about everything."

Setting the mask beneath the bed, Eke shuffled backward on the soft mattress to lean his back against the wall and folded his arms across his chest as he sighed. Chief Madu tilted his body to his right and gave Eke sidelong glances.

"How do you know the gunshots have anything to do with the king?" Eke said.

"Well, I don't. But considering that things have not been right around his palace for two or three days now, it is only sensible to take an educated guess that it is related to him."

"Well, if you are right, then I do not know what to say. He is his own worst enemy. The venerable ones made it clear that this fight is unnecessary. And now, by hook or by crook, he is dragging us into it. He could and should have just let the temperature cool down and found a secretive way to silence the woman and her cohorts for good. He should have realized that he has more clout than his opposition, and his words of denial, if the fact about the ritual ever came out, would have been believed more than the opposition's view of the matter. Now, they are constantly looking for ways to checkmate him, and, according to you, he has lost all his henchmen, lacking physical protection. He is also losing his mind. He looked a shadow of himself when we were driving around. Why does he take a sideways look at our methods?"

"Remember, it is a sin to speak ill of your king," the chief said.

Huffing out his sudden irritation and cracking his knuckles, "Sure," Eke retorted. "That is what he has often said, but it is not part of the law of the land, and nobody has ever been found out, let alone punished, for committing that so-called sin. It is just his manipulative way of staying in control and demanding respect."

The vehemence of Eke's answer surprising him, "None of us is flawless," the chief retorted. "You were also, just two nights ago, found wanting in following our methods to the letter."

Eke stayed quiet for a long, maddening moment.

"Well, whatever it is, we have no choice, or do we?" the chief continued.

"No," Eke said. "Not when the only two options one has are: doing it as he wants by one's choice, or doing it by his force, and that is the part that saddens me. Him having merited and received powers equal to, or greater than those of the hundreds of peace warriors across Igboland combined, hence wielding so much control, makes it impossible for me to even consider going against him as much as I would have liked to."

"It is always pleasing when you and I agree on something," the chief said. "You know, you, too, can agree to further shorten your life…then you will begin your journey toward meriting the same nature of his powers."

"Hmm, though I desire more power, I do not possess that kind of guts. Taking one year off my lifespan in sacrificing Ijezie is all I can give up. How does one enjoy to the fullest all the things one desires by becoming a peace warrior if one has an ever-shortening life span?"

With a nod, "So, as the one who did what others could not do, thus was chosen by the Evil One to run his otherworldly operations in Igboland, we must remain loyal if we intend also to increase our ability to operate in those realms," the chief said. "So, I ask that we go and find out what is going on at the palace and help him out, if need be, and by so doing, help ourselves out too."

"He is supposed to be spiritually powerful beyond imagination…Seemingly even more powerful than Tamir, who is supposed to have rubbed out more people, and doing things that Tamir clearly has not done. Why does he need our help?"

"That is a very good point, with 'supposed to be' being the operative words…And he has shown that he still has a brittle human mind. If you had seen him over the last two to three days as I have, you would have agreed that he has been somewhat weakened both physically and mentally and more prone to errors. We can be the adults and civilized ones in this if he wants to remain all emotional about it."

"What if he was shot at, do you want us to be in the line of fire, too?"

"I do not believe it would be that easy to hit him with a bullet," the chief said. "He is still more spiritually powerful than your average human, and you have agreed as much. I am only saying we should show up and give him some support. All peace warriors are capable of dodging bullets by becoming invisible. You are aware of this."

"I am aware of it, but I have never faced a bullet. It could travel faster than I can go out of sight, especially if my energy is low."

"Well, tidy up, eat some food, and let's go. An opportunity to test it beckons," the chief said. "Who knows, after we win this, he might help convince the venerable ones to endow us with more powers and we won't have to lose any years."

"Just had lunch—and it is now that you are beginning to make sense. Though hard to come by, of the three options for gaining more supernatural power, recommendation from a superior warrior is the one I prefer," Eke said as he sprang off the bed. "I had not thought about it. I was focused only on the venerable ones choosing to give me more powers as payback for recruiting and maintaining more peace warriors into the fold, which, I must say, is not that easy. The one I finally succeeded in recruiting two days ago, Mr. Odimegwu, killed himself early yesterday morning."

Shaking his head, "It was strange of him to do that. He was on his way to becoming spiritually powerful and wealthy," Chief Madu said, and after a momentary lull, he added, "But come, your compound is way too quiet for someone with young children and, again, on a Sunday!"

Hanging his head as he dressed up and avoiding eye contact with the chief, "Uche and Adaobi have gone to stay with their mother's parents. I had to send them away. They were crying for their mother too much. They will be there for some time, and they will be going to school from there also. Udo is in his room, doing his homework but also has seemed a bit under the weather since I rubbed Mama Uche out. Shouldn't you be wearing your chieftaincy outfit to see the king on a matter this serious?"

"We are not going there on official business," the chief said. "I hope this is not your way of abandoning her children for good."

With a half shrug, "Who knows what will happen? I am busy, and as Mama Udo sees looking after them as 'slavery,' they are better off there."

"Hmm, I see. By the way, where is she?"

"Kitchen…Washing up lunch stuff."

Chapter 57

Being the odd one out amongst all the Pneumas, Adaku found no usefulness in their adventure wherein they'd continued to prevent King Ajutu and his spiritual associates from inhuming their remains.

"Still can't see or hear Ijeoma," Adaku said in a quiet mumble as she watched Adure and Adure's catch, who had Isioma on a piggyback ride, walk down a path that opened out into a glade to be greeted by squirrels that darted in and out of sight and raced across the dell, romping through the trees.

Existing next to a smooth, snaking streamlet that was lined sporadically along its low bank by saplings and had two-thirds sunk stepping stones dotted across it as well as eddies of mist at its periphery, the opening was also proud with boulders. Saturated with water, the fresh air was tainted by hints of the scents of earth, animal scat, dew, the mustiness of moss, and the fusty tang of decay.

Adaku had observed Isioma and Adure's every activity except for the very short moment Adure had vamped the young man into having an intimate encounter with her; though Adaku knew what had transpired as it unexpectedly did enkindle her own desires.

Following that awkward moment, she'd continued to track them through to when he'd tied his unclean underwear over the bullet holes and successfully stemmed the bleeding from Isioma's right thigh. She'd also noted how the young man had seemed happy to be in the company of three sylphlike belles—hence the reason he'd tried his utmost to impress them by not complaining about being exhausted from traveling tens of kilometers on rugged terrain, much as he was obviously way-worn.

"I am in your debt, ladies, for agreeing to stop for me to get some rest," the young man said. "Thank you."

Resting the big book atop one of the featureless rocks, Ijeoma bent over the babbling brook to wash her face in its clean water as Adure helped the huffing, loose-limbed man set Isioma down on the ground, leaning her back against the same, large, smooth-faced stone.

Wiping her hands on her hips, Ijeoma looked up at the interstices of the arching trees to enjoy the little sunshine that filtered through.

Chumming around, Adure and her catch took their time to wash their faces and drink water.

Ijeoma grabbed the tome, settled down next to weary Isioma, and, as an afterthought, "Would you like a drink of water?" she asked, looking rightward at Isioma.

Isioma shook her head, and Ijeoma began thumbing through the hardback, opening it at near the middle.

Straightening up and staring at the young man, "Can't believe that we've come this far, and I still don't know your name," Adure said.

Still squatted down at the bank, he looked up, "Well, Adure, there was no time for a formal introduction, though I learnt your names as you ignored me and spoke to one another," he said as his eyes darted from her, and he picked up a small pebble, skimmed it across the water, and watched as it glanced off its surface and hit a tree trunk downstream. "My name is Kenna Ogene."

Nodding, "Nice to finally know, Kenna," Adure said. "Did you like what we did back there?"

Smiling as he got to his feet, Kenna nodded, "But it was way too quick… I prefer to take my time with it."

"We can take our time with the next one," Adure said, gave him a sleek smile that emphasized her words and turned around to be by his side, reaching out her right hand to take his left hand. "Shall we?"

Still all smiles, "Uh-huh," he said and laced his fingers into hers.

"We'll be right back, girls," Adure said without looking back at the duo. And setting off at a jog with Kenna in tow, she herded him into the woods in the wink of an eye.

Looking up from the page she'd been perusing as they disappeared, "We have a long way to go, and we cannot run because of Isioma," Ijeoma shouted, then smiled, and with a sidelong glance at Isioma, she said, "Would you like to hear more about the pregnancy thing that I discovered in this book, which Adure is trying her hardest to accomplish? And you too ought to attain."

Isioma's head moved in an almost-imperceptible nod.

"Okay," Ijeoma said. "Hear this: '[W]hen it comes to a situation where a negergized-lifeforce inhabits a body that didn't originally belong to it, it seems that one certain way of claiming the body forever, well, at least until age or health defines the body's mortal limit, is by allowing a separate life to grow within that body. Of course, pregnancy as a way of achieving this phenomenon is practically possible only in female body occupations. Nonetheless, this phenomenon has also been documented in male body occupations; it having occurred through a process that can also occur in female occupations when passing through the zone of unification; the last such case having been reported in the early 1970s…' um, the rest of this is not relevant…' Then listen to this: '[T]he duration of such a pregnancy would depend on what the usual gestation of the different components of the chimera is. For example, if the pregnancy resulted from fertilization that occurred between an ailuranthropic lifeform whose feline form usually has a pregnancy length of 90- to 100-odd days, and a human with a usual nine-month gestation, the chimera offspring may be born anytime between 90 days and nine months inclusively after the onset of the pregnancy. This would depend on which component of each of the paired genes dominates the other…' So, it means that I could give birth anytime now—and not knowing when exactly that would be, my plan is to run away from the king, give birth, and only return to him if it is a boy."

Giving a nonchalant nod, "What does it say about resisting control?" Isioma spoke with a voice that had a catch to it.

Gesturing with her right index finger, "Hold on, I marked it," Ijeoma said and leafed through the book for a little. "Here: '[I]t has been documented that in body occupations in which a negergy was the occupying lifeforce and the body succeeded in producing an offspring, that that negergy not only was able to stay in that body until the body's life limit was reached but had also gone on to take full control of its own existence during the body's lifespan…'"

"It looks like the king had been reading those highlighted portions in the book when he made the request of the queen of the coast to make us," Isioma said.

"He definitely was," Ijeoma said. "It was the yellow markings he made over the sentences about felines, humans, and pregnancy length that drew my attention to those paragraphs when I first rifled through the book."

"We cannot be so sure that it was him who left those marks," Isioma said. "It may also have been Adaku."

"Possible it was Adaku, but unlikely considering that we were made felines," Ijeoma said. "And the king existed long before Adaku."

"I wish I knew if it was Adaku who did," Adaku murmured to herself, then, sensing that Somto must be done with his latest thrill as he'd begun to yearn for her, she switched off from watching and listening to Isioma, began drifting away and got lost to view.

A little while later, a sense of expectation hung in the almost-vacuum surrounding Somto as Adaku crept up on him, focusing her energy. Though he couldn't see her, he felt her presence and passion for him as the latter had begun to increase further in intensity. It wasn't until she planted a peck on his cheek did he realize that she was quite near to him. Concentrating his impetus in a snap, he shut his eyes and turned his head toward where he expected her face would be. Closing his arms around where he hoped her body would be, he puckered up his lips.

As she materialized in that instant, his lips met hers, and she brushed hers against his for a beat, then closing her eyes, she locked lips with him.

Enfolded in a visible flame of passion that shone through their smoky form, they became the light of each other's existence not just in a metaphoric sense but also in literal terms.

Letting each other go a little and maintaining strong eye contact with minimal blinking, "You said we would not be able to participate in this sort of intimacy," Somto whispered.

"Wasn't aware of how creative we could be then, and I was also getting to know you…Now I know anything is possible and I want it all with you."

"Did your maiden friends get you hot with passion?"

"No, it was you who got me hot with passion. Adure merely made me stop fighting it. I have strong feelings for you, Somto."

With a beam and a glow to his cheeks, "I have strong feelings for you, too, Adaku," Somto said, and after a short moment, asked "And what do you mean by 'strong feelings'?"

Resting the side of her head on his chest, she said, "It means that you have become an important part of me, and I will do my utmost not to hurt you. What does it mean to you?"

"That I have decided, consciously, to give you every part of me—my all in every sense of the word 'all.' That I will be patient with you and tolerate you…That I would treat you as I want to be treated—which is with respect…And that I will continue to decide to be this way with and to you."

Locking gazes, for a few beats, they embraced and, as each submitted to the other's will, began to float away. Wrapped in each other's arms, they gradually faded out of sight.

Chapter 58

Arriving at the turn-off from Farm Road to Palace Road East, Eke and Chief Madu sighted Sergeant Fric and stopped.

Their first instinct was to keep out of sight behind shrubs that weren't at all remote from Eke's shrine.

"Looks like the king has decided to enlist military men," Eke whispered. "So, there you go—the reason for the gunshots you heard…Maybe as a way to deter those who are against him."

"He did not mention the use of military men to me," the chief said. "He promised to keep me in the loop."

"I think the king is safe. We should get back to minding our own businesses, and I have things to sort out. I travel to Agudagu first thing tomorrow."

Tilting his head, Chief Madu's skepticism was apparent, "I do not believe that he would contract soldiers without telling us chiefs. It is an act that requires agreement amongst us. Spiritual mission aside, we are still a polity with laws that he knows ought to be obeyed. My instinct tells me something is off. Let's go and check."

"Well, there is only one way to enter the palace without being noticed by the military men," Eke said. "And just in case those soldiers also happen to be against the king, I think it is better we port ourselves into the most likely place His Majesty would be around this time of the day."

"I agree," the chief said. "And that would be his caucus room, studying that massive book."

And the iniquitous duo grew unseen in no time.

Chapter 59

Chief Madu and Eke were left aghast, standing face to face with Odera and Namdi respectively.

Had they walked through the palace whilst remaining invisible rather than teleport straight into the caucus room, they might've had time to prepare for what they met, considering that Ijezie had made us aware of their pending arrival through Ejizu and the queen.

Slack-jawed, they screwed their necks around and scanned about. Looking like men who'd become caught in the traps of their own deviousness, they gazed at the rest of us, perhaps trying to see if the king was also in the room or wondering about what we might've done to him.

Glancing at each other for a moment and with split-second timing, Odera, and Namdi lunged at the men, grabbing them in exceptionally tight chokeholds.

They'd probably, in the prior moment, concluded that they mightn't be fast—or effective—enough in using their machetes, given how very close the men had been to them.

Gasping for air, the men failed in their attempts to become invisible, as their energy stores declined fast, given their precarious oxygen supply. Chief Madu managed, though, to keep his wits about him enough to thumb a button on his Mkpó. And in one swift and desperate movement, jabbed Odera in the right thigh with a knife that had thrust out of the walking stick's distal end, then flailed it overhead across Namdi's face in a sort of right-to-left clockwise arc.

Wincing, Odera reflexly shoved the chief away and moved back a pace whilst clutching at his right thigh. Transfixed by the pain in Odera's face, I flinched as Namdi moved his head back, ducked, and missed the knife's swing, unwittingly loosening the chokehold on Eke. Each drawing a quick gulp of air, Eke and Chief Madu vanished into thin air without waiting to regain their breath just as the captain squeezed the trigger of his gun; the shot blasting through the empty space that Chief Madu had occupied and whizzing past Odera by millimeters as he bent over to examine his thigh. The bullet smacking into a hardcover book on the shelf.

For a brief period, I hesitated as my heart pounded and I could hear nothing else but my own breathing. Then I moved toward Odera. As I approached him, he ripped open his pants' right leg and looked up at me with wide eyes.

Seeing the gash in his thigh begin to repair itself, I was stunned. Stopping dead in my tracks, I gaped at him in incredulity, then at the others behind me whose heads hung slack in attitudes of despair as I pointed at the muscled-up part above Odera's knee.

Seeming to be none the wiser about the reason for the occurrence, Odera shut his eyes and opened them again to look. The proximal segment wound had completely mended. Save for the blood smear on the identical khaki combat pants Anika had provided for him, Namdi, and me, there would've been no sign of any injury.

Looking over to Namdi just as Namdi straightened up, "Something happened to me," Odera said as he pulled out King Ajutu's chair and sunk himself in it, revealing his left arm and hand. "See, no sign of any wounds. Must be related either to the contact I had with Jadue's acid, or the burn to my hair by Kadiye, or both. More likely to be the acid though—it was soon after it happened that my injuries began to heal."

Shaking my head as I arrived to crouch down before Odera, "Now is the time to tell everyone," I stated with strong eye contact, pointing at his left wrist. "What's happened to you has to do with that watch. He knew you were his, and he gave you powers."

Walking toward us, "Who knew what?" Prince Ikuku asked as Odera leaned back.

Odera hesitated before he elected to disclose what he knew, "Everyone needs to stay calm," he said, motioning for us to reclaim our seats and we sat on the edges of our chairs. After a long, contemplative silence, he said, "I am going to keep this simple: as a little boy, King Ajutu always called me 'son,' and I thought it was just his way of endearing himself to me, but about an hour or so ago, I learnt that he is my father and I—"

Shuffling in his chair and sitting back, "I won't pretend that I am surprised, because I am not," Prince Ikuku interjected. "I would believe anyone who says Ajutu is his or her father due to the way he conducted himself with women. I did wonder why you were not as sad coming out of your back-neighbor's house as you had been before going in there. Now I know."

Standing up and walking toward Odera as the queen canted her head to observe Odera with intensity, "That doesn't mean he didn't care about the man he knew as his father," I said with tenderness in my eyes. "It's only natural to worry less when there's no need to."

Leaning back in her seat in surprise, "Now I see the resemblance," Queen Nena said. "I can't say I didn't have my suspicions going by the way he forced me to let you come to our home to play with Ejizu, and your mother was all too willing to let you spend a lot of time with us."

I arrived next to Odera and linked my right arm with his left arm.

Odera continued, "And Nkem is right, I believe that he gave me his kind of powers—"

"Which should now be to our benefit," Captain Iduto quickly added as though he were trying to reassure himself that we then had a solid plan of action.

"Though I don't know its full extent, it is not the kind of powers that I would have asked for had I the choice."

"Yes, you mightn't have chosen whatever power he gave you, just like we don't choose to be born into this wicked world, but you can dictate what you do with it, just like we decide what we do with our lives for the most part once we've escaped childhood if we don't get killed," I said with passion, then glanced at the queen before darting a sidelong gaze at Odera, locking eyes with him as I felt my impulsion begin to grow. "Everything possibly happens for a reason. I have this sudden strong feeling, an unshakeable belief that fate—that God has ordained you the one to defeat him. We, on our part, are destined to help you accomplish that, and the children of the shadows are determined to protect us all."

"This is perhaps the best thing that has happened to Akagheli, ever," Namdi said. "We not only have a capable heir to the throne, but we have a superhero in the making, and we shall call him 'The Punisher,' and soon, our island nation of Naïjerland will be on Wakanda's heels."

Chuckles emanated and gales of laughter erupted from us six for a few beats as a feeling of relief descended on the room and then, "Was only teasing," Namdi said, resting a hand on Odera's left shoulder and sensing a similar kind of growing inner strength as I'd just experienced. "We will find a more befitting name that will include 'Prince' in it."

"I believe that Akagheli is better off a democracy," Odera said. "So, thanks, but no thanks. I may be a part-blood prince, but I'm not going to be king."

"Let us assume that we defeated Ajutu, which is ever more likely considering that I now have a nephew who, it seems, has the wherewithal to do so," Prince Ikuku said. "Akagheli will still need a steadying hand during the transition."

"That is easy," Odera didn't hesitate. "Her Majesty, Queen Nena, will be that hand. We will all rally around her."

Prince Ikuku looked over at the queen who nodded and shrugged. She was exceptionally dumbfounded, "What more would I learn about Ajutu? And about you all?" she mused. "And no kingdom in Igboland has ever accepted the rule of just a queen, and Akagheli won't be the first."

"Then Prince Ikuku will act as the king," Odera said hurriedly.

"Good. No qualms with that," Prince Ikuku said with a half shrug. "I will do whatever it takes to get Akagheli thriving. Now, where is Ajutu?"

Driven by impetus that had materialized out of the blue and seemed to grow very quickly within me, as everything else began to make sense regarding how I'd begun to better deal with Dike's demise in such a short time period, "You all stay here and wait for him," I said, grabbing Namdi by the hand and thrusting for the door. "Namdi and I will go after Chief Madu and Mr. Isigwe. Captain, I need a rifle. Odera, I'll take your bike."

Looking astounded, to say the least, Odera wondered about the origin of my sudden audacity and when the heck I'd learnt to shoot a gun or ride a motorbike. But before he could articulate his thoughts, perhaps to dissuade me from putting myself in peril, I'd already swung the door open.

And dragging Namdi in tow through it as Captain Iduto rose to his feet and grabbed his handie-talkie, we arrived at the caucus-area passage in a trice.

"Private Dabir," the captain spoke into his communications device. "I need two semis immediately. I am on my way to you. Out."

Not wanting to miss a probably ephemeral opportunity to confront the king, Odera stopped himself from coming after me.

Getting onto the main passage, I set off at a jog. Against his wish, Namdi's slow steps changed to leaps. Moving abreast and mirroring my speed as the captain maintained a bounding stride behind us, Namdi started: "How do you even know where they are?"

"I don't," I said. "But I know where they'll eventually be. We'll wait there for them, if need be. Grab a rifle and head to Chief's house. Your machete may not be sufficient. I'll head to Mr. Isigwe's. Stay hidden and shoot at sight. This battle can't be over if those two and many others like them remain alive. We're never going to see all of them congregated in one place, so we have to take them out piecemeal."

"Many others?" Namdi inquired, sounding bewildered.

"It appears that anyone who has killed for Mkpátáku possesses the sort of power we just saw those two men display, and you already know that where Dike and Bute are, there are many like them."

Shaking his head, "Going with all guns blazing is reckless," Namdi said. "I have a bad feeling about doing this without Odera."

Standing pat, "To be able to do something about the evil in our community and not do it is reckless," I protested. "I will feel horrible if I don't do this and won't forgive myself. Odera can't be everywhere at the same time. He already has his hands full as it is and needs us to take a share of the load."

Chapter 60

Surrounded by no breath of wind and beneath a sky that had become less leaden because of enfeebled dust haze, the atmosphere was relatively noiseless with no trees swaying or birds singing aloud. Well, until I made Odera's motorbike's engine cough, wheeze, and roar into life as Namdi stood by his bike and took his time to get moving.

Carrying a rifle with its muzzle up across my back with the aid of a padded carry-strap sling, I settled my feet on the heavy two-wheeler's broad footboards. Revving it as its wheels shrieked, and the privates and sergeants continued to gander at me in incredulity, I tore down Palace Road East like grim death.

Reaching the junction, I screeched it leftward around the corner at top speed. Slowing down, I jinked the twists and turns on Farm Road left and right and, with incomplete success, made attempts at skirting small tracts of mud that were scattered here and there. With the bike bouncing and joggling on the earth path's bumpy surface, I blasted onto Mr. Isigwe's compound, leaving dust trails.

Surprised at, though gladdened by my newfound ability, I wondered what more abilities I'd been able to extract from Odera.

Braking hard, I brought the sporty vehicle to a squealing halt, tracking the concrete ground up with dirty tire prints. Positioning it on its kickstand, I sprang off it as its engine thrummed and swung the rifle around to get it at the ready as I ran toward Mr. Isigwe's room.

He wasn't there when I barged into his dwelling. Dashing out, I headed to the kitchen as Mama Udo came running toward me. She probably heard the whine of the motorcycle's engine.

Stopping in her tracks as she saw me with the rifle, she turned on her heel, lifted her arms, and prostrated herself on the concrete ground, "Please, don't hurt me, please."

"I don't care about you," I blurted out as I surged forward around her and, with rampant dislike, discharged the semi-automatic rifle wildly into the air with its carry-strap sling for shooting support and my finger planted firmly on the trigger to show my determination. "You'll live to see how the evil that you've been a major part of will come after you."

"Please, don't hurt him," she shouted. "He has no energy left, and he is trying to eat."

You must be kidding. So that he'd then have enough energy to fight me? Not a chance!

Ignoring her, I entered the rectangular, fully walled, door-less, utilitarian kitchen, which had open windows in each of its four walls, just as weary Papa Udo's attempts at passing out of sight continued to fail him.

With a slab of bread in his right hand, he seemed to have hung back in the shelter of the kitchen upon the realization that he'd already expended most of his available energy perhaps during his last apportation and needed to re-energize by eating, which was a quicker way, than by sleeping it off.

Making one attempt at transforming into a two-legged dragon with a rooster's head, he gave up, "Spare me, please, I beg of you," he said as he made a sudden move toward me with my eyes following his every action. "In the name of—"

Squeezing on the gun's trigger before he could complete his sentence without my body kicking back with its recoil, I took no chances as I was unsure whether he'd eventually succeed and for fear of what he might do to me on becoming that creature, considering that he didn't spare Mama Uche.

Instinctively dropping the thick slice of bread and stretching out his arms to block the discharge, the multiple blasts sent him flying diagonally upward and backward to land hard against the kitchen's back wall.

"For Dike," I said, the words erupting from me in an angry rush as I released another set of bullets.

"For Mama Uche," I said and let fly even more shots.

"For Ijezie." And with a final burst of gunfire, "For all the others that I don't know."

With his back hard pressed against the wall, he dropped, smearing blood on it. Knocking off kitchen utensils and clattering them to the floor, he landed limply atop a cabinet, making the wooden cupboard groan. Coughing out blood, he stared wide-eyed at the gaping holes on the front part of his torso, most of which were in the left side of his chest, just about the exact position I'd seen a knife sticking out of Dike's body. Then, he looked at me as his lifeforce gradually diminished, and I was still poised. As if to say something, he perhaps waffled as his throat rattled; and with a succession of gasps, he breathed his last.

Starting to feel in much better spirits, "One down," I murmured. Tossing the rifle over my shoulder, I wheeled around. And Mama Udo had whisked out of sight.

Looking around the compound, Uche and Adaobi were nowhere to be seen, confirming what Ijezie had told Dike, and neither was Udo nor his mother.

No chance that I will leave Akagheli without my godchildren.

Adjusting the weapon across my back and mounting the bike, I screeched out of the compound. Arriving onto Farm Road, I stopped for a moment as I heard Mama Udo and Udo scurrying in the opposite direction and screaming for help.

"This is only the beginning," I muttered, letting my voice trail off, then zoomed off toward Palace Road East. "Wonder who will consider providing her any aid or comfort when everyone gets wind of what they've been doing."

Chapter 61

Wondering how Namdi was fairing, I took a left turn into a vicinity that was spotted with tall coconut trees and dwarf kernel plants.

I got onto the straight paved alley, which led toward the four chiefs' bungalows. It was strewn with yellowed fronds and in line with the gap between the two middle houses. Then, I caught sight of Namdi looking up and aiming his rifle but not getting any shots off.

Following his stare, I saw another abomination through the burning, long-feathered leaves at the peaks of the trees. At once, my hands felt clammy and my breaths burst in and out, "Keep calm," I told myself.

A massive fire-breathing creature that fluttered its wings hung high up in the air over the roof of Chief Madu's house. With a reptilian torso, it had a dragon's head and wings, two limbs, and a long, barbed tail with an arrow-shaped tip.

Nearing Namdi, I could see the occupants of two of the three other chiefs' residences sneaking a peek at us from behind their curtains. The inhabitants of the bungalow to the immediate right of Chief Madu's appeared not to be at home.

Angular-faced Chief Ikeme was the only person who came out maybe in his attempt to find out the reason we were disturbing his neighborhood. He'd see the creature and would quickly run back into his home, slamming the front door shut and pulling his curtains tight.

Switching off the engine and as I jumped off it, I let the motorbike rest on its left side. Whipping out my auto-loading gun with my trembling hands, my right index finger found its way to the trigger in no time and blazed the beast with bullets.

With sidelong glances at Namdi, "Why aren't you firing at it?"

With his usual sangfroid, "It's no use wasting any more ammunition," Namdi said. "He absorbed all of my shots."

Feeling rooted to the spot, "Where the heck did it come from?" I shrieked with a shrill voice, looking all around but mostly behind me, scared stiff.

"That's Chief Madu. When I blasted through his door, he saw me, then attempted to vanish but failed. Instead, he ran out of his house through the back and changed to that. I saw his arms become those wings before he flew off but didn't see the rest of the transformation as I ran back out through the front door. So, that is him. Good news on the other chap?"

With a mulish expression on my face, "Snuffed out," I said as I let a few more fruitless shots fly at the hovering dragon in frustration. "He tried to change into a similar creature but with a cock's head, and I gave him no chance. On my way here, Dike said Somto called it a cockatrice when Ijezie described it to him."

Perhaps in a display of his intimidating power on sighting me and perchance because of the disdain he felt toward me for being obstinate at firing at it, the beast emitted a threatening growl and a loud roar.

"I'm guessing it ignited the burning tree."

"Yes. He tried a few times to set me ablaze, got angry after Bute absorbed it all, and struck the treetops."

"Why isn't he flying away?"

"Well, my guess is that he has realized that we can't hurt him. Also, this happens to be his home, and where else would he be safe? Perhaps he also doesn't have much energy to fly since it was difficult for him to disappear. He might also be concerned for his wife. She fainted on seeing him change to that. There is really no way to be certain."

"Dike just said Bute described this creature to Somto, and Somto called it a Wyvern. What do we do?"

"I don't know whether knowing exactly what it is makes any difference," Namdi said. "I say we head back to the palace and rethink our strategy with Odera."

My nerves on full alert and the front and underarms of my sweater sousing in perspiration, "Knowing what it is might help us discern its nemesis," I said, able to draw in a stronger sniff of my body odor as my nerves went on full alert and the front and underarms of my sweater became almost soused in perspiration, "Let's," I said, backing away and sweeping beads of sweat from my forehead with my left hand. "And thanks to Chief Madu, his neighbors have begun to wake up to his hole-and-corner ways. Word can't wait to spread throughout the village."

Arriving at his bike, "More people will likely now be thrown into jeopardy," Namdi said as he bestrode it and started the engine. "We should have waited for Odera."

Lifting my hefty motorcycle with ease and mounting it, "We took the right steps. Stands now to reason we've got to get our acts together and finish this quickly," I said as I cast a further glance at the buildings and saw that all window shades had been drawn.

"I hope Odera has the abilities to match a flying beast," Namdi added as he waited for me to ride ahead of him.

Descending from the air to alight on the ground behind his house as he saw us leave, the wyvern changed back to Chief Madu.

Chapter 62

At the same time, with faces wreathed in smiles, and skin and clothes smudged with dust, Adure and Kenna appeared from the woods, hugging each other around the waist to stop at their assembly point.

Slumbering like content newborns, Isioma had the left side of her head and neck pillowed on her left arm that rested on the book atop Ijeoma's lap, whilst Ijeoma had the right side of her head and neck on Isioma's right flank.

Due to a strengthening haze of dust, the sun had become a huge, deep-red disk in the sky, and almost everything as far as the eye could see continued to be a study in the shades of rufous.

Whistling and swaying somewhat on his feet, "What now?" Kenna asked, glancing rightward at Adure.

With a deep, gratifying sigh, "We wake them up and continue on our trek," Adure replied, casually anchoring her right hand on his right hand that rested on her hip.

"How come you don't know where we are going, yet you follow Ije blindly?"

"You wouldn't understand. We've been together for so long and have submitted to one another's will. We go where any of us goes without asking questions."

"Wow! Wish I could find friends this loyal, caring, and daring."

"It's indeed rare amongst your kind," Adure said. "Many are selfish. I've come to realize that much."

"What does that mean, 'your kind'? You mean men?" he said, sounding addled.

Adure almost shook her head before she changed it to a weak nod. "Never mind, though," she eased herself from his hold and headed toward her fellow maidens. "Let's get on with it. Dusk falls very quickly these days and even quicker within the forest."

Responding to Adure's shake of her shoulder, Ijeoma passed from deep sleep to wide awake in a flash. She seemed to feel an oddity about rising to ambient forest sounds as it compared with the sensual mood that she'd been accustomed to within the king's great chamber. Overcome for a moment with acute nostalgia, it fleeted away on hearing Isioma's groan of anguish.

Rising to her feet abruptly, "Can I help you up?" Ijeoma said as Isioma continued in her seemingly fruitful attempt to stand up.

"Not yet," Isioma said through searing pain that shot up her right thigh. "Let me give it a try rising by myself. I feel a bit stronger."

Experiencing a flash of her own kind of wisdom, Adure paced forward and whispered into Isioma's ear, "Now that you're stronger, do you want Kenna to get you pregnant? If you miss this opportunity, you'd have to wait until the middle of February, and he might not be here."

Shaking her head in almost slow motion as if it hurt a lot, and barely able to focus, "Not now," Isioma murmured with a frustrated half shrug. "Not while I am still in pain. We would have to keep him till then or find someone else. It should not be that difficult. The men around here are easily anyone's."

Her leg still weak, Isioma stumbled and fell against the rock. Ijeoma and Adure tried to help her up, but she declined.

"I will do it on my own," Isioma groaned.

Getting to her feet again, she hobbled, then waddled toward the stream that meandered further away between bosky banks dominated by reeds and rushes whilst Adure and Ijeoma as well as Kenna, who remained a few paces behind, watched on.

Unable to reach down for a drink as she leaned over the bank, she transmuted into her cougar. Bending all limbs, the right hind one in an awkward stance, she just about balanced on the slope. Surveying the vicinity for a moment, the slender cat voiced a low-pitched growl before it dipped its shoulders, neck, and head down and lapped its tongue atop the water surface.

Frozen to the bone, Kenna's eyes went wide. And shaking like a leaf, he backed away. Gazing around and appearing like he sensed danger, his left heel tripped over tangled mass of undergrowth, and he went down, landing backward with a crash, crushing dry twigs and hitting the back of his head with a hard smack against an elevated root.

Hearing him groan, Adure looked back at him for a moment. Flashing him a placid smile, she looked forward again.

Raising his head, Kenna rubbed his occiput. Looking at his right palm, there was bright red blood. Ignoring it, he gandered at the stream whilst wiping his right palm on his pants. Isioma was limping lightly back toward the rock to join Adure and Ijeoma who continued to watch her with less and less concern.

In his own time, Kenna got to his feet, still touching the back of his head, and, each time, he felt less and less pain as the ooze of blood slacked off. Unbeknownst to him, his wound was gradually sealing.

With a wan smile, Isioma walked across the space, looking down at her right thigh, stamping her right foot, testing the strength in her right leg. Directly opposite the brook, she got to the limit of the clearing, at where the woods began, and about-faced. Ambling back toward the rock, "We should make a start on the rest of our trek," Isioma said as she ripped off the bloodied underwear around her upper right thigh and flung it away. "I can now manage. Looks like the wounds have healed."

With thumbs-up to Isioma, "Discard him if you are done. I sense trouble with him," Ijeoma whispered to Adure, then walked toward her book.

Closing in on the group, wide-eyed, "Did you see what I just saw?" Kenna said, motioning toward Isioma. "Isioma becoming a puma?"

Picking up her book from the ground, Ijeoma contemplatively bit her lower lip as she and Adure exchanged knowing glances.

"Nope," Adure and Ijeoma chorused with bullish demeanors without looking at him. "What you saw was a forest illusion—a trick of the light that filters through. I won't give it another thought."

It was obvious that they'd perfected those lines and had used them innumerable times.

With a shrug, "I guess," he said. "So, Ije, where are we headed? You should be able to tell me even if not the others. As a man, I can protect you three."

Gazing at each other for a moment, the maidens shared knowing smiles. And not wanting to meet his eyes, "Somewhere you have never been and probably would and should not want to be," Ijeoma's reply was a retort that rang with contempt. "And don't call me Ije. To you, it shall be Ijeoma."

Motioning to the other maidens, "Shall we?" Ijeoma added.

Feeling more and more uncomfortable, Kenna squished his eyebrows together at Ijeoma's tone of voice as it dawned on him that he'd overstayed his welcome. Glancing around, he shaped what he'd say, "I must head back home.

It's clear you lot no longer need me. Glad to have helped Isioma. Nice to have met you, Adure. You can check up on me anytime. You know where I live. So long!"

Adure tried to go after him as he turned on his heel, but Ijeoma grabbed her by the arm, "Leave him be," she grumbled. "You do not want to get too attached to him. He is not one of us."

Muttering a self-reproof as hair on the back of his neck bristled, he walked off in a huff and cleaved a path through the woods.

"You don't like him?" Adure said.

"Does not matter whether I like him or not," Ijeoma said in a muted whisper. "Do you think he is going to stay quiet when he figures out who we are? That what he saw was real? What will happen then? We cannot trust that he would not want to get our bodies destroyed. Can you bank on him not doing so? Your guard will be down with him around and so would ours, and we will not see it coming."

Whilst he continued on his way, razing dry shrubs to the ground as he gained distance from the maidens, Adure's eyes met Isioma's and Isioma shook her head.

"You're quite right, Ije," Adure said. "We'll find someone else for Isioma."

"Good," Ijeoma blared.

Chapter 63

In the interim, scores of kilometers north-northwest of Akagheli, within a clearing in the middle of thick bush that spread as far as the eye could see—a countrified ambience with no residential huts, or buildings around, King Ajutu seemed lost as he bent over and leaned his elbows on his thighs, staring at his Akupé.

Creaking in the wind, the shrine he was sat in was dark, diabolically embellished, outmoded, mud-walled, and thatch-roofed, and had no clear-cut trails that led to it.

Shaking his head, "Success is fast slipping through my fingers," the king murmured amidst heavy breathing without shifting his gaze. "It had been within my reach—two days ago when that woman was still at the palace and I could have taken care of her myself, but I trusted Odera. I was such a stupid fool.

"Nothing feels right anymore—I no longer control the things I once did. My number-one henchman has deserted me, my number-one maiden and my supernatural henchmen are rubbed out, my other maidens have begun to hide things from me, my health is less and less in fine fettle, I have lost more years to live for nothing, the venerable ones have flatly refused to partake in my ordeal, I am on the verge of losing the loyalty of my subjects and likely my kingship, and, to top it all off, I have no preferred heir apparent."

Sitting next to him, deep in the shadows, atop ridged-up earth, his oblong-faced host, who looked equally as spent as him and tried to catch his breath, put his right arm around the king and gave him a brief consoling pat on his right shoulder.

As his breathing normalized, the king raised his voice: "Though we have not achieved any success," he said. "I am thankful to you, Mr. Udochi, for traveling with me whereas others made excuses, and I will make them pay."

Still huffing, "Not at all," Mr. Udochi's deep voice echoed. "Please, don't blame those who refused to go with you…They must have had good reasons. We are one in this brotherhood."

"We shall see," the king said. "I had thought it would be different in *Idumeli* village than it was in Akagheli, but I was wrong. Wishful thinking, perhaps."

"I was at six shrines with you. How many have you managed to cover so far?"

Still staring at his Akupé, "17 all together," King Ajutu said with a wavering voice. "Not even scratched the surface yet—still have at least 690 to cover across Igboland, going by what my map indicates."

"Not advisable to do that, and I won't recommend it if you asked me. The outcome will be the same," Mr. Udochi said. "Those spirits are very coordinated, determined, and industrious…I mean, look at how they stopped every bulldozer operator we came across from taking up our offer even with the promise of doubling or even tripling their pay. They are not budging an inch, and we have no powers over them. If I were you, I would conserve my energy for the fight against the humans. I believe that if all those people you mentioned are rubbed out, the spirits of these children will have no choice but to lay low. After all, we only started hearing of them in the last couple of days even though they must have been in existence since as far back as when the ritual first happened, and we are talking decades here. It appears that this Okanka woman is their driving force, and once she is silenced for good, I believe there would not be another who will be as outspoken as she has been, and if there happens to be another who comes to you to report as she did, we will be in a position to better handle them."

Rubbing the back of his neck, King Ajutu drew in a huge breath, then exhaled. "I appreciate your wisdom in this, honestly, I really do, and, in theory, it is a perfect plan," he said with a strained voice. "However, I am up against not just the woman but a renegade who is perhaps physically the strongest man alive, and the irony is that I wished for him to be so. His powers continue to evolve, and he can spread it to people and things around him. To even begin to consider defeating him, the advancement of his powers must be stopped by first cutting out no more than the black area on his left wrist. As I understand it, the directive from the most venerable one was that '… Odera's indestructible machete must not only be in the possession of the one who must be in complete opposition of him, but can only achieve its goal if used to extract the revelatory scar, and done within the zone…For out of it his powers came with fierceness and to it may they be cast aside without his blood…'"

"So, it can only be done with that weapon at the place of its origin, in a process that must result in no blood spill and the excised scar must not be accompanied by any normal skin?" Mr. Udochi summarized.

The king nodded, "How likely is it that one would be surgically precise with an instrument as big as a machete? How possible is it to be exact if he is not unconscious? How can he be put to sleep when he is too strong to be captured and too smart to be deceived? It is a terrible no-win situation."

With an intense, cold stare as his own words settled in, King Ajutu seemed to experience a sinking feeling.

"You are equally powerful," said Mr. Udochi.

Scrunching up his face, then releasing it to regain some calm, "Supernaturally, but not physically," the king said. "I am told that because my human body is weak, I can only become nearly as physically strong as him when I transform, but then I lose supernatural abilities once the transformation is complete. The venerable ones' objective, it appears, was to prevent bringing to existence an all-powerful being."

"But why do the venerable ones dangle the idea of utopia for peace warriors but make it so difficult, even impossible, to achieve?"

With a hint of a grin, "Julius, it is obvious that you are still a novice peace warrior," the king said, seeming to welcome a discussion on a slightly different subject. "The Evil One makes whatever rules he wants, gives nothing for free, and it is difficult for any human to fully furnish him with all he requires in return for his gifts. It is also as a constant test of our loyalty to him that we must jump through hoops in our quest for power. In the end, since they themselves do not possess everything—considering that they have no physical abilities, only supernatural, they cannot and will not, even if it wasn't nearly impossible, give us everything…There must always be a deficiency, a weakness…And they can't be happy to give what they themselves don't and can't have."

"It has not been two years yet since Rapulu was sacrificed, so you are right that I am still learning," Mr. Udochi said. "Which is why I agreed to go with you, to continue to familiarize myself with our methods, and so that when the time comes, you may also recommend me to the venerable ones for more supernatural powers. And I can see why you've decided to go about this fight this way. But why did you ask for this man to be made like that?"

"I think you are definitely going about your education the right way. About the man, it is a long story, and I will make it very short. After I received my powers in the 'Zone of Unification' as is tradition when one has become a peace warrior because the Evil One has accepted one's oblation after one has sworn to never accept The Prince of Princes while intoning the incantation, I also asked to be made physically strong as part of the mandatory request afforded a spiritual leader, but the venerable ones refused as I have already explained to you. But they would agree to endow any non-peace warrior of my choosing, upon my request, with the powers I had sought for myself. Looking back, I think it was their way to either keep me in check, knowing fully well that humans betray one another easily or inveigle whomever I chose into the netherworld, as they are always looking to get souls on our side. Back in the day, I did not anticipate that things would turn out this way. Had I known!" He paused and shook his head. "Then a boy, I had expected him to grow into a man who would remain loyal until the end, especially because he is also my son—though he is not aware, I think."

"Maybe if you made him aware that you are his father, he might switch allegiances."

After a long, contemplative moment, "Who knows?" the king said. "The way things are, it seems impossible to even snatch Ejizu's bones, which is tangible, from his mother. How can I expect something intangible from someone who has already betrayed me? Can I trust any loyalty from him even if he offers it?"

Heaving a heavy sigh, "So what's the way forward then? What are you thinking?" Mr. Udochi asked. "I have never seen you like this."

Wiping away the mist of perspiration that began to dampen his temples, King Ajutu seemed to feel more and more tense as the moments wore on, "I have never seen myself like this…I am not used to accepting defeat, and in no case ever have I even been close to discussing the possibility of my downfall for that matter," he said, then paused. And with a long, low sigh and appearing distrait, he stood up and patted Mr. Udochi amiably on the right shoulder with his Akupé. "To prepare to fight him. Though I don't know it yet, there is surely a way to get him. I doubt that he can defend against all of my supernatural powers—everything has its nemesis…I must do this as soon as possible before his powers progress even further and he begins to recruit others into his flock…people who will possess similar strength and make this battle many folds more difficult."

Within a blast of smoke, the king vanished without a trace, and, not long after, Mr. Udochi disappeared also.

Chapter 64

In a fit of pique and flashing a black look in the direction of his front door, Chief Madu walked over to where his wife laid motionless on the floor, within the space between the dining area and the hitherto-curtained doorway that closed it off from the kitchen. A sense of dread seemed to have begun to hang over him.

The drape had been inadvertently consumed by the fire he'd breathed when he ran through the entrance to the kitchen as he rippled and transformed.

Muttering to himself and pinching his underlip, "Adane probably has just one more midnight to stay alive. The venerable ones would be demanding her life during tonight's meeting for being in contravention of the first four subsections of section three; after which I would have to end her life before the next meeting, unless I manage to permanently get her away from my personal and social space before that time is up and convince the venerable ones beyond any reasonable doubt that I have done so. Should I rub her out right away and be over with it already? To avoid the embarrassment of being told to do it by the venerable ones in the presence of all and sundry. If not, how would I explain to her the need for us to never again be in each other's company unless she promised not to retain any thoughts or say any words regarding what she saw? Would that not entail letting her know that I am a peace warrior? Could she be trusted to not think about it? And with her tongue as loose as it is, can I trust her not to speak about it?"

Standing astride her with his tense arms akimbo and muscles quivering, he gazed lovingly at her flawless, milky-chocolate-skinned face. "Namdi must shoulder the blame for leaving me in this quandary," he huffed out his overflowing annoyance, then hoisted her over a shoulder as her flowing, luminous, silk-brocade caftan made crinkling sounds. "For now, I must stop her from running out of the house after she wakes up and babbling about what she saw—until I can make up my mind about what to do with her."

Arriving in their bedroom, he laid her facing up on the draped and canopied, massive four-poster bed and, using items of clothing, tied her four limbs separately to the vertical columns.

Stomping off toward the front door, "Death to Namdi and his cohorts," he muttered under his breath as he dematerialized in a puff of smoke.

Chapter 65

Across the road from the chiefs' place of residence, Sergeant Fric felt constrained by his still-small voice to retain his captain's standing order as he watched a swarm of people approach his position.

The clamorous crowd, a few scores strong, were chanting on top of their voices in Igbo[17] language—some of them trailing behind, looking haggard and disheveled. Though the sergeant didn't understand a word they repeated, he was certain they weren't coming that way to make friends.

Whilst the women, some of whom had young children on piggyback rides, brandished sticks, and the older children had sizeable stones in their hands, the men either scuffed their cutlasses against the ground or beat their bare chests with the hands that were clenched around the hafts of the short, curved swords as they stamped their slipshod sandals and slippers, or bare feet hard on the ground.

"Captain, there are protesters heading our way," the sergeant said. "Women and children included. Does your previous command stand? Over!"

"Any weapons? Over!" the captain's voice rang out of the two-way radio.

"Cutlasses, sticks, and stones, but no obvious guns. Over!"

After a momentary pause, he said, "Previous order is overridden. The queen's instruction. Calm them down. We are heading that way. Out."

Chafing at the bit for a fight, the group made their way around the military vehicles to come to a halt before the wide-open palace gateway.

Uttering not a word, Sergeant Fric gestured meaningfully with his rifle for them to keep quiet and settle down. Obliging with immediate effect, the crowd's growing chorus of complaint died to near absolute silence except for the intermittent cries of poorly dressed, half-starved infants and toddlers who

---

[17] One of three major tribes in Nigeria. Also, the main language spoken in Igboland, southeastern Naïjerland.

were more likely irritated by hunger, or the chill in the dry air rather than by the antecedent brouhaha.

Before long, Odera, Namdi, Queen Nena, Prince Ikuku, Captain Iduto, and I arrived in the gateway.

Odera had his hand on the helve of his sheathed, double-edged, 61-centimeter bush machete; the captain had his handgun drawn, whilst I and Namdi—with his sheathed machete dangling by his side—had our rifles at the port.

Believing, at first, that the group had come to complain to the king about what they'd begun to hear regarding Mkpátáku, my mind changed the instant I saw Mama Udo arrive at the helm.

Shaking with rage and pacing back and forth at the front of the muster, Mama Udo's breasts heaved as she retied her wrapper. Rousing herself to a pitch of indignation and eyeing me with open hostility, "She is the one," Mama Udo said, locating me through a mist of tears and pointing at me. "That woman, beside our queen, is the one we have come to report to the king. She came into my home and killed my husband in cold blood with that gun she has by her side. We want the king to sentence her to death and for her to die by that same gun."

The crowd of indigent-looking locals—some of whom continued to yawp and jaw away, and I couldn't make head or tail of their utterances probably because they were made in patois that I still couldn't understand or perhaps due to the fact that nearly my entire focus was on Mama Udo—then chorused again and again: "Sentence her to death…Let her be killed the same way she killed our Chief *Díbià*."

And with her heart whamming away as though a frenetic drummer had begun to exist within her chest cavity, the queen glanced at me, then stepped forward, signaling to address them.

I'd been told that the last time she'd done anything of the sort was decades earlier, at her and her husband's coronation when she had to address the citizens for the first time as their queen. Then, it was all smiles, happiness, and joy, as the potential for prosperity hung in the air and the people were happy to finally welcome a queen after more than two decades without one. Also, that time, there was nothing impromptu about her set speech, which had been prepared weeks prior and tweaked innumerable times to perfection.

The contrast between then and now couldn't have been starker.

But I was glad that she was taking the bull by its horns in reclaiming her spot in Akagheli's story rather than, according to her, while away her often-long days burrowed deep into her bed.

Quietening down, the adults amongst the group paid her their respects as talk continued to flow freely amidst them, albeit in murmurs.

"My fellow Akaghelites, *Ǹdêwó nu o*[18]*,*" the queen started. "I greet you all—"

Interjecting the queen, "Long live our queen," they chanted in concert.

Her heartbeat slowing down, she said, "It is clear why you have all come here today, and anyone who says otherwise does not have their eyes and ears open. You have come to seek justice for one of your own. Am I correct?"

They chorused a noisy, "Yes, Your Majesty."

"One thing I like about our people is that we find ways to stick together even in times of strife. Am I correct?"

"Yes, Your Majesty," they said as one again.

Nodding, "On your way here, you must have also seen the military vehicles that are stationed on this Palace Road, am I correct?" the queen continued. "If you haven't, please take a moment to look around you."

"Yes, Your Majesty," most of them said with one accord, some of them glancing at the sporty bikes and armored four-wheelers.

"Are you aware that even though our country is ruled by the military, the only time we need their help to protect us in our communities is when there is a civil disturbance."

Muttering incomprehensible words that crescendoed for a moment, the group's protests stilled before their chattering faded away as the queen raised her hand.

"By your responses, I can safely assume that you all are not aware, so I will explain to you all what is happening in our village," the queen stated. "As we speak, your king is not here, and we are waiting for him to return. He is traveling around Igboland visiting Mkpátáku shrines. Are you aware that the ritual that his father, King Otubu, abolished a score and ten years ago has continued to exist?"

---

[18] An open hearted, endearing formal greeting in Igbo language that's extended to an individual or a group of people.

Murmuring, the adults amongst the horde glanced at one another in waves as tears of disappointment pricked Mama Udo's eyelids. Ill at ease and backing away whilst the tears slid down her cheeks, Mama Udo flurried through the ruck and blended less conspicuous amongst them, perhaps hoping to be lost in the shuffle.

Chapter 66

Meanwhile, Chief Madu materialized within Mr. Isigwe's room but didn't find him there. Exiting from the dwelling, "Mama Udo? Are you there?" he yelled as he dashed toward the back of the compound, peeking into one dwelling after another. "Where is your husband?"

Arriving in the kitchen, he froze upon sighting one of his closest allies sat atop his kitchen furniture, stiff and stark, with his head bowed and the front part of his clothes riddled with bullet holes and drenched in his own blood.

The chief's cold eyes assumed a flinty stare, and much to his chagrin, he stomped off, "They have clearly thrown down the gauntlet and I have accepted it," he huffed in sheer anger. "I now fully understand why the king feels the way he does. I must go home, quickly re-energize, and show these non-entities who I truly am."

Baring his teeth, he gritted them. Fighting waves of nausea, he passed out of sight.

Chapter 67

In the meantime, recovering from the energy-sapping encounter involving the Wyvern and bracing himself for the possibility of another, Bute waited with bated breath as Dike and Ejizu huddled together with him.

Somto and Adaku were still nowhere in sight. Every Pneuma knew that the couple had remained invisible to keep all and sundry out of what was transpiring between them. Nonetheless, no Pneuma seemed bothered. Somto and Adaku needed their space.

Having expended energy in stopping their fathers and occultists, among others, from burying their remains when it came to the respective shrines of their sacrificial deaths, the rest of the Pneumas preferred to re-energize in preparation for whatever else might come.

With great effort, in addition to what Dike and Ijezie, others included, had achieved at Mr. Isigwe's shrine, the remaining Pneumas had pulled several stunts.

Clearly thrilled to death, "I'm indeed glad that we were able to pull this off," Ejizu said. "That we could give every bulldozer operator significant fright that made many of them not agree to drive to the shrine or caused them to run away after arriving at the destination was a considerable feat."

"I mean, causing the engines of some of those tractors to overheat by transferring energies to them," Dike gushed. "I would never have thought of that all by myself, or the fact that at some locations, we were able to generate strong winds that buffeted the seekers of Pneuma remains and made it impossible for those overpaid, resolute, and unswerving men to dig manually in the absence of any functional tractor."

"The most interesting for me was when a handful of Pneumas were able to get their mothers, siblings, and local, for-hire thugs to rally and drive back the eager men," Bute said. "That capped a memorable adventure for me. A marker has now been set down."

Smiling, "Bute, it appears you had something to say about your sister—sorry that it may have appeared like I was fobbing you off," Ejizu said. "I was only paying attention to my father while he was with Rapulu's dad. What did you want to talk about?"

"Nothing really," Bute said. "I was only concerned for her. She seemed stressed—Odera's mother had been crying inconsolably. I wanted to sound your opinion."

"Being there for her every reasonable need is probably the best she can offer her…For your sister to comfort her when she weeps…Console her when she needs consoling…And listen to her when she whines," Ejizu said. "But her melancholy should get better with time."

"Though not in those exact words; that's sort of what Dike suggested as well and what advice I gave her."

"I give her a few weeks—six months tops—and she will join him," Dike said. "It was not long after my mother's mother died that her husband passed on too. I think it was just a few months."

"I don't think it is as set in stone as you say it," Bute said. "My mother lost my father nearly 16 years ago and she is still with us. So many factors are often in play, of which social-support network perhaps comes out on top—"

"And a good spiritual life and network," Dike interjected. "But going back to what we were saying, you are right Bute…I don't think my mother would have suffered to the extent that she would find herself in the depths of despondency to the point that she gives up her ghost because she lost my dad. So, the strength of the relationship matters. She has already moved on and has fallen head over everything in love with Odera. You should hear the kind of things she says to herself about him and—she is going to say she will kill me for saying this, but since I am already dead, I will say it: you should have seen how she touched herself when she thought about him and heard the sounds that she made two nights ago."

"I sense that she can't wait to have a life with him," Ejizu said. "Same with my mother, she wishes my father gone already—she just can't wait to be with Uncle Ikuku…To relive the good old days."

"And Namdi mentioned Anika," Bute added. "Everyone seems to be finding happiness in their other half."

"Oh, the transience of happiness," Dike muttered. "I would not go that far. Happiness is, in my opinion, transitory in nature…There seems, with the passing of time, to be an inevitable wane in enthusiasm for everything in life, and the search for a replacement. I don't think it is right or fair for anyone to put the burden of their being happy on another person. Humans just need to find a way to be fine with themselves regardless of what happens…To not look to others for approval…To look to something higher, something that will not fade, something like—"

"Like The Almighty," Ejizu interjected. "I have a confession, and I will say it now that Somto seems to be insentient. I knew exactly where I had been during the last 30 years—just didn't want Somto to be distracted from the matter at hand."

"We didn't even sense that you weren't being forthcoming," Bute said. "You concealed it quite well."

"For all his good points, Somto is quite excitable," Ejizu added. "Over three decades, he has remained the same in that regard—responding too readily to anything new."

"I think he would have heard what you've just said," Bute said. "And he has grown in other aspects. Helping his brother study has taught him a lot. I wish I had that kind of opportunity. Azuka is the only person who could have afforded me that opportunity, but all the while I have been here, she was either in secondary school, learning things I already know, or, right now, spending most of her time trying to make money to pay for her teacher-education program."

Shrugging, "It's okay if Somto hears it," Ejizu said. "And you can learn from him."

"We can if he actually dedicates time to teaching us," Bute said. "He has so far spent most of his time with his brother and Ijezie, and now that Adaku is here, that will be even less time for any of us."

"You would have to formalize any teaching sessions and apportion a time period dedicated to learning from him," Ejizu said.

"I have to go," Bute said as he began to change realms. "It looks like Namdi, and Odera might be needing me. A commotion is brewing in front of the palace."

"So, what is up with your father?" Dike said

"He has just left Idumeli," Ejizu said.

"And where is he headed?" Dike said.

Shrugging, "He didn't mention," Ejizu said. "Only said he has to get ready to fight Odera, which we already knew would be the case."

With a smack of agitation in his words, "But you said that he always informed his host of his next destination before ever he left them," Dike said. "Call me paranoid, but this shift in his method gives me the impression that he is going back to the palace. Have you informed your mother? I will inform mine immediately."

"Oops! I better do that right away," Ejizu said, and as they both switched realms in a trice, Somto and Adaku materialized.

Shaking his head and smiling, "I've been cozened by a mere child, and he would've to answer for it when I catch him," Somto murmured.

"He has a good reason," Adaku replied.

Regarding her with a contemplative eye, "Perhaps," Somto replied. "Well, if he's going to keep secrets, then I have to reconsider telling him about his father's illegitimate child. So, what's happening with your maiden friends? Anything new?"

"What's new is that I can't now see or hear Adure as well. And if I'm going to hazard an educated guess, I'd say that she, too, has become pregnant since I couldn't also see, or hear Ijeoma who they said is pregnant. And Adure was recently involved in an act to get herself pregnant."

"So, we'll depend on Isioma to know what's going on with them."

"Yes, but she says very little."

"We'll have to hope she starts to say much more then," Somto said.

"She now knows that it's also in her best interest to be pregnant. She's been saying it to herself."

"Potentially three more were-felines to contend with," Somto said.

"All of whom we're potentially not going to be able to see, or hear from again," Adaku said.

"In that case," Somto added. "Ejizu must now change course and inform his mother."

"And you definitely have to let him know about his half-brother Pneuma," Adaku said. "Don't be childish or else I will blab."

"Well, I've got no choice now, have I? He must've heard what we've just talked about."

Chapter 68

A long moment of considered thought later, Queen Nena continued, trying her best to ignore Ejizu's attempt at connecting with her as she got into the swing of her re-engagement with her subjects: "Did you know that by getting rid of that man, this woman that you are asking for her life has done us all a huge favor in initiating the purging from our community of all of the Mkpátáku ritualists? Agreed that the way it happened is not exactly how King Otubu wished, but is it not true anymore that anyone involved in that ritual must die as decreed by the late king? Is that man, therefore, not a lawbreaker?"

"God forbid bad thing," said some of the men and women together. "If it is true, then he met the right end."

"*Alu eme!*" said others united. "This is an abomination! The woman probably did well."

Glancing around at her subjects and nodding, "Or do you want proof?" she continued. "Do you want us to go to that man's shrine so that you can see for yourselves?"

"No, Your Majesty," they said as one, many of them also swinging their right arms over their heads in a quick, circular motion and snapping the thumbs and middle fingers as they lowered their arms—a sign of their rejection of what they deemed was unacceptable.

"Let us, therefore, not kick against the pricks," the queen stated. "So, before you join the bandwagon in demanding an innocent life, first of all, ask questions. Spread the word…not only within Akagheli but beyond it—to all corners of Igboland…to Wusaland…and to *Orubaland*[19]. Let everyone know that we are at war to defeat the evil that some men are perpetrating against our children all over the country. Keep your eyes peeled and ears pricked up. And

---

[19] One of the three autochthonous and ethnic lands that make up the island nation of Naïjerland. It is in the southwest of the island.

let nobody throw dust in your eyes because this is no fallacy. There are living witnesses amongst us," then indicating me, she continued: "Mrs. Nkemjika Odimegwu, the woman whose life you all came for, is one such witness. Now, does anyone still desire her life?"

As I caught a glimpse of Mama Udo and Udo pushing their way through the crowd, taking to their heels, and disappearing around the corner onto Farm Road, "No, Your Majesty. You have spoken well," the gathering said in near harmony, the men's heads assuming a bullish hang and the women curtsying. "Your wish is always our command."

"Now go in peace and join in the brewing crusade against this deathly conduct, against every man and woman of evil bent," the queen said and, in that instant, the feeling that the community had begun to ride on an inevitable wind of change grew much stronger within me. "Every village has a story, and this has become ours…Go and begin to tell it to all listeners as we strive to become a community imbued with a sense of fairness and social justice."

****

No sooner had the rabble done a volte-face and spread down Palace Road East in droves and we turned around to return to the palace than the locals began to stampede, scattering like the wind.

The commotion would alert us to the crackling and spitting of sparks from orange-and-pink flames that shot up into the air whilst engulfing what was left of the bits of dried, previously burnt, and, at that moment, smoldering, fan-shaped leaves, which crowned some of the palm trees that were directly opposite the palace.

Looking further behind the tall, unbranched, evergreen plants as wafts of sulfurous vapors lingered in the airspace around it, we saw, behind their cover, the monstrous, bug-eyed wyvern reappear in the sky, breathing fire and flapping its wings with wrath.

Standing on the middle step of the front stoop and flanked by Odera, and Namdi who watched on as the beast made a beeline for our position, "That's the creature we told you all about," I shrieked, then ushered the prince and the queen toward the doorway, sighting Papu within his usual location. "Everyone, inside, now! Captain, instruct your sergeants not to waste any bullets on that creature…They as well as your privates must immediately leave their positions and seek refuge within the palace. Odera, Namdi, come on."

Reacting to my anxiousness, "You heard her," Captain Iduto barked as the queen suddenly halted and faced me. "Soldiers, into the palace! At once!"

"Ejizu said he thinks that the king is on his way back to the palace," Queen Nena asserted to Odera's hearing, trembling at the thought of what the king would have in store for us upon his return, going by what his chief had reshaped into.

Darting knowing glances at me and Namdi as the four privates and Sergeant Fric trooped through the gateway and toward the palace front stoop, Odera swept up the steps and through the passages to arrive at the caucus room ahead of everyone else, in readiness for the king.

Barging into the king's lair and invading Odera's personal space, "What do we do about Chief Madu?" I asked. "You've had some time to think about it."

Standing behind the door and keeping it from shutting as the rest of us entered the room, "We wait for him here," Odera replied with hesitation.

Facing him, "Really?" I retorted; my voice low but vehement. "He's not going to come in here after the last time, and he's not going away either. So, do you want us to have to fight him together with the king when it's late?" Glancing at his watch, I continued, "It's a minute after four o'clock. We have less than two hours until sunset. Do you want us to still be fighting when it's dark?"

Forcing the slow-closing door shut, he leaned his back against it, closed his eyes, and drew in a deep, meditative breath. Exhaling with equal speed, "No," he stated as he faced the door, yanked it open, and strode out. "Namdi, we fight him like we did the other beasts. Ejizu, inform us immediately the king shows up."

Thumping his rifle down on the conference table, Namdi dashed out. Initially following behind Odera, he caught up with him in no time. In tandem, they drew their machetes.

Somewhat numbed by what was to come, "How do you know where he is going to be?" Namdi said.

"I don't. You should head to the courtyard. I am going to climb to the roof to lure him there."

"How do we fight him in the air?" Namdi said.

"He is the one who is coming to us, so if he wants to fight us, he will have to come down to our level. According to you, he already knows that his aerial assault with flames will do nothing to us. He is going to have to try something different."

Chapter 69

Seething across the palace and toward the three-storied, northwest section, Odera cascaded up the stairs.

Arriving in the hallway adjacent to Papu's lookout room and with a sudden, upward bounce, he yanked down the roof-access ladder in one attempt.

Odera climbed the metallic set of steps two or three rungs at a time, pushed the hatch to swing open with a bang, sprang onto the roof that was covered in brown dirt and immediately jumped down two stories to the west-roof terrace, sending up clouds of dust.

Glancing down into the courtyard, Namdi was poised for action. Spinning around to look in a northerly direction, Odera caught sight of the immense wyvern. Silhouetted against the smutted sky, it flapped its wings, hovering, perhaps wondering what to do next.

Then, suddenly, it flashed a sulfurous glance at and locked gazes with Odera.

Pulling backward for a moment and with a predatory gleam in its huge, green, zoomable eyes that exuded an aura of evil and hatred, the wyvern arced forward.

Thrumming from its mouth and nostrils, it glided at ferocious speed, dead aiming for Odera. And as it advanced, its scales just glinted in the all-but-absent sunrays, sending off turquoise streaks.

Odera observed as the remorseless being, going through wild and unpredictable twists, swallowed more and more of the intervening space, closing in on him, and his heart whammed harder whilst fighting a swelling foreboding.

Leaping from the terrace, Odera somersaulted toward the courtyard and landed on his feet like a raptorial feline, next to Namdi, on a ground that had once been gravel and sand over earth but had begun to welcome rampant weeds all around, including over King Otubu's burial site that was centered within the garden.

As the cold-blooded brute that would, at times, become the despair of the duo swooped down and shot toward them, Odera tossed his machete onto his left hand and charged at it.

Breathing and roaring its fire at Odera, Odera jumped up in a gravity-defying flip and dodged the blaze. Landing atop its face, which was encrusted with sharp projections less so than the rest of its body, and immediately hopping off it to soar head over heels, Odera came within a centimeter of being caught in its snapping jaws as it twisted its neck toward his direction of flight. Somersaulting in the air over the monstrosity, Odera slashed its flesh down its middle and landed on his feet behind it, glimpsing his machete that then was blood-soaked a third of the way up from its point before he faced the creature and watched in anticipation.

Stung by this and shutting its thick eyelids over its maddening eyes, the fiery red-and-black dragon-like creature writhed about in pain. Tripping over King Otubu's marble-bordered barrow that had weeds straggling along it, the clumsy brute lurched backward. Dropping to the mound, the thumping sound caused the innumerable feeding birds to take to the air, chirping louder many times over. Flailing uncontrollably toward the southeast corner and rocking the terracotta effigy of King Otubu, which was stationed on a pedestal, it fell with a crash and *kwok* that shattered it into a myriad of fragments. Composing itself and holding steady on its massive and powerful legs that each bore four huge talons, the non-reasoning, not-less-than-five-meters-tall creature twisted its neck to watch, as did the brothers in arms, the deep and bleeding linear laceration, which ran along its spine from the base of its head, splitting the large frills on its neck, to the beginning of its tail, rapidly heal itself.

Realizing the full extent of the work they then had before them, Namdi forward rolled to stand ready, next to Odera, "What now?" Namdi whispered.

Glimpsing palace workers, including Papu, gaping through the windows that dotted all the walls, which separated the passages from their verandas, Odera probably sensed that I'd be amongst them. Darting determined glances counterclockwise from the west, then southward, then eastward, he descried me with my rifle in my right hand, peeking at them from behind one of the east passage windows just as he stopped his eyes from flickering to the north-side windows.

Giving him thumbs up, I mouthed as he looked away, "You can do it."

Flapping its great, leathery wings, the viscous adversary rapidly lifted toward the brothers in arms and tried to squash them with its fearsome claws that looked capable of lacerating any flesh to mere strips. Dodging the swing of its claws, Namdi and Odera thrust their machetes into the soles of its feet. "I am still thinking," Odera retorted.

As the pain seared through its core, the vile-tempered animal struck Odera in his chest with the point of its flailing, powerful, and long tail. The bone-crushing jab sent Odera crashing against the pedestal of King Mbanegu's statue at the northeast corner; the carving rocking a little without falling. Rapidly wrapping its sturdy tail around Namdi's waist, it lifted him up in the air, squashing, twisting, and turning him.

Falling to the ground as shattering pain seared through the center of his chest, Odera's thoughts were a whirling storm of doubt and fear. Then, he felt the rent over his breastbone begin to heal, and, in a trice, his bodily and mental vigor took a turn for the better.

Even as Namdi groaned in anguish and saw stars, the animal pulled the machetes out of its claws one after the other with its beak-like jaws that boasted four massive and pointed canines and flung them away. As the machetes clattered to the veranda and struck sparks from it, the gash in the beast's feet mended. Touching down on its renewed limbs, it spun its neck around and exhaled a blade of fiery breath at dizzy Namdi's head.

Bute blocked it.

Rising to his feet with renewed determination, Odera shut his eyes for a moment and drew in a deep breath. Puffing out, he opened his eyes to see a mournful Namdi in a lethal squeeze. Making a dash for the east veranda, he scooped up the two machetes. Wielding both weapons, Odera let rip toward the brutish chromatic, hopped onto the wooden pedestal on which King Otubu's graven image had once stood, and leapt toward the creature's tail. "Namdi, catch," Odera roared as he threw Namdi's machete in his direction, probably to help Namdi stay alert. And raising his own machete with both hands, Odera drove it with a powerful, downward motion, severing the bumpy tail from its body and landing next to the bust of King Igungu at the southwest corner as Namdi fell toward the ground, the tail's distal remnant unwrapping itself around him.

Crash-landing, Namdi failed to catch his weapon as he vomited. Striking out for his machete with a crawl just as the end of the foul beast's tail landed with a startling smack by his feet, Namdi grabbed his weapon. Inspirited by a further surge of adrenaline as he recovered from the harrowing experience, Namdi managed to forward roll to Odera's position and staggered to his feet.

Grasping that the situation presented no options for freezing or fleeing, Namdi maintained a resolve to fight to the finish.

As Odera gave Namdi a once-over to ensure he was fine, roaring in torment as its tail regenerated, and, without warning, the evil-natured creature swiveled counter-clockwise at breakneck speed, crouched as it did and forcefully knocked the distracted duo off the ground with its outspread wings.

Sending the groaning pair flailing helplessly in the air, they landed with a thump atop the south-roof terrace.

Breathing fire at them as they tried to rise to their feet, arching, and rubbing their backs in agony, Bute absorbed it again.

It plunged its chin to crush the brothers in arms and its jaw crashed hard against the concrete sundeck as Namdi and Odera, who huffed and puffed with every breath, just managed to roll away in opposite directions in split-second timing.

"Bute said he is not sure how much more of these fires he can take," Namdi grunted and heaved. "We must overcome it sooner or we get burnt alive."

There was a momentary pause as Odera cogitated, "How do we do it?" Odera shrieked with a hint of displeasure at his inability to proffer a way forward. "The swift thing has too wide a neck to strangle or chop off, and it regenerates damn too quickly for me."

"I may be clutching at straws here, but can Ejizu help out?" Namdi roared. "At least to buy us some thinking time."

"He has no connection with you and can only shield me, so the quick answer is, no, I don't think he can help us individually, if he could, he would have," Odera retorted as the foul-looking creature recovered from the intense pain that jabbed up its jaws and head.

Staggering to their feet, the brothers forever glanced at each other for a second, "Can he at least try?" Namdi said.

Appearing to ignore Namdi, Odera pointed two fingers of his right hand at his own eyes. With Namdi understanding the plan, they went like lightning toward its head.

"Never have I come across anything as complex as understanding the creative abilities of these Pneumas," Namdi mumbled to himself.

Jumping onto it, each man thrust his long, pointed knife into the ipsilateral eye, Odera the left and Namdi the right, and twisted the unyielding metal, each gnashing their teeth in rage in lockstep with the other man. Yanking out their weapons and performing a backward somersault down toward the courtyard as jelly-like material admixed with blood flowed out from the creature's eye sockets, it thrashed its head about and tried to summon its remaining senses.

The duo landed on either side of the creature and waited a long moment.

Sniffing with the symmetrical, slit-like openings at the tip of its long snout, listening with its colossal, pointy ears that pricked, lashing its huge and red-carpet-like tongue about, and whipping its tail back and forth, the wyvern tried in vain to capture either of the men.

Realizing that the blasphemous life-form was unable to self-restore its sight, Odera reckoned that any part of it that was directly linked to its nervous system might struggle to regenerate since the eyes hadn't. "We go for its brain," Odera roared with the reassuring tone of a man with growing mastery. "Come this way."

With an excited breath and knowing fully well that Odera was rarely wrong, Namdi galloped toward Odera. As he closed in on Odera, Odera ran the other way. "Throw your machete to my right hand when I am up and continue to distract it," he said as he thrust his machete at just above the oafish creature's hindquarters.

Flinging his machete toward Odera, Namdi began running back and forth. Spearing the wyvern, Odera hopped onto its barbed, sturdy tail and using it as a step, sprang to hang from his machete with his left hand as Namdi's weapon came spinning in the air toward him.

Reaching for Namdi's machete as the blind beast twitched and swung its head hither and thither to spoor Namdi, Odera gripped its helve with his right hand.

Stabbing the wyvern that reeked of smoke and sulfur further up with Namdi's weapon as Namdi sensed Bute trying to say something to him, Odera yanked out his own weapon and stuck it hard, higher above Namdi's.

Twitching and giving unearthly yells with each knife prick and pull, the animal healed the puncture wounds again and again.

Alternating between pulling out and plunging into its back his and Namdi's machetes higher up each time as Namdi tried to draw his attention by shouting his name, focused Odera rose upper and upper, managing to hold on as the creature thrashed about, occasionally losing his grip but averting any falls by the skin of his teeth, until he got to its head.

Still oblivious to Namdi's attempts at getting his notice and using Namdi's machete as anchor, exuding extraordinary strength, Odera struck with his left hand, piercing his pointed machete into the top of the desperate beast's skull, through its head and exiting at the center of its lower jaw.

Pulling the weapon out, Odera transpierced it again and again at multiple points until the creature gradually succumbed to the clutches of mortality and its eerie growls faded away.

Turning on his heel as he sensed the presence of his king strengthening and having seen enough, "Everyone, back to your duties," Papu screeched again and again as he strode up the west passage whilst the uniformed and petrified members of staff scuttled across the soft floor in all directions. "The king is home."

Heading through the north passage as it also emptied of people in no time, with doors swinging open and slamming shut, Papu arrived at the gaping palace entryway. Looking about him and seeing no-one, he vanished.

At the same time, jumping off with both weapons as the animal slumped against the ground and landed with a loud thud and shrunk to become an eyeless and lifeless Chief Madu, Odera forward rolled to Namdi.

"Ejizu told Bute that the king has just appeared in the palace and is heading for the great chamber," Namdi said as Chief Madu continued to bleed out from atop his head, eyes, and below his jaw. "He said he had tried to let you know himself, but you would not connect with him."

Nodding, Odera's eyes flashed anger as he got to his feet. Lobbing Namdi's machete in Namdi's direction, he about-faced and pelted across the courtyard toward the south veranda, "Head to the caucus room in case he changes his mind and ends up there," Odera said. "I am off to his chamber."

Chapter 70

At the same time, whilst the maidens were on a quiet saunter down a track that inclined through the darkening forest, Isioma's trek had a slight halt to it as her right thigh twinged.

Taking to their heels as Isioma was jolted to a stop the instant the sound of King Ajutu's call had pealed in their ears, setting the fleeing duo's teeth on edge, "I wasn't expecting it so soon, going by the last time he teleported," Adure and Ijeoma shrieked in a chorus as they gained distance from Isioma.

Glancing backward for a moment, Isioma reluctantly willed herself to follow Ijeoma and Adure.

Arriving to run side by side with them, heading further away from the palace, "Are you sure we should not be heading back to him?" Isioma asked. "The queen of the coast will not entertain this."

Adure and Ijeoma darted irritated glances at Isioma, then looked forward again without as much as a break in their running pace.

"Adure has certainly conceived," Isioma murmured, her voice swallowed by the forest's ambience. "Though I had my doubts about the role pregnancy can play in helping to kick against the king's control, I believe it now. These two are clearly experiencing that freedom, while I am still having to fight the temptation to return to him—the propinquity I share with them, which has been forged over 20 years, clearly stronger than my desire to obey his call and the only reason I have carried on with them. I ought to do as they've done at the very next opportunity if I want to maintain this relationship."

Nimbly changing directions left and right between and amongst tree trunks, the trio also leapt across streams and over masses of vegetation, grabbing tree branches and swinging off them in a Tarzan-esque style and switching to their feline forms as was necessary to negotiate any difficult terrain they encountered.

"Yippee!" Ijeoma exclaimed. "I am forever free. Could never have imagined that a time such as this would come when I would hear that annoying sound and be happy to ignore it—"

"And not care an iota," Adure added, then looking rightward at Ijeoma as Ijeoma continued to express wild delight. "I know we can't and won't return to a place where the odds are that we'll be killed, but is there an end in sight for our coddiwomple? What's the plan?"

"Adure, it is obvious that you are a hundred percent with me on this by the fact that you agreed to let your man friend go and did not look back a short moment ago when we heard the king's call," Ijeoma said. "But I am not sure of Isioma. What if Isioma decides to return to the king after I tell you where we are headed, then he cajoles her into telling him of our whereabouts? I mean, she had to think twice about continuing with us after he beeped for us."

"How many times have we betrayed one another?" Isioma retorted.

"Not many, but we can't beat our breasts and say never," Adure said. "So, it's always a possibility."

Snorting with a dismissive laugh, "I understand," Isioma said as she felt a wave of disgust. "But Ije's worries make little sense, if at all, since I will eventually discover where we are headed when we get there."

"Well, since I have not mentioned our final destination, wherever we end up may turn out to be a stop off until you have achieved freedom."

Nodding, then shrugging, her gaze darting between Adure and Ijeoma, "I agree," Isioma said with a rising voice. "And I am not going to return to him, and even if I do, which I doubt, I will not be ratting you two out. So, how can I win your trust then?"

"It is not so much about trust as it is about you not being in total control of your will, which is clear," Ijeoma replied. "And you would have to get pregnant for that to happen."

Puffing out a noisy breath as her eyebrows lowered, "And I now know that for a fact," Isioma retorted as she flipped her long, naturally wavy, and flowing hair with a toss of her head and, in the wink of an eye, scraped it back into a high chignon. "But there is little chance that it will happen before we get to our journey's end."

Drawing her eyebrows closer, Ijeoma cleared her throat and with a hesitant nod, "Who knows?" she said. "Anyway, um, so, we will hope to sort that out at our first port of call before continuing onward. It does not seem hard to find a man in the forest doing this, or that. We just must remain vigilant."

"Should it not strictly be at the middle of the month?" Isioma asked. "Should we not wait until next month, to time ovulation better?"

"It can be any time after the middle of a month," Ijeoma said. "The book suggests all that matters is that the womb is in a state capable of carrying pregnancy. In none of its 1,500 or so pages did it mention ovulation."

Following a long moment of silence as the maidens galloped along, "I have an overwhelmingly disturbing feeling that pregnancy and this free-will thing are not all good," Isioma said. "I will say it again…In the last few weeks, Ije has become meaner than usual."

Looking to her right at Isioma, "Who said it was all good?" Ijeoma said, lifting the book up and indicating it with her head. "Again, this book makes it clear that if we take full control of our existence, our willpower will totally dominate, and we will be unleashed. So, there should be no ambiguity."

"I don't like the sound of that," Adure said. "Evil is our nature, and it does sound like we are going to become a bunch of completely unchecked troublemakers. I'm worried that we're going to put ourselves in harm's way and risk our bodies being rubbed out while we flex our uncontrolled free will."

"Well, it is not like we were not doing a lot of evil already," Ijeoma said.

"Then, we were protected by the king's control," Adure said. "With pregnancy and being away from him, we won't."

"Our free will can still be controlled, I think," Ijeoma said, glancing at Isioma. "We just do it on our own terms. And I hope you are not changing your mind, Isioma, because you will have to leave this group if you don't get pregnant. The world is fast becoming our oyster, and I do not want a lame duck or lame feline as it were."

With the atmosphere suddenly full of menace, "Yes, madam," Isioma retorted as it appeared to dawn on her that without the king, she will have no-one else to turn to if she were to be abandoned. "I intend to remain a positive force in our group."

"Good," Ijeoma said, then launched the book high in the air. Leaping up toward it as she morphed into her leopard, she plucked the weighty volume with her jaws as it dropped. Landing majestically, she sped off without breaking stride.

Gazing at each other for a beat, Isioma and Adure shrugged, then transforming into their respective feline forms, they charged after the golden leopard.

Coincidence, predestination, or sheer will, it didn't matter which, as the slight pain Isioma had felt in her right thigh seemed to completely resolve.

Chapter 71

Walking with leaping strides down the east passage, I reckoned we had to act quicker. Not only was sunset not far away, and the king could ask for the generator to be switched off, plunging the palace into darkness, and making the already-difficult battle even harder, but my eagerness was bursting at the seams.

No-one was going to tell me otherwise, not even Odera, the man for whom I had the utmost respect. Once I got wind of King Ajutu's whereabouts from Dike, I'd resolved to fight alongside Odera. The temptation was too strong to resist.

Ghosting from the west passage toward the first step of the stairs that led up to his great chamber and with just a wooden door blocking us from catching sight of each other, the king was oblivious to my approach from the south passage.

On looking to his left upon gaining access to the south passage from the south veranda, Odera was surprised to see me with my rifle at the ready as I bounded down the south passage. Shushing me with a wave, he motioned for me to slink behind him. With a twitch of annoyance, I wondered why I had to stay quiet when I was that close to getting the better of the person who'd wanted me silenced for good.

As the glow of the lighting in the passage cast a long shadow of the door that we'd passed through two days earlier, on our way to visit the queen, the ordeal she and I had been through came flooding back. With the king being at the center of it all, I firmly ignored Odera's wishes as quivering hatred for the king settled in my bosom and I blasted through the door that would normally incline into the southwest passage.

Shuddering with horror as he was hit by several stray bullets, King Ajutu fell face down against the steps. Screeching with pain whilst clutching his left lower back, he turned and eyed us with hatred as we burst through the door, spraying splinters everywhere.

Drawing a deep, unsteady breath as his right hand thumbed harder on the three stars that lined his Akupé's handle, suggesting that he'd been trying to summon the maidens long before we waylaid him, "You two have the nerve to come back here," he groaned, still glowering at us.

"It's no use activating those maidens," Odera growled as he transferred his machete to his left hand and moved toward the king who appeared out of breath. "They are not at the palace. You have nobody now."

As Odera reached for the king's hand fan, the king uncorked a kick in a blink and Odera felt the king's sole of the right foot stamp, hard, against the center of his chest, sending him backward through the air.

Letting a couple of rounds whiz from my weapon as Odera crashed against the wall that closed off the southwest veranda from the namesake passage, the king vanished before he was hit and the slugs rebounded off the marble steps, the loud sound ricocheting around the passage.

"We are scheduled for so much fun tonight," the king's high, grating voice mocked, coming from the top of the stairs, and fading away as I helped Odera up.

"What were you trying to do?" I whispered. "Why didn't you stab him or something?"

"Yea," Odera said as he staggered to his feet. "I wasn't thinking right. I thought your bullets had gotten him, and I wanted to get rid of that mysterious fan. He also happens to be my father and you should not be here."

"I'm wherever I want to be," I stated as I pulled him by the hand. "No second thoughts…Remember that he wanted you killed and he's now getting away!"

Sweeping the stairs, we arrived at the landing adjacent to the great chamber as its doors slammed shut. Blowing the doors open, we peered into the room, then entered it.

Reappearing with the wound in his left lower back having healed, he quickly inhaled twice from his puffer and set it on his dresser. Leaning against the furniture, with his legs crossed at the ankles and arms folded across his chest, "You dare to attack your king?" he said, flashing a black look.

Taking a few careful paces forward, "A king looks after his people," Odera retorted. "You care only about yourself."

"You are no king. You have shown that you can't be trusted and, therefore, not fit to lead us," I spat with escalating anger as I sidled to Odera. "A king knits people together, not allow for divisions."

"It is a sin to speak evil of your king," the king said with a sneering curl to his top lip.

"It is a sin to mete out evil on your subjects," I retorted and, with an explosion of anger, fired a rapid succession of shots at him, though blue smoke instantly began to swirl around him, absorbing the machine-gun fire.

In hysterics, "Whatever those child spirits can do, I can do better," King Ajutu said and flashed an amber-green beam of light at me.

Odera, on instinct and in less than no time, dropped his machete and dived on me. He landed atop me on the soft floor and the flash missed me by millimeters as it sailed past us. With my trigger-happy right index finger involuntarily letting slugs fly upward to lodge in the middle of the west cornice as we fell, the strong streak of amber-green light struck the nightstand and ripped a massive hole in it.

As Dike seemed pleased at the fact that Odera had been quicker than him in saving me from the flare, considering that he was then able to avoid another energy dump, conserving his own impetus, my heart pounded three times faster on seeing the damage to the wooden set of drawers.

Lunging with fury at the struggling-to-levitate king through the blue smoke that suddenly and inexplicably wreathed upward in wisps, Odera met him head-on. Dropping into a low kick, he swept the king's legs out from under him. Just as the evidently sapped king landed on his side before the dresser and my momentary daydream about lovemaking with Odera, induced by the warm glow I felt within me as his chest laid pressed against my breasts passed, I arose, scooped, and tossed Odera's machete to him.

Catching his weapon, he leapt toward the king to stab him in the heart, with both his hands gripping the haft. Quickly beaming his alternating amber and cyan eyes at Odera, the king passed out of sight, and Ejizu absorbed the flash.

Falling on his weapon as its point struck the plush carpet, puncturing it and cracking the marble beneath, he turned, looking troubled as I began to appreciate the extent of his machete's power.

Gazing at me as he got to his feet, "Dike and Ejizu will have to let me know where he shows up," Odera rumbled, feeling a rising unpredictability.

"Let us know," I said. "He might be heading for the caucus room, and Dike just said that Ejizu has informed the queen."

"Since he won't be expecting it, Bute, let Namdi fire at him as soon as he cracks the door open or appears in there," Odera roared as he streaked across the room, grabbing me by the hand and pulling me in tow out of the great chamber. "That should slow him down till I get there, even if it doesn't kill him."

"Till we get there," I snapped. "You clearly need me to bring you into line."

Chapter 72

Though relatively quiet, still, the late afternoon percolated with unexpected fear that ranged from simple worry to outright terror in parts of the community as the serious matter at hand, especially after the recent sighting of a dragon, continued to filter into the consciousness of some of the villagers.

It'd been only a question of when, not if, that pockets of people would huddle together for gossip in whispers; some of them time and again. After all, Akagheli's motto was, *united we stand, divided we fall*.

Within a hundred-meter radius of Akagheli's only public elementary school, baby Ugochi's shrill cry, which pierced the air, was the only additional, audible sound other than the sigh of the wind.

Rising to his feet in the hut that was dim with lantern light, "Mama Ugochi, broken bones shall knit again," Papu said as she walked with him to her doorway that was closed off at the time with a reed mat, cradling her baby in her arms. "I must set off, as I have to still visit the others and let them know to meet you at the usual place—we are getting closer and closer to what you all want, so take heart and continue to brighten up."

Lifting the mat and turning around in the doorway of the mud hut, Papu bowed with praying hands.

The cockles of her heart seemingly warmed, "See you soon, Papu," Mama Ugochi said with more verve as Papu turned on his heel. "You have been a reliable friend. I hope it all works out. We can't all continue this way, living in fear."

With a no-look wave of his gnarled right hand, Papu dashed out of the hut and toward the exit from Mama Ugochi's dust-covered compound. Arriving on School Road and seeing no-one, Papu passed from sight.

Chapter 73

Not long before, Chief Ikeme poked his bald head through his front door, lowered his thick glasses that sat on his big, pockmarked nose and looked around, scratching his sparse, bristly white beard.

Looking less fear-stricken, he stepped out perhaps because Namdi and I were no longer there with our weapons, there was no longer the commotion that had been across Palace Road East, and the wyvern hadn't showed up again. Walking across the front yard, he knocked on Chief Egwu's door, then, moments later, on that of Chief Jokum.

In a short while, he was joined by Chief Jokum.

"You are dressed for the occasion. Good that we are thinking alike," Chief Ikeme said. "The king must be informed about what is going on."

"Did you call Egu?" Chief Jokum said.

"You want him to scream my head off again?" Chief Ikeme said. "Have you forgotten that he wants us three so-called 'junior chiefs' to be ready before ever calling him to join us for any official duty?"

"That's correct; it totally skipped my mind," Chief Jokum said. "Let's wait for Chief Egwu then."

And not long after, Chief Egwu stepped out of his house and looked around, "Chief Ikeme, Chief Jokum," Chief Egwu said as he shut his front door and ambled away from it toward the two chiefs.

Both men towering over Chief Egwu and staring at him, their faces looking a question, "Happy Sunday to you," Chiefs Ikeme and Jokum said as one.

"Now that we are complete, let's go and get Chief Madu," Chief Ikeme said.

With raised eyebrows and gazing with focus, "I greet you two," Chief Egwu said in a quick manner. "Why are you both dressed in your chieftaincy attires? Why have you decided to disturb my family's Sunday rest? Why do we need to get Chief Madu?"

"The question should be, why are you not wearing your own garb?" Chief Ikeme said. "Is the king not supposed to be made aware of what happened? For us to know what to do? Is it no longer our duty to be his eyes, ears, nose, and taste buds on matters we assume he is not yet privy to?"

Looking a question as his posture perked up, "Know what to do about what?" Chief Egwu asked with an uncertain tone.

"Did you not hear the commotion…The gun shots?" Chief Ikeme said. "Or see the dragon that suddenly appeared in our village?"

With his eyes widened, "A dragon?" Chief Egwu asked, then chuckled. "Get out of here, you joker—"

"I thought you saw everything," Chief Ikeme interjected, pushing his glasses up.

"Don't mind Chief Egwu," Chief Jokum said. "He was probably with the pastor when it happened."

Realizing that his associates were dead serious, "You are right. I was in church with my wife and daughter…and on our way driving back, we saw people either crowded around in places, or moving around in a confused mass. They mostly looked agitated to say the least," Chief Egwu said as his expression changed in an instant from that of astonishment to that of worry and he walked across toward Chief Madu's house.

"Now you are talking," Chief Jokum didn't hesitate to add.

"So, where is Chief Madu then?" Chief Egwu said. "Chieftaincy attire can wait. He has to lead us right away to the king to discuss this matter before our people start asking questions."

Seeing the door to the oldest chief's house wide open and hearing a faint voice calling for help, Chief Egwu's gaze flitted around the vicinity and his eyebrows drew together even more. Motioning for the other chiefs to wait for him, he hurried into the head chief's house. Following the source of the ever-loudening voice, he entered Chief Madu's bedroom and found Adane tied to the bed.

Untying her, and before he could offer her his help, "Don't touch me, you beast," Adane snapped as she ran out of the room and the house, screaming on top of her tremulous voice, panting, and quaking, tendons standing out in her neck, "Who are you people? What are you people? Did you not see my husband turn into that creature? What is going on in this village? Why are you people standing in front of our house? What are you planning? Did you all become chiefs by joining the occult?"

Rushing out of the house as the other chiefs gazed wide-eyed and slack-jawed at Adane and at each other, "Calm down, Adane—" Chief Egwu said, looking around.

"Did…did…did you not hear the woman?" Chief Jokum stuttered, interjecting as his unblemished oval face grew a frown. "She just said that Egu turned into that dragon, or whatever it was that we saw. How…how can she calm down?"

Restlessly tugging at her long and loose caftan as beads of sweat appeared above her top lip, "So you saw it," Adane shrieked, gritting her teeth, putting her hands on her head as she continued to pant, sticking the index finger of her right hand between her teeth. "I am not safe. I knew that he was hiding something. Now I believe he killed our son for powers."

Raising his right hand to cup his small chin and his left arm across his abdomen as realization dawned, "So, it is true, all these rumors we were hearing about Emenozo?" Chief Egwu said. "All the visions Pastor Omenka saw? I should have prayed more."

With a heavy sigh, "You are safe with us," Chief Ikeme said. "We are not like him. Come into my house. Chichi, my wife, is at home with Ify. We are heading to the palace to discuss these things with the king unless you want to come with us."

With widened eyes and jerky movements, Adane squirmed, "Me? Never. I am not stepping foot in that palace—before they kill me, too, like Emenozo," she barked as she sprinted toward the bungalow that was two blocks on the right of hers. "I will stay with Mama Ify; thank you, Chief Ikeme, for offering."

Marching without any word passing between them, the three chiefs arrived at the wide-open palace gateway before long, and as Chief Egwu pressed the bell multiple times, "Something is definitely not right with this village," Chief Jokum said. "Why is the palace front gate sawed off?"

"Very strange," Chief Ikeme said as he turned his neck around. "And what's with the military vehicles? Did the king ask them to come to help with the commotion?"

"Who knows," Chief Egwu said. "Though he obviously did not tell us about it, we must wait to hear from His Majesty first instead of making assumptions."

Waiting for Papu who they expected had seen them from his look out, Chiefs Ikeme and Jokum stood arms akimbo, drawing in heavy breaths and shaking their hanged heads whilst Chief Egwu cupped his right elbow and tapped his lips with his right index and middle fingers; their eyes darting hither and thither.

Chapter 74

Before long, Papu materialized within his stark room and heard the sound of the gate bell that had been shrilling through the palace.

Peeking out the window that looked out over the front yard, he saw the chiefs gathered in a discussion.

Inclining the aluminum sash-casement outward, "Good afternoon, sirs," Papu said, his voice unfolding as a dry croak. "I assume that you are here to see the king—"

With a tight smile flashing across his oblong face, "Yes, yes, Papu," Chief Egwu said and tramped through the gateway, motioning for the other chiefs to follow him. "Please let us in."

Clearing his throat, Papu raised his voice. "But he is not home. I will let him know that you called." Worn to a frazzle probably due to a combination of age and the energy he'd expended in teleporting to several locations within a space of a few minutes, he slammed the frame shut with a clang and hasped it. Pulling the shades together, he slumped in his lookout chair. Letting his hands pillow his forehead atop the adjacent table, he murmured. "I hope this ends tonight…I am much too old for this hurry-scurry."

"How do we proceed now?" Chief Ikeme asked.

Shrugging, "I don't know," Chief Jokum said. "Perhaps go and talk with Adane to see what more she may know."

"Yes," Chief Egwu said. "And later return to check up on the king?"

Nodding, "Definitely a good idea," Chiefs Jokum and Ikeme said together.

Turning on their heels, the chiefs traipsed away from the palace, rubbernecking all the way.

"Where can the king be when he has military visitors and again on a Sunday?" Chief Egwu said. "And where is Chief Madu?"

"Something is definitely not right," Chief Ikeme said as he adjusted his glasses. "I don't know about you two, but Papu has never spoken to me through his window. He had always taken the time to come down here to speak to me."

"That's right," Chief Jokum said. "It's unusual of him to behave that way. He seemed out of breath, too. Respect from the palace has definitely flown out of its windows."

Chapter 75

A little while later, against the growing backdrop of an orchid, yellow, orange, and red sunset, a group of women, a few tens strong, were circling the wagons within a yard somewhere near Church Road.

Deserted and overgrown with dust-mantled fringing and ubiquitous plants and smelt of mildew, the almost-square compound had four roofless and sooted mud houses at its four corners as well as badly charred wood and tree trunks here, there, and everywhere.

Shrouded from passersby by the crumbling structures and by the cohort of women who were shuffling with unease on ground that was bestrewn with sand, and litter, Mama Ugochi had Ugochi secured in a piggyback by a wrapper as she stood in the center of a small circle formed by the forlorn figures, many of whom either had their swaddled babies in their arms, or also on piggyback.

"Thank you for heeding Papu's call," Mama Ugochi said in a hushed voice. "Thank you for taking the time away from your busy schedules to meet me here."

"We, the M.F.F.S, are always honored to be here. We came here in a hurry because he suggested some good news," the women chorused in low but serious tones. "What is going on?"

Nodding as she gently swayed on her feet to keep her daughter in a sleep state, "Though she was not part of us but was dear to us—to me, when she was still active in church, it was sad news for me when I heard that Mama Uche, Ugochi's godmother, is no longer with us. It is unfortunate that she did not listen to the advice some of us gave her about her husband and she would end up losing her life for nothing," Mama Ugochi continued in a low voice. "But the good news is that her husband, who not only was Akagheli's chief Mkpátáku occultist, but who we believe also silenced her for good, has now met his end, too—"

Letting out a collective gasp, then sighing with relief without warning, many of the women squealed with delight and made the sign of the cross as others hugged one another, or waved their arms in the air, or did both in turn. There were tiny, tattooed letterings visible on the inside of the right arms of those who were brave enough to wear sleeveless tops in the weather of that day perhaps due to being in a rush to leave their homes for that August meeting.

Quickly and with darting eye movements, Mama Ugochi shushed them with a motion of her hands, "I am not saying that we should not rejoice but not this way," she said. "Let us do it inwardly, or in our homes."

With their mouths curved in smiles, "We understand," they said in concert.

"Equally, Chief Madu, who most of us believed was second only to the king, supernaturally, has also been taken care of," Mama Ugochi said in haste whilst still motioning with her hands to keep the women from whooping it up again. "Papu also said that he believes the king will meet his end before tonight. This means we are beginning to rid our village of this menace that has caused us mothers so much fear, which we were scared to speak about in case we were also silenced. It is true that we don't know all the men in our village who are so inclined, but since two of the top three are gone, it should send them a clear message that it is only a matter of time before they, too, are found out and executed as well. But until we are sure of this, let us not be loose with our tongues."

"We agree with you, Mama Ugochi," the women said in harmonious whispers.

"Now, who wants to go with me to meet Prince Ikuku? Papu said he is in the palace now," Mama Ugochi added sotto voce and ambled away from the center toward a path that opened up as the women parted. "I know many of you cannot because of your children. But anyone who wants to go with me should meet me at the junction between Market Road and Farm Road. Let me go and give my sleeping daughter to her father. We will leave once we are at least ten in number."

Chapter 76

A little while earlier, King Ajutu appeared within Chief Madu's house, huffing and puffing. He scoured through the home and much to his irritation, found no-one, then vanished.

****

Becoming visible within Mr. Isigwe's compound as wailing came from the backyard; the king entered his chief occultist's room and found it empty. Rubbing the back of his neck with jerky hands, "Where the hell are these men? Never around when you need them the most. Unreliable," he bawled as he exited the dwelling, his gaze bouncing from point to point, and bustled toward the keening voice that tore into the otherwise-silent, late afternoon.

Arriving at the open entrance to the kitchen, he stopped and stood still on seeing Mama Udo who was smeared all over with blood. Sitting splay-legged on the floor and lamenting the death of her husband whose body rested between her legs, her arms cradled his head. Behind her, Udo, who looked sad and stunned, knelt with his arms enfolded around her neck as the side of his face rested atop her head.

Looking up at her king with tear-soaked eyes, Mama Udo shook her head and sniveled, "It was Nkem—she shot him like he was a criminal who was facing a firing squad; Your Majesty, she has finished me. We must get our revenge—help us!"

Staggered by the sight and absolutely incensed, King Ajutu backed away. Gazing down as he drifted in and out of view, he clenched his fists as he struggled for control, "Most Venerable One, you must now come to my aid, please," he muttered as hot rage surged through him and his Adam's apple bobbed. "The execution of our high priest is a clear signal that the ritual is being attacked. Barring my execution, nothing can top this. This is no longer just my fight. I shall entreat you in my shrine with supreme propriety."

Turning on his heel, he right away got lost to view.

Chapter 77

Coming into sight within the caucus room, which had remained suffused with its usual soft, fluorescent light, King Ajutu's front was sent smack against the shelves by a quick succession of shots into his back from Namdi's rifle as he tried to thumb the button that opened his shrine.

Dropping on his right side to the floor, he landed with a loud thud. Coughing up blood from his mouth as he lay supine on the floor, he looked with his half-lidded eyes to his left to see Odera, Prince Ikuku, Queen Nena—cleaving to the bag of Ejizu's bones, Namdi, Captain Iduto, the two sergeants, the four privates, and me on our feet, nervously staring back at him.

Fear capturing my face as he feebly struggled to arise, with my fingers pumping and my blood up, I exploded a series of shots into his chest that, again, flattened his back against the floor.

He shut his eyes.

Watching as blood and air rushed out of his lungs and his breaths spaced out further and further, we exchanged glances with one another as the feeling that we, when all was said and done, had gotten the better of him began to well up within me; the others, except for the prince, looking equally pleased.

What happened next wasn't as unexpected, as it'd seemed impossible to imagine. Had he become a beast like the others Odera and Namdi had fought and defeated, there might've been an overwhelming feeling within me at the time that we still stood an imminent chance against him, but that wasn't what happened.

With his eyes making rapid motions whilst still closed, his face warping and his body jerking, King Ajutu was a blur of streaks, shimmering lights, and colors as he went through at least five transformations. Happening so fast as the bullet wounds closed in no time at all, and as though he found it hard to choose what creature to turn into and instead preferring to improve on who he was, he began to assume a jauntier version of himself.

Flicking his amber-turquoise eyes open and fixating on Odera's left wrist, he jerked his neck leftward and grinned as I involuntarily fired more shots. Levitating in a trice, he continued to dodge the slugs—twisting and spiraling as he fully transfigured until all I could hear from my weapon were the clicks of the trigger.

Exchanging rifles with frozen Namdi, I continued to eject shells. King Ajutu inclined vertically as I sizzled the air with chunks of lead and floated as he cracked his neck, palming the bullets away hither and thither; with the royals and military folks taking cover beneath the table.

With a stressed expression on my face as fear continued to rage within me and uncertainty swallowing any words I tried to utter, I knew that Odera would see the fight as his and his alone, and that the only weapon to matter was his machete.

And as fate rushed at Odera and as though we both had the same thought, Odera motioned for everyone to leave the room. Becoming poised with both hands holding his lifted machete, Odera set his feet wide apart, and heels lifted a touch.

As Namdi and I bustled the others out of the room, the king blasted a beam of lightning in our direction, which Bute, Ejizu, and Dike shielded us from.

"I knew that would happen," the spryer-looking king mocked. "No harm in trying. We'll meet again. Now, Odera, my son, and viper in my bosom, what am I going to do about you?"

"What am I going to do about you, Father," Odera rasped, drawing a look of surprise from the king.

"So, you know, huh?" the king snorted as the door shut.

"Did you think I wouldn't find out what you did to my mother? What you did to many other women?" Odera roared.

"So, you had always known and just played along?" the king said.

"I wish I knew much earlier than today. I would have gone against you sooner.

The king furrowed his brows, "So, Namdi also had the guts to disobey me in that regard," he scoffed. "And who amongst those two would have had the nerve to go against me and tell you this? That nebbish stepfather of yours who can't be anyone's rock and should never have been called Peter…Or is it the unadventurous Evelyn who wasted all her life with him?"

Contemplating for a moment, Odera's brows turned inward and downward, "She is a much better human being than you could ever be," he said in a blaze of anger. "Your intimidation of them was always going to end. Everything, good, or evil, eventually will come to the light. Your focus on yourself and on the palace intrigue between you and Chief Madu as well as your mingling with your spiritual compeers and sanctification of an ancient deathly conduct allowed for gross abuses of human rights under our very noses. Disaffection with the way you rule was spreading and some of us were bound to find out. One malcontent victim was always going to break the laissez-faire attitude of most of our people. Even a long-suffering person will resist or retaliate if pushed too far. Nothing lasts forever…Might is not always right…And, tonight, your pride shall be pocketed."

Rolling his eyes and knotting his left fist, "Your growing mastery of the English language is evidence that the powers I helped you get continue to strongly manifest in you," King Ajutu had a cold, supercilious tone. "But rather than impugn my honor, what do you intend to do about our practices besides killing Mr. Isigwe—"

"And Chief Madu, if you didn't already know," Odera interrupted. "And what I intend to do is to destroy you too."

Hot under the collar, the king's shoulders sagged. And after a long, meditative moment, "You have proved more disloyal than I anticipated…" the king growled, feeling spurned, looking forlorn, cocking his head to the side, studying Odera's left wrist and machete, "and have made me abandon all the lofty plans I had for you. I can't believe that I helped you become who you are now only to be at the receiving end of your wrath."

Sensing a hint of distraction about the king and a window of vulnerability, Odera charged at him, with his machete ready to chop, but slammed into the bookshelves, as the king sidestepped to Odera's left in a flash, dodging his advance.

Striking sharply with the side of his right hand to disarm Odera's left hand of his machete, Odera's left fist was immovable. And quickly, faster than the king could think of his next move, he hemmed the king into the corner between the shelves and the east wall. Flicking his wrist to slash the king, the king held out his left arm and parried Odera's attempt with contemptuous ease. Palming Odera away, hard, as his Akupé transformed into a sword, the king emitted a growl of fury, tightened his grip around the weapon's haft, and aimed a wide, sweeping stroke at Odera. As Odera evaded this with fast, backward steps, a rapid swordfight ensued that was fraught with only near hits.

Hacking at each other at lightning speed as sparks flew, both men moved back and forth without breaking stride, lunging, spinning across the floor in blindingly fast sashays, applying their weapons with the same force as they used their feet as well as the fists of their weapon-less hands.

With the atmosphere feeling the force of the king's bitter and depressed spirit, they fought with elan, clanking away, hammer and tongs. Staving off all potential strikes at each other and keeping each other at bay, the books on the shelves tumbled out when they could bear the brunt of Odera's ferocity no more.

As Odera sweated and panted, and King Ajutu exuded calm, there was a major hit.

Chapter 78

Meanwhile, as twilight neared and the stench of evil pervaded whilst the atmosphere remained saturated with tension, the resplendent throne room in the meantime was bathed in light.

Pacing up and down the area immediately before it's doorway with my rifle about me, I impatiently poked my left thigh with the fingers of my left hand.

I couldn't help puzzling over what I'd just seen. I was certain that I'd seen, within the king, as he transfigured, a black panther, as well as each of the creatures Batu, Diko, Jadue, and Kadiye had been able to change into. I was doubly sure that the others had witnessed the same going by the horror that was in the air.

How will this end? Surely Odera had once fought these creatures and prevailed, he can repeat it. But then again, he wasn't alone at the time. Now, he is. Though he's got the power, still, he might be overpowered. Had it been before I began to feel his force grow within me, it'd have made sense for me to abide by his want and stay away from danger. Now, I'm a hundred-percent certain that he's given me some abilities, albeit still nascent. Shouldn't I be using it? Isn't this the purpose for having them?

My inaction, at a time Odera had his hands full, brought me to the brink of exploding, and I gave myself up to impulse, "Namdi," I said, my eyes flashing with dawning recognition of what must be done; my words flinging out at him like an accusation. "The thought that things don't go well when I'm not front and center in them often devours me. Call me impulsive, hyperactive, or paranoid, it doesn't really matter, I've heard them all before. You can sit by if you want. I, on the other hand, can't just sit tight and sit on my hands. I'm going to join Odera."

"Don't go; Odera indicated—" Namdi said.

"I know what Odera indicated, but I'm countering it. You should, too. Swap weapons or reload. I shouldn't have left him—only did to help get the queen, the prince, and our military friends, who don't have powers like you, and I now do, safely out of harm's way," I interjected, the words bursting from me in a passionate rush, oblivious to the look of concern on Namdi's face.

And then, before he could perhaps frame a better reply, I streaked out of the room whose door was flanked on the inside by the captain and his sergeants to my right and the privates to my left, all of whom were a study in fright, had their weapons at the ready and stared down the passage time and again.

Seeming to ponder the ramifications of either my bizarre action, or of his continued passivity, Namdi darted a glance at the queen who was perched on the throne and clung onto the bag of Ejizu's bones, which was atop her lap, with her head, on a neck that had disappeared as her shoulders were pulled forward, hanging, and shaking in a slow, back-and-forth sweep, and her feet trembling. Flickering his gaze at the prince on the queen's right who sat collapsed in his seat with his brows folded inward above eyes that ping-ponged whilst his lips were pressed together and arms were crossed at chest level, Namdi heaved a heavy sigh as all his visible muscles twitched.

It was apparent that he itched to fight beside his brother in arms.

But what is stopping him? Is it just because Odera has so indicated? Is it because he believes Odera is always right? What will it take for him to disobey Odera for once—to realize that three isn't a crowd in this situation?

Turning left, as Namdi continued to pace the center of the room back and forth with his arms crossed behind him, I barged through the first door to the caucus room.

With a soft shake of his head as he scratched his neck and heaved a weary sigh, and with a despairing look, Prince Ikuku hauled himself to his feet. "You all would have to excuse me," he said with a pensive tone that lacked enthusiasm. "Nature is calling."

Chapter 79

At the same time, within an ambience impregnated with the hum of dragonflies, the whine of mosquitoes, and the flow of water in riffles, the maidens approached the grassy banks that edged the rippling, silt-less water of a shallow river, which purled as it flowed over cobbles, rolled around boulders, and coursed whilst it swashed about tall trees that hemmed its meandering flow.

Glancing at one another and jumping in, "Certainly deeper than the last one," they said with one mind as Ijeoma flung the book onto the top of the bank.

"We couldn't enjoy the last one because you were still in pain," Adure added as, with a soft squish, they landed their bare feet into the knee-high water's muddy bottom and soil oozed between their toes.

As a gentle current flowed around their bare ankles and drifting twigs brushed their legs, they sat down on the bank. Staring skyward through the treetops, shades of evening continued to draw on as sunset pearled the sky beyond the hills.

Rolling her neck on her shoulders, Adure then looked to her right at Ijeoma. "If the king dies in this fight…" she said. "What then?"

Much to her irritation, Ijeoma shut her eyes, "We have agreed to not go back, so it matters not whether he is dead, or alive," she said.

"I mean, with regards to the child," Adure rephrased. "Since it will be the heir, will you not at least let the village know of its existence?"

"I do not know what the future holds for my would-be child, but now is not the time to worry about it because it totally depends on what gender it is. We have talked about this already."

"Doesn't the gender matter only if the king is still alive?" Adure said.

With a half shrug, Ijeoma opened her eyes, "I guess," she said as her gaze dropped toward the water. "But these people have never been ruled by a queen. What if the king dies and my child is a girl?"

"We can change that," Adure said. "I'm just worried that the child may grow up really fast and you would have lost the chance to claim the monarchy for it. You may not be believed the longer it takes if they haven't already seen you pregnant with it and suddenly you show up with a child you claim to belong to their king's lineage."

Turning her head and flashing Adure an askance stare, "You are assuming that I want anything to do with this village," Ijeoma said.

"We may struggle to fit in wherever it is we are headed, as we won't know the custom," Adure continued. "The palace, where the king does whatever he wants and allowed us do the same, is all we know. I know you don't want to go back to the king; what about going back if he dies? Isioma, what do you think?"

Glancing leftward at Ijeoma and trailing a hand through the clear water, "I have nothing to add, really, at least until I conceive," Isioma said. "Or else I could be labeled a traitor."

"I think we will adapt wherever we end up," Ijeoma said. "If people don't like how we behave around them, then we rub them out. As for the monarchy, if and when I make a decision about it and the king is no more, then every villager will certainly learn of it. But until then, I have a life to own and enjoy."

Turning her head rightward and pinning her ears back, "On a different note," Isioma said with nonchalance as she got to her feet. "I can hear a woman screaming and a man's voice trying to keep her quiet—sounds like she's being forced to make whoopee. Do you hear them?"

Nodding, "Quite far away from here though," Adure said. "Nonetheless, this is your opportunity, Isioma. You are bound to be more beautiful than whomever the woman is. So, go and get what you need."

Hot to trot, Isioma transformed into her cougar in a trice as a steady breeze ruffled the leaves of the trees. Loping upstream of the upland for a little, she discerned her direction of proposed travel. And then, zoom, she went like a streak amongst the trees.

Smiling and looking rightward at the disappearing feline, "Go girl," Ijeoma said with her left thumb up. "We will wait here."

Chapter 80

A little earlier, Odera had thrust his machete downward in a flash.

Pulling it out of the king's body, between the king's hands, slashing the king's palms, he retreated.

With his eyes wide open and brows furrowed, King Ajutu's jaw dropped. Struggling to hold stance with his legs quivering, he lowered his head as he dropped to his knees. Glancing down and through his pullover, he saw the deep rent in his anterior abdominal wall, which ran from just below his breastbone to his navel, pulsating, and filling with bubbling blood. Gritting as huge stabs of agony shot through him and with a slow, disbelieving shake of his head whose neck veins bulged, he sneered as he lifted his head and sent a long, pained gaze at Odera.

Watching on and not knowing what to expect, the whole of his machete's distal half bloodied, Odera readied his weapon.

With his body crumpling in on itself, "I may not be able to heal this, but this is only the beginning," the king rasped as his sword landed on the floor and reverted to his Akupé. Going limp and breaking eye contact with Odera, the king slumped as he bled out, and I barged into the room without knocking.

Whirling his neck around so quickly that he almost ricked it, Odera acknowledged me for a moment and motioned for me to wait at the door.

Backing away toward me, Odera's eyes refocused on the king. As King Ajutu shut his eyes and grew more and more pallid, what I'd anticipated would happen, did, though it wasn't in the order I'd thought.

Morphing into a healthy black panther in a snap, King Ajutu charged toward Odera. Feeling a tedious familiarity about the unfolding situation, "My God!" Odera groaned as he staggered back in disbelief, heaved a helpless sigh as he tensed up, and his stomach knotted.

Lunging his machete at the furiously snarling and nimble cat, it swerved to its right and leapt over King Ajutu's chair onto the table, faster than Odera could swing his machete at it.

Obvious to me that the feline's interest wasn't in attacking Odera, perhaps having learnt from previous experience, it pounced, catching me off guard as I wasn't fast enough in positioning my rifle to get a shot off.

Knocking me down sideways, I smacked my right hip on the floor of the thin-carpeted, short passage. Scrambling with its four limbs, its jaws reaching in furious desperation to fasten on my neck as I rolled onto my back, Odera dived at it.

Transpiercing its abdomen through its left side, Odera shoved it with Herculean strength off his machete.

"Thank you," I panted as the feline's claw marks on my body slowly healed.

Grunting, bleeding, thrashing about, and tumbling as it fell away from me, it quickly transmuted into the lion-headed stallion.

One transformation later than I did expect.

And with thunderous roaring, and snarling, it galloped up the short passage. Striking lightning, it ripped a hole out of the door ahead, leapt the three steps, and crashed through what was left of the carved wood barrier as bullets from my rifle lodged into its hindquarters, knocking it off balance.

Frowning, "You shouldn't have returned," Odera said as he jumped over me and headed toward the caucus-area passage. "Stay away this time."

Sighting Namdi on the caucus-area passage who opened a spray of bullets at it, it careened rightward around the corner, scraped its side, and began to bleed. Then quickly healing as it streaked down the east passage whilst Odera gave it chase with Namdi in hot pursuit, its king cobra tail flew off its hindquarters.

In the air, the long and huge snake lifted the front third of its body. Flaring out its hood, it emitted a spine-chilling hiss as it moved forward to attack Odera. As the reptile lunged, aiming for Odera's throat, Odera leaned left, skirting around it, and, with one down-up stroke, chopped its head off as it flew past him, then rubbed the snake's body into pieces with fast swings of his machete.

Rising as my heart thumped away, I realized that King Ajutu was using up the lives afforded to his body by the negergies that had inhabited his four henchmen's bodies as well as Adaku. Believing that he then had four lives left, I rose to my feet, loped forward for a little, began to run, then tripped like blazes after the brothers in arms with my rifle at the ready.

Arriving at the east passage just as the creature emitted another tremendous shaft of lightning that rived and splintered another door, I couldn't blaze it away with my weapon as Odera and Namdi, both running in sharp, long strides, blocked my line of fire, and I suspected Odera was blocking Namdi's too.

Closing on it as it battered through the split door, which splintered as it charged across the veranda, Odera dived at it and stuck his machete into its left loin. Dragging Odera along as he hung from his machete, it saw Chief Madu's lifeless body and, in a fury, turned and flashed lightning at Odera.

With its attempt blocked by Ejizu, it then struck the machete.

As the heat transferred from Odera's weapon's metal to the stainless-steel cross guard handle, Odera felt his hands scorch. Pulling out his machete on instinct, he let it fall to the ground, and as he recovered from the burn, Namdi and I took the driving seat.

With the creature healing, changing back into the panther, and leaping onto one garden furniture after another, on its way to the west roof terrace, we fired away at it with total abandon as confusion fogged my brain. Having believed that its feline form's life had already been extinguished, I didn't expect to see it again.

Still five lives left then: the panther, the liorse, the komodion, the Ammit, and the lieagle?

Crashing to the ground, it quickly healed and transformed into the lion-headed eagle. Flapping its wings and hovering, it roared a ball of fire at Namdi and me. Flinging my rifle in Odera's direction near the east veranda, I backflipped across the ground toward Odera to evade the blaze whilst Namdi cartwheeled away toward the northeast corner, stood poised, and continued to fire at it.

Odera grabbed his not quite cooled-down machete as I picked up my rifle, "Hold your fire, Namdi," he roared, running toward the beast as it took off.

Jumping, Odera reached for one of its large talons with his right hand. No sooner had he latched onto the claws than its Inland Taipan snake tail, snapping its jaws with vicious intent, delivered a series of rapid and accurate venomous strikes. Leaving multiple bloodied rents in Odera's right sleeve, Odera didn't flinch.

Looking the snake square in the eyes with fury as it bared its fangs and moved in to coil itself around his neck, Odera chopped the snake into fine bits with sizzling and, in one fell swoop, thrust his long, pointed, red-hot knife into the bird's underbelly, twisted the weapon, and eviscerated it with a gush of blood.

Letting go of the ugly avian as it plummeted, Odera dropped to the ground and rolled away toward the southeast corner. Rising to his feet, he tore off the right sleeve of his jumper and watched as his skin quickly absorbed the venom and the puncture wounds rapidly healed.

The creature landed with a thump, changed into the komodion, and heaved its acid like a waterfall in a counter-clockwise arc over all that was in the vicinity of the east half of the courtyard, releasing its tiger-snake tail into the air.

Four lives left: the panther, the liorse, the komodion, and the Ammit?

Watching as Chief Madu fizzed and dissolved in a snap to bare bones and everything else animate and inanimate foamed and seethed like mad, we realized that we hadn't been affected much by the fluid that also wetted us to the skin.

Glancing at each other in incredulity as our clothes and rifles, but not our bodies, or Odera's machete, began to succumb to the acid, the tiger-snake aimed for Odera.

Distracted, "Your guns are no use now," Odera said, clearly confused by what had just transpired. "Go get your machete, Namdi…Nkem, you need a change of clothes."

Sensing that Odera was still trying his level best to get us out of what he thought was harm's way despite that it should've become obvious to him that we'd become nearly, if not completely, as invincible as him, "You both need new clothes, too," I protested. "You can't get rid of me that quickly, you know!"

"I am staying here with you," Namdi said as he blasted the tiger-snake's head just before it closed in on Odera whilst baring its fangs. "We are not going to get hurt if that's what you are worried about."

Looking to his left as the entire snake shattered in a sheet of searing flame that traveled through its body, Odera heaved a huge sigh. "Suit yourselves."

With a shrug, Odera charged toward the center of the courtyard at the creature that looked daggers; possibly because we hadn't succumbed to its acid, or because we'd destroyed its snake. With a sudden spring, Odera leapt off the burial mound and flipped over the beast. Landing behind it as it turned around to face him, Odera decapitated it in a flash with a down-up strike.

Three lives left: the panther, the liorse, and the Ammit?

As its head rolled away toward the southwest corner, the king's multiply negergized-lifeforce regenerated into the Ammit. Lunging at Odera as it released its mamba tail to fly toward me, Odera crescent-kicked it with all his might and it flew back toward the west veranda, sliding, and smacking against the wall, creating a massive dent in it.

Recovering, it charged at Odera at speed and my shot struck the mamba, disintegrating it in the air to smithereens. Dodging the beast's attack, Odera helped it on its way through the air. Landing against King Mbanegu's sculpture, it knocked it off its pedestal and the statue shattered to pieces on the northeast veranda.

Lurching into the courtyard, its gaze alert and ferocious, the maddening beast stopped.

Odera pushed up what was left of his left sleeve, the right sleeve no longer existent, and drew in a deep breath through his nose and exhaled through his mouth. Standing poised, Odera readied his machete. With the creature engaging in a stare down with Odera as a look of brutal determination remained across its face, Odera's visage hardened.

And then bang, with a glow in my eyes as my breath came in short bursts, I fired at it just before what was left of my rifle's trigger dissolved away.

Darting its angry gaze at me, it charged toward me. As I froze, the rifle fell out of my hands and Odera mirrored its movement.

With a leap, it pounced. Landing square on the point of Odera's machete, it knocked Odera down atop me. Hitting the ground, Odera rose instantly and pulled his machete out with exceptional strength as he counter pressured with his right foot. And with anger and ferocity, and at breakneck speed, Odera hacked the creature again and again with a series of sickening strikes that jarred every structure in its body, then, suddenly, unexpectedly, it exploded like an empty pod.

Two lives left: the panther, and the liorse?

Without warning and utterly bewilderingly, and with the soft, rapid suck of the earth against the creature's multifarious parts, whatever was left of King Ajutu vanished completely into the ground without a trace.

Looking around for a moment and at each other in puzzlement, our gazes then fixated at the very spot we'd last seen any part, or form of the king.

And what the heck just happened? The panther and the liorse hadn't yet been exposed to life-ending injuries. So, where's King Ajutu? Is it possible that he has, at long last, gone the way of the flesh?

Chapter 81

The close of day rapidly made its way, and with the trees looking tenebrous in the half-light, the cougar felt something anew within itself as it descried its destination within a clearing.

Skulking forward without noise and curling its lips, the felid emerged from the trees behind the man who was down on his knees. Focused on his back, which blocked its view of his sufferer, it crouched, ready to spring.

As the woman continued to struggle in vain, making forlorn attempts to free herself, "It would be over before you know it," the man roared, almost pleading. "Just wait now, I will be gentle, okay?"

Perhaps its need from him getting the better of its predatory instinct, the cougar thought twice about attacking the man, who wasn't in a good, physical shape, and, instead, transformed to Isioma.

Seemingly overwhelmed again by the same predacious feeling of the moment before, she flinched, trying her hardest not to revert to her feline form. Muttering to herself, "I am not pregnant, yet my free will is keen on dominating. Does another way to be free exist rather than allow this filthy man anywhere near me?"

As the man with significant middle-age spread persisted in his attempts at forcing himself into the bound and gagged young lady whose clothes were rucked up, Isioma snuck up to him and towered over him. On seeing the woman point at her, Isioma's conflicted state became resolved.

Scared out of his wits in the semidarkness, he spun around to catch sight of Isioma standing behind him.

"What the heck are you doing?" Isioma said. "You ought to be ashamed of yourself."

Freezing as he tried to get to his feet, sweat stood in pearls along his receded hairline, and he tripped on his pants that were down at his ankles, falling backward atop the woman.

Isioma grabbed the front of his shirt with exceptional strength and flung him away, "Stay there," she said, then, as the man cowered, she ungagged the woman and began to untie her. "How old are you, young woman?"

"17."

"How did you get here?"

On her feet with arms crossed tightly over her chest, head inclined, and shoulders pulled inward, and with a cracking voice and through tears, "I came to send him my condolences, then he told me he had something for me that he had kept somewhere in the bush and—"

"Never mind," Isioma interjected. "I get the gist. You are free now. Never again follow any man into the bush. Many of them are notorious in this village for their sexual depravity."

Setting the wasp-waist teenager on her way, Isioma turned toward the man as he tried to zip his pants up. Approaching him, she shoved him back to the ground and tugged his trousers off. "I told you to stay," she said. "Now, I am going to bind and muffle you like you did to that young woman so that after experiencing the shame and pain of it, you will not ever do it to another woman. Then I am going to do to you what you wanted to do to her and much more."

Looking up at her, "Please," the man with a somewhat wonky nose and crooked mouth said. "I will not do it again. I can see that you are no ordinary lady. By the force with which you pushed me, I am sure that you are more powerful than you look. Please don't hurt me."

"You know, I heard her beg you from far away, and I heard you hit her and threaten to kill her if she continued to resist. Why did you not listen to her and let her be?"

"I am sorry," the man said as tears began to streak his face. "I just want to go home. I fear the forest when it is dark."

Straddling the man, Isioma stood over him, "You should have thought about all of these before bringing the lady here. Who was she by the way?"

"She was my son's girlfriend."

"Your son's girlfriend, huh," Isioma snorted. "What do you think your son would say if he heard what you did to his friend?"

"My son is dead."

"What is your name by the way?"

"I am Mr. Ben Nzule—"

"And then, Mr. Nzule, you decided to take advantage? What do you think he would say if he was watching you as a spirit? What would your wife say if she heard it?"

"My wife, too, died in the same house fire—I have just been a weak person since I lost my family."

"I sense that you are saying all of these so that I show you mercy, but I really do not care. You brought this upon yourself. Rather than find yourself a woman who is willing, you assault vulnerable ones and blame it on your loss?"

"Most of the women of my age are not free, and no young woman will look at me at this age, and I have needs, especially now."

Rolling her eyes, "Well, I have needs, too, and I need you to stretch your arms out like this," Isioma said, reaching out her arms. "And then put your wrists together. I am going to tie them, then do the same to your ankles. After that, I will gag you."

"Are you going to kill me?"

"Death is an easy way out of the punishment you deserve. By the time I am done with you, you will never look at another woman, talk less of lay your filthy hands on her."

Chapter 82

A little while later, we were still agog to find out where on earth the king was. Whilst we stood atop King Otubu's grassed-over tumulus at the center of the courtyard, waiting, staring at one another, the sky dusked. And as our shadows got long and hard, Ejizu still couldn't feel, or see his father anywhere.

As hundreds of lantern lights were kindled almost in concert within the sprawl of huts across the village and began to shimmer in the gloaming, Odera and Namdi each dropped their weapons and commenced their bond greeting.

"Considering that you are a prince and that it also became obvious to you that you had powers after that Komodion's acid dropped on your skin," Namdi whispered in Odera's ear. "I am not sure which of 'Dragon Prince' and 'Lion Prince' would be, for you, a more befitting superhero name."

Smiling and with the skin around his eyes crinkling, Odera remained focused as they completed their greeting.

From the downslope, I watched the brothers forever pick their machetes up. My eyes riveted on Odera as his eyes continued to shine with triumph, I began to revere him as a figure of heroic mold.

For me, it shall be Dragon Prince all the way. No question!

Chapter 83

Adaku looked sick as a parrot, as she closed in on Somto, Dike, Bute, and Ejizu, who continued to hug one another in delight.

"I think, with a high degree of certainty, that all the three maidens are now pregnant. I'm no longer able to see any of them," Adaku said, looking a question. "The last time I saw Isioma was when she walked in on a man who was about to force his way with a young woman—she saved the girl, forced the man into copulation, became her cougar, and…" Adaku paused, then leaned in toward Somto. "Ended up biting his erect manhood off, and I've never heard a man scream as loud as he did," she whispered, then continued. "So, now, I've no clue if they're still on their journey, or if they've ended up somewhere."

"And given that they achieved pregnancy within minutes of the act, you are concerned that they might also give birth way earlier than nine months?" Somto said and Adaku gave a few frantic nods.

"This isn't good news at all," Ejizu said. "We won't know when any of them gives birth. But telling Mother now will lead to a wild goose chase, as none of us can send them in any meaningful direction."

"I say we tell her nonetheless," Dike said, glancing at Bute.

"I guess it is still up to Ejizu at this point," Bute retorted. "Unless you tell your mother and she in turn tells the queen."

"I don't want to go against Ejizu," Dike said. "I will let him decide. I promised not to be cantankerous."

"What worries me though is how I am able to see the strangers Adure and Isioma were intimate with when they were in the same vicinity but wasn't able to see Ijeoma at all even when she was in the same place as Adure and Isioma at a time I could still see both of them?"

"If you can fully see a human simply by wishing to see them, it's because there was a connection with them while you were human, and if you can see only their heat signature, then there was no connection be it direct, or indirect," Somto said. "You could see Adure and Isioma because you knew the bodies that now harbor those negergies and explains why you could also see, indirectly, any human they were near for the duration of that interaction. That you couldn't see Ijeoma at all means that Ijeoma's body was no longer the body of the friend that you knew and had a connection with—in other words, it was no longer the exact human body you knew; meaning that her pregnancy altered that body to something else that you had no connection with whatsoever and also couldn't see while it was around Adure, or Isioma because the necessary energy field didn't come into play. Same goes for the pregnant Adure and now Isioma. Certain chemicals of pregnancy must be interacting with the negergy and have altered the processes that make it possible for more than their heat signatures to be seen by anyone who had once been able to see them."

"Now, that sounds complicated and exceptionally scary," Ejizu said and quickly drifted away. "Nothing's going to stop me now. I have to tell Mother."

As Ejizu changed realms, "If what you say is true, Somto; how is it then possible that I can still see the men Adure and Isioma were intimate with?" Adaku said.

"Simple," Somto said. "During the act, the maidens that you had a connection with must have rubbed off on the men something that once made the maidens visible to you—"

"By that same reasoning," Adaku said. "Since Ijeoma was pregnant by the king, why was I not able to see him?"

"I'm not sure I have the correct answer to that. It could be that whatever was transferred between the maidens and the men they copulated with is only temporary, or there could be another explanation."

"Or the king was so powerful that he was able to negate whatever was transferred," Adaku said.

With a nod, "That's a strong possibility," Somto said.

"Our past life never ceases to spring up new surprises," Dike said. "It's one thing after another. No moment to rest."

"Somewhat…But still I disagree in a way, Dike," Somto said. "Many things may be out of one's control, but one's lack of peace, or inability to rest is, for the most part, because of one's own choices. Humans for the most part are the ones who complicate their own lives by dabbling in things that they shouldn't."

Chapter 84

At the same time, Odera fastened his weightless gaze on me, and as my desire lit up, despite my inner conflict against allowing myself to enjoy the pleasures of the flesh so soon after losing my only son, he beamed at me.

Noticing this and with an understanding nod toward Odera, "I better change clothes," Namdi said and headed off.

Absentmindedly, "Check my room," Odera said with a calm expression as I remained transfixed by his sheer brawn. "Be there shortly."

With a chortle, "You clearly will be needing that room," Namdi said. "I will find something my size in Jadue or Kadiye's room."

As Odera strode to me in a sure-footed manner, I grew weak-kneed. Taking me by my left hand as Namdi walked toward the north veranda, Odera kissed the back of it, pulled me to himself and wrapped his right arm around my waist. Entrancing me, he lifted my face to his, brushed his lips against mine, then kissed them with tenderness, warmth, and want.

As he withdrew from me, I wrapped my arms around his neck and pulled him in for more. With half-lidded eyes, I slipped my tongue between his parted lips, and we stayed in a lip-lock for what seemed like an eternity.

Easing off, we nose-rubbed for a moment, and my eyes sparkled as my passion mounted up. Letting his machete fall from his left hand to the ground, he lifted me whilst we continued to gaze into each other's eyes. My heart fluttering, I wrapped my legs around his waist, and he carried me on an easy, unhurried walk across the veranda.

Odera set me down as we arrived at the north passage, and my gaze was all over his tattered-looking clothes, which just about covered his private areas, revealing his rippling muscles.

"Take me with you to your room," I said with a warm, caring tone as my eyelashes flickered.

With an easy smile, "But I have nothing in there that would fit you," he said.

Dragging him by his right hand and delightfully free, "You definitely do!" my voice rising in delight as I stopped myself from staring at his crotch and dashed toward the northwest passage with him in tow.

Through the lounge, we arrived at the door of the room I knew to be his and pushed it open as he twisted its knob. Spinning around in the doorway, I grabbed the sides of his face and planted a wet kiss on his apposed lips as my desire for him went up multiple notches.

Lifting me again as I moaned with pleasure, he shuffled into the room and slammed the door shut.

Chapter 85

Not too long after, Odera and I, each of us in a fresh set of Odera's pants, top, and sandals, and pleased as punch, headed toward the throne room.

With easy and loose strides, we walked through the doorway with hands clasped. Then letting each other go and paying the queen our respects, we settled to stand to her left, and I faced Namdi. Smiling at Namdi as it was obvious to me that he'd been unable to find a set of shirt and pants that fitted whilst still wearing his acid-damaged boots, I wondered where everyone else was, "Did we miss anything?" I asked. "Where're our military friends? Where is the prince?"

"We are waiting for Papu," Namdi said. "Prince Ikuku excused himself, and the captain has gone with his men to guard the palace."

"And why're we waiting for Papu?" I asked.

Still perched on the throne since the moment we'd left Odera and the king in the caucus room, "Papu came to say that a group of women at the gateway wishes for an audience with me," the queen said.

And I sensed that the news that Akagheli was succeeding in the fight against Mkpátáku had begun to disseminate amongst affected and at-risk groups of women like a raging, rapidly spreading conflagration.

Before long, Papu walked into the throne room in between a group of women who were in two files. He appeared to be in a jocular mood—one that I suspected neither Odera nor Namdi had ever seen going by the look on their faces. Whilst he exchanged occasional whispers with the woman at the top of the line to his immediate right, I remembered getting acquainted with her through Mama Uche because Mama Uche was her daughter's godmother although we never really palled around.

As Papu bowed to the queen and stood on Namdi's left hand side, the 15 women bobbed curtsies and dropped to their knees in three rows of five before Her Majesty.

Inclining their heads as the queen leaned back in the ample throne and relaxed her posture, they chorused: "Long may you live, Your Majesty, for granting us this impromptu audience," their voices largely timorous.

Nodding to them, "Welcome, my people," Queen Nena said, darting open glances, in a clockwise direction, to her left at Odera and me, then to her right at Namdi and Papu before her eyes rested on Mama Ugochi in the middle of the front five women. "To what do I owe this visit?"

"Your Majesty," Mama Ugochi said, raising her head whilst the heads of the other women remained hanging. "We heard that two powerful Mkpátáku spiritualists are dead, and we came to hear for ourselves if this is true amongst other reasons. On arriving here, we also heard that the foremost Mkpátáku spiritualist, His Majesty, King Ajutu, is no more."

The queen remained quiet and after a long moment of fraught silence, she leaned forward, glancing nervously around, "And who gave you this information?" she said as her eyes came to rest on Mama Ugochi.

Involuntarily casting her eyes over her left shoulder toward Papu's direction, then bowing, "We heard through the grapevine, Your Majesty," Mama Ugochi said. "Is it true?"

"What is your name, madam?" Queen Nena said.

"I am Mrs. Abigail Onu, Your Majesty, but my friends and family prefer to call me Mama Ugochi."

"I don't know who might have told you this, but I cannot confirm either way, Mama Ugochi," Queen Nena said. "This is not how we disseminate information. But tell me more about your group, please. Papu said you are known as 'Mothers for firstborn sons.'"

"Yes, Your Majesty, we call ourselves that," Mama Ugochi said, then looked up. "And it is not because we lost children to Mkpátáku as you might suspect, but it is because out of fear of the known; we gave up our first sons so that our husbands will not be tempted or forced to sacrifice them—so that they might live. There are scores of us, but not all of us could come tonight for different reasons."

Shifting in her seat and making sidelong glances whilst her head remained still, "How do you mean, Mama Ugochi?" the queen asked, crossed, and uncrossed her arms, then tightened her grip on the bag that was atop her lap.

"Your Majesty, when it was time to give birth, we made sure our husbands weren't there. If the child turned out to be the woman's firstborn boy, we didn't let our husbands see them before we abandoned them far away from their homes, then lied to our husbands that the child was stillborn. That way, we ensured that our firstborn sons survived."

Shaking her head and darting a terrified glance at us, "Where did you leave these children?" the queen said. "And what type of husband will not ask to see their child's dead body?"

"Many of the fathers did ask, but we had agreed to lie that they had to be immediately buried because they were carrying an infection that might spread to other people, Your Majesty, the midwives at the birth houses were fully aware of our plan," Mama Ugochi said with a keek in Papu's direction. "After that, we traveled and left them at bus stops, car parks, and playgrounds in Agudagu…as it is the only place where Mkpátáku sacrifice does not happen as far as we know, and we heard that Prince Ikuku was doing a good job with the orphanages there. We knew how irresponsible it was to leave our children that way, but we kept watchful eyes on them until they were discovered by people. Also, when we learnt that there was an edict that any child found abandoned had to be taken straight to the main orphanage, the subsequent groups of women went directly to that orphanage and lied that they found the babies, which were in their possession, abandoned. The reason we came tonight is to confirm that the evil of Mkpátáku is no longer a threat to our children, all of whom are still below 18 years of age."

"It must have been difficult for you all," the queen said with a voice full of compassion. "And if I may ask, what is your relationship with Papu? I know he is the one who told you about the events that earlier occurred at the palace, considering that you've been eyeing him a lot."

"We were not allowed to say, Your Majesty, we agreed not to disclose so that the king did not learn of it," Mama Ugochi said. "Now that you know, we will not lie to you since the king seems to be no more. Please do not punish him. For that, we will agree not to tell anyone else about what might have happened to the king."

After a long moment of considered thought, "It appears you have wholehearted trust in Papu and that's fair enough," the queen said. "And I shall not tell a lie to you, too—my word is my bond as long as yours also remains your bond. It is important that we don't cause a different kind of unrest, which may be the case if people start to think that they have no king and no heir—until I have formally addressed them."

With a hint of a grin, "You have nothing to worry about, Your Majesty," Mama Ugochi said with another furtive peep at Papu. "We also came to find out from Prince Ikuku how to get our children back, so that we can go and look for them and bring them to their families who love them. We know that he is here."

With a wandering gaze at Papu, "I will discuss with him, and we will send Papu to you to let you know what to do about it. You may go now so that Papu may explain certain things to us. Tell the other women in your group that there is nothing to fear anymore starting now. The people you see in this room have made sure of that and will continue to do so."

"Thank you, Your Majesty."

Not long after the last of the women left the throne room, "So, Papu, tell us?" the queen said as she attempted to make strong eye contact with Papu. "Who really are you?"

Lifting his head and straightening his shoulders, Papu darted forthright glances at all of us before locking gazes with the queen. With a heavy sigh, "Your Majesty, I was a messenger from the netherworld," he started. "They sent me to deliver powers to Master Odera through a wristwatch and to provide him with his 'one-of-a-kind' machete, the weapon of choice for the king's henchmen. I was also instructed to ensure that the king did not avail himself of the powers they had meant for Master Odera and to guide Master Odera until he was old enough to look after himself—"

Odera shook his head with a hint of a grin and interjected, "Who would have thought that you replacing my driver was for a reason. So that's why we became close, and you helped me out with almost everything!"

Nodding, "Until Namdi came along, and you wanted nothing to do with a man who was over 40 years older. And don't worry, I hold nothing against you."

"Do I have the same foreign spirit that the king has?" Odera asked.

"They are known as negergies, and the answer is no," Papu said, clearly having found his groove, then faced Odera. "That had been the sneaky venerable ones' original intention, but for some reason, probably because you were still a child and didn't yet know good from evil, or for some other reason that I don't know, the negergies didn't take to you, though, inexplicably, you obtained physical abilities. Perhaps it had to do with characteristics of the place that is called the Zone of Unification, also known as the Unification Zone, or

Unification Center. Let me put it this way, it is a seen-unseen realm where evil and good, as antithetical absolutes, meet, partaking of both, belonging to neither…Where the human world, the seen realm, is believed to interface with the spiritual world, the unseen realm, and considered the spiritual root of the tree of knowledge of good and evil. While some people say that any person can extract either mostly the good, or mostly the bad from anything that comes from that zone though never both in equal measure, that one must supersede the other depending on which of good, or evil a person has done more, yet others say that it works out of the existence of free will such that if one's free will was tended toward evil at the time of going through the zone, the zone magnifies evil and if one's free will was geared toward good, the zone enhances one's goodness…But I can't be sure of any of these theories. The people of the netherworld are often evasive when it comes to matters concerning the zone…"

"Go on," I was eager.

"Incidentally, it is also the part of the earth where water, fire, and wind coexist in harmony…Where the earth brought forth the best metals known to the visible and invisible worlds and the king, the venerable ones, and I, on July 27, 1967, the same day that he gave you that watch…and exactly day nine of my coming into existence as well as of him making the pleas that inadvertently led to my being created, observed your machete being forged as *fire* made the metals into a molten mixture that is known to the unseen world as 'Devil's alloy' but looks like silver to the human world, *wind* carved it into shape and fashioned its handle, and pommel, and *water* cooled all its parts to retain its form. It is also where your wristwatch, the knives known as athame, as well as other Mkpátáku chattels were created. Even so, as you grew older, the venerable ones tried other ways including using Adaku to get their negergies into you, having failed with the wristwatch and perhaps the machete as well, but you heeding my warnings probably helped you."

Odera assumed praying hands, "Thank you for looking after me."

"Then she came after me, right?" Namdi said. "Did they send her to me?"

Nodding, "Yes," Papu said. "As Odera's ability passed onto you and without the king being aware, they used her to try to get you on their side of the spiritual warfare, but you also obeyed Odera's caution."

With an incredulous gaze whilst a smile built, "You are saying that I am able to pass on my powers to others?" Odera said, his voice rising in its pitch as Papu nodded. "I should have quickly realized that following that acid downpour."

"You were clearly locked in your fighting mode," Namdi said. "Nothing else often matters when you zone out like that."

Odera cast his eyes at Namdi as Namdi spoke, then at me, and we each gave knowing smiles in turn.

"You ought to have discovered this long ago," I said, and Odera nodded contemplatively as his shoulders loosened and his eyes brightened, becoming vacant.

The queen's eyebrows flashed up and held whilst darting a glance at Odera, "Do you still have any powers?" she asked as she remade eye contact with Papu.

"Anyone from the netherworld is expected to have certain basic powers," Papu said. "For one, I am still able to sense that the king is within this world although in a weakened way. This is the first time I haven't been able to fully feel his presence outside of the hours from midnight to six o'clock in the morning when his body remains in the human world and his negergized-lifeforce is in the netherworld. I was able to fully feel him even when he teleported, or became invisible, though I could never say exactly where he was, because both his body and lifeforce were still in the human plane during those times."

"So, there's a chance that the king is no longer in this world?" I asked.

With a weak nod, he faced me, "In the human world as body and lifeforce, yes," Papu said. "But I wish I could say his lifeforce is gone for good from the human plane."

"Is there a chance that he could be back?" I squawked.

"I don't know the exact answer to that because his body cannot be seen," Papu said. "Namdi described that it disintegrated and got sucked up by the earth. That phenomenon seems to me like an extenuating feature for him…One that was made available to him by the netherworld—much like saving him from being completely rubbed out—"

"Rubbed out?" I interposed.

"I mean killed. Die. Pass on to the afterlife," Papu said. "So, I won't say it is impossible, but it is far easier to return if the body remains in the human plane when the lifeforce exits the human plane.

As a not-unusual, vacant look of disinterest about any discourse regarding the king came over the queen's visage, and she all but stopped her ears, "If your purpose was to protect Odera, why didn't you depart when it was clear to you that he no longer needed you?" she said.

"Well, to put it mildly, as time went on, I became able to override the will of the ones who sent me. I think it was possible because Odera managed to rub some of his good powers off on me due to a caring relationship that existed between us at the time. To continue to avail myself of this, when I was unable to drive him around because Odera no longer needed me to take him places, I begged the king to make me the chamberlain just so that I could stick around. Also, considering that the alternative would have been for me to return to the venerable ones and probably sent elsewhere having served my purpose and since my will was to stay around Odera, I found myself a wife and had a son. Through Odera's influence, I had learnt that true love is all-conquering…and it became clear to me that developing loving relationships that were unconditional helped avert being controlled by the men and women of the underworld."

With a pleased nod, "And your relationship with those mothers?" the queen asked.

"It started when they would come to the palace seeking an audience with the king because they feared Mkpátáku and the lead henchman before Odera, as well as Odera, wouldn't let them in until it was noon. Knowing that most of these women had to go to the market to sell and make a living and coming during those stipulated hours was impossible for them, I took pity on them—so that each time any of them came, I would ask for their reason for coming.

"When it dawned on me that they all had similar reasons for wanting to see the king, I linked them up with one another for support. Later, after I learnt from the king of what Prince Ikuku was doing for Agudagu and knowing fully well that by being part and parcel of Mkpátáku the king wouldn't have been in any position, or cared at all to help them, I advised them to send their children there."

"When did this sort of abandonment start?" the queen said. "When was the last child abandoned? How will those women know which child belongs to them?"

"Your Majesty, the first group sent their children that way 17 years ago, and the last group only during the rainy season of last year," Papu said. "I, and my son on some occasions when he was not displeased by me, helped tattoo the name each woman had chosen for her son, along with the first letter of their surname, into the inside of the right arm of each woman, near their armpits, as well as on the same part of their son's arm. That way, there should not be any mistakes and, on the flip side, omitting their full last names also meant that the family they came from couldn't be traced easily."

Nodding, clearly impressed, "I don't know why you've been secretive about what you did for those women because it is laudable and must be rewarded—" the queen said.

"I could never have said anything with the king still around, Your Majesty," Papu interjected. "Those women would have been in danger. We agreed to keep our affairs clandestine for that reason alone."

Nodding, "I now understand," the queen said. "So, since these women trust you, you will become Her Majesty's women's affairs' liaison officer and be the connection between the women of Akagheli and me. Your wages will be doubled, and you will give me a list of whatever else you might need to help make your job easier—like a bicycle or motorcycle. You may leave now."

Papu paid homage and padded toward the exit.

"On second thought, please also get me your son, I mean the bellman," the queen added as Papu wheeled around to face her. "I must address Akaghelites sooner before those women let it slip that their king is no more as they go about their merry-making…We must get ahead of the story. Let him wait for me in the throne room."

Bobbing his head again and flashing a hint of a grin, "Thank you, Your Majesty, your wish is always my command. It is wonderful to have you back."

Hunching forward, "Thank you, Papu," the queen said. "One other thing; did you also tell those women the lie to tell their husbands about the 'infection' thing?"

"Yes, Your Majesty," Papu said. "I had heard the king and Chief Madu talk about it many times."

"Same thing the king told me about my son," the queen said. "You may leave now…Thank you."

As Papu left the throne room, Queen Nena turned to Odera who still exhibited a dazed disposition, her expression changing to that of serious concern. And with a quiet voice as well as hands that all but trembled, "Ejizu told me a little while ago that those three maidens are now pregnant, one of them by Ajutu, and our people have to know so that they stay vigilant. Also, there is a child spirit whose mother is locked up and must be set free."

Grimacing, "Does Ejizu know where the maidens are?" I asked as the queen drooped her head.

Queen Nena shook her head on a bent neck, "None of them know," she said. "And they are worried, as we ought to be, that the child will cause trouble when it realizes it is heir to the vacant throne."

A calm and still silence descended on the room for what seemed like forever as glances were exchanged between one another.

With his stare more focused, "Considering that I became an heir before it, it will have to go through me first," Odera stated with emphasis.

Stepping down from the throne and shouldering her bag, "Ikuku has been gone for too long. I wonder if he is giving birth to a child," the queen casually said as I curtsied and Odera and Namdi bowed their heads, each of us trying as hard as was possible to suppress a laugh. "I must go and change into a better outfit and don my diadem. Nkem, please walk with me. I might need help to get into my sheath-like robe if it still fits."

"Yes, Your Majesty," I said with my hand over my mouth that remained curved into a smile as I stole a veiled glance at Odera's wristwatch and murmured to myself: "6:11."

"Odera, when Ikuku returns, let him know that I am on my way to my quarters. Go with him to his brother's room and grab the coronet. He must stand in Ajutu's place as we address our people. It shall be our word against those mothers' words. We can't completely trust them. And let Juno, my chauffeur, get my car ready for us and bring it around to the front. Let Ikuku also decide whether the military folks stay here or go with us. You, Namdi, and Nkem are certainly going with us."

"Yes, Your Majesty," Odera and Namdi said as one.

"Namdi," Odera said. "My room is free now. Go get yourself better clothes and shoes."

With a smile that reached his eyes, Namdi made for the exit.

Chapter 86

Switching his gaze in turn between his mother and Odera as she and I dispersed from the throne room, "Something weird is happening," Ejizu said. "Quite similar to what Adaku described—"

"How so?" Somto interjected.

"It's becoming more and more difficult to see Odera, or to connect with him—" Ejizu said. "It first happened when he was fighting the wyvern...Then, I could still see him clearly. I thought he was just too engrossed in the fight to connect. Now, I can just about see and hear him, and comparing him with Mother, his figure has gone out of focus, and his voice has faded too."

"I would have said you stole my thoughts if not that this is a serious matter," Bute said. "I, unlike you, have stopped seeing more than his heat signature, or hearing him altogether."

"Can you still see Namdi?" Ejizu asked.

Nodding, "Yes," Bute said. "As per usual."

"I wonder if it has to do with the powers he received and is now giving away," Dike said.

"Perhaps," Ejizu said.

"Mother said that it seems anyone close to him is able to harness some of his impetus—" Dike said.

"If that's the case," Somto said. "Dike, one question is: does it mean you too may become unable to see your mother? I think what Bute and Ejizu are experiencing answers the question, without a doubt, of what might make it impossible for a Pneuma to connect with a human they were hitherto able to connect with—"

"Exceptional superhuman abilities," Adaku said, drawing a smile from Somto. "My turn to steal your thoughts. His cells must be changing at a rapid rate perhaps to replenish whatever impetus he is losing to others; thus, accounting for the visibility issues."

"What do I do about Mother?" Dike said with a cracked voice. "Tell her to stay away from Odera?"

"That's going to be more difficult than telling Namdi the same, and I'm not going to try because I know it's a no-go area," Bute said. "From what you said, she is quite consumed with desire for him. You don't want to risk her saying she prefers relating with humans to Pneumas. I'd be much too hurt to hear that or feel that from Namdi—just like Feanyi felt."

"Dike, do you still see her?" Somto asked.

"I do," Dike said. "Nothing has changed, though I couldn't watch her get it on with Odera a little while ago."

"If you still see her, and Bute still sees Namdi, then we have to play the wait-and-watch game," Somto said.

Glancing at Dike, "If what Papu said is true, and Odera started giving off his powers to Namdi at least ten years ago, then it is probably going to take a long time, if at all, so nothing to worry about for now," Bute said.

Absentmindedly, "Sure, Bute," Somto said. "Though the strength of the contact probably matters also, and I expect Odera and Dike's mother to remain intimate in a way Odera wasn't with Namdi if you get my drift, it therefore might not take that long for Dike's mum to reach the point, if there is one to reach…The other question is, can the humans still see the Pneumas they were once able to see? Dike, find out from your mother if Odera is still able to see Ejizu, or Bute as normal."

Turning to drift away, "I will get on it—" Dike said, then drew up. "What if he cannot?"

"If he can't," Somto said. "Then it's something I don't yet have an answer for as to how we might proceed. I didn't envisage this. We'd have to put heads together on this one. But one good thing that has come out of it all is that no new Pneuma came down that portal after Tochi, before last night's cycle ended. My hope is that it stays that way during tonight's round while we continue the fight—"

Hanging her head, "A fight that is going to get tougher—on the one hand because of what could amount to no communication between the Pneumas and humans that matter, and on the other hand because the maidens now very likely now have even more extraordinary powers," Adaku said.

"While I share your pessimism, we're still dealing with probabilities here, even possibilities. We're not, by any means, certain. Let's retain hope as we figure out a way forward," Somto said and began to rack his brain.

"Ejizu, shouldn't you tell your mother to stay away from Odera," Bute said as a contemplative Somto flowed toward Adaku.

Shaking his head with nonchalance, "Odera can only transfer powers to my mother if there is a mutual loving relationship between them, and there is presently none," Ejizu said. "I heard my father, and not long ago, Papu too, say something of that sort. All there is, right now, is a cordial relationship.

"Though Odera and Mother had a bond during the time I was alive, they grew apart after I passed on and even further apart when he left for boarding school, and he rarely came around while he was a henchman. Now that he has Dike's mother, I don't think he would have much of the relevant affection to send my mother's way, I hope…And same probably goes for what there might be between him and Uncle Ikuku. Let me check up on him. He's been trying to make contact."

"Let's not be all panicky and jump to conclusions," Somto said, "things may yet normalize regarding who sees who."

Chapter 87

Sitting slumped against the sofa in the waiting room, Prince Ikuku continued to gaze leftward at the portraits of his father and brother for a moment longer as his eyes glazed over, then he dropped his head in his hands.

Feeling Ejizu's presence as he appeared, the prince looked up, "Don't tell your mother that I'm here if you haven't already. Let her continue to think that I'm in the gents," Prince Ikuku said, leaning forward a little. "I just need time alone to digest everything. I can't believe that Ajutu will meet his end today."

"Okay," Ejizu said. "But he has already met his end, and I didn't, and won't, tell Mother where you are."

Losing eye contact with Ejizu as he felt heat behind his eyes, Prince Ikuku felt his head spinning whilst an aching feeling of loss came over him. He lowered his chin to his chest as his hands went limp to hang by his side; he slumped again in the chair, turned his head to his right, and screwed his eyes shut. "I wished there was another way," he said with a cracked voice, then heaved a dolorous sigh. "Though we had our differences, we had many good times…Those good memories should have been enough for him to still be here with us."

Arriving next to Prince Ikuku whilst concentrating his energy, Ejizu patted him on his left shoulder, "He asked for it," Ejizu said. "You shouldn't feel sorry for him. You two may have had good times, but he ultimately chose to create evil ones and live by them."

With wheezing breaths and a long, low sigh, Prince Ikuku opened his eyes. "I know," he said with a thickening voice. "But he was the only family I had left."

"He has now passed on, and you now have Mother all to yourself, again."

With vacant eyes, "I could have saved him—" the prince said.

"Don't be hard on yourself," Ejizu interjected, lifting his voice. "Only The Almighty could have saved him—"

"I remember when he first mentioned Mkpátáku to me—Christmas eve, 1962," the prince continued. "It was our 26th birthday. You were about 15 months old then. He said he had overhead Father's chiefs, then, talking about it with Father about how they were planning to investigate and bring it to an end, and all I did was dismiss him. I didn't think that he would ever become interested in it and end up harming you. I should have talked to him more about it…how evil it was and all. I could have told Father about it, and all this might have been averted."

"There was no way you could have known what he would do."

Nearly in tears, "I don't know," the prince said. "I might have been able to stop all these from happening…Things might not have come to such a pretty pass had I looked after him as a brother should. Instead, I spent most of my time being angry at him for taking Nena away from me and for getting her pregnant to marry her as well as paying too much attention to the many demands Father placed on me in regard to succeeding him as the king. He must have felt alone with our mother not being around and with Father pouring all his attention on me—not getting enough notice definitely drove him down the wrong path."

With an emotionless stare, "He chose that road," Ejizu said. "He wasn't a child who didn't know that what he was doing would be fraught with consequences. He had many opportunities to not continue down that evil road. You can beat yourself up all you want, but it won't bring him back. We are all better for it that he is no longer around. He helped stalk Akagheli with relentless evil, and who knows how further he might have gone had we not stopped him. I see much more than you humans see and much more than I let on, so believe me when I say he is, according to his own usage, 'good riddance.' You don't want to know where he is heading to right now…Who he is going to meet."

"You can still see him?"

"Yes, I see him."

"Can he see you?"

Shrugging and with his eyes still empty of expression, "If we are in the same realm and I stay visible to him, yes…But I have decided to stay invisible to him like I am to the leaders of his spiritual order."

"Is it possible for you Pneumas to mingle with them? Are they able to harm you?"

"Posergies and negergies do not ever fraternize. Pneumas, by default, become invisible to negergies at the slightest chance of an encounter."

"Good to know. And I also know that you hated him for what he did to you, I can tell from the way you talk about him. I hated him for what he did to Mother, to your mother, to me, and to you. But I was willing to forgive him."

Leaning away, "I hated the evil, not the man. Well, I must go now, Uncle. I thought you had something more important to say. I'll be around when you want to talk about other things. Pull yourself together…No more repining. There is work still to be done. Mother needs you to assume the role of king when she addresses the villagers later tonight and going forward. Odera is waiting to go with you to collect Father's crown from his bedroom. And whatever you do, don't ever connect with Father. He must not be trusted. He and his group must have a plan for having maintained his lifeforce in the human plane, only now calling it to join them."

"Lifeforce?" the prince asked.

"A person's soul or spirit."

"I see."

Patting the prince on his left shoulder again, Ejizu disappeared.

Chapter 88

Having experienced a moment of sudden insight, "Ejizu, if you were to quantify, how much of Odera would you say you are now able to see or hear compared to what it had been?" Somto said whilst still arm in arm with Adaku not long after Ejizu reappeared in the crossroad's world; hoping to find a way to settle the growing anxiety amongst the Pneumas regarding some's sudden inability to stay connected with humans and the rest wondering if it was a harbinger of what was still to come.

Following a long moment of focusing on Odera as he walked with distraught Prince Ikuku toward the great chamber, then of contemplative thought, "50-percent give or take," Ejizu said.

"And you are half siblings?" Somto said.

"What's your point?" Bute said just as Dike switched back to their realm.

"It's possible, though counterintuitive, that superhuman abilities whittle away the connections to our world, fine-tuning it to what it should be familial-wise," Somto said. "So, since Ejizu and Odera share the same father but not the same mother, Ejizu has only half a familial connection with him. In Bute's case, the connection with Odera is completely lost because there was no familial connection at all. This, I believe, means that Ejizu, Dike, and Bute will not lose connections with the queen, Nkem, and Namdi respectively even if they obtain impetus from Odera."

Looking at one another as a shadow of a smile creased their mouths, "I hope you are right," Dike, Ejizu, and Bute said as one.

"So, what's left now is to find out if Odera still is able to see Bute and Ejizu," Dike added. "I have just asked my mother to do so."

"Does it then mean that I might start to see less of Uncle Ikuku?"

"I don't think so, even though it might appear to be the case," Somto said. "This is because he has the exact make-up as your father—thus the same familial connection between you two as between you and your father…same way Dike and his mother and you and your mother, hopefully, will not lose an iota of connection even if they receive powers from Odera."

"I hope so," Ejizu said.

"Somto, just because you considered it contrary to common-sense expectation, and earlier on suggested that things might normalize, is there a chance that the issue with some of us not seeing supposedly superhuman beings will be transient?" Adaku said. "That what happened to Odera and the maidens are, by no means, permanent?"

"I know you want that, and we all want that, too…And, yes, it's a probability, and I hope it's truly going to last for only a short time," Somto said. "It is likely that after Odera's body comes to terms with whatever it is going through, like his cells, as you suggested, settling down, he might become fully visible to Bute, and Ejizu again…And it's also possible that after the maidens give birth, you may begin to see them again. Let's retain hope."

"That would be terrific for the sake of our loved ones," Adaku enthused as Somto drifted toward Ejizu.

Quickly taking Ejizu aside, "There's a Pneuma called Kaima who arrived here around the same time Ijezie showed up," Somto started. "He said he was 12 when he joined us. Two nights ago, during our usual meeting, he finally spoke up after I made a speech that gingered all of us up. In a nutshell, he said he could see your father but not the man who sacrificed him—"

"Meaning that his mother was pregnant by my father, and he didn't have a good relationship with a man that's in fact his stepfather?"

Somto nodded.

"And that his stepfather definitely didn't know; to have thought he was his firstborn son," Ejizu said.

"And never stood to benefit from the sacrifice," Somto added.

Ejizu shook his head, "What an absolute waste of everything."

"Indeed," Somto said. "You know, I heard you say you held back information from me, so tell me where you've been all this while."

"This might shock you," Ejizu said, "but I was at a place where the multitude there were peacefully asleep."

"And nothing else happened?"

"Absolutely nothing!"

"Well, what can I say?"

Shrugging, "What can anyone say that will change anything about what happens to the dead?" Ejizu said.

Chapter 89

Humidity remained low as the temperature plunged, and the dust in the air settled not, eddying around the bellman, worsening the haze as draft gently whirled leaves and blew them across the landscape.

By his lonesome as far as anyone could see and wearily dragging his feet past compounds as he made his way from Farm Road onto Market Road, sending more clouds of dust into the air whilst straining his eyes to see through the murk of the foggy evening, and calling for silence and attention, the lanky, wan, bleary-eyed town crier with an untamable thatch of thick, black hair rang out his handbell.

Glancing at his lapel watch, "Listen up, the people of Akagheli," he megaphoned. "The queen has requested that all patriotic citizens of Akagheli and all loyal subjects of Their Majesties King Ajutu and Queen Nena must make their way to the Market Square for an important announcement at 7:30 tonight. Nobody will be excused for not attending. Those of you who have children below the age of 18 must take them along with you; I repeat, do not leave any child that is not yet 18 at home, alone. It is important that everyone hears what she has to say. I have told you all. A word, they say, is enough for the wise. Be wise, spread the news, and be there tonight. It is just over half an hour until she starts her address. She has also said that there is nothing to fear regarding the event of earlier this evening, which some of you witnessed…That everything is now under control."

Stopping in the road, he slumped against a tree at the edge of the forest, his head drooping back. Swayed by emotion, he set his megaphone on the ground and placed the bell in his armpit by its handle. With palms facing up and eyes shut, "My ancestors, I ask again, please help me change my lot in life. Grant me, Nonzo Belagu, powers like you gave my father…Powers that he is not aware that I know about," the bellman muttered to himself. "These dead-end jobs are no longer for me. They pay very little…I cannot prosper just doing them, and at 29, I ought to have found a wife and left my father's compound. I promise to use whatever powers you bless me with in a way that pleases you."

Opening his eyes and looking up for a moment as the evening continued to fall and the waning, gibbous moon peeked out of the white-pink sky, an unseen voice purred, "Ask of me, and it shall be given to thee, but be careful what you ask for and from whom you ask," while a jumble of nebulous forms jostled for his body.

Leveling his gaze, he turned his head around in search of the source of the fiendish words but couldn't quite see anyone. In the wink of an eye, as all but one of the shadowy figures dematerialized, his eyes glinted amber. As the bell landed with a clang, then a thud, he hit the ground backward with a flop across the edge of the bushes whilst his body began to contort in spasms.

He managed to rise to his knees, then dropped forward on his hands. On all fours, screaming and caterwauling with aggression, he struggled against the excruciating pain.

Forced to prostrate himself on the ground, he then tossed from side to side as he slowly and involuntarily transformed. With bone, flesh, and muscle rearranging and reshaping his face, fingers, and all that made him human, he rolled into the bush and disappeared amongst shrubs.

Not long after and with low, guttural growls, a black panther leapt out from the bush, looked around for a little, and glanced at the megaphone. Seizing its strap, along with the bell, in its jaws, it padded off with a low, continuous, vibratory noise along a side path that ran down deeper into the forest.

Chapter 90

Far in the remotest regions of the depths of the earth, two spectral figures slid out of the dimness. Becoming more visible, one towered over the other. As they wended their way through the shadowy space, the silence was eerie until…

"The Evil Lord is delighted that the negergy that was once Adaku has successfully re-hosted," the most venerable one boomed as they drew to a stop, and he turned his ghoulish face to the other figure.

Smiling with a trace of mockery and looking up at the most venerable one, "That should begin to teach Papu a lesson," King Ajutu's voice snorted as his figure drooped its head a little. "Imagine that he did not just betray the netherworld but also me…Even after I employed him, gave him a good existence, and also gave his only son a job when he was languishing at home!"

"Negergies choosing independence once they are in a human body happens from time to time…I am not at all surprised that Papu chose independence. His unification at the zone was a bit odd…But we often get back at the bodies that allow these negergies go against us. That's why he has begun to pay back with his son's body now being under the control of a negergy. The Evil One is always willing to take back whatever he gives," the most venerable one boomed. "That said, the next issue at hand is how we resettle your other myriad negergies…though I still don't know how you managed to host that many when you should have had no more than 13."

Looking up with indifference, King Ajutu asked, "Was competing for his body the only way my negergies could have possessed it?"

Clasping his hands behind his back, the most venerable one said, "You had too many negergies, and this made it difficult to just pick one and possess him with it…Nonetheless, when something doesn't belong to you, to own it if it is willing to be owned, you must work for it. Also, that's the only way to make it fair and give each negergy an equal chance of a host-body—winner takes all."

"How was the winner decided?"

"Your bellman's mild manners meant that the negergy with the softest features won. By your will, Adaku's negergy wasn't made a warrior one, as all the others had been, and your bellman's inner self attracted it."

Assuming praying hands and bobbing his head, "Please, since they were all made for me, let me go back, Your Most Venerable…" King Ajutu's voice boomed, "and host the others again."

Folding his arms across his chest, "Only 13 negergies were made for you, not all of them. I don't know how you got the scores of others…But you make me repeat myself. You are no longer able to return because your body no longer exists," the most venerable one roared. "It exploded because it was too weak and couldn't handle the five new negergies on top of the multitude you had been harboring. You were warned."

"But you gave me a new body—I saw it!"

"We tried, but because your outward appearance was all we could prettify when we passed you through the zone during your fight with Odera, it still couldn't host all those negergized-lifeforces. Though we patched up the injuries, we couldn't freshen the damaged internal structures. This meant that your inner being, which is what really matters when it comes to being able to host any negergy, remained precarious."

"You said I was a Leviathan."

"In more ways than one, yes, you were: a king of pride and of repression who was availed of the power of serpents…But if you are referring to the great Leviathan of the deep, the dragon in the sea, the Evil One's beast of all beasts, then you must remember that we can't create something out of nothing. The Leviathan you wanted required a strong body. Your body, when it was still in existence, had been weakened not only by the pigeon disease but as well by the heavy drinking and smoking of your youth and adult life, and the multiple, poorly treated, sexually transmitted infections you contracted. In the beginning, I explained to you that though humans lose most of their strength upward from their 70s or 80s, no human has a set time to expire from the human world—that it depends on how well their bodies are taken care of by nature and nurture and whether, or not their organs continue to support life as determined by injuries, or afflictions. Nonetheless, even if this was not the case, you wouldn't have been availed of much of the powers of the Leviathan you so desired, for it couldn't survive long enough outside of very deep waters for the only deep water around you, the Naïjer Sea, already is ruled by the queen of the coast and cannot welcome two masters. And she tops you in hierarchy. You know all of these."

"You should have allowed me fight with the negergies for my bellman's body then," King Ajutu's words came out somewhat in a huff.

"Only negergies can find their way into any living body and fit in it. Your unique lifeforce cannot fit into just any human body."

"If I am unable to go back, am I then rubbed out? Is this the end for me?"

"You know fully well that a peace warrior's lifeforce might exit his body by any of three ways: transiently when its raven, leaving the body behind, takes it to the zone for unification during Mkpátáku, or on our nightly missions after becoming a peace warrior…When it is salvaged by the netherworld before expiration so that the lifeforce may remain in the human plane, making it possible for it to dip into the spiritual plane from time to time but not to remain in it permanently…Or when it permanently passes on to the spiritual plane after the body succumbs to mortality. The first two mean the lifeforce is returnable because a connection is present in the human plane, while the last means a total rub out with an unreturnable lifeforce. By the fact that you were so deep in the Evil Chief's cause, and I was able to harvest your lifeforce before your body exploded, you are, strictly speaking, salvaged, though you may technically be considered rubbed out…"

"Huh!" King Ajutu's voice huffed; his face assuming a more menacing look and his form sagging, "Oderaaaaaaaaaa! You have indeed succeeded! You have rubbed me out!"

With both men glaring at each other and King Ajutu's shadow's eyes flashing, a long moment of preternatural quiet ensued until, "Unless a body that has the exact make-up as your former body accepts your lifeforce that we made capable of staying in the human plane," the most venerable one rumbled on. "You read about these things in your book that is currently in Ijeoma's possession."

With a nod and a face that suddenly began to glow, King Ajutu's figure raised his eyebrows and with a questioning expression, it seemed like his mind flitted to Prince Ikuku. He probably could see that the prince was sat in the backseat of a state-of-the-art, black Mercedes sedan, staring at a coronet on his lap whilst the fingers of his left hand were interlocked with those of Queen Nena's right hand atop the middle seat.

"I did, but one is not expected to remember everything in that big volume," King Ajutu's voice echoed. "On a different note, what would it have taken for you to engage in my fight? The rubbing out of all peace warriors?"

"The Evil One holds sway when it comes to getting unsaved men to become peace warriors by getting them to kill their firstborn sons, so, I am afraid not."

"When Wusaland and Orubaland begin to suffer the same fate?"

The most venerable one shook his head.

"Hmm" King Ajutu's specter grumbled. "What then?"

"This is the question you should have asked in the beginning to have avoided the situation you're currently faced with," the most venerable one boomed. "Two conditions exist under which we would get involved. The first is: if a human stops the birth of would-be first sons and that has a zero chance of happening. The second is: if a human succeeds each time that he, or she attempts to prevent the sacrifice from taking place and firstborn sons no longer get rubbed out—"

"And what is the chance that a human can stop those rubbing outs from happening?"

"Low, but not zero," the most venerable one rumbled.

"So, for all intents and purposes, I was on my own?"

Wheeling around and starting to drift away, "There was a good chance that you would have, for what is left of your entire life span, been on your own on that issue," the most venerable one clasped his hands again behind his back. "And I hasten to add that you asked for it though…You were warned…And it's now time to meet up with the other venerable ones."

Watching as the most venerable one floated away, "Why are we meeting them?" King Ajutu's lifeforce purred. "What for?"

Without looking back, "To choose your successor," the most venerable one rumbled in a somewhat puckish tone. "Now that your race in the physical world is at the least held in abeyance if not on a probably indefinite break, we must begin preparations for tonight's anointing. The work of he who has the road map to the human mind must continue…It never ceases. Remember that he is the artful enemy of creation and destruction is his manner."

Arriving to flow in tandem with the most venerable one's ethereal form and looking up rightward at it, "Who will it be?" King Ajutu's voice boomed. "Who has the wherewithal to fill my lofty shoes?"

"Mr. Udiwu…Going by the number of non-peace warrior rub outs for Igboland, he is second only to you—seven as opposed to your 13."

"That means my Igboland will fall to third behind Orubaland."

"That's correct with Chieftain Jukutu's 12," the most venerable one said. "But it is forever a fluid situation. Mr. Udiwu has the chance to even move ahead of Tamir's 16, in a short period of time, should he so choose."

King Ajutu's specter shook its head, "Mekanna is faint-hearted," King Ajutu's voice rumbled. "I doubt it. By the way, is there a chance of me becoming a venerable one until I can return to earth? I know that the enigmatic Lord of Evil never reveals himself to people of the earth, preferring to send his negergies. Any chance I can see him now that I have become a bona fide part of the netherworld?"

Looking straight ahead, unwaveringly, "You are still on earth; we, too, are on earth. What you mean to say is the human world, the physical world," the most venerable one boomed. "But Ajutu, you want so many things…and don't get me wrong for saying this as these are welcomed by the accuser of the brethren, but the greed as well as the vanity of the desires of your will steered you to the mistake of creating a superhuman Odera whose abilities continued to be beyond your ken as of when you still had a human body. You were not supposed to love the earth, including your erstwhile world and the otherworld, or what it offered. You are not bona fide yet…still transitioning, as your lifeforce is still attached to the human realm. Only salvaged lifeforces that have resolutely transitioned from the human plane can be bona fide. Only bona fide lifeforces can see him, and only negergies stand to be considered when there is the need for a new venerable one. So, do you want to be a revenant, or become bona fide? If a revenant, he most definitely will not reveal himself to you so that you do not go telling the physical world what he is like. But before you decide, I must let you realize a few things. In your previous world, you had your own free will, and the Evil One only overrode it if you allowed him. However, everything to do with this netherworld is within his purview and his alone. He makes the choices and will begin to control your lifeforce the moment you become bona fide. Also, be aware that a precondition for being salvaged is that the condition for a return pre-exists or is in the process of coming into existence, otherwise we wouldn't consider carrying it out…So, take your time to think about these things in depth before committing to one path or the other…To conclude, until you are able to return, you could still, from here, influence humans to do his bidding through graven images—"

"I see. Is it not demeaning of my status to be represented by a carved idol?"

"You will be doing the bidding of the Ruler of the World, and as you are not one of his negergies that can take full possession of a human body with or without their consent or knowledge, the surest way for you is through your lifeforce's familiarization with the only human you are able to possess while waiting for that body's unwitting and voluntary subjection. Us binding your lifeforce to a graven image that the only available human you may return in has an attachment to has given you the chance. Now your role here, if you so choose, is to get that human to make strong and continuous physical contact with that image for your lifeforce's transfer to be engendered. You know this already. That book did inform you on all of these things…"

With a nod, "I remember that the book indicates that 'strong' contact must be for exactly one hour, 51 minutes, and 26 seconds a day and 'continuous' contact must be daily contact for seven consecutive days."

"For a total of 13 hours."

"The book did say so…You also earlier attested to—and the book makes clear—the fact that once we are rubbed out, we are no longer connected to life, yet the Children of the Shadows seem to disprove that fact, why is this so?"

"Yes, when a body is disconnected from its lifeforce, either permanently, like in their case, or transiently, like in your case, hopefully, the creative part of the lifeforce may become activated from the unseen world and is able to interact with the seen world. In those children's situation, it's because they remain unburied and, in your situation, it's because your lifeforce is effectively still within the human plane, tethered to one of the skulls your twin owns to avoid, for you, a complete rub out from the human world."

"Hmm," King Ajutu's shadowy form expressed, scratching his temple with his left index finger as his stare flitted from the most venerable one to the special chamber within Prince Ikuku's house, where two, padlocked, metal-bound, oak chests were set on a shelf.

"If you ever thought that your brother procured those crystal skulls of his own free will without a nudge from the fons et origo of evil, who considered that the likelihood existed that his most loyal human servant in Igboland could end up in this situation, then you must think again."

King Ajutu's figure gave a winning smile, "As there is a chance that I will return, we must then ensure that the peace warriors do not make the people of my village and far-off aware that I am no longer in their world."

"Though you will always remain a part of our spiritual journey and the warriors shall continue to see you during that period hence have no reason to suspect that you are no longer body and lifeforce in the human world, tonight, we shall swear those who might be expecting to continue to relate with you outside of this realm to secrecy with unspeakable consequences for any warrior who disobeys."

And as a hair-raising hush fell over the two wights, they vanished without a trace; the taller one a beat ahead of the other.

The End...
... Of the Continuation

Human Characters

LAST NAME	FIRST NAME	ROLE AND ALSO KNOWN AS
Odimegwu	Nkemjika	Nkem, Mama Dike
Odimegwu	Ebubedike	Dike
Odimegwu	Obiageli	Oby, Nkem and Papa Dike's Daughter; Dike's younger sister
Odimegwu	Ibe	Ibe, Papa Dike
Njoku	Odera	Odera, King Ajutu's Lead Henchman; the Commander
Njoku	Evelyn	Odera's mother
Njoku	Peter	Odera's father, Papa Doka
Njoku	Doka	Odera's Oldest sibling Odera's Oldest brother
Njoku	Ileka	Odera's immediate older sibling Odera's immediate older brother

Ezeogu	Namdi	Namdi, Second-in-command Henchman to Odera
Ezeogu	Azuka	Namdi's younger sister, Odera's parents' house help
Ezeogu	Akudinma	Namdi's mother
Ugodi	Ajutu	King Ajutu, the king
Ugodi	Nena	Queen Nena, the queen
Ugodi	Ikuku	Prince Ikuku, King Ajutu's identical twin; the prince; Uncle Ikuku
Ugodi	Otubu	King Otubu, the former king
Madu	Egu	Chief Madu, Oldest chief; Head of the chiefs; Head of Utolo clan
Madu	Adane	Chief Madu's wife
Madu	Emenozo	Dead son of Chief Madu
Duru	Izundu	Chief Madu's house boy
Ileka	Onuka	Chief Madu's house boy
Odia	Grandpa	Caretaker of the Communal Well
Jokum	Isaiah	Chief Jokum, Head of Itoga clan
Jokum	Neomi	Mrs. Jokum, Chief Jokum's wife; Headmistress at Akagheli's public school

Ikeme	Joe	Chief Ikeme, Head of Ozumba clan
Ikeme	Chichi	Mama Ify, Chief Ikeme's wife
Egwu	John	Chief Egwu, Head of Amakwe clan
Isigwe	Eke	Akagheli's Chief Occultist, Papa Udo
Isigwe	Chika	Mama Udo, Mr. Isigwe's first wife
Isigwe	Ama	Mama Uche, Mr. Isigwe's second wife
Isigwe	Ijezie	Dead son of Mr. Isigwe/Mama Udo
Isigwe	Udo	Second child (son) of Mr. Isigwe/Mama Udo
Isigwe	Uche	First child (daughter) of Mr. Isigwe/Mama Uche
Isigwe	Adaobi	Second child (daughter) of Mr. Isigwe/Mama Uche
	Ezinne	Ezinne, Queen Nena's adopted daughter
Belagu	Papu	King Ajutu's Chamberlain, Messenger from the netherworld
Belagu	Nonzo	Akagheli's Bellman/Town crier, Papu's son
Ogene	Kenna	Kenna, Adure's fling within the forest
Nzule	Ben	Mr. Nzule, Rapist within the forest

Onu	Abigail	Mama Ugochi, Leader of MFFSs
Onu	Ugochi	Mr. & Mrs. Onu's daughter
Onu	Amos	Papa Dike's friend at the beer parlor, Mama Ugochi's husband; Papa Ugochi
Bakiri		Mr. Bakiri, Northern-based Herbalist
Omenka	Pius	Pastor
Tinkle	Madam	Beer Parlor owner, Mama Bomboy
Tinkle	Bomboy	Madam tinkle's son
Ofuzo	Batu	Henchman
Ibaga	Diko	Henchman
Efudu	Jadue	Henchman
Imuno	Kadiye	Henchman
	Ijere	Henchman
	Idiche	Henchman
	Duna	Henchman
	Amalu	Henchman
	Adaku	Head of the palace maidens, Negergy that morphs to a black panther
	Adure	Palace maiden, Negergy that morphs to a black jaguar
	Ijeoma	Palace Maiden, Negergy that morphs to a golden leopard

	Isioma	Palace maiden, Negergy that morphs to a tawny cougar
Odinaka	Buka	Somto's younger brother
Odinaka	Manda	Somto's younger sister
Odinaka	Aham	Peace warrior, Somto's father
Udiwu	Mekanna	Peace warrior, Mefule Udiwu's father
Duru	Amaechi	Peace warrior, Jikeme Duru's father
Udochi	Julius	Peace warrior, Rapulu Udochi's father
Bioma	Amadi	Peace warrior, Tochi Bioma's father
Delvue	Anika	Friend of Prince Ikuku
Omali	Juno	Queen Nena's chauffeur
Iduto		Captain
Fric		Sergeant
Brymo		Sergeant
Dago		Sergeant
Dabir		Private
Imala		Private

Pneuma Characters

LAST NAME	FIRST NAME	ROLE AND ALSO KNOWN AS
Odinaka	Somto	Somto, Serendipitous leader of the Pneumas
Odimegwu	Ebubedike	Dike
Isigwe	Ijezie	Ijezie
Ezeogu	Bute	Bute, Namdi's older brother
Ugodi	Ejizu	Ejizu, Dead son of King Ajutu/Queen Nena
Ofor	Adaku	Adaku, Human lifeforce that used to own maiden Adaku's body
Duru	Jikeme	Jikeme
Udochi	Rapulu	Rapulu
Udiwu	Mefule	Mefule
Buchi	Feanyi	Feanyi
Ruba	Kachi	Kachi
Agulu	Deobi	Deobi
Ngala	Fedi	Fedi
Diwem	Kechi	Kechi
Dunus	Chikwe	Chikwe

Bioma	Tochi	Tochi, Youngest, and newest Pneuma. First seen in Unearthing the Ritual
	Kaima	Kaima Pneuma half-brother to Ejizu